DOLLY
AND
THE
STARRY
BIRD

DOLLY
AND
THE
STARRY
BIRD

DOROTHY DUNNETT

Vintage Books
A Division of Random House
New York

First Vintage Books Edition, September 1982
Copyright © 1973 by Dorothy Dunnett
All rights reserved under International and
Pan-American Copyright Conventions. Published
in the United States by Random House, Inc.,
New York. Originally published in Great Britain
by Cassell & Company Ltd. and in the United
States by Houghton Mifflin Company under the
title Murder in Focus in 1973.
Library of Congress Cataloging in Publication Data
Dunnett, Dorothy.
Dolly and the starry bird.
Reprint. Originally published: Murder in focus.
London : Cassell, 1973.
I. Title.
PR6054.U56M8   1982   823'.914   82-40045
ISBN 0-394-71158-0   AACR2
Manufactured in the United States of America

CHAPTER 1

I HAVE NOTHING, even yet, against bifocal glasses. I know some very nice pouffs and a couple of stock-brokers and a man who keeps a horn mustache comb in his jumpsuit. I'm a girl who doesn't shock easily.

Or so I thought until I first met Johnson Johnson, which was outside the Rome zoo in November.

He was there because he was waiting for me, although I didn't know it. I was there on a day's leave from the Frazer Observatory. If I'd stayed on leave, none of it might have happened.

You have heard, of course, of Maurice Frazer, the most famous actor-manager of his day, and also the prettiest. When Maurice retired to Italy and bought a villa in the Tibur Hills with two observatories in the garden, his chums put it down to senility.

3

An error. Having chosen, so to speak, his new theater, Maurice proceeded both to act and to manage it. The large observatory, which was made of seven kinds of marble and situated above the rose bower by the swimming pool, was cleaned, refitted, and the telescope checked. The smaller observatory, a pillared Folly hung with wisteria, was emptied of its inadequate resources and left, a shrine awaiting its Mufti. Then Maurice wrote straight off to the Zodiac Trust for astronomers.

He got two, and I had to be one of them. I acquired the observatory with the telescope, and shared digs with my running mate, a photographer called James K. Middleton. The Folly went to an American, Innes Wye, for an electronic experiment in which the Trust took a passionate interest.

We had a project as well, Jacko Middleton and I: to photograph a series of stars through a fifty-inch telescope and send the negatives back to the Zodiac. The Zodiac Trust is the Santa Claus of worldwide astronomy. A private foundation richly funded by fish paste, it makes grants to struggling centers. It also processes and disperses information, computerizes statistics, discovers sponsors for expensive projects, and even helps choose the staff to direct them.

I knew the Zodiac people. I trained with some of them. I was an orthodox astronomer for years, until the existence of Charles made it cleverer to move into the more free-wheeling fringes of the profession.

Jacko was a scientific photographer who could take pictures through an astronomical telescope. Charles Digham was a self-employed photographer who could and did take pictures of practically anything, provided it was visibly groovy. Outside that, he pursued a life of simple hedonism, composing and collecting doggerel obituary notices and working hard, he reported, on other guys' test-beds. Charles and I, in spite of this, had what our friends call a stable relationship. That is, we had lived together for years, and it suited us.

I believe I wondered what my landlady would say when she heard my boy friend was coming to join me in Italy. In the event, I need hardly have worried. She opened another bottle of vino and pushed the spare bed from Jacko's room back into mine, which fouled up Jacko's personal relationships but pleased Charles immensely.

That was in October, when Maurice Frazer had had us for three of the four months we'd booked for. By then I knew that whatever Murice might take exception to, it wasn't an irregular life style. I was glad. I liked running the Frazer Observatory.

The Frazer was built like a wedding cake, and was referred to as the Dome, because of the cupola over the telescope. The ground floor had a lush rest room, a kitchen, and offices. The middle floor, reached by a white marble staircase, held the darkroom and workshops and storeroom. Between the middle floor and the telescope was a steep spiral staircase in iron.

Every observatory is round and has spiral staircases. That is why astronomers go everywhere in single file with their elbows tucked in, which is quite comfortable, except in bed sometimes.

Jacko and I took turn about with night duty, or sometimes split up the night work between us. Our digs were ten minutes away in Velterra, but you could bunk down in the rest room if you wanted. Singly. In the Dome, science was science.

You could say the same of our U.S. friend in the Folly. Innes Wye, from Wyoming and Wakefield, ran Mouse Hall, the smaller pillared frivolity housing the object we called Innes's Incubator. No one knew what it was except Innes and the Zodiac Trust. Rumor had it that he was testing a new way of infusing tea by passing an infrared ray through a Chianti bottle, which was a sick joke (Jacko's) because Innes didn't drink and we couldn't. Innes and Jacko didn't like one another.

Usually I got along with them both, except when Jacko arrived at the Dome as he did this November morning, and strolled straight into the rest room where I was sleeping. I flung an ashtray at him, which made its usual nick in the door as he banged it shut, snickering. He called through it, "Had a thick evening then, angel?"

I'd had a long, boring night as he very well knew, up in the breezy dark of the Dome, with my eye on the telescope cross wires. When I trailed through to the kitchen ten minutes later he had the kettle on and the Instant on the table and was raking among the developing liquid in the fridge for last week's Supermercato wrapped bacon. Innes, who doesn't like Italian food, keeps the Dome kitchen stocked up with tinned corn and peanut butter and Sanka and eats there instead of at his digs, which are in a different part of Velterra from Jacko's and mine.

This is all right, but leads to a certain amount of friction when improvident people like Jacko and

Charles and myself become peckish on duty at night-time, or can't be bothered going back to our digs for breakfast. Or have two breakfasts, like Jacko. He said, still raking, "Hell of a bright was your beloved, at breakfast. He's got a new obituary notice for you."

I said, "I hear Innes coming. What breakfast?"

"My first one," said Jacko. "This is my second one. I'd have a third one if that American bastard would eat like a Christian. Why let Charles lay you, and not your old physicist buddies?"

"Because he writes good obituary notices," I said. I was meeting Charles at three on the steps of the Villa Borghese, where he had a photo assignment with four models and half the Italian fashion collection. Jacko was on duty tonight. I poured out the coffees and found the olive oil for Jacko's bacon, and sat down again with an apple and the *Messaggero* open at all the film advertisements, while Jacko stood with his frying pan over my shoulder reading aloud all the entries on the opposite page under MASSAGES ESTHETICS.

They ranged from *AAAA Very young attractive masseuse, independent house, every afternoon, to AAAAAA Ambiente elegants, brave brave manicure* and explain why Rome's principal newspaper is nicknamed *Il Massaggero* and never gets into the red. We were just working out the price of forty-two capital A's at L. 210 a word when Innes's voice said, "That's my bloody bacon!"

Innes Wye is a very clever man, but he is small, and his voice is rather high, and he is apt to talk about a role of soft galactic X rays in the alignment of dust, for example, in the coffee break.

7

"And I'll tell you something else!" said Innes to Jacko. "You've got your bloody playmates all over my darkroom again!"

He had, too. The developing tanks were all full of busts and bottoms and blowups of Jacko's latest models. What was more, Jacko knew that Innes would see the pictures and Jacko knew that Innes would be offended, so I said, "Yes, I was going to say to you, Jacko, I want to do my plates before lunch."

"I'll get them out," said Jacko casually. "Bacon, Innes? Shirred Eggs with Thick-Cut Salami and Straw Taters? Old Plantation Blueberry Pancake with Wild Berry Syrup? Spaghetti?"

"Shut up," I said. I fished in my basket and tossed out yesterday's shopping: some eggs, a tin of caffe solubile and two gold packets of salami, L. 250. "I don't see why Innes should feed us. Shove it in the fridge somewhere."

"He has enough to do, feeding Poppy," said Jacko. "How's Poppy, Innes?" And as Innes still stood there, glaring at him, Jacko added in exasperation, "Give us a break, mate. We're all big, grown-up scientists and we can drink and smoke and go to X films and everything. My God, I wonder you don't put a G-string on Poppy."

Poppy (or Poppaea, according to Innes) is a white mouse who lives in Mouse Hall by the Incubator. She is trained and looked after by Innes, who feeds her sunflower seeds and cleans out her cage on a Saturday.

Innes said, "It is nothing to any of us, I imagine, how you spend your spare time. But you have heard Ruth say she wishes to develop her night's work.

8

I imagine she hardly wishes to do it in the ambience of a low-grade Soho nightclub." And bending, he brought out two chaste eggs and cracked them.

I finished my coffee and got the hell out of it. I had my log to write up and my lists to tick off and my plates to develop, once I had stacked Jacko's porn where it would attract less attention. I had time to be pleased that Jacko was on duty that night. Two more weeks and we should all have left Italy and scattered for Christmas. Winter skies are no good for photography and electric storms interfere with the power lines, so that I was reduced sometimes already to opening the cupola of the Dome with my muscles, not to mention manhandling the whole bloody weight of the 50-Inch. When Charles dropped in, he was able to help me.

We shared my digs, as I have said, because I was tied to Velterra. The rest of the time he spent in Rome, in a rather lush flat with a bar fitted into a sedan chair. I shall never, I suppose, get to the end of all Charles's friends but I knew Sassy Packer, the idiot he was sharing it with, and most of the set who wandered in and out half the day and all, but all, of the night. I never did discover whose flat it was in the first place.

We gave a party or two there, but it was easier to live near the observatory. Gradually, Charles's gear landed up in my wardrobe and he only went to the flat when he was working. Today he was working, and the car had broken down anyway, so I changed, and repainted, and yelled "See you at the party" to Innes, and then caught the Rome train at Parassio. I wonder—I often wonder—if the car hadn't been out of use, what would have happened.

Rome in November isn't beloved of tourists. The visitors are mostly businessmen, doing the rounds with their secretaries. The pavement pavilions in the Via Veneto were steamed up with the resident foreign element having a quick hamburger and cappuccino, but your Roman proper had gone off to lunch. I climbed up the street, feeling underprivileged, to the Aurelian Wall at the top, walked through the crumbling arches and over the park to the villa.

The Villa Borghese (17th C., the property of the City of Rome) shuts at two, and the run-out of picture fakers and art students and culture vultures usually starts before that: the attendants want to get at their gnocchi. From the uproar floating down from the vestibule, I gathered that Charles and the four leggy ladies were still doing their stuff around the Titians. The closed-circuit TV in the entrance hall showed six empty rooms and then Charles's back, very kinky in jodhpurs. He was talking to an Afro-wigged model in a transparent two-piece sexytunica who, I saw to my sorrow, was Diana. I walked forward into the sculpture hall saying, "Help for the photographer," and two men with collars and ties on followed me in without buying a ticket.

Before we got to Room I, one of them drew alongside and opened a smiling conversation. By Room VII he wanted to know where I was going to lunch. Charles was in Room VIII, and when we greeted one another, my opportunists politely retreated. Italian manhood does a lot for one's ego, especially when confronted with three scowling Art Deco chicks and Diana Minicucci, whose mother was Berna-

10

dette Mayflower of Hollywood, and whose father is Prince Minicucci, the industrialist. I stood with Charles's hand in mine and said, "Hul-lo Diana. We've seen you already this morning. You're absolutely all over poor Jacko's developing tanks."

She groaned in a desultory way, above almost as many unclothed molecules as had been on view in the darkroom. "He has the *coldest* hands," she said. "I do blame your telescope. Or is it his circulation?"

"It doesn't make me cold," I suggested.

The six pairs of eyelashes considered me. "Ruth sweetie, you haven't a chilly pore in you. And if you did, dammit, you've got your own heating system." She glared at Charles, who blew a solid raspberry at her. The terrible thing about Di Minicucci is that she is rich and pretty and fearfully likable.

"Wait," said Charles gravely, "for the seasonal lull. That's it, girls. I'll be five minutes, darling."

This to me. I looked around at the lighting man and the dressers and the hairdressers and the couturiers' men, and the gaggle of attendants and illegal gaggle of onlookers and finally, at the TV screen out on the landing, which showed two men in collars and tie, standing somewhere surveying a Rubens. "Where for lunch?" I said to Charles hopefully. It was a long, long time since my apple.

Di had pulled off her wig and, bare to the waist, was preparing to let drop the rest of her dress. With a hiss of offended propriety, the group at the door drew closer and then was shepherded reluctantly away. "I thought," shouted Charles, over a ripple of pink female fleshpots, "of the Rome Zoological Gardens."

The zoo it was. A sample of Charles being whimsical. A sample too of his childlike conviction that wherever he chooses to take himself something astounding is bound to turn up.

In this he was perfectly justified.

We said goodbye to everyone and left our gear, all but his house-trained Zeiss Icarex and my basket with the lighting man and set off to walk through the park, which was leafy and mostly deserted. The sun shone and the wind blew through my hair and Charles's as he swung along with his hands on my elbow, murmuring confidingly exactly as follows:

> *"Full fathom five my father lies*
> *He fell in off a tender*
> *The herrings come up pickled there*
> *On gin from father's bender."*

I groaned, which was what he expected.

With its substance reverently adjusted, that crap was due to go off with eleven others to the obituary files of Charles's favorite publisher, for future selection by sorrowing relatives. Some early girl friends, worried by his morbid inclinations, had tried to switch Charles from Mourning Cards to Anniversaries. But it just wasn't Charles. Charles was Obituary Verses, and there was no point in trying to change him.

Outside the yellow stucco triumphal arches of the zoo there was a red truck with OCCHIALI GIOCATTOLI, otherwise Toy Spectacles, on the front of it full of flags and films and cameras and hopping dogs and balloons. Charles bought me a large red balloon with a cardboard fish dangling inside, and I carried it after him through the barrier and past

12

a llama standing about patiently under a fine date palm roaring with sparrows.

"You don't wish," I said to Charles, "to be photographed in Agfacolor con il lama?" A nun with a string of five children paused to read the notice on her way out, and someone entering behind us also stopped at the truck and bought a large blue balloon. It was November and an hour short of closing time: the Giardino Zoologico di Roma was not going to be seething with patrons. We strolled past the carousel and the monkeys and Lo Yack and Il Gorilla, who was playing lightly with motorcar tires, and the Moorish palace occupied by the giraffes.

"I'm hungry," I said, with some feeling, and seizing my hand Charles took to his heels so that we ran together up the broad tree-lined slope to the restaurant, which was, being November, quite shut. So we sat under the closed sun umbrellas on the piazza and ate finger rolls and Panfrutto Motto supplied by the kindhearted barman. A fountain hissed and the sun shone benignly and a lot of red geraniums bloomed among tubs of laurel and myrtle. There was a faint scent of corpse-fed Rapaci wafted from the condor enclosure behind us. Charles said fretfully, "And what about this bloody party?"

"Di is going," I said.

"You said that for no other reason than to make me say To hell with Di, poor little Di," said Charles fluently. "You're a sour, sex-starved cow and I am not going to friend Maurice's party." Under the table, his knees had trapped mine and he was uncorking and pouring into the two water glasses before us the contents of his silver hip flask. The man with the blue balloon came into the piazza, looked vaguely around him and went and sat next to the condors. The child, if he had a child, was not immediately visible.

I sighed. I refolded my newspaper and said rapidly, *"La Vendetta di Tarzan?"*

"No."

"Il Figlio di Frankenstein?"

"No. No films. No plays. Maurice's party if you like, but very, very late . . . Oh, come on, Ruth," said Charles flatly, and rising, pressed the back of his hand against my cheekbone and then went off to square with the waiter. A moment later he said, "Where the hell's my bloody camera?"

It had been where he had slung it, on the next wrought-iron table with my basket. My basket was still there, but the Zeiss Icarex had quite vanished.

The sun, losing its grip, slid behind the restaurant roof. The sound of sawing machinery stopped, and the man who had been painting the railings put the lid on his paint and walked off. A woman came out of the bar and took down the wall cage of budgerigars; various stoutly built men in faded blue cotton trousers who had been leaning against walls or sitting on the customers' benches came erect and began treading about, dimly purposeful. The park was about to close for the night.

I jumped to my feet. Charles was already weaving around the piazza, saying things in restrained Italian to the white-coated waiter and the woman with the cage of budgerigars still hanging from one finger. When my balloon burst we all jumped as in an old Bogart film, including the budgerigars. The cardboard goldfish, dangling exposed from its stick, had *Fall Fair, 500 L.* neatly marked on its stomach; a price which only a financial moron like Charles would have paid for it.

It reminded me of something and I looked across at the white-collared condors, who stared back, their raw flesh peeping coyly through the black feather boas on their bosoms. The man who had been sitting there had gone, and his big blue balloon with him, at that. I said, "He came near the table."

"So he did," said Charles. "Stay here. He's probably juiced to the eyeballs." And vaulting over the myrtle hedge, he bounded off down the path past the condors. I followed him.

The Zoological Gardens of Rome occupy about thirty acres of gently undulating ground. Anything could hide there with utter impunity. The inmates of the cages are far too much taken up with their indigestion to pay any attention to interlopers.

But the zoo was closing. We belted down that path without overtaking or seeing the slightest sign of the thief of Charles's camera and then we did the sensible thing: we returned to the entrance and, concealed behind the broad, fluffy flanks of the llama, scanned the trickle of patrons emerging.

Our quarry came, too, strolling past the flamingos with one hand in his pocket and the other still holding his stupid blue balloon on its stick. The sunset, glaring red in his face, showed me what I had missed in the piazza. The thief was one of the two who had entered the Villa Borghese behind me.

I squeaked. It was not, as Charles made out afterward, an animal ululation. But it made the llama twirl on its neck. The man turned. Charles, revealed, made a headlong dive in his direction, with me following. The man whirled and, running like hell, disappeared behind the flamingos again. The last visitor strolled through the zoo gates and the gates were loudly locked.

At this point, naturally, we should have summoned the police and the director. Instead, we raced after the disappearing patter of footsteps until Charles stopped and I cannoned into him and Charles said, "He's hiding."

The sound of footsteps had vanished. Charles said, "He could be up a tree." We looked up. The trees, like Di, were in the autumn seminude mode and quite empty. "Or," Charles added, "he could go out the same way as the keepers."

"Except that he hasn't," I said. "He's here, or we should have heard him. What about the Ippopotami?"

The circular marble hall of the overweight brigade was not yet closed. We slid in and looked: an Ippopotamo, hoping to be fed, came into its show cell and gazed at us. The ten cells in the rotunda all appeared to lead to the outside enclosure. Charles said, "Hell!" and vaulting in beside the Ippopotamo, which still looked as if it expected to be fed, he disappeared through the back of its premises. Across the mudbath behind we could see, distant in the dusk, a man with a balloon, galloping. We bounded soggily after him.

If you ever feel like tearing across a deserted zoological park let me dissuade you, especially at nightfall. No astronomer works with the light on. In every observatory the grounds are in darkness. But the walls don't normally overhang a ten-foot sheer drop to the lion pit. The notice said it was strictly prohibited to Accostarsi Agli Animali, and my heart bled for the animals as I switched off my torch and blundered into the next pile of dead leaves and branches. A plane roared overhead and a smell of fish just warned me in time of the seal pond. I switched on my torch and a blue balloon hysterically bobbing, ran along the hedge top just beyond it. I yelled to Charles and charged stoutly onward.

We met on the other side of the hedge and were running together when the footsteps stopped and we had to creep about listening again. My finger roll sat in my tonsils. Charles said fretfully, "Why doesn't he burst the bloody balloon?"

"Because," I said patiently, "the noise would give away where he is. What did that camera cost you?"

It was a rhetorical question, but he answered it. "The same as yours. A hundred and twenty quid sterling and no customs receipt," said Charles, breathing heavily. "Are you a man's woman, or a body-clinging knit like Diana?"

"I'm a cripple," I said angrily. "I've been attacked by a shark."

Charles grabbed the torch and turned it on, regardless. I had tripped over a water point. From the tap, a long green hose snaked wetly away in the mud. "Ha!" said Charles, and turned the tap on with a flourish. The hose got up and bounded; we ran alongside till we both reached its nozzle, and had a brief difference of opinion over where we should point it.

Charles won. There was a strangled gasp from Gli Elefanti Marini and the torchlight wavered on a streaming figure with a blue balloon which rose behind a wall and lit out across the grass, going as if the pumas were coming.

He led us full pelt across the whole width of the zoo, with the leopards roaring and the volpi barking and the gorilla knocking hell out of his ropeful of Michelins. We chased him out past the llama stand, over the entrance piazza and through the trees to the sloping walls of a disused Egyptian temple. Shadows veiled the crumbling hieroglyphics and carved rhinoceroses over its entrance. Darkness hid the doorway, and the forty-foot hole of mud, grass and rubble excavated in front of it.

We didn't know about the hole. Charles fell in first, and I fell on top of him. The torch broke and went out. The night contained only the sound of running footsteps, lightly retreating, and the solemn music, many decibels strong, of the entire strength of the Ark complaining about the living conditions. I sludged off a faceful of mud and remarked, shouting, "I have news for you. You are going to buy me a new chamois shirt in the morning."

He got to his feet, to my private relief, and swore, in a decidedly undamaged way.

"And a new torch," I added. Very soon the uproar was going to rouse somebody.

"Come on," he said abruptly. "The wall by the restaurant is the lowest."

I didn't argue. I had other plans for the evening, besides explaining to a group of large shirty keepers why we were running about in the darkness plastered with mud and Accostarsing Angli Animals. And since Charles doesn't enjoy giving up any more than anyone does, I walked beside him back up the dark slope to the restaurant with my mouth firmly shut.

It was, I suppose, pure coincidence that the man with the blue balloon thought of the same low wall out of the Gardens. And that he believed us sufficiently out of commission to risk doing something before he went over it. We had just caught the first spicy wind of the condors when Charles stopped me dead with his arm and said, "See it?"

I saw it. Down the path, flickering dimly, was a small wistful light in the Gents. "I pass," I said, whispering.

"Right," said Charles, and picking himself off the next pile of rubble he felt about and lifted a billet. "If I come out of this I shall buy you a new shirt and a torch and a wall-to-wall bed, and by that I am defining your future environment."

"Well, watch it," I said, without much ingenuity. What I think about Charles doesn't fit into words very readily. And then he walked away into the darkness.

He had gone three paces when the loo windows went white and then red and there was the crash of a violent explosion. I saw Charles, silhouetted, stop moving. Then, as the echoes rolled cracking away, he began to sprint fast to the building.

There was a moment's stunned quiet in the Gardens, followed by a howl of protest from the denizens. I began to run after Charles.

Before I got there, he backed out of the toilet. He had switched on the lamp by its doorway. In the light his face was green with shock. He said, "Don't go in. I'm going to be sick," and was. I dragged out two paper handkerchiefs and gave them to him.

My hand, I found, was shaking. There was a sack of dead leaves onto which Charles, recovering, had subsided. He said, around the handkerchief. "He had blown his head off."

I said, *"Shot* himself?" It was unbelievable because it was so unlikely. He had stolen a camera. He had escaped from the owners. He didn't know Charles was on his way there. I added, "He might have shot you," and then, "Is your camera there?"

"I didn't look," said Charles. He looked a little better.

"Then we'd better get it," I said, and walked in fast before I could change my mind or Charles could stop me.

It was all true. The camera was there, blotched with blood, and I had no more paper hankies. Charles snatched it from me and swore all the time I, too, was being sick. Presently I was able to collect my senses. "Charles. He didn't knock himself off. There wasn't a gun in the cubicle."

"To hell with it," he said with abrupt violence. Somewhere in the distance whistles were blowing and you could hear men's voices here and there above the bickering animals. He pulled me up and helped me run up the pathway. "It might have been a grenade," he said as he ran.

"No," I said. I drew some punctuated breaths and added, "The film had been pulled from the camera."

I could see his face as he looked around at me, startled. "Right out? Exposed?"

"No. Gone," I said. "There was no film in the camera and none in his pockets. I patted them.

And the camera had been loaded. I noticed. Half the reel had been shot off already."

We ran in silence up to the restaurant plateau. The street-lights over the wall showed my basket, standing dim on the table. I said, "Charles. He was stealing the fashion shots?"

"My God. I suppose so," said Charles. He paused, a little distractedly, by the white marble fountain which decorated the wall we were scaling and added, "In which case he's got them."

"Or someone has," I said. "Charles, there were two of them in the Villa Borghese. Do you think they met in the Gents, and our man passed the roll of film on to his mate?"

"And then blew himself up," Charles remarked. He pulled himself together.

> *"We will not build a cross for you*
> *With angels all a-simper*
> *Because, my friend, you left us with*
> *A bang and not a whimper."*

His foot, slipping off a defaced marble elbow, landed in a pool of pale slimy lily leaves. He swore and began climbing again.

"Or was killed by his mate for the film." I had got to the top of the wall and was in no mood for obituaries. I said, "Charles? Shouldn't we go back and tell all to the police?"

He was too busy at that moment to answer, so I jumped first into the darkness of the Via Ulisse Aldorrandi.

I didn't fall. I was caught by two waiting hands, one of which patted my head and then gripped me. The same grasp received Charles and arrested him likewise. Limp as shot game birds, we hung side by side on the pavement.

"I shouldn't tell them, you know," said our unknown captor, vaguely surveying us. "The Roman fuzz are so old-fashioned, like Directoire knickers. I have a car, if you want to push off discreetly."

It was too much. I could hear Charles begin to gasp with incipient hysteria and I had trouble, myself, with my uvula. I said, "Who are you? We don't know you, do we?"

"My name," the man said, "is Johnson Johnson. A man of regular habits, with the fastest vertical liftoff in Italy."

CHAPTER 2

WE TOOK THIS MAN Johnson Johnson to Maurice's party, and if that seems unlikely, you haven't considered the problem.

We got into this beaten-up Fiat 500, and the man said, "Where to?" and Charles said, "The railway station would be marvelous," with what I can only call prodigious presence of mind.

"Nonsense," said Johnson Johnson. He was English, that went without saying, and I have seldom seen a man less remarkable. You would remember nothing, not even his coloring, if it weren't for his bifocal glasses, glittering under the peak of a golfing cap. He had on a Harris Tweed jacket, and under it a hand-knit jersey, the cuffs of which nearly covered his knuckles. "Nonsense," he said. "Where to? I'll drive you all the way."

"Brindisi," said Charles, and I would have kicked

23

him had we been sitting together. I said, "We stay north of Rome, at Velterra. I work at the Maurice Frazer Observatory."

"Do you?" said Johnson Johnson with interest. He had not yet started the car. Over the wall, we could hear shouting and see the light of torch beams glancing through the tree branches. "I thought it was owned by a film company."

"It's been refitted and modernized," I said. "The Zodiac Trust are encouraging Maurice to use it for projects."

With lemurlike innocence, the glasses surveyed me. "So you're an astronomer. And is your friend an astronomer also, or are you merely cohabiting?"

At this point, Charles opened the car door. The light, coming on, illuminated in full technicolor the bloodstained camera lying on the car seat and also brought us, full strength, the volume of shouting from over the wall. He shut the car door very gently.

"Charles," I said with some effort, "is a photographer. We were chasing after the man in the zoo, who had stolen his camera. We think he wanted to pirate his advance fashion photographs. It would be lovely, really, to be taken to the station; it was so nice of you to rescue us. A police thing would be very boring."

"I do agree," said Johnson Johnson. "Especially if Charles is the Marquis's son. Charles Digham?"

"Digham," affirmed Charles sweetly. My heart sank. "And this," he added, "is my friend, Miss Ruth Russell. You haven't said, sir, what brought you to the zoo?"

The glasses stared at him. "I thought I had," said Johnson mildly.

"I mean . . ." said Charles.

"What am I doing here? Oh," said Johnson. "I'm painting the Pope. I shan't blackmail you if you won't blackmail me. Now then. The Maurice Frazer Observatory. Do help yourself to a tissue," he added, "if you want to wipe the blood off that camera." And he put the Fiat into gear and tooled off.

We got to the Dome in forty minutes, having done the Piazza Galeno in one dizzy circuit and roared past all the tarts on the motorway, doing roughly a hundred and twenty miles an hour. Whatever was under the bonnet of that Fiat wasn't cinquecenti, and Charles and I by tacit consent gave Johnson Johnson the address of the Dome and not the address of the humble lodgings we both shared with Jacko. We had not only been picked up by a nut: we had been picked up by a well-off and dangerous nut and were likely to be exposed either in print or in prison, whatever we did about it.

At the Dome we asked him in for a coffee, which unfortunately he accepted, and I went ahead and yelled up to Jacko, who was fixing his plate-holder on the swing-up shelf which bars the other side of the cupola door and makes sure that idiots don't march into the dome with their torches on.

He came down a few minutes later to make sure we had all the blinds closed but actually to see what Charles had in his hip flask. Astronomers are not allowed to drink before they go on duty: you can get enough straight hallucinations just looking for eight hours through a telescope without resorting to alcohol. Charles, an intuitive man, poured him a noggin for afters into a yellow Melamine cup and related the event of the evening in four succinct sentences while liberally lacing our coffee. Jacko went becomingly white and said, "Christ. The Zodiac Trust'll have kittens."

The top brass of the Trust, in the person of one Professor Hathaway, does not expect its projects to get mixed up in murders or suicides. "It won't," I said. "It'll have baby lawyers with letters of dismissal all ready for signing by Mr. Frazer." I stared at Jacko with what I hoped was a message of despair in my eyes. "Maybe," I added, "since Mr. Johnson got us away, the police will never get to hear how it happened. Mr. Johnson," I added with emphasis, "is here to paint the Pope."

"I know," said Jacko. His color was coming back. He twisted the nearest messianic lock of his hair. "Would the Pope help?"

I sometimes think the only reason Di goes to bed with Jacko is that he asks such damned silly questions. I was about to answer this one when Charles, heretofore much subdued, said suddenly, "How do you know?"

"We met last week at Castel Gandolfo," said Jacko. "My God, where did you get that damned cup from?"

Castel Gandolfo is the Pope's Summer Palace. It also houses the Vatican Observatory in an elegant house by the lakeside. If Johnson was there, at the very least it was with the Pontiff's permission. I said to Johnson Johnson, "I beg your pardon."

"Granted," he said.

26

"Where the hell did that come from!" said Jacko. He was talking about Charles's cup. Charles pointed to a cupboard, and Jacko ran and fell on his knees in front of it. Then he put both hands around the handle like oven mitts and opened the cupboard a fraction. A white mouse with red eyes sneaked out of it and ran under the stove.

"Poppy!" I said accusingly.

"I was going to put her back," said Jack hurriedly. "That bastard Innes tore up all my pictures."

"I'd have torn them up too if I'd thought of it," I said with exasperation. Open war between Jacko and Innes was all that I needed. "Now you'll have to take them all over again. Think of that."

He didn't hear me because he was lying full length under the stove with a broom. Charles had found some All-Bran and was emptying it on the tiled floor while Johnson Johnson, with great presence of mind, had shut the door and stuffed dishtowels under it. A stream of oaths flowed from under the stove, broken by a flurry of activity. Jacko jabbed with his broomstick, swiveled, rolled over the bran heap and stabbed at the legs of a table. Charles crouched twitching beside him while Johnson, moving from cupboard to table, began methodically to wall in the floor space with Supermercato packets of groceries. A doorbell rang somewhere in the Dome and Charles said, with prescience, "That'll be Innes." Johnson began methodically to put the packs back again. We all got to our feet.

That was all we had done when Innes shoved open the door, after batting it a few times against the dishcloths, and looked with surprise at the bran mash on the floor and Jacko propped on his broom-stick and heavily profiled in cereal.

"We were taking an impression for posterity," said Charles with great simplicity. "What can we do for you?"

Innes looked around at us all. Then he looked straight under the table and shouted.

Johnson Johnson yelled at the same moment. They leaped forward together, colliding heavily into the cereal; Johnson, his arms outflung, was a yard nearer the table than Innes, who lay blowing into the bran and then rose uncertainly onto his knees.

"Hell," said Johnson with feeling. He looked at us. "That was a rat. Did you see it go past you?"

The door was wide open.

"Yes," said Jacko. "It's all right. It went out the front door."

"We wondered," said Charles, "who had been spilling the bran. Are you all right, Innes? Have some coffee."

"And some brandy," I said.

"I think," said Johnson, "I had better be go-ing." He was holding his wrist.

"You've hurt yourself!" Innes said.

"No," said Johnson reassuringly. He doubled up and then sat down quickly. "Charles and Ruth will look after me anyway. Unless I'm keeping you all back from something."

We all said no, and Innes delivered his message, which was a pressing invitation to Jacko from Mau-rice. Jacko said sulkily, "I can't go to his flaming party. Someone has to stay with the 50-Inch."

"Look," I said. "Go and have a couple of hours.

You needn't drink. I'll look after the plates if you'll put out the chart and coordinates."

He was dying to go. "We tossed for it and I lost," he said appealingly.

"I know. But if the weather had been thick you would have been able to come. I don't mind," I said, and I meant it. I avoided catching Charles's eye in order to continue to mean it. Jacko was still arguing in an unconvinced way when Innes left and we all made a dive for Johnson, who was doubled up screeching with laughter and continued to laugh while we got his coat and tie off and finally opened his shirt.

He had a winter-weight woolen vest underneath it, and Poppy. I helped him dress while Jacko lit out for Mouse Hall to return her. I admired Johnson's jersey.

He was pleased. "I have an uncle who knits them in Margate." He added, with a faint wistfulness, "Is Maurice Frazer giving a party?"

One forgets how famous Maurice is. Long before he bought the villa and the garden and the observatories, Maurice had wintered in Italy on the proceeds of his work in the theater. Everyone in Roman society came to see Maurice. And English and French society. And American. And South American, even. And every pretty girl in the civilized world, whether in society or not. Maurice is seventy or more and Timothy, who looks after him, is his hostess. They are past scandal, but never past gossip. Maurice's is the finest center of gossip in Europe.

I said, "Would you like to go?" because it was

easy. Anyone with his wits about him can get into Maurice's. But to be asked twice to Maurice's you must be very good company indeed.

You observe therefore, humble pie, Ruth Russell quite as naïve in her own way as Jacko. I did my stint in the Dome; I went home and dressed up like a bottle of Mille Fiori d'Alpi and I walked fifty yards to the white marble gates of the villa, where Charles met me in someone's Alfa Romeo and conveyed me the mile and a half up the drive. He had been two hours at the party already, and behaved like it.

"And Johnson?" I said, when I got him to stop making tensile tests all over my bodystocking.

"Never mind Johnson," he said.

"But I do mind Johnson," I said. "And I want to get to this party. And if you stop the car once again, I shall leave you. Did Maurice take to Johnson Johnson?"

Charles made an expansive gesture, and then corrected the ensuing diagonal. "Your friendly neighborhood portrait painter," he said, "has been given the key to the executive washroom. Maurice has always wanted to meet Johnson and Johnson has always wanted to meet Maurice. A series of portrait sittings has been arranged and will begin this very week, London papers please copy."

I stared at Charles, and made a number of mental apologies to Jacko. "Aha!" I said.

"The artist will, of course," said Charles, "be staying at the villa with Maurice."

"Oho," I said vaguely.

"You thought," said Charles accusingly, "that he

was going to paint you and me and the Pope in a triptych."

"No," I said thoughtfully. "No. But I know who's going to go for him. Di and Timothy."

I was dead right at that. Timothy is tall and pink and helpful and Lithuanian, and anything as hand-knit as Johnson was bound to be whipped in and licensed. Timothy met us among the arum lilies at the top of the twin marble staircase and kissed us both while he unwrapped Charles from his ankle-length wolfskin. "Darlings," he said. "You have brought us a beautiful present. The Master is thrilled with him. Truly."

"Look at all the nice things you give us," I said. "You do such lovely parties, Timothy."

"Oh, well," he said pinkly. "except that you keep all the little treasures to yourself, don't you? Hasn't Charles any nice friends?"

"Only you and me," I said grinning back at him. I said it before. I have never minded pouffs. Charles was mine and I was his, and even people like Timothy knew it. Then we got to our food and awaited our summons to Maurice.

The excuse is Maurice's age; but Maurice always held audiences, even when he lived in the Penthouse Suite in the Dorchester. At the Villa Sansavino he held audience in his writing room. During the day, he would be enthroned behind his antique sarcophagus desk. During a party, in velvet jacket and slippers, he would be sitting erect in his antique Sicilian armchair beside the roaring fire, the flames gleaming on his chaise longue, his desk and his books and a quantity of handsome appointments, generally aged eighteen or under and single. All Maurice's interviews were conducted over the heads of a bevy of girls, many of them related to him, and all of whom knew the time of day to the last double entendre. You needed to watch what you were saying at Maurice's.

We made our entry together, Charles and I, because Charles had not been summoned alone in my absence: Timothy is careful about such things. We left the hot, polite uproar of the supper room and, shepherded by Timothy, stepped through the paned door carved with the princely arms of the family who had built the villa and laid out the gardens and erected the first Dome, that obligatory plaything of princes, on top of the gradient.

Then Charles shrieked. He shrieked, and gripped my arm and, turning, rushed from the threshold, dragging me with him.

I can tell you precisely what I thought. I thought, Maurice has blown his head off.

Then I heard Maurice's voice saying, "Well I saw Beatrice, Timothy darling, but where's Dante?" and I said to Charles, "What is it?"

I had to say it again before he stopped, and then he put his hands to his head and just stared at me. *"Don't you hear it?"* he said.

I thought, Meningitis. *Lord Digham Serious. Lady Teddington Flies Out to Photographer Son.* His face was yellow white and his eyes had black slopes cut out under them. I said, "Sit down. I'll get a doctor. Don't worry. To hell with Maurice."

He didn't sit down. He said, *"Don't you hear it?"* in a voice rising distinctly toward panic. It was not the Charles of the obituary notices. But then, it had not been fully Charles of the obituary notices ever since what we had found in the zoo. I expect I looked pretty grotty as well.

Timothy was coming toward us. I said, "I don't hear anything. Whatever you hear, it must be in your head."

He was saying, "It's not. It's not, Ruth," when Timothy came up beside us. He said, "Aren't you well? Ruth, isn't he well? He must come and lie down then, darling. Along here. It's my room and ever so comfy."

Charles stared at him, his hands still held over his ears. "It's something in his head," I said. "A noise. He thinks he hears a terrible noise."

Timothy blinked. Then, turning slowly, he glided back to the room he had left. We heard his voice, speaking to Maurice, and Maurice's voice saying, "Yes do, do. How exciting!" Then, as if a command had descended from heaven, Charles's face altered. His hands eased off and then left his eardrums. He said, "It's stopped!"

Timothy's head, appearing in Maurice's doorway, called dulcetly, "You can come along now!"

We went in.

We were confronted by ten pretty faces and Maurice, whose face was pretty too. It was a beautiful face, fine and aesthetic and cynical, and upholstered with the finest white hair, like a porcelain vase with white mink on it. He said, "Ruth darling. You must have Digham tied off or divorce him. I won't have you become preggy by someone who can hear Mouse Alarms."

I said, "We're not married" in the same moment

as Charles exclaimed, "Mouse Alarms!" which gives you a rough idea of our respective order of priorities.

Maurice was with me. He said, "Are you living in sin? Why, of course you are. I remember it all. What is the basis of morality? It is a loving relationship, one not to possess, dominate and exploit another person but one in which two people try to understand and care for one another. But how very exhibitionist of you to refrain from marrying. Think how lucky you are, being of opposite sexes. Although you do give me a moment's worry, Ruthie dear. Career women always do."

"Timothy," I said, "is quite safe from me. Maurice, explain the Mouse Alarm."

Maurice stared inimically at me. He said, *"You* are the scientist. It is *your* world we poor creatures of Nature are trapped in. Do I not pay you with shekels to succor us?"

"He doesn't like mice," said Johnson mildly. I hadn't seen him, there in the shadows; neither had Charles. We peered at him, and the bifocals flashed redly back. Diana Minicucci, almost topless and earmarked like the Passover with cake blusher, was lying reclined at his feet.

"So," said Timothy, "we had this Mouse Alarm fixed to scare them off. Too high for human hearing, or so they said. I'll write and tell them. Imagine. How they will foam!"

I looked at Charles. "You're a freak," I said. "I suppose you hear dog whistles too?"

"I've never been whistled at," said Charles, "by a dog. Do you have the bloody thing on all the time?"

"Yes. Especially tonight. Tonight was a Red Alert," said Maurice peacefully. "We heard a certain rumor from Jacko. What a ridiculous name. Almost as ridiculous as its owner."

I said, "You know, this is a little story I'd hate anyone to tell Innes Wye. He doesn't know Poppy had wandered."

Maurice stared at me with such disfavor. "Ruth darling, if you must give a rodent a name, why let your choice fall on a flower? Why not look to the earlier cultures, the strong, the primitive nomenclatures. I often feel," said Maurice with gentle melancholy, "that God was less than fair to the Shittites."

One of the blossoms at his feet raised her fair face. "Hittites, Uncle Maurice," she said.

"In my book," said Maurice gently, "it was Shittite. Tell Innes, Ruth, that if he cares to bring the creature to me, I shall rename it. In a vat. With some sulphuric acid."

"I once painted a mouse," said Johnson Johnson.

"What?" said Maurice sharply.

"Green," said Johnson. "It looked very pretty."

We left soon after that.

From the loggia behind the French windows you could see the top of the hill and even the mosque shape of the observatory black against the night sky, with the segment of denser blackness where the cupola was rolled back for the telescope. We left that way because it was quicker, and we looked up at the Dome because we were together, and Jacko was alone, and hadn't got either Di or her photographs.

That was how we came to see that tonight there was no segment of dark but a golden triangle. Tonight the cupola was pouring out watts like a lighthouse.

I bumped into Innes as we raced for the steps. He took one glance where I pointed and joined us. No one spoke. Even Charles, the outsider, knew enough to recognize what was the matter.

At night the full lights in the cupola never go on. They would spoil the plate, and ruin your night sight. Sometimes, when you lose sight of the wire and begin to see streets and people and cars in the lens, you can relieve your eyestrain in the dim light of the console. But you can't, of course, abandon the telescope. The motor might stick: the telescope might fail to follow the arc of your subject; atmospheric changes might make your star become fuzzed or the light become jumpy and splintered, so that you have to center it back on the cross wire.

On a clear night like this, with exposures going on all the time, the cupola light is never on. Except in an emergency.

We got to the Dome and I found the front door, which is always locked, had been forced open. Charles swung around the emergency generator and dashed for the stairs to the cupola. I stood in the hall shouting "Jacko!" while Innes closed the door and dragged a chair over to jam it. We heard Charles reach the second floor and then the ring of his feet on the steep iron steps to the telescope. Then a door on the middle floor opened, and a moment later a man came out of the darkroom.

He looked down and I looked up, and I recognized him. It was the second of the two men from the Villa Borghese.

I shrieked. I heard Charles's answering cry

from the Dome. Then suddenly all the lights vanished.

It was Innes who surprised us that evening. As Charles's steps came thundering down from the top and the steps of the intruder, even louder, came down the lower staircase toward us, Innes shoved a chair into my hand and said, "Stand there. We'll get him between us."

We did, too. The footsteps came flying toward us: I could smell him, that polite gentleman with collar and tie and neat haircut, who had asked me in the Villa Borghese where I was lunching. Then Innes moved. There was a thud, and a gasp, and I brought my chair down with a crash just as the intruder came blundering between us.

I had grasped his jacket when he tore himself free and, turning, ran back upstairs again. There was another crash, and a series of thwacks and harsh grunting. He had run into Charles's fists this time. Somewhere behind me was a fire extinguisher. I felt for it and ripped it off its hook. Then I said, "You guard the doorway" to Innes, and, running, made for the fight on the staircase.

It had moved upward before I could reach it. From the sound of it, they were fighting in and out of the darkroom and then through the workshop and into the storeroom. I thought of all the tools in the workshop and called Charles's name in the darkness. He shouted back something which sounded reassuring. Then he said more clearly, "Ruth? I've trapped him. Tell Innes to stay by the door. Try and untie Jacko. He's been left in the darkroom."

I ran blundering along to the darkroom. The lights were smashed; the floor was a mess of crunched glass, but someone lying on it was pounding for attention with his feet. It was Jacko, with ropes at his wrists and his ankles. I touched his face, and found a cloth tied also over his mouth. I loosened it, and he spat out a hunk of wet cotton and said, "Put the power switch on."

The power board is on the wall of the darkroom, and I was dimwitted not to have thought of it before. I left Jacko and scrabbling over the wall, found and pulled it. A moment before that, a clatter of running footsteps echoed suddenly from the circular passage outside. Charles, my phlegmatic Charles, exploded at the top of his voice, *"Ah, God damn it to hell!"* and then called more distantly, "Innes! Innes! He's left through the loo window. Do you see him?"

There was a bang as Innes opened the door, and another clatter as Charles rattled down the marble stairs to the bottom and then ran out to join him. Their voices receded, calling.

I looked at Jacko in the reflected light from the passage. He was covered in blood, mostly from the cut glass, but he did not look concussed, only furious. I said, "How did it happen?"

"He hit me on the head from behind," Jacko said. "I was changing the plates, and I'd left the bloody Vee filter here in the darkroom. When I woke up, he'd bound me."

I said, "What did he want?" There were plenty of knives. I had him half freed already.

"He didn't tell me," said Jacko sarcastically. "But I can tell you, he made a hell of a mess of Charles's camera. Then he smashed the lights and I had to stand on my shoulders and kick on the Dome power switch. Look at my bloody jacket."

"We lost him," said Innes, coming in with a torch at that moment. He turned it on Jacko. "Come on, let's get you into the bathroom and sponged down. We lost the guy in the bushes. But I'm going to get on that phone as soon as you're fixed up and get the police onto his tail." He swept his torch around the wrecked room. "What in hell do you sppose he was after?"

"He's smashed up Charles's Zeiss Icarex," said Jacko for the second time. "He'd left it in the Dome and I'd just brought it down when it happened."

"Not my camera. Hell," said Charles from the doorway. "That must be your camera, Ruth. The man must be bonkers."

Jacko, mopping his face with a handkerchief, was moving with Innes's guidance to the door. "No, it's Charles's," he said. "I found it there when I came on duty. *Digham* it says under the lid." He stopped, and looked at us, as Charles and I stood both staring at him.

Charles said slowly. "Then . . ."

"Then," I said, "it was my camera they stole in the zoo. You took *my* camera to work with this morning."

His face was marked, just a little, by the fighting. The graze stood out against the paleness of the rest of his face. He said, still staring at me, "I thought there was more unused film than I'd expected. So it was your film they pinched."

"Some tasteful shots of the Fontana di Trevi?" I said. "Preceding some even more tasteful shots of Di's sexytunica from the Villa Borghese this morning. What was in your own camera?"

He turned the torch on it. It lay, a warped, twisted wreck on the work bench. It had been attacked, repeatedly and efficiently, with a hatchet. There was no film inside it. I said, "He didn't want you to take any pictures with that one again. And he's got the film."

"With yesterday's fashion batch on it," Charles said. "Which was, as it happens, top secret." He whistled. "I'll have to tell the couture houses. Thank God I sent the other exposed film back with the van. I rang this evening. It's all perfectly safe."

"Police?" I said.

"Yes," said Charles.

"No," said Johnson, arriving unheard in the doorway. "One, the couture people won't want the publicity. And two, the police will link you with the recent nasty occurrence by the condor house. Two cameras mysteriously wrecked in one evening is too much of a coincidence."

"We met him in the grounds," said Charles very sweetly, answering my unspoken question. "He went back for some small reinforcements."

"I brought them too," said Johnson, and opening a duffel bag, displayed three bottles of champagne and three others of vodka. "With Maurice's compliments. He was sorry to hear that poor Jacko had tripped down the stair shaft. Shall we adjourn, would you say, to the kitchen?"

We started with the champagne and then we finished the three bottles of vodka, a passable feat for five people, and blew the fuse of the stove while boiling up coffee. In between, we swapped obituary notices proper to what had been a stirring evening:

> *We could not say our last farewell*
> *Nor even say goodbye*
> *For you were gone before we knew*
> *And only God knows why.*

CHAPTER 3

THE NEXT DAY, Sunday, we all spent nursing our hangovers in bed and searching the papers for Gothic accounts of the headless form found in the zoo park toletta. We didn't have far to look. Even the llama got into the picture, although there were no sensitive camera studies of Lo Rapaci. The police were treating it, they said, as obvious murder. Charles and I got up for lunch, and then went back to bed again.

At four o'clock, the iron shutters went up like gunfire, and the village prepared for its promenade. At four-thirty, with a bang louder than gunfire, Charles slammed the door of our joint digs and left me.

By then it was no news to the village. Charles and I are normally rather muted performers, but whereas I quarrel also in very low gear, Charles's voice rises in anger; and he had been very angry indeed. In retrospect, I put it all down to its being Sunday.

Although all the museums are free, not even Innes goes into Rome on a Sunday. Every ruin is packed like a biscuit box. And between eleven and twelve, fresh out from late Mass and present unto the third and fourth generation, the whole of Rome packs itself into its Fiat 500's and sets off, driving slowly, for Parassio. Or Neni, or whatever. After lunch, it returns, driving even more slowly and not all that straight, for reasons not at all to do with the health of great-aunt and the bambini.

To visit Rome on a Sunday is suicide. Particularly if you are Charles in a rage. More particularly if you are Charles in a rage and your Alfa Romeo is still having its brakes fixed. There are nine motor repair shops in Parassio, and I could only hope that he'd forgotten which one he'd left it at.

He didn't come back that night, and I was at work all day on the Monday, with a wrecked stove and a temper. Jacko and I have an arrangement, because the Rome shops shut that day. I work, and he goes to the Spanish Steps and picks up new subjects for his photography. By November, the German blondes and sultry Philadelphians have disappeared, but the Rampa and every other staircase in Rome is thick with homesick students reading their letters. Jacko merely looks at the postmarks and addresses them in the language of origin. One day, someone will smash Jacko's camera. One day, someone will smash Jacko if he is not very, very careful.

I was packing the plates when Maurice came to

pay one of his state visits to his seigneurial property. In the weeks since he brought us to Italy, Maurice had become quite knowledgeable about the observatory. He sat and talked while I went on boxing them, each plate in its transparent envelope with a card giving the date and exposure and atmospheric conditions obtaining. There were plates for every day: the Zodiac Trust would expect a full record to process. I even included the plates we had spoiled. There would be a few from Saturday night, for example, to explain away.

There was nearly another that moment. "You ought to know, darling," said Maurice. "Timothy has lent Charles the old Maserati. He really can't take dud brakes to Naples."

I released a plate and cased it, unfractured. Then I said, "No, Maurice. No gossip this morning."

"I can guess what it was, anyway," said Maurice, quite undisturbed. "He offered to marry you. I do sympathize, I do really, darling. I'm like Timothy; I'm *militantly* Fem Lib at heart. I should never marry a man unless he was poor but brilliant. Look at darling Di's mother. Eight starring vehicles with Rock Hudson, and she never saw Minicucci again after she got him to the altar."

"Really, Maurice," I said. I checked the supplies in the fridge. All fine photographic stock comes from America. Because the Roman heat plays hell with the emulsion, the bulk supplies go straight into the stockroom meat safe, and from there to the fridge in the darkroom. Maurice, looking particularly elegant with the white mink combed, and his hands crossed on the Malacca cane under his Thai

44

silk stock tie, was more than a little in my way. "She had Di, didn't she?" I said.

"Oh, but that was *before,*" Maurice said. "Didn't you know? A breech delivery six weeks after the wedding, and she couldn't have another thing, poor darling; not even free range for the test tube. She died of overeating; you wouldn't believe what she looked like. A Givenchy Pekinese sitting on two fake fur pouffes. Di *loves* your Johnson."

"I thought he was your Johnson now," I said. He had brought me some Alemagna Tintin chocolate and eaten most of it himself because I hadn't a light for his cigar: Charles and I were out of matches. In any case, I was damned if I was going to stop before I was ready. Jacko had put away his porn pictures, but the tube from the nitrogen cylinder had been left partly unhooked: it ran all the way around to the sink, where there were instructions in green felt pen all over the wall beside the Intermittent Gaseous Burst Valve, including a poem using three four-letter words and an Italian one I hadn't heard of before. I rubbed it out, for the honor of the team, and rehooked the tubing and checked the lists for the evening's work.

Maurice said, "I'm sure, darling, he'd paint you for nothing; I can see he adores tall, busy girls. You don't even know who he is. You know he painted Ladybird, and all those strong-faced people in Persia, and he has this fabulous yacht called the *Dolly?*"

I laid down my pencil. "Maurice. When I want to swap Charles for Johnson, you will be the first I shall tell. I promise you."

Nothing ever shakes Maurice. "I'm so glad,

darling," he said. "These small woolly men are often quite energetic. Di says he's lovely, and I don't think she's even got him into bed yet."

I wasn't feeling witty. I got rid of him by saying that I had to go along and visit Innes, and did he want to see Poppy.

Next day I treated myself to a trip into Rome, and went and bought shoes at Samo's, which may not seem the gesture of defiance it is if you don't know Samo's prices. Then I went and had a coffee at the Greco.

Di was there, which was nice. She had on dark glasses and a long coat of gray glacé snakeskin, edged from neck to floor with lime green rabbit fur, and lime green stockings to match. She was alone, and reading the *Daily American* with a Wodka Moskoskaya Martini in front of her. I sat down, and she turned over a page. "He's gone to Naples," she said. Under whatever unusual circumstances Minicuccis were born, it wasn't yesterday.

"I know," I said. A tailcoated waiter brought my drinks and a glass of water, and put them on the round marble table. I said, "Thank God he isn't with Johnson. Maurice had persuaded himself he's a sex maniac."

"That's Maurice's wishful thinking," Di said. "You can just imagine all the slap and tickle he's hoping for out of ten sittings. This paper has the most peculiar advertisements. *Dynamic experienced poised bilingual executive secretary needed for financial office in center, Italian hours.*"

I considered it. "It sounds almost normal."

"Yes," said Di. "That's just what I mean. Well, what about this one? *WHO has white American*

Turkeys for Thanksgiving? The Zoo Farm. Order yours now."

"No, thanks," I said. Another advertisement had caught my eye. It said, FALL FAIR, 7th Nov., 2:00 to 5:00, and underneath: *Museo Nazionale, Palazzo Barberini, Tuesday Nov. 7th. Bring the kids. Home-baked Goodies; Ready-wear Rack; Games; Tombola; Genuine Auction.* A chorus of loud cries, rending the scarlet plush baroque ambience of the Greco and causing the antico oil paintings to tremble on the silk damask walls heralded the arrival of Di's current party on a wave of Patou and Madame Rochas. I gave Di her *Daily American* and lit out.

Gladioli and carnations and roses were massed at the foot of the Spanish Steps. I walked there behind two soldiers with black tricorn hats and broad red stripes on their trousers; their tailcoats beat in rhythm like blackbirds all the way past the fountain and up the first flight of steps. A group of Indians with a guitar was sitting on the steps just above, strumming and talking with a man in a brown woolen pullover who was accompanying on comb and tissue.

It was Johnson Johnson. He got up as I stepped around the pendants and said, "Well, Christ, at last. I take it you've left Di behind you?"

He was jacketless and his trousers were bagged. The bifocal glasses glittered under a lot of black hair. I said, "She's at the Caffe Greco," and moved my skirt away from the guitarist's expert fingering. I added, "Waiting for you."

"Hardly," said Johnson. He jerked his head toward the big yellow hotel at the top of the steps.

47

"I'm at the Hassler. I saw you both pass from the roof terrace. If you don't believe me, come and have lunch with me."

"Instead of Di?" I looked at him. "Hardly," I added.

"Instead of Charles," said Johnson politely.

That is the great thing about Rome. Everyone knows everyone else's business.

I am not in want, but I don't lunch every day at the Hassler, either. Among the other reasons why I accepted Johnson's invitation was the conviction that anyone who could stand up to Maurice's twin-urn burials of his friends' reputations could stand up to a mad portrait painter with an eye to the main chance like Johnson. Ah, well. Ah bleeding well, Russell.

The Hassler is built on the Pincio Hill. Through the plate-glass walls of the roof restaurant you can see all of Rome and her hills and monuments and bits of the Tiber. You can also see, as Johnson reported, the Piazza di Spagna and the steps. I sat at a window table with Johnson and had an amber antiseptic negroni with lemon and ice balls, and watched the corner into the Via Condotti to see if Di would come out and where she was lunching. Johnson said, "You don't think he's in Naples?"

I said, "Do you live here? Or are you living with Maurice?" Monogrammed napkins had appeared; iced water, rolls and butter in ice. The headwaiter drifted around us in his gray jacket like a shadow, smiling when the bifocals glittered.

"I stay with Maurice for the gossip," Johnson said. "I come to Rome for the action. If you want to know where he is, I can find out for you. I have a boat at Naples, with radio telephone."

"The *Dolly*," I said. The lenses, dazzling into my eyes, reflected the yellow-fringed swags of the pavilion. I said, "Did Maurice send him to Naples?"

"Maurice," said Johnson, "is a legal escape clause to himself, as you will recognize. All I have said is that if you want to speak to Charles, I can arrange it."

I said, "I'm not interested in where he is now. I only want to know where he wants to be."

There was a pause. "Married to you, I imagine," said Johnson.

The dining room filled. Roman matrons sat facing each other, bouffant head to perfect bouffant head, the straight cashmere backs rippled with corseting. The businessmen, American, German, Italian, drank and discussed slipped disks and smoking and hotels they had stayed in at Frankfurt. Johnson said, "People with good taste don't change overnight."

"You think not?" I said. I thought of Maurice and all his awe-struck encomium of Johnson and his cosmopolitan living. I said prosaically, "Then why should Charles suddenly want to marry me?"

I waited for him to flunk it, or bish it, or paper it over. Instead he thought, and then said, "To protect you?"

I stared at him. They were serving us with brochettes of lamb, slipped off the charcuterie wire, with tossed salad glistening beside them. A flagon of Antinori, Chianti classico 1966, had arrived instead of champagne. It was all quite different from what I had expected. I said, "It was you who said there was no need to go to the police. We've done nothing wrong, except hide the fact that we were in the zoo. We didn't see the man die."

"But," said Johnson, "you know two things the police haven't discovered. You know who was with the dead man. And you know why he died. You know what was in Lord Digham's camera."

"So do you," I said. "So do Jacko and Innes and Diana and the couture house and Maurice, for all I know, as well as poor Charles himself. If I need protection, then so do we all. How shall we pair off?" I added.

"Morally, genetically or aesthetically?" Johnson inquired. The sweet-trolley stood to one side, awaiting us: I could see fresh strawberries and a deep bowl of cream; gooseberry tart, pears in brandy and gâteau. The waiter replenished my wine. Johnson said, "Who do you imagine killed that man in the loo? Mila Schön or Carlo Palazzi in person? The pirating of a season's fashions can make the fortune of a wholesale house and bankrupt a couturier. Where big money is involved, big operators are hired. The two men you saw together in the Villa Borghese might even have been rivals. There was a struggle for the film in the toletta, and the first man had his head blown off." He broke off. "I'm sure he had an obituary."

He had several. I recited the most recent one, rapidly.

"Just as you were, you will always be
Treasured forever in memory

50

*Death came and gently kissed your brow
God has another angel now."*

"Mr. Johnson—"

"Johnson," he corrected me. "It's confusing, I know, but my Christian name and surname are the same."

"All right," I said. "I'm Ruth. And it would be nice if you didn't keep calling Charles Lord Digham. But if they were rivals, and not meeting each other, why did the first man have to go into the loo. I mean—"

"There is a time for everything, and that wasn't it," said Johnson. "Yes. Well, my guess is that he knew someone else had his eye on the camera, and he was looking for a quiet place to wind up and take out the film. He could hardly do that while you were spraying him with hoses in the rhinoceros compound or whatever. Then if he was attacked, all he stood to lose was the empty camera." He finished partitioning his brochettes through the lower half of his bifocals and inspected me through the upper. "You still don't want to go to the police?"

"No," I said.

"No," he agreed. "They might ask how your camera and Charles's got mixed up in the first place."

I went on spearing cucumber because I prefer not to show when I have been shocked. I said, "Charles is around the Dome all the time. He was there before his Villa Borghese session. I suppose he picked up the wrong camera."

"The police," said Johnson prosaically, "might

think you gave him the wrong camera. It certainly left his lying where anyone could get at it."

"Yes . . ." I said slowly. "But that would argue that *three* people were after Charles's film. Do three lots of people really want to know whether backless dresses are going to be in again this year?"

"Or your two men from the Villa Borghese were really together, and one of them was killed and the film stolen by a different party?" said Johnson. "Or no. That won't wash. Unless he developed the film from your camera, the Villa Borghese survivor wouldn't have known it was the wrong one. Assuming your Zeiss had no identifying mark on it."

"No," I said. "It hadn't." I gazed at the sweet tray. "You know, you have a lot in common with Maurice."

"Charm?" said Johnson.

"Gâteau, I think. Charm, of course. And a wholly misdirected talent for mischief. If I wanted to pinch all Charles's pictures, I should only have to take prints from his negatives. He develops half of them in the Dome while I'm working, and I could always take a contact print while he's having a coffee. The same applies to Jacko and Innes. They come in and out. They've seen his stuff lying around. If any of us had pinched his pictures, we shouldn't want Charles's camera lying around in the Dome. We'd want Charles to take it, and pray that someone pinches it from him. So you see," I said over the gâteau, "we may be rather out of favor among the criminal classes, but there isn't a police case against us."

Johnson had chosen gooseberries. "But you don't want Charles or the Trust on the front page of the

News of the World," he said thoughtfully, and arranged a passable sneer on his features. "I am a well-known sexual deviationist. Pander to my aberrations or I shall tell all the media."

"Well, naturally," I said. "We all thought of that."

"And?" said Johnson. He seemed to be enjoying the gooseberries.

"And we decided all you wanted was an introduction to Maurice," I said.

"Money isn't everything," Johnson said. "And Charles is in Naples."

I felt very cool, and very spiteful and extremely self-possessed. Or it may have been the Chianti. "And where were *you*," I said, "when all the fun and games were going on in the toletta?"

"Waiting in the restaurant piazza," Johnson said, "for Charles to come back for your basket. I followed you both to the zoo. But I didn't buy a balloon. You've spilled your cream . . . Ruth?"

I had. But the spot on my hand wasn't cream: it was a tear. I put my fork down and sat looking at it and daring another to fall. Johnson made a little movement, and I felt the plates being taken away and a tray of coffee and colorless liqueurs arriving in their place.

"I shall pour," Johnson said, and pushed a cup under my nose. "Black coffee and Sambucca and good intentions. I do some things for money, but I do other things from love. For example: You have never asked me what it feels like to paint the Supreme Pontiff, and indeed in one way it is like painting any other portrait. Except that I am summoned to each sitting by a phone call from the

Maestro di Camera and admitted at eight in the morning through the Bronze Doors of the Vatican, inside which is my room, with easel and table and Pontifical chair. And once there, I am alone with my sitter, who talks a great deal, but not in English."

He smiled suddenly. "Does it sound alarming? But then, the element of risk is what gives savor to dull professions like painting and astronomy. Are you frightened, when you go into the Dome at night, and put off all the lights, and shut the door at the top of the stairs?"

"No," I said. And it was true. You shut the door, and you put up the bench bar across it and then touch the dimmer so that all the lights sink low. If you work in the fall it is cold, because hot air distorts, and heating is never allowed in the cupola. Above you is the high aluminum dome in silvery orange-leaf sections, and you pull down the long spring switch which hangs from the rim of it and press the button and allow the spring to fly up as the loud drone of the retracting section begins. It opens ladderlike and very slowly from the outer rim inward, and reveals bit by bit the night sky, and the cold. You put the lights off and climb the pair of gliding steel steps and look at your sky and find your constellations and climb down again and then press and hold the switch by the door. Above your head the dome begins to revolve, slowly and groaningly, and the open sector sweeps the night sky until there is your star cluster. You stop the cupola. And then you uncap your lenses and begin to set the declination and advancement of your telescope, and it is quiet.

"You observe alone," Johnson said.

I drank my coffee. The Sambucca had three coffee beans floating in it. "Yes," I said. "Some find it boring and like to work in pairs, one observing and one taking notes. Here we do from six to ten exposures in a night, depending on when our stars set. Then the negatives are sent to the Trust and the findings computed. That is how you evaluate what you are doing. Back at the Trust, they'll be reducing material from all their protégés, and comparing the results with other researchers. It's what gives our work here its significance."

"According to Innes," Johnson said, "you and Jacko don't believe your work *has* any significance."

He was looking at me over the top of his glasses. I said, "That's because Innes doesn't know much about people. I don't suppose you run on much about the significance of art, for God's sake, either. You take it as read, and run about making up . . . obituary notices."

"You've known Charles a long time?" Johnson said.

I said, "Yes. He was engaged to someone else. She was furious." I paused, and then said, "His parents want us to marry."

"I should have guessed that," Johnson said.

There was another pause. No one moved or spoke around us. It was only when I turned my head that I realized we were alone in the restaurant. All the tables but ours had been cleared. But no one hovered and no one even looked near us. Such is the power of money. I said, "Thank you for the lunch," and there was another silence.

Then Johnson said, "Whatever you may think, I

am not motivated by mischief. I think you know something you haven't told Charles, and I think this could be dangerous for both Charles and you. Will you trust me?"

"If I do nothing," I said, "nothing will happen."

The glasses watched me. "Is that a scientist speaking?" said Johnson.

I said, "There was a goldfish inside the balloon."

He said quickly, "Which balloon? The one you had?"

"Yes," I said. "It burst. There was something inside. I thought it was the maker and price. It said, *Fall Fair: five zero, zero.*"

"And?" said Johnson. He was sitting very still.

"You'll need a *Daily American*," I said. "But I saw it in Greco's. An advertisement for a Fall Fair. And the hours are from two P.M. to five, zero, zero. Today."

"Then," said Johnson, "let's go."

CHAPTER 4

THE FIRST PERSON WE SAW at the Fall Fair was
Innes Wye, clutching a bottle of ketchup, which
figures. Sometimes one forgets that Innes is American and conscientious, but not for long.

The railings of the Palazzo Barberini are up-
held by marble weightlifters with beards and gri-
maces of incipient hernia. There were American
cars parked under the palm trees beyond and
American children with explosive grins and busty
cult-figures on their sweat shirts were charging up
the façade, chased by an assortment of incoherent
doorkeepers.

Inside, as I have said, there was Innes. If the
place was a gallery, it was not immediately dis-
cernible. At the top of a staircase, a suite of large
rooms hung with blazing crystal chandeliers was
full of brilliantly barbered Americans. The girls

57

were thin, trouser-suited and purposeful, with Pat Nixon hairdos. The men tended to be silver-haired, statuesque and faintly cultured, and to be standing about with a harem of richly dressed and well-preserved silver-haired ladies. There was a bar, patronized by a milling throng of desperate non-Americans, a side room selling soft drinks and ices, and a large, hot salon full of small empty tables at which sat a number of elderly patrons, looking as if their feet hurt them but smile, brother, smile. The rest of the tables almost equally empty, had held the Christmas Gifts, the Home-Baked Goodies, the secondhand clothes and used books of the bazaar. There had been a run on everything but tea cozies and babies' socks. Off that was a smaller room full of silent mothers with raging children, and a litter of toys. In a corner an earnest middle-aged man with glasses like ploughshares was telling a fairy story, with gestures, to a half circle of mesmerized toddlers. His voice, a seductive Irish-American, welled back among the baby socks and mingled with the voice of the auctioneer from the salon, pushing a De Luxe 4-Egg Chick Incubator with Thermostatic Control, plus a 32-page booklet with pictures on how the egg becomes a chick. "Don't they *know?*" inquired Johnson austerely.

I said to Innes, "Never mind. You'll come out all right in the yen revaluation. Let me carry the ketchup." He had a raffle ticket pinned to his jacket.

We accompanied him to his hoard. He had a paper carrier of Trappist jams and a box which said *Electric Callous Eraser. Have Better Looking*

Feet, $4. Di appeared with Timothy, of all people, in tow.

Old Home Week. Of course, it had been her *Daily American.* Snakeskin and lime green fur flipped past the pants suits and drawing up with the dark glasses trained full on Johnson, Di said, "And what groovy goodies have *you* got?" to me.

I said, "I paid full market prices. Hullo, Timothy."

"You forget," said Diana, "the law of diminishing returns. Timothy wants to buy something."

"Well, there you are," I said against the din of the auctioneer's voice. "Throw pillows, patio fruit cake or babies' bootees." Below the glasses, there was a dissatisfied look about Di's frosted pink eye makeup. I said to her, *"Timothy,* dear?"

"I met him outside," said Diana. "He has a thing going for Innes. He *had* a thing going for Innes. What are you doing with Johnson?"

"Nothing, yet," I said. "But I'll lease him to you, if you can cut out Timothy."

"Thanks a million," Di said pointedly. Timothy, holding Johnson by the arm, was just disappearing into the room for the little ones. A moment later the reader of fairy tales, looking slightly harassed, emerged and went over, in a distracted way, to help at the book stall. Di, toward whom men were gravitating from every quarter of the suite, started to giggle. Innes, still holding his bottle of ketchup, lost his head and hissed at her. "Will you please take Mr. Frazer's secretary out of there and go away? This is a charitable occasion." A woman with silver hair, cleaving her way through the throng, said, "It's Diana Minicucci, isn't it? How nice of you to come along. Now you're here, I wonder if we can persaude you to pick out the raffle tickets . . . ?"

Unperturbed, Diana walked off, surrounded by units from Pan American, the American Academy, the American Episcopal Church, the American Express, the Ford Foundation and Coca-Cola. Innes fell back and disappeared. I was sorry for him but you have to remember that Di is not only the basic subject of Jacko's more enterprising photographs; she is also the daughter of Prince Minicucci and Bernadette Mayflower. I went off to find Johnson.

He was in the kiddies' room, sitting cross-legged listening to Timothy telling the story of Little Red Riding Hood to about twenty-five children who were sitting watching his nice pink Lithuanian face and listening to every word, even the bits he was putting in for Johnson's benefit. I sat down beside Johnson and whispered, "It's five o'clock."

"Spoilsport," he said, and got up. Timothy, telescoping the wolf's eyes, ears and mouth and unzipping Grandma in three well-chosen sentences, got up too. The twenty-five children started to cry. A well-coiffed mother with three offspring and a prenatal outfit covering possibly several more said, "You should send back Mr. Paladrini."

"Of course," said Timothy kindly, and slid out after Johnson into the deodorized heat of the salon. Di came toward us, laden with a packet of bread sticks, some crochet work and a 1903 Baedeker, from which she was reading aloud, when she could get a word in edgewise from the crowd hanging over her shoulder.

". . . Chapter Five. *Intercourse with Italians.*"

(Happy applause.) "Guides . . . Gratuities . . . Waiters. *If too importunate in their recommendations or suggestions, they may be checked by the word Basta.*" (Ironic cheers.)

I said, "Di? Who won the raffle?"

"Guess who?" said Di, and lifting the dark glasses down again on her nose, looked at me through them. "Innes Wye."

I said softly, "Di?" Poor Innes, ticketed like the Mad Hatter for all to see, had been easy meat. "Di," I said. "What did he win?"

But even before I finished speaking, a certain muted confusion was making itself felt from the raffle stand. Among the heads turning, I noticed, was that of Timothy's predecessor, the teller of fairy tales, presumably about to return to his post. An odd idea stirred somewhere at the back of my mind. "First prize," Di said lightly. "Jungle After-Shave, the Essence for Men Born to Conquer. I'm rather afraid I gave him the Organizer's crocodile handbag, too."

Growing cries from the raffle stand told all too plainly the perfect success of the project. Further cries defined the extent of the tragedy. There had been two hundred-dollar bills and a Cartier cigarette case in the crocodile handbag. The crowd seethed and then began making off, in a surge, down the length of the room to the staircase.

I said to Johnson, "Mr. Paladrini. The story-teller in glasses."

"Yes?" said Johnson. Pursued by Timothy we were being swept forward by the crowd; the last I saw of Di she was settling down at a table and being brought a drink by a boy from the Embassy.

I said, "If you took off his glasses, he would be the spitting image of the man at the zoo with the balloon cart."

I had, for once, Johnson's fullest attention. "The storyteller?" he said. "Then let's have a chat with him. Can you spot him, Ruth?"

A man in a shortie raincoat who had been walking just behind us suddenly slipped sideways and began unobtrusively to forge ahead in the crush. It was Mr. Paladrini. "Oh, damn," I said. "He heard us."

"And he doesn't want to know us," said Johnson, accelerating. "Isn't that interesting?" He began, with the greatest politeness, to thrust through the crowd in the wake of the vanishing storyteller and, as best I could, I followed him.

I dare say, if you lost a crocodile handbag with two hundred dollars and a Cartier cigarette case in it, and saw it vanishing across a room and downstairs in the possession of a small unknown man with a shopping bag, you would lose your razor-cut head and go ape over it. I don't know who started the cries of "Stop thief!" but I strongly suspected Mr. Paladrini. At any rate, they were taken up with touching enthusiasm by all the unlucky raffle contestants and most of the Organizer's friends who up till then had been trotting rather self-consciously through the marble halls, and suddenly Johnson and I found the pursuit had turned into a gallop. It began to look, indeed, as if with a little encouragement it would turn into a lynching squad. And ahead of us, a bobbing spectacled face in the throng, was the escaping person of Mr. Paladrini.

I shoved. Kipper ties and fine jersey knits flinched from me; I stood on a handmade shoe and wriggled through the resulting small gap. Johnson, I saw, with considerable expertise was making even more progress than I was. I heeled around three children and met up with him again in the middle of what appeared to be a logjam. The pregnant mother was next to him and busy talking. "Mr. Paladrini? Isn't he sweet? 'I'm used to entertaining children,' he said, and just walked right in. I sure hope the Organizers give him a vote of thanks at the next committee meeting."

We had started to move forward again. Over three shoulders Johnson called, "Who brought him?"

"He just came," she yelled back, and we were off again.

I suppose Innes, walking sedately down the stairs on his way back to Mouse Hall and Poppy, had no reason to connect the bustle upstairs with his winnings. When people started to run, he probably thought that the fair had concluded, and the Voice of America was about to arrive in a body and fill all the seats on his trolley bus. So he started to run downstairs also. When the court case came up afterward, people said that he turned at the first shout of "Stop thief!" and then, faced with a solid wall of shrieking people sweeping down the wide staircase after him, he whirled around and most wisely beat it.

He tripped and fell six stairs from the bottom, and the leading hounds tripped and took off right over him, followed by their near neighbors. Rather stylishly, in a glistening wave of manicured hands and blue glassess and other crocodile handbags, the entire body politic of Little America overturned and slid like a pack of cards straight down the staircase. At the bottom in a pool of scarlet lay Innes Wye, covered in Trappist jam, money and ketchup. And Jungle After-Shave, the Essence for Men Born to Conquer.

Glissading down the side of the staircase was Mr. Paladrini, his spectacles no longer visible. I took a flying leap over Innes and, with Johnson pounding ahead of me, followed them both out into the courtyard.

Outside, it was the rush hour. I think I have mentioned before that Rome has a worrying problem with traffic. The street was full of taxis, but all of them were bumper to bumper and motionless; ahead, dimly, Mr. Paladrini was pounding up the vestigial pavement. He paused, looked around, and then began running downhill to the Via Nazionale and the buses. A large green double-decker bound for the Piazza Venezia swung out from the curb, and he plunged through the doors as they hit him. We could see him haul out a fistful of money.

In Rome, there is a pathological shortage of small coins. For change, the little shops tend to use candy. Johnson said, "Come on!" and set off down the Nazionale, running.

I could see the point. At the rate the traffic was traveling, we had as good a chance of getting to the next stop on time as the bus had. The pavement, it must be admitted, was crowded and not with polite Americans, but deploying his palette-holding arm, Johnson turned out to be more than an adept at barging. A stream of Italian oaths followed us on the whole of our free downhill slalom, which entailed ignoring the ALT's and treating the AVANTI's like a springboard. We got to the next stop just as the bus was drawing in, with a brooding face looking down from its galleria. The doors opened. One person got off, and only one person was allowed on. And it wasn't one of us.

"Ah, well," said Johnson. And again, holding my wrist, began running. We battled our way through the parked cars at Trajan's Forum and got to the bus stop just as Mr. Paladrini descended there. He saw us, turned, and got back in, against the physical and vocal resistance of all his fellows. The door shut and the bus trundled across the Piazza to the Via del Plebiscito, where he got off again.

We were badly behind him that time. To cross the Piazza in the rush hour in full sight of the policeman standing there and chirping at you, whistle in mouth, is the quickest way to the British cemetery I know. We made it in time to see our quarry disappear into the maw of a black archway opposite the Palazzo di Venezia. We raced after him.

Outside, the row of brass plates appeared to indicate the usual colony of lawyers, dentists and insurance companies, with possibly a minor resting place of the Banco di Spirito Santo. Inside was a dark vaulted tunnel of pure seventeenth-century magnificence with a pebbled floor and arcaded walls through which we groped in the meager daylight which penetrated from the street. The only other light came from a small concierge's room at the end, next to the locked double doors which ended the tunnel, and from a hint of daylight to the left, from a small courtyard overlooked by tall buildings. Fragments of ancient marble: masks, broken draperies and fractured Latin inscriptions were built into the vine-covered walls. Among tubs of flowering plants rested a small cherub fountain, pouring thinly under the inscription NON POTIBLE. The tunnel itself was full of small cars.

We ran about, looking for Mr. Paladrini. "I bet you don't know Napoleon's mother died here," Johnson said.

> *"A million times I've needed you, Mum,*
> *A million times I've cried*
> *If love could have saved you, Mum,*
> *You never would have died."*

"Hell," he said abruptly. "He's gone through the shoe shop."

We had missed it first time around. But on the right, near the entrance, an archway led down some steps and into a lit arcade which proved to be just that: the shoe shop at the foot of the Corso. We plunged through it and into the street. Dodging up it was Mr. Paladrini, in the middle of all Rome going home to its wife and bambinos in suede jackets and knitted jackets and shortie overcoats and very long overcoats and enough polo necks to outfit the entire British Raj, and better filled, at that. We belted after.

They used to hold horseraces in the Corso, which runs for a mile uphill between the Venezia and Renati's, and the horses must have needed corks on their shoulders, because the pavements are about three inches wide and the road not much better. It is lined with continuous blocks of shops and churches and palaces, broken by monumental squares. The palaces are the kind made of faceted marble where the barred windows start three feet above the top of your head and the gardens are full of palm trees and gardeners and the private art collections are uninsurable. We charged up it and came to a halt finally in the open space of the Piazza Colonna, with the Marcus Aurelius column towering fervently above us. "Hell," said Johnson. "He's gone across to the Galleria."

The Galleria is a maze, and any self-respecting criminal would make straight for it. We had got halfway across the road with a screeching of brakes to encourage us when Johnson swung me abruptly around and raced back the way we had come. "No, he hasn't," he said, and at that moment I saw Mr. Paladrini, walking slowly and deceptively up past the monument and over the piazza.

Halfway across, he glanced around and saw us and, spinning around, started off, fast, in another direction. Two Fiats, an Alfa Romeo and a Mercedes-Benz allowed him to pass and met, uncontrollably, in his absence. There was a bang, followed by a quartet of long, tinny rattles. Mr. Paladrini, in a burst of imperishable speed, nipped onto the pavement and vanished down a flight of steps signposted SOTTO PASSAGGIO PEDONALE, followed by an erratic file of afflicted motorists, a number of bystanders, two carabinieri, and us.

The Piazza Colonna has been referred to as the bellybutton of Rome, and the only way to get from one side to another is under it. Once you get down the steps the foot passage is wide and crowded and brightly lit, and lined with shop display windows and showcases. It also has as many exits and entrances as a badger sett. We had hardly fought our way in when a flight of steps reared on our left labeled, P. COLONNA: MONTECITORIO. From the fact that a red-faced man with a bleeding nose was pounding madly down it, we deduced we were still in the ranks of the pursuers. We ran hopefully on.

Steps to the right: Galleria Colonna, blocked by one of the carabinieri attempting to form a one-man cordon. More steps to the right: the Palazzo della Rinascente, full of people running both up and down and colliding with one another. Further steps to the right: the Piazza Silvestro, with six people standing on the stairs waving their arms around and arguing. The stairs up, at which was standing the other carabiniere, listening to two drivers and a waiter shouting at one another. Johnson and I came to a halt.

"What a pity," said Johnson. "I rather hoped they would catch him for us."

I said, "We've lost him, then?"

"Not at all," said my friend Johnson. "You underrate the speed and resourcefulness of any Roman citizen who thinks he has suffered an injury. If no one is running up those steps yelling blue murder, it is because Mr. Paladrini hasn't run up those steps either. In which case he's still here."

"In the shop?" I said. LA RINASCENTE, said the shop sign beside us. Behind double glass doors we could see a busy lit interior full of men's clothes and executive briefcases.

"Right," said Johnson mildly. But he didn't leap into the shop. He stood inside and, raising his voice, called in excellent Italian to the carabiniere at the end, "Here! Your man went in here! I saw him just now in the shop here!" Then he stood back, holding my arm, while every man in the passage poured past us and in through the doorway.

I looked at Johnson as the shop door swung to, and a ruminative quiet returned to the passage. "You didn't see him," I said.

"No," said Johnson. "But I know where he is." And walking six paces back he came to a halt by the Rinascente staircase, now empty. At the bottom of it was an erection like a small telephone booth, with a sign above which said FOTO-TESSERA AUTOMATICO, and a curtain closing the doorway. The curtain trembled, and Johnson addressed it.

"Mr. Paladrini," he said. "They're going to come back. And then I'm afraid you're in trouble. Why not come with me? Miss Russell and I just want to talk to you."

Silence. The curtain stopped moving.

"Mr. Paladrini," I said. "We think someone asked you to pass on a message about the Fall Fair, and it got to the wrong person. We know about the theft of the fashion pictures, and we don't want any publicity. If you'll come and tell us about it, no one will do a thing to harm you."

I tried to say the right things. I was thinking so hard that I didn't notice that Johnson's hand had slipped between the curtain and the edge of the cubicle. There was a chink of metal and then from inside the box a volley of brilliant white flashes, followed by a terrified cry. The curtain was wrenched back and the exponent of fairy tales tumbled out, just as the sky above the Rinascente steps was darkened by a column of people pouring down them.

I had forgotten that the main door of the department store debouches on to the street up above. The pursuit had raced through the shop and, finding nothing, had simply descended into the passage again. I heard Johnson swear feelingly just before we were bowled over and Mr. Paladrini, setting off like the hammers, tore along the rest of the passage with the four drivers and two carabinieri and the audience in full cry after him.

I gave, sitting there, a passing thought to the four impacted cars, still presumably blocking the streetway above us, but justice is justice after all, and a clearway at the rush hour isn't everything. We walked slowly after and stood at the top of the Corso steps watching. After twenty yards the shouting increased and then died away; so did the action. They had lost him.

"Heigho," said Johnson, and halted at the foot of the Rinascente steps. The automatic booth stood just as Mr. Paladrini had vacated it, with the curtain half torn off its rings. From the side protruded, limply, a long strip of glistening paper.

Johnson extended a hand and removed it. "Mr. Paladrini," he said, and passed the whole strip over to me.

It held six pictures of Mr. Paladrini, working from the top of his head to his ear tip. The middle two showed the whole of his face very nicely. It was plain that, beyond any conceivable doubt, the seller of balloons and the teller of fairy tales were the same man.

"As a tonal composition," Johnson said, "it lacks confidence. But as a clue they don't come any better. All you and I have to do now is find him."

CHAPTER 5

AT THAT POINT, I revolted. "Oh no, we don't," I remember announcing.

" 'The Struggling for Knowledge hath a Pleasure in it like that of Wrestling with a Fine Woman,' " said Johnson. "The late Marquess of Halifax. You can retire if you want to. The police are bound to have street traders' records. I'm going to find out who Mr. Paladrini is."

"If you do, they'll arrest him for jaywalking," I said. We were on the surface again and making, it seemed, for the Hassler.

"Not if I don't tell them why I want him," Johnson said. He remained unmoved by the idea that he would outrage the Trust, involve the Dome personnel in a court case and probably have us all extradited if he pursued his silly detective work. He fed me at the Hassler, and then mentioned that he had work to do at the villa, but would spare the time to drive me back to my digs in the Fiat. How Di ever got the idea he was a sexpot I cannot conceive.

In my pocket were two tickets, bought before his desertion by Charles, for a performance by Il Gruppo Teatro Libero. The theater they were appearing in is called Il Kilt, which was enough to account for Charles's interest. As I have indicated, he has an overdeveloped sense of the ludicrous.

Charles, I understood, was in Naples. Di, if I was not mistaken, would be at the Number One with one or more of the boys from the Fall Fair. Timothy had last been seen bending tenderly over the ketchup-covered form of Innes Wye and was possibly even now conveying him back to his bedroom, or even possibly Timothy's bedroom in Sansavino. Jacko's whereabouts I knew precisely. He was at the Dome, on duty until I took over at midnight.

There seemed to be no one to take me to Il Kilt but Johnson, who said he had seen *Il Barone Rampante* and why not hire a bedroom instead and play contract.

I said, "Bridge? Why bridge, for God's sake? It needs four bods."

"So Di has noticed," said Johnson. "Her erotic reputation rests solely on her habit of inviting three chaps to her bedroom and all stripping off for a rubber. I know. She asked me in once, but the lights failed."

"What a waste," I said, playing for safety. It seemed unlikely that he was reading my mind, but I made a determined effort to clean up my think-

72

ing. I said, "Do you follow the form in the newspapers?"

"That's why I took up the game," explained Johnson. Someone had brought the old Fiat to the front of the Hassler and he held the door for me. "I think Di is going through life hoping to meet those chaps North, South, East and West. You know. *East felt an itch to overruff Dummy?* I'll take you to Il Kilt if the Pope isn't there. You can go about too much together."

In fact, he never did take me to the Kilt, because as we drew up at the front door a man came through the crowd and stood a little way off, on the pavement, just looking.

It was Charles, with the Maserati covered with dust parked beside him.

"Goodbye, Ruth," said Johnson. "How was Naples, Charles?"

"Neapolitan," said Charles. He was still looking at me. I got out, and Charles shut the door of the Fiat and added, "I saw your yacht there. Much admired by the neighborhood. Your man sends his regards and says the dynamo's fixed and she's ready."

He didn't need to prove that he'd gone where he said he had. I didn't mind whether he had been to Naples or a European Grand Masters' Tournament with Omar Sharif, so long as he had decided, of his own accord, to come back. I said to Johnson, "I'm sorry. You've been so kind. You wouldn't like two tickets for *Il Barone Rampante?*"

Charles was already standing at the door of the Maserati. Johnson smiled and shook his head and drove off in a roar of high octane fuel while Charles

73

got hold of me in full view of the clientele of the Rampant Baron and kissed me.

I relieved Jacko at midnight, which may or may not surprise you. Charles refused to come to the Dome on the grounds that he would only distract me, which was certainly true. I left him in bed, received on my way out the felicitations of our landlady and had to hammer on the door of the Dome when I got there, because the locksmiths had replaced the burst lock and Jacko had forgotten to hand out the new keys. All Jacko carries in his head are thousands of coordinates and the correct meter readings for three-dimensional natural objects, preferably moving.

He is, however, a hard-working and reliable duty man. He had been observing since seven o'clock, although the weather impinged on the hazy. A cloudy sky up till midnight means, in our own code, that you can turn it in after that if you want to. I wished that night that he hadn't been so hard-working.

He had made me coffee, and we had it in the Dome while I checked over what he had finished. I would develop his plates with mine in the morning, and by the end of the week we could pack them up and send them on to the Trust. It was the last pack we should send there this season. The week of the full moon started on Saturday, and that meant no photography. And by the end of the next week we'd have reached the end of our contract. I began to hum under my breath as I perched myself up on the ladder and Jacko, about to open the door to the stairs, said, "Don't tell me. I'm clairvoyant. Charles is back?"

I said, stricken, "Oh Christ. Jacko, I'm terribly

74

sorry. We've got the bed again. I meant to put it back in your room as I left."

"The way I feel," said Jacko, "it doesn't matter. Timothy tells me you all had a gas at the Barberini. He dropped Innes off at his digs, loaded up to the eyeballs with aftershave."

I revised my opinion of Timothy's kindheartedness and tried to think of a way of not telling Jacko what he was asking. The trouble with Jacko is that he really does go for Di. I said, "You'll never guess who we saw in the Barberini. The man who sold Charles and me the balloon outside the zoo. We ran after him and lost him somewhere in the Corso."

"At the Fall Fair?" said Jacko, arrested. "You're dreaming. The Yanks wouldn't let a street trader in—not if he went through a car wash and wax spray with Dettol. Ruth, precious, you've seen too many teleromanzos on the goggle box."

I said, "He was specially scoured for the occasion. Johnson's got a photograph. I couldn't stop him. There is shortly going to be a sonic boom at the Trust which could be felt in three continents, and I only hope I'm not there to hear it. In the meantime, that unfortunate star is going to set in forty minutes."

"I'm off," Jacko said. The cool air flowed in from the cupola. Warm from bed, I felt it on my face, but not at all through my thick jersey and anorak. In the dim light Jacko's face looked like a clown's, with sad eyes and tangled hair and Zapata mustache. I said, "I'm going back after five to have breakfast. You can bunk downstairs here, if you want to."

"Thanks," said Jacko morosely.

"Without service and back-up facilities," I called after him, and heard him make a rude noise as I shut the door and swung up the bench and prepared the filter and plate for their holder. I heard his footsteps ring down the spiral stair, and then clack on the marble one lower. An inner door shut. He was going to stay.

It had happened before. We didn't bother each other. Work was work, and like Charles he occupied himself as a rule in the developing room, or reading, or listening to the British Forces Network or the Voice of America and making endless cups of coffee before turning in. I would be brought a mug and a sandwich, or perhaps join him in one halfway between exposures. But most times the place would be dark if I went downstairs, and Charles, or Jacko, asleep. Innes, who had been known to work all night on his Incubator, never came into the Dome in the evening.

But tonight Charles was asleep in my digs and Innes, it seemed, tucked up in his, stoned to the eyeballs. For slights received, Timothy had taken vengeance.

The telescope reared black above me, its cold metal bulk like a cannon, with the finder and guider tubes ranged alongside like gun barrels. The stepladder glinted in the starlight, and behind it stood the skeleton of the quarter-ton crane. Once a year, through the trapdoor below me, the mirror would descend for its aluminum coating. Mirrors are heavy, to avoid warping. I have known them to weigh almost a ton.

I switched on the power for the rings and the

green slot light which showed the declination numbers and pointer. The 50-Inch was an old one, with Roman numbers. I like Roman numbers. I set and clamped it.

The right advancement is more difficult: you have to subtract the number twice from the sidereal clock before setting. I did it, and fine-set it and then unclamped the main movement and pressed the switch which starts the telescope moving.

However quick you are, you must always be accurate. The filter must be put in right side up, with the surface mat and not shiny. You must remember to uncap all three of your telescopes. You must remember to take the time as you slide in the plateholder, and to open the shutter at the end of the 50-Inch. Then you must watch, all through the exposure, that the telescope follows the arc of its subject, with the slow-motion button held in your hand.

You learn as a student how to relax, how to look steadily with one eye and not to screw up and weary the other. At first, you are allowed to cover the idle eye with your hand. Then the knack comes to you and you can stare with one eye into the lens of a telescope while the other looks into darkness, seeing nothing. I have known Charles to move soundlessly across the dome and touch me before I have been aware of him. It is, in a sense, a form of professional oblivion. It is less welcome when there are pleasanter things to do and to think of. And if you are in neither a state of depression nor a state of euphoria, it is the best source going of simple perspective.

Footsteps came up the marble stair and the loo fizzed, and the same footsteps went down again. The rest room door shut. I settled down to my constellation.

Normally, as I have said, there are no lights in an observatory after dusk. The outside door is locked, and once the door into the dome has been closed and the bench raised inside, no one can interrupt the observer. For good reason, since the incident of the wrecked camera, Jacko had had locks put on the bathroom window and any others big enough to admit an intruder. There was no reason why anyone should come near me that night except Jacko with coffee; and Jacko always took good care to clatter up the stairs and yell first, to find when the next plate would finish.

But Jacko was in bed. I gave myself a five-minute break at the end of the first two-hour session, and, taking my torch, opened the door and walked down to the ground floor through the most profound darkness and silence. The rest room door was firmly closed and a certain rhythmical obbligato which came through it indicated that Jacko had been treating his problems to Carlsbergs. I snitched a biscuit and a tumbler of Innes's quellingly microbe-free milk and climbed back upstairs to the dome, leaving the top staircase door madly open.

That was how I first heard the footsteps so clearly.

I was in trouble just then with the cross wire. As a star begins to decline it sinks toward the thick part of the atmosphere. Mine was dancing about in the haze. I heard the steps as I centered it with the slow-motions. I finished what I was doing, and then, swearing, plunged over to shut the door before Jacko's torchlight could hit my exposure and wreck it.

I had my hand on the door when I realized the steps weren't Jacko's. To begin with, there wasn't a light showing anywhere; the whole hollow building was in darkness. Then, as I moved, the footsteps had broken off suddenly.

The dome floor is noisy to walk over. The sound of my movements would have caused Jacko to come up and call to me. But, on hearing them this person had halted.

I told myself I was hallucinating. The front door of the Dome was fast locked, and so were the windows. Jacko and I were quite alone. I was hallucinating, or else it was merely Jacko suffering the results of an excess of birras and unwilling to attract my attention.

I looked at the black bulk of the 50-Inch, breasting unaided the vagaries of the Roman atmosphere, and with an unvoiced apology to the Trust I took two silent steps out of the door and then closed it firmly behind me. I couldn't fake an equally firm tramp across the dome floor to the telescope, but if anyone was there, I hoped he'd imagine it. I breathed as slowly and lightly as my heartbeats would let me, and waited.

Nothing happened. Behind the door, the 50-Inch motor buzzed. The central heating creaked, and a tap dripped below in the developing room. One of the electric clocks gave a whirr and a grunt and fell silent. I bent down and, sliding off first one shoe then the other, I took three steps down the metal staircase and peered over.

This time, I could see the front door. And the

front door was slightly open. I could see moonlight, in a crack, down the standpost.

So what?

Yell for Jacko. It may be Jacko I have heard, opening the door and stepping out of the Dome to look at something.

Unlikely. Even Jacko wouldn't forget to shut the door and leave me protected. Besides, he has the key.

Yell for Jacko. He may have heard a knock on the door and let someone in, forgetting to close it.

But he wouldn't have forgotten. See above. And then why the stealth?

Yell for Jacko. Someone else may have got in, unknown to either of us, and is lurking now in the bathroom, the developing room, the stockroom, the offices, the kitchen.

The staircase was clear. I drew a deep breath and raced down to the stairs to the ground floor, giving the front door a slam as I passed it. I burst into the rest room, yelling for Jacko.

He lay on the bottom bunk, snoring, and the room stank of beer. I banged him hard on the funny bone with my torch and when he made a loud and incoherent protest I said, "There's someone in the dome. There's your torch. Come on."

The kitchen was next door. I left him sitting ejaculating and ran there, switching on my torch and flinging open the door with some bravado. There was no one there that I could see, and the cutlery drawer was two paces away. I jerked it open, snatched a couple of knives and raced back to Jacko, who was upright, saying "What?" with his torch on. I put a knife in his other hand, grabbed his wrist and dragged him into the hallway. "Not again!" Jacko said.

"Yes, again," I hissed at him, and switched the lights on. The hall and staircase were flooded with light. A rush of footsteps coming down the marble stairs came to a halt and then the steps changed direction and receded in great leaping strides upward.

Jacko said, "Christ, you were right," and took two bounds toward the foot of the stairs. Then he slowed down and said, "We've got him. He can't get out. You phone the police and stay by the door. I'll go up after him."

"Don't be silly," I said. "He may be armed. He could hurt you. I'll phone the villa." Then I thought and said, "Jacko. He could get out on the cupola."

It had been done. Every now and then the dome sticks, and the workmen get up there and fix it. From there, the climb down to the ground isn't impossible. Jacko said, "Hell," and then, "All right. I'll follow him upstairs. You go outside and watch, and yell if you see him."

Upstairs, silence had fallen. I said, "I don't think he's gone up the iron stairs. I think he's in one of the middle rooms, Jacko. Then if I go out and you go to the top, he can open the door here and walk out of it. We'll stay together. We'll go upstairs together and search every room till we get him. For example . . ."

The lights went out.

"For example," I said, "that's one reason why he's on the middle landing. He's in the developing room."

It was like the repeat of a nightmare, only worse because there were only two of us. We didn't run anymore. We walked up the stairs side by side, with our torches searching the landing, but our quarry was one step ahead of us. Before we reached the door of the developing room we heard the footsteps ringing on the spiral iron stair just above us, and the door to the telescope banged. A pang for my exposure blipped through the high-performance funk in six colorways which was gripping me: I switched off my torch and Jacko, from years of sheer bloody brainwashing, did the same.

So we crashed through the door at the top of the stairs into darkness, and didn't even stop to wonder why our intruder hadn't paused to slide down the bench shelf that would bar it. The telescope loomed in its dome and the segment of sky, frosty with stars, twinkled behind it. Beside it was the lattice giraffe of the Eli Hoist Company of Philadelphia, with something solid and moving within it. A man was climbing the crane jib.

I cried aloud. Jacko didn't waste time on utterance. He jumped for the steps and caught the spring with the dome switch and pressed it.

There was a grinding roar and, above us, the slice of cold sky began dwindling. The roof of the dome was rolling shut on its ratchets.

The intruder realized it too. I have never seen a man move so quickly. He went up the crane like a lizard, one arm outflung to catch the spring switch and reverse it. Jacko jumped off the steps and dashed forward.

I had a better idea. I hopped with one foot on the ladder and raced it across the full width of the dome floor to jam him.

I was never to get there. Just in front of the telescope the floor disappeared altogether. The stepladder dropped into nothing and threw me, and we went through the hole in the floorboards together.

I have always had little use for screaming ladies.

I was screaming that time without knowing it. I screeched as I fell through the trapdoor, and screamed again as one leg of the steps struck and trapped me.

Everything stopped. The ladder stopped, jammed half through the opening. And I stopped, entangled in slippery alloy, and dangled there with a drop of three stories beneath me.

I heard Jacko's footsteps racing over, and had enough sense to yell, "Mind the *trapdoor!*" Then he arrived and plunged to his knees by my shoulders. He got one tough, cold hand around my wrist and he gripped it, while he tried to pull my limbs free with the other. The polished metal swung and slithered on the edge of the trap, and juddered and clanged with every move of my body. I got my second arm free. Then the hinges closed and the ladder slid through the opening, dragging my legs and my bruised body with it.

Jacko grabbed my other hand and tumbled backward. There was a jangle of metal; a pause; and an almighty crash from the base of the building. Jacko and I, in a shivering heap by the hole, lay and listened to it.

"*Dear Mr. Frazer,*" said Jacko, in a trembling voice. "*Owing to an unfortunate accident, I am writing to requisition one new collapsible aluminum stepladder . . .*"

"Dear Jacko," I said. "Owing to an unfortunate accident, you were nearly writing to requisition a new collapsible female colleague." His mustache, not by accident, was moving toward me and we had a long and satisfactory kiss. Then he said, "I suppose the bastard's got away," and helped me to struggle up, panting. That is the realistic, not to say sensible, streak in J. Middleton.

The bastard had, of course, got away, and not out of the dome ceiling either. As I fell through the trap, he must have nipped down the crane and fled past us. From that moment on, it was simple. While Jacko was hauling me out, a colliery band could have marched down the stairs to the front door, playing Purcell's Trumpet Voluntary if they knew it. When we had redeemed my plate and capped and clamped the 50-Inch for the night and retired to the kitchen for two therapeutic mugs of black coffee, we had reached a few shaky conclusions.

The intruder must have had a key to the front door.

He must be familiar with the dome, to know about the trapdoor used for silvering.

Since imagination boggled at the idea that two men could be impelled to visit us, it seemed likely that this burglar was the same as the previous one. That is, the survivor of the two from the Villa Borghese.

In which case, what had he wanted? More pictures?

"Couldn't be," said Jacko. "He'd smashed Charles's camera. In any case, if he's clever enough to get hold of a key, he's clever enough to find out that Charles had been in Naples and hasn't developed any pictures here recently."

"Then what?" I said.

"Let's search," said Jacko. "Then let's call the police. That lark with the trapdoor wasn't burglary. That, dearie, is what they call obsolescence planning. We're in deep, and we're not going to get any deeper."

I didn't say anything, but I helped him search. Nothing was out of place and nothing, so far as we could see, had been taken. We flooded the building with light, even to the sacred precincts of the dome, and all we found were the chips and scars from the fall of the steps, and the spray of castors and screw nails and hinges strewn about the ground floor by the wreckage. We began to clear it up.

It was then that Jacko said, "Hullo?" and I went over to look.

He was holding up a key. "Look what I found in the shovel. Middleton's deviant filing system. I knew I'd dropped it somewhere."

I toured my sweeping brush around a few boxes. "Keep going. You should find my entire nervous system down here somewhere. And what gold-plated coffer did that sacred key open?"

"Fort Knox," said Jacko, "is quite safe from me. It's the key to the plate store. The damn thing is empty in any case."

"Give," I said.

He stood holding the key. "You don't trust me."

"You're quite right I don't," I said, and caught

it as he chucked it over. "And while we're about it, what about my key for the front door?"

"What, now?" he said.

"Bloody now," I said. He had saved my life but at that moment his lack of grip on the subject of keys had got on my nerves. I pocketed the new key he delved for and gave me, and then trudged pointedly upstairs to put the other key where it belonged. I said, over my shoulder, "How many new front door keys are there?"

"Yours and mine," Jacko said, gazing upward. "One to Innes, for breakfast; one to Maurice because he paid the locksmith. You could defrost that thing while you're about it."

I forebore to say that that was precisely my errand. I walked into the stockroom, which we had searched in some detail already.

We kept our store of plates in the largest deepfreeze on the market, which happened to be an immovable tank of a meat safe. Stock are run-down at the end of the season, and the last plates transferred to the fridge.

Once empty, the freezer is switched off and promptly defrosted. If, that is, you haven't mislaid the means to unlock it.

I introduced Jacko's key into the lock, turned it and dragged the big freezer door fully open.

Inside, the safe was not empty. Inside, picked, packed, freeze-dried and dead as a cod steak in batter, lay the second man from the Villa Borghese.

> *Your photograph is faded now*
> *The rose you picked me, flat and sere*
> *Your love-notes faint*

Your violin still
And gone the bliss of yesteryear.

We did not dream then, you and I
As hand in hand we trod Life's way.
That here that warm and loving heart

Would lie so chill (−18° C) in death today.

CHAPTER 6

"SO, SCOTCH-KILLED SIDE in the meat safe. If you were in Wyoming, you could have a Wyoming steak fry," said Maurice next morning. "You're not a prude, darling?"

"She's not a prude," said Johnson firmly. "But she doesn't want to start her morning watching you get out of the bath either. Shut the door."

"She could do worse," Maurice said, his voice echoing comfortably from among all the verde antico and clouds of bath oil.

He emerged, draped like Lucullus in terry bath sheet, and settling himself on his pillows said briskly, "Hostess corner, Timothy. Five coffees please, and nothing exciting on the sugar. This is our morning for being practical. Now, Ruth dear. Now, Jacko. Tell Maurice everything."

It had been my idea, after a long and heated

discussion with Jacko, to telephone Johnson from the Dome at first light that morning. And it had been my misfortune that the voice from the villa which answered had been Maurice's. Stonewalling an eminent and inquisitive playwright who wants to know why you are telephoning his house guest at seven in the morning is not very easy. In the end Jacko simply took the phone from my fingers and told him. As he pointed out to me afterward, it was up to Maurice after all to decide what you did with a corpse in your meat safe. It was his house and his Dome and he was the permanent resident. Then we spoke to Johnson, and here we all were, in Maurice's bedroom. The Pope, Johnson said, had canceled his sitting that morning.

"He probably had a Message," said Maurice. "You must be quite, quite careful, you know. You can upset the balance of nature. A definite *implosion* of corpses."

"Two," said Jacko succinctly. He looked terrible, and he had had four more hours' sleep than I had. We had never been in Maurice's bedroom before. It was decorated like a carpeted tent, with a twelve-foot four-poster bed covered with the Rape of Persephone in petit point. The tables were crowded with skyphoi and kylikes and psykters and there was a bronze figure of a warrior in prayer, standing life-size by the drawn curtains: like the Romans, Maurice thought daylight unhealthy. Apart from the loot there were five modern works of art, one of which was plugged into an electric outlet on the baseboard. "You like it?" said Maurice, who had earned his living, after all, by observing his fellows.

It consisted of a panel of hardwood, thickly furred with fragile wire filaments. Timothy brought in the coffee and the wires shivered like dogs in the eddy. Then the door shut and the wires went on slowly twitching, individually and erratically, first in one quarter of the work and then in another. My eyes jumped about, trying to catch them at it. Maurice said, "Your coffee, darling. And was your second friend headless as well?"

"He'd been shot," I said shortly. "A little, round hole through the temple."

"And out again?" Johnson said. The filaments twitched.

"And out again," Jacko confirmed. "And the wound wasn't blackened, so we know he was shot from a distance."

"Well, of course he was," said Maurice. "He was shot when he was running away from the Dome four days ago after wrecking poor Charles's camera . . . You have, I take it, settled your doctrinal differences with Charles?"

I stared at Johnson and the bifocal glasses stared back at me blandly, lightly steamed up with coffee. Since my phone call Maurice had been brought up to date, it seemed, in the Dome's affairs. I said, "Yes."

"And since the dead man was frozen quite solid," continued Maurice, selecting a cigar and preparing to light it, "he couldn't be your second intruder, particularly as the meat safe had been locked and the key lost ever since the first break-in. How convenient, by the way."

Timothy, Johnson and I all looked at Jacko, who

went beige under his coiffure and said, "Lovely; but don't forget, I found it again."

"Naturally," said Maurice, leaning back and blowing long, expensive smoke rings among the festoons of his canopy. "Your ally had failed to extract the body, and sooner or later the meat safe would be forced open for defrosting. Better divert suspicion from yourself immediately."

"Except," said Johnson, "that Jacko could have removed the body during any one of his duty spells with no trouble at all. Don't be provoking."

Jacko's face began to return to its normal color. "If I can't be provoking, I'm not going to play," said Maurice happily. "Timothy, ring up the police."

Coffeepot in hand, Timothy looked at him. "You know what will happen. Television cameras. Reporters."

Maurice breathed out cigar smoke, coughing, and glared at him. "Sunk in oblivion, neglected, dragging out my meager existence in this stinking backwater, does it matter that the world has forgotten Maurice Frazer? It shall be reminded!"

"You can't do it," Timothy said, frowning. "You have two drinks parties, a Discussion Group at the British Council and dinner with the Marchese already."

"On the other hand," said Johnson gently, "there is a body to explain away. Who shot our friend from the Villa Borghese and why? Who took the key, and who returned it? Ruth?"

"I don't know," I said. My head ached. "The murderer, I suppose, took the key, and came back last night to remove and dispose of the body." I looked toward Jacko for help. "Then he must have dropped it. When he bent over the trapdoor in the dome, it must have slipped from his pocket. We found it below, in the wreckage. Jacko?"

"Check," said Jacko. "Let's call in the television cameras."

"You heard," said Johnson. "Maurice is busy today. Then who was the murderer?"

Inspiration visited me. "Of course. The *balloon man!*" I exclaimed.

Everyone, it appeared, knew about Mr. Paladrini and our chase up the Corso. There was a ripple of animation. "Except," said Johnson, "that one wonders how Mr. Paladrini was able to find his way about the Dome. Even to locating a trapdoor in darkness?"

"And," said Maurice, smiling bewitchingly, "to possessing a new key to open the front door with, my darlings."

"You had a key, Maurice," I said. "Who did you lend it to?"

Not a hair in the white mink was disturbed. Smiling, Maurice gently applauded me, the cigar notched with grace in one finger, and said, "No one. But then, I can't shoot. Italians can't shoot either. They come here every Sunday, poor dears with their elephant guns and the sparrows go *berserk,* but marksmanship, no. On the other hand . . ."

"Yes?" said Johnson. He had an envelope on his knee and was doing little sketches of Maurice with a red ball-point pen: as I watched he gave him a cloud, a harp, a pair of wings and a halo.

"Astronomers are perfectly unbelievable shots,"

said Maurice fondly. "All that work with the cross wires. I tell you. Take Ruth or Jacko or that other young man with the machinery to any rifle range and I guarantee you. Two shots out of three straight into the gold. Or the temple. I can't of course speak with any certainty about Digham. But photography, I should have thought, needed *the* most accurate eye. I thought you sent for him?"

"I did," said Johnson. I was beginning to change my mind, too, about Johnson. I had appealed to him that morning as to an ally. And since then, it seemed to me, he had taken altogether too much upon himself and his nasty bifocals. I said coldly, "He's probably out shooting Landrace Cutters with a submachine gun."

"Don't be bitter, dear," Maurice said. "Why shouldn't it have been Charles on the Dome roof last night? He knows the observatory better than most. It was his camera, if I remember rightly, that our frozen friend wrecked. Might he not have been a little carried away the other night outside the Dome and shot him?"

"He might," said Johnson. "Except that he hadn't a key to the Dome. Neither had Ruth. And according to both Ruth and Jacko, a key was used to open the Dome door this evening. The lock hasn't been marked or splintered or in any way forced." He paused and then said, "In any case, there is something we are all forgetting. Whoever entered the observatory last night opened that trapdoor deliberately, with the intention of killing either Ruth or Jacko, or both. It was only thanks to Jacko in fact that Ruth survived . . ."

The wall panel twitched. Maurice suddenly

ground out his cigar and said, "Yes. Then who else had a key?"

"Innes," said Timothy dulcetly. He laid an arm along the back of Johnson's chair and gazed at his drawing. "I emptied his pockets last night: keys make such a difficult bulge, and you can't ask *too* much of bespoke work. Maurice, he's got you exactly. And all those clouds, like my chintzy hop pillows. Maurice thinks I'm a fusspot, but I swear they make me sleep like a baby."

"Like Innes," said Jacko.

"Oh, well," said Timothy. "He was knocked out, you know. One had to try to revive him with *something*."

"Aftershave lotion," I said this time.

"Yes," said Timothy. "Silly me."

Johnson contemplated his drawing and then, detaching the page, proceeded to fashion it into a splendidly contoured paper dart. "And do you think," he said, "that Innes, resuscitated from his aftershave, could have nipped about climbing cranes yesterday evening?"

"No," said Timothy with regret. He opened his palms as Johnson launched the dart in a graceful parabola near him. The dart sailed past him and landed on Maurice's bedcover. Johnson's hand, at the extremity of its sweep, brushed the coffeepot and a full cup, poised just beyond it, tilted and emptied its contents against Maurice's artistic wall.

There was a flash of flame, a barking report and a wisp of smoke traveled lazily up to the putti. The thicket of filaments, arrested in mid-twitch, hung on the wall, inanimate as the corpse in the freezer.

Make a wall happy this weekend. Johnson said, "Oh dear. What have I done?"

There was a little silence. Then, "Made your point," said Maurice dryly. "Or do I mistake a subtle gesture of reproach when I see one? Take a note, Timothy: a telephone call to the electrician. Also, I think Lord Digham is trying to enter the room."

I got up and sat down again. It was true. The door had opened and Charles was standing there, his oldest cloak slung over his shoulders and, I suspected, his pajama top lurking underneath his scarf and sweater. He said, "Ruth?" and then, "Christ, I thought I'd never get in. I've been standing out there for fifteen bloody minutes, trying to get your bloody staff to knock on that door, Maurice. What do you need, the Keys of Saint Peter to get into the Throne Room?" He said to me, "Are you all right?"

I was used to urbanity. Not having urbanity was, I found, perfectly agreeable too. I said, "Yes, I'm all right. Why couldn't you walk in yourself? Oh, Charles, of course. The Mouse Alarm?"

"The revolting noise," said Charles, "that this former matinée idol in his dotage chooses to inflict on human beings because he is frightened of mice. I couldn't get into the room. I couldn't get anyone else to come in and tell you to switch the bloody thing off. All I know is that someone tried to kill Ruth in the Dome. What's been happening?"

"Dear Charles," said Maurice. "Matinée idol I may have been, but I don't recall ever being reduced to using the word *bloody* three times in six sentences, even in someone else's feeblest dialogue.

If the noise offends you, why are you here entertaining us now?"

"Because it's stopped," said Charles. "It stopped this moment. Ruth? What happened?"

Maurice sat up. "You've wrecked my Mouse Alarm," he said to Johnson.

But Johnson, rising, was leading Charles gently to a seat beside me. "I've wrecked his Mouse Alarm," he said kindly. "It's a long, long story and Ruth and Jacko will tell it. In the meantime—"

The telephone rang and Maurice snatched it up pettishly. He said, "Pronto?" and then held it out at arm's length toward Johnson. "I wish," he said, "that you would ask your friends *not* to telephone before lunchtime. It spoils my appetite."

"For what?" said Charles dulcetly. The urbanity, I was sorry to see, was making a comeback. Johnson, on the telephone, was saying, "Oh? Where? No, but I'll remember. What number? Right. Thank you." He listened for a few moments longer and then said goodbye and hung up. We all looked at him.

"Well," he said. "Thanks for the coffee."

"You're *going?*" said Maurice.

"It was the Pope," suggested Jacko.

"Actually," Johnson said, "it was a man who knows a man who hád his photograph taken recently."

He wasn't looking at anybody, but I got up and walked over to him. "Mr. Paladrini? You've got Mr. Paladrini's address? Charles, the man who sold the balloons at the zoo. We're going to find him."

"Why?" said Maurice's voice baldly behind us. "If, of course, one may ask."

It was a little difficult to recall why. I stared at Johnson and Johnson said cheerfully, "Because there was a message in the balloon Ruth received making a rendezvous of some kind at the Fall Fair. She got it clearly by accident, and didn't even realize until later what it was. At any rate, we went to the Fall Fair and recognized the balloon trader in superior guise taking part in it. We chased him, and he ran away from us."

"I'm not surprised," said Maurice huffily. "And for no other reason you are going to call on this gentleman?"

"Well, for one other reason," Johnson said. "The balloon may have been intended for one of the men from the Villa Borghese. It is, at least, a possible link with them. And anything which might lead to an explanation of what has happened so far in the Dome can't be altogether a bad thing, I imagine. That is, unless you want to call in the police. Pacifists, vegetarians and anti–blood-sport enthusiasts, make your opinions known. I don't like murders and I like nice girls like Ruth Russell, but we can all go home and finish our knitting if the majority verdict prefers it. Charles?"

"To hell with knitting," said Charles. "I'll come with you. But not Ruth. She's had enough trouble."

"You can't come," I said. "Charles, you have to retake all those pictures this morning."

Charles stared at me. "I'm coming," he said.

"I beg your pardon," Johnson said mildly. "I'm not asking for volunteers, merely a vote of confidence. Jacko? Timothy? Maurice? Paladrini or policemen?"

"You don't mean—" said Timothy. "Not Mr. Paladrini who was so nice to the weenies?"

"The same," answered Johnson.

"Oh but do go," said Timothy. "You have his address?"

"Sit down, Timothy," said Maurice. "You aren't going. I don't see why anyone need go. Wheel the body out of your meat safe, and I shall tell the gardener to bury it. There are plenty of places in the garden."

"And the police?" Jacko said.

"This," said Maurice, "is nothing to do with the police. It is on my property and in my observatory."

"But leased to the Trust," I said quickly. "And if it all came out anyhow, think of the row. Why not take a half measure? Leave the man in the safe, and give us two more days to make some inquiries. If we can't do it by then, Jacko will make his dramatic discovery of the body. How's that?"

"All right," said Jacko. Everyone nodded. Jacko added, "So who goes with Johnson this morning? All of us?"

"It's an interesting thought," Maurice said. "I take it you are trying to *avoid* the attention of the police?"

"Actually," said Johnson, "I'm going alone. Don't worry. I have on my tearproof mascara."

There was the grinding noise of a number of people changing their minds. Then Jacko said, "Well, if you want to. I've got film to develop anyway. But Charles could go. You've forgotten, Ruth. He doesn't need to retake all his photographs."

"Why?" said Charles. He looked, poor darling, as if he could have done with some of our coffee.

98

"Because we found the film on the body," Jacko said. "The film he took out of your camera, Charles, before he smashed it and ran out and got shot. He'd shoved it into his sock but it was rolled up and properly sealed. Ruth has it."

An elegant howl left Charles's lips. "Madder music," he said, "and stronger wine: this is my birthday, love, today." I delved in my handbag, found the roll of film and tossed it to him.

Johnson, rising between us, thoughtfully fielded it. "I'm terribly happy for you," he said, "but let's keep our heads. If we have to call in the police, this is evidence. You know what's in it, Charles. You don't have to take these pictures again. I vote we leave the roll here with Maurice. I'll sign it" (he did so), "and put it out of sight . . . there."

There was a clink as he dropped the film inside an Attic vase rampant with satyrs and maenads intent on creative play projects which ought to have cost Maurice half the proceeds from his last West End run but probably didn't. It seemed the right spot for Diana, if only in the negative, and Charles was perfectly complaisant. He turned in the doorway as we were leaving and, sinking his chin on his chest, delivered himself, I remember, of one of the gems of his collection:

> "Sweet Mem'ry's Chord
> Was Touched Today
> They Came and Took
> Your Teeth Away
> Your Wig has Gone
> Your Gas Limb Too
> The Plastic Joints

That Rivet You
Your Contact Lenses They Removed
And All About You that We Looved."

I went back and had breakfast with him, and then left him to go and finish my work in the Dome.

But I didn't go to the Dome. I waited at the gates of the villa and made Johnson take me to Rome to see Mr. Paladrini.

CHAPTER 7

I SLEPT MOST OF THE WAY into Rome, curled up on the passenger seat beside Johnson. He drove fast and steadily and when I finally awoke we were through the Porta San Lorenzo and into our first bout of traffic jams. There was a rug over me which hadn't been there before, and my cheeks were wet.

I dried them, and Johnson said, "He's in the Via Margutta, behind the Via del Babuino. But I think we deserve a drink at Renati's first." He had made no fuss, to my surprise and relief, about taking me with him. He had not, come to think of it, even appeared amazed to see me. He was, of course, one of your homespun types, invincibly phlegmatic. Like me.

It had begun to rain when we got to Renati's. Johnson parked the car, presumably on somebody's doormat, and joined me at a pink table. I had a gin fizz, and said, "I thought we were in a hurry. I thought you were going to rush to the Via Margutta, fling open the door and say, 'Ha!' "

"You can't say, 'Ha!' in Italian," Johnson pointed out patiently. "You say, 'Ah!' Or perhaps, 'Ciao!' "

"Then he shoots you," I said. "Shouldn't you be painting somebody? It's less dangerous, and presumably you get paid for it."

"In other words," said Johnson, "don't go to the Via Margutta?"

There was a pause. "No," I said.

"I see. Then what," said Johnson, "are you suggesting instead? A high-stake rubber of contract?" He stared at me, the black eyebrows raised above the obscuring bifocals, and then when I opened my mouth, forestalled me smoothly. "No. Stinging rebuke followed by abject contrition. But if I don't do this now, the police will merely do it in two days' time, Ruth. All I shall do is threaten him with the polizia. This is only Red Riding Hood. What I should like is a look at the wolf."

"And if the wolf is one of us?" I said.

He took his glasses off. There was nothing wrong with his eyes underneath, except that they were chilly and narrowed. He said, "It probably is. Are you suggesting that he—or she—should be allowed to escape?"

I saw I had made a mistake. An irretrievable, hopeless mistake. "I thought that was why you were doing this," I said. "I thought you were the only one who realized it had to be one of us. Someone from the villa. Or someone from the observatory. I thought you would help us to—"

"Sweep it under the carpet?" said Johnson. "Or

bury it all in the garden? It'll be the making of Maurice's organic tomatoes."

At the next table a middle-aged lady with long, shining fingernails poured a little cream delicately into her saucer and held it under her bosom. A miniature white poodle attired in a black knitted tube like a sock emerged from the overhang and began to lap with a scrap of pink tongue. She conversed with it, in miniature Italian.

I looked back at Johnson. He had put on his glasses and all I could see was beer and bifocals again. I said, "I suppose not."

"I suppose not, too," Johnson said. "Tolerance, yes. Decadence, no. People don't laugh at comic obituary verse because death is funny. Quite the reverse. On the other hand, you can stretch your sense of proportion on light years until it can't apply itself to the human dilemma anymore. Hence the mystics." He finished his beer and continued in the same tone of voice, "So you really think Charles wants to murder you?"

The saucer at the next table tilted and shot a trail of cream upward; the poodle, craning forward, lapped it up neatly. All the blood in my veins rose as through a hose pipe into my face but I didn't look away and I didn't gasp and I didn't lose my head. I said, "All right, my adrenalin blipped. The rest of the experiment was a failure. I don't think Charles is trying to murder me. I don't think Charles has any more to do with all this than I have. I live with him, remember?"

"When he isn't in Naples. He *was* in Naples, Ruth. The message on the fish couldn't have been for him. He wasn't at the Fall Fair and, alone of you all, he didn't have one of the new keys to the Dome and he didn't have any possible access to one. He couldn't possibly have murdered the man in the zoo: he hadn't even reached the loo when you heard the shot that killed him. And lastly, if he didn't want you around, he would hardly have come back to you after Naples."

Johnson grinned at me and turning to the woman at the next table said, "We're rehearsing a play." She smiled tremulously and then, ducking her head, began to collect her gloves, her handbag and the dog like a native of Vesuvius reacting to the first smoke ring over the crater. Johnson turned back to me and I said, "I know all that."

"Then why were you crying?" said Johnson mildly.

The woman at the next table had gone. I said, "I was asleep. My God, I'm not responsible to anyone for my dreams, am I?"

"And yesterday?" the irritating voice went on persistently.

It was unfair. It was unfair to me and to Charles, and it was nothing to do with Johnson. And, more damnable than anything else, I could feel my eyes beginning to sting once again. Johnson said, "I know. You love the man. But you *have* been worried. I wonder if perhaps Charles seemed to have more money than you ever expected? And if perhaps I'm right in thinking that your camera and his have quite clear distinguishing marks?"

I didn't know what to do. I didn't have to do anything. My face gave me away.

"I see they did," Johnson said. "So you expected Charles to remark on it at the zoo, and when he didn't, you jumped to conclusions. But, you know, he might have had a very good reason for letting people think that it was his film which had been stolen, and not yours. He might have realized that his own camera must be lying about unprotected, with even more important couture pictures still in it. Or he may have remembered that he left a film in his camera which he didn't much want anyone to see anyway for quite uncriminal reasons. People who are good with cameras shoot funny things with them sometimes."

"You guessed," I said.

"I guessed," said Johnson. "What was on Charles's film? Girlie pictures?"

"You could call it that," I said. Maurice had asked me if I was a prude and he was right, I was. I was a heel, too. I had sent Jacko to Maurice's party on Saturday night after the zoo, and I had carried Charles's camera down from the dome where he had left it and developed the pictures inside it. It had only been half full, like mine. I said, "Some of the pictures were couture ones, the important ones which the Villa Borghese men must have been after. The rest were just straight sexy portraits like Jacko's."

Johnson said, "What did you do with the negative?"

"It's well hidden," I said, and produced a grin. "I shouldn't like any modest souls to be outraged. I put a new film in the camera and clicked through the first half in darkness."

"So the film our frozen friend pinched later on the same evening was a blank one? What an unsatisfactory thing," said Johnson, "to be shot for. But at least you can acquit Charles, surely, of committing murder and mayhem to preserve a little smut and a change in the hemline. *Now* what is eating you?"

"Charles will be so worried," I said. "He'll find he's lost all his fashion pictures."

"He can reshoot them," Johnson said. "And they haven't got into the wrong hands. Surely that is what matters. He'll put it down to a fault in the camera, and since the camera is in five hundred pieces, no one is likely to dispute it . . . How nice," he said, breaking off and then recovering smoothly. "If you breathe in when you do it again, you won't fog my glasses."

"Hul*lo*," said Diana Minicucci above us. She bent again and kissed Johnson, thoughtfully.

It was, I had forgotten, one of Di's other haunts. She had been done over at Giulio's again and was wearing a long, thin olive suede coat and huge tinted glasses with yellow rims and her own hair, coiled over her cheeks and knotted in ladylike fashion at the nape of her neck.

Johnson surveyed her in exactly the way that he had looked at Innes's mouse which she adored and which was a change, admittedly, from poor Jacko, who treated birds and ring-pull cans as one problem. Johnson said, "We're running away to get married. Where's your photographer friend?"

"Looking for Ruth," said Di, eyeing him. "When he called on her at the Dome, she wasn't there. Panic. All sittings postponed till further notice."

I said, "Where is Charles now?" Johnson had paid the bill and we were all standing politely being buffeted and/or pinched without even noticing it.

"Dashing around Rome like a rotary lawn mower," said Diana callously. "If I meet him, I'll tell him you're having a total immersion oil-painting course. If you want him, you'll find us all at the Villa Borghese at two. Back to the prologue."

She didn't interfere, because Di doesn't interfere. But her lashes indicated that she was standing by on the secondary runway for the moment I chose to take off. Johnson said with complete unexpectedness, "We're going to call on the man who sold Ruth a balloon outside the zoo, the day the man stole her camera and got killed. How much are you insured for?"

Diana smiled. "May I come? Really?" she said.

"We're not getting married till after lunch," I said. I wasn't at all sure if Johnson knew what he was doing. "What about the Villa Borghese?"

Outside in the Piazza the rain was coming down as if a tank had burst, drowning the noise of the fountains and beating hell out of the glories of Rameses II and Merneptah (c. 13–12 B.C.) as celebrated on the ancient obelisk in the center. There was a crash of thunder, a flash, and the lights went out everywhere, busily.

Di Minicucci spread her gloveless hands. "Celestial endorsement. Not even Charles can take pictures without any power. Do we take your car or mine?"

We took neither: if a Roman junction during one of the four normal rush hours is suicide, a Roman junction while the traffic lights are off resembles nothing so much as a herd of myopic rhinoceroses meeting eye to eye with a herd of dim-witted elephants and attempting to copulate. We crossed the

Piazza to the astonishment of the sheltering natives and entered the Via del Babuino without melting. Johnson's hair dripped gently inside the shapeless tweed collar of his jacket and my trouser suit stuck to my body. Diana remained totally immaculate. I congratulated her on her appearance.

"But darling," she said. "Absolutely new and too easy. The closest any woman can come to the tingled air-washed look of a country-freshened face. So it says on the pot. You must try it."

The Via del Babuino is where most of the art dealers dwell and the streets around about it are occupied by the artistic colony and the voluntary bodies who serve it. The Via Babuino closes from lunchtime till half-past three in the afternoon. It was nearly lunchtime now. Between the brass rings of the eight-paneled portals the cinquecentis were filing out from their patios, leaving patches of oil by the statues. Peering through lightless windows you caught glimpses of classical busts, painted bureaus, furniture French and Italian, Dutch paintings on easels, Florentine prints on boxes and bookends. On the left, a familiar red and white street sign said CARNABY STREET, while below, a white arrow on red said VIA MARGUTTA.

"Think nothing of it," said Johnson, and, leading briskly, turned into the street of the balloon man.

The Via Margutta is a quiet street. On the left, behind the parked cars, stretched a row of shops selling dresses and icons and paintings. On the right there was a line of mews buildings, whose faded wood doors were closed with cumbrous latches.

On none of them was the street number Johnson

had been given. "I'll ask," I said quickly, and went into the first shop that seemed open.

It was a small leather boutique dangling with belts and shoppers and shoulder bags, with racks of suede skirts and rawhide jerkins with fringes. A male Italian with liquid eyes and a long, unwavering nose and a perfect jawline with silky black sideburns was lolling on a wooden chair absorbing instant football from a transistor, while beside him a signora in knee boots was jabbing holes in a belt with a hand-punch. Bags of eyelets and staplers and wooden shoe molds and lengths of cut leather littered the floorboards. The smell was ecstatic.

I explained I was looking for a street trader who sold Occhiali Giocattoli.

Against football, no woman can expect to compete for attention. The perfect head swiveled around in my direction. The man's cigarette hung from his lips, and his thumbs were tucked into a belt so low it was practically garters. But his lips did not move, neither did his mind swerve from its primary task. The girl said, "For Marco, another visitor."

Which was sad. I said, "Oh. He has someone with him?"

"Ah, frequently," the girl said, and I didn't need my crash course at the language laboratory to follow the nuances. "Four people to drink with last night, and already another this morning."

"Drink, then, is his trouble?" I said. I smiled at the gladiator by the transistor, who fluttered his eyelashes.

"Why not?" said the girl, forcing an awl through a wadding of pigskin, her arm muscles rippling. "You cannot imagine he chooses to earn his living making Occhiali Giocattoli, now can you? He is an educated man, well brought up by his family."

"You know him well, then?" I inquired.

"He is a neighbor," the boy friend intervened lazily. "No, we do not know him well. He has accepted a coffee when he comes for his cart."

"Where does he keep it?" I asked.

The girl jerked her head at one of the faded doors opposite. "In the mews there. His studio is two stairs along, next the dress shop. On the first floor. You will see the name, Marco Susini . . . To-to!"

To-to turned, with flattering reluctance, from studying all he could see of my kneecaps.

"Cavallette!" the girl shouted suddenly, and flung up her fist with the awl in it.

The awl was pointing at me. And the sharpened steel flashed in the candlelight.

The boy friend sprang to his feet and, snatching a broom, plunged toward me.

I flung myself sideways. There was a crash, a flurry of scattering handbags and a grunt from To-to, engaged in tolerating stress poorly among the cape leather slough-offs. Through the plate glass window I could see Johnson and Di standing outside in the rain, their hands in their pockets. I screamed, and snatched up a bullwhip of plaited kangaroo leather. To-to got to his feet scowling faintly.

"There is a plague of them," the girl said obscurely, and lowering the awl, resumed stabbing the pigskin. To-to said, "Two stairs along," and began, irritably, to pick up the handbags. "You wish the bullwhip?" he added.

It cost twelve bloody pounds and I bought it. I hadn't the nerve to refuse it. Then I left the shop and showed Johnson the stair to the studio. He set off for it right away, but Di lingered, unrolling my bullwhip.

There were twelve feet of it altogether. We trailed it up the chipped marble staircase after Johnson and stood in total darkness outside the door that said *Marco Susini*. "Fourteen pounds," said Diana. "Come on, Ruth. Charles doesn't need it."

"Neither does Jacko," I said, outraged. Now that Di wanted it, the bullwhip seemed the most sophisticated possession since suspenders.

"That's what you think," said Diana. "Fifteen pounds. And my pot of Fresh Air Make-up Base." Johnson was ringing the bell.

"Listen," I said. "Mr. Paladrini is in there. And very possibly Mr. Paladrini's visitor, with a muzzle-loading gun and a guilt complex. The bullwhip is mine and I'm hanging on to it. If you want a kangaroo of your own, go and catch one." Johnson rang the bell for a second time.

Di said helpfully, "The door's open, darling."

And so it was. A thin crack of daylight, widening and lessening in the draft, showed where it had been left on the latch. "I want my mother," said Johnson, "to have an Interflora Sympathy basket. It will be cheaper if you send it from London." He pushed open the door very slowly.

The room inside was large and empty of people. The glazed roof and windows, heavily coated with dirt, on which the rain frothed and spattered, told that it had indeed once been a studio. It was now the stockroom of the balloon man as well as his living space. A frayed armchair stood beside a battered stove, on which a pan thick with pasta was sitting abandoned. Packets spilled out of a cupboard onto a small table holding the remains of a meal, and one or two wooden chairs stood about.

The rest of the room, bare of carpeting, was occupied by long trestle tables containing layers of cards loaded with clockwork mice and toy sunglasses and plastic tea sets and Vampire Fingernails and cardboard masks and glutinous reptilia and tinny cowboy guns with *Super Bum-Bum* on them and packets and packets and packets of limp assorted balloons.

We stood in the doorway, taking it all in. Then Diana said, "There's no one here, what a sell. Now *I know* who would like a clockwork mouse," and swam forward to the nearest table, bubbling. Johnson and I followed after her. I had the door in my hand when it was wrenched out of my fingers and slammed shut behind me. A hard hand striking my shoulder sent me tripping forward to crash into Johnson. He whirled around and Di, a clockwork mouse in her fingers, looked up, the eyelashes open like daisies.

Standing with his back to the main door and barring it stood Innes Wye, and the gun in his hand was pointing straight at us. "I don't know anyone who would like a clockwork mouse," said Di, her voice shaking, and I can't think when I've admired anyone more. Then Innes said, "Drop that whip," and I realized it was still in my right hand.

I didn't make any jokes. I dropped it.

I have said, I think, that Innes Wye was a little man with a high voice and equivalent principles which none of the best scientific workshops in the world had apparently succeeded in shaking. There was little more I did know of him, except that he came to the Dome for his calories, and that the rest of his life, it appeared, was devoted to his white mouse and his bloody Incubator, with sundry forays into bestial license in the Museo Nazionale Romano and the Pinacoteca Vaticana on holiday.

He had, for example, torn up poor Jacko's painstaking photographs, and made the Fall Fair the Fall Fair of the century. He seemed, in fact, a character of quite regrettable consistency until you noticed the fact that he *had been* at the Fall Fair. That it was his falling downstairs which allowed Mr. Paladrini to escape. And that he had the new key to the observatory.

I looked quickly at Johnson. Johnson was standing with his hands hanging at his sides looking at Innes, and demonstrating the melancholy fact that it is not the habit of eminent portrait painters to carry offensive weapons about in their jackets. He said gently, "Dr. Wye. What are you doing here?"

"Oh, no," said Innes. "Oh no, it won't wash. Put your hands in the air, all of you. And get over there, away from the table. This time, Miss Minicucci, I don't get pushed around. This time, Mr. Johnson, you won't get your friends to do your dirty work for you. This time you all get what's coming to you."

It is another unfortunate fact that in moments of stress all human exchanges are conducted in unerring clichés. The exception proved to be Johnson, who said merely, "Why?" followed after a moment's thought by "What?"

"You'll find out," said Innes firmly over the revolver. He sidled along the wall toward the door to the inner room, near which, I suddenly saw, was a wall telephone. I wondered if Mr. Paladrini— Marco Susini—was inside the other room and if so, why he hadn't come out to help his colleague. I wondered what possible connection Innes Wye could have with the houses of Antonelli or Schön, and then realized that those who earn their living by dealing in secrets don't necessarily confine themselves to fashion houses. I wondered what exactly was inside Innes's mysterious Incubator that none of us had been allowed to gaze upon, and if in fact there was anything at all except, say, a Mickey Mouse eight-day alarm clock.

Sitting there in his shed, engaged in intergroup transactions with half the scientific establishment in Europe, no one could deny Innes was neatly placed: as central as the fish in my balloon. I wondered if he had put the fish in my balloon, and whom he had meant the message for. There were fish on the table, rather inefficiently cut out of cardboard, with the string and the rubber studs all ready for fixing. Beside me Diana, her hands stretched up high with the fingers pointed outward like Plate 193 of the Kama Sutra, said, "Don't phone, Innes. The police know we've come here."

Innes smiled, his hand on the telephone. "Bluff," he said, and took down the receiver.

"They do, Innes," I said with equal earnestness, not to mention mendacity. "Look, don't make it worse. You can't possibly overpower three of us and get away without anyone noticing. All we came for was to talk to Mr. Paladrini."

The revolver was pointed straight at my head. Of course, for his work, Innes's touch had to be steady, but I wasn't keen on the spillover into small arms. He said, still smiling stiffly, "I have no idea who you are talking about. There was no one here when I arrived. The whole affair was a trick and I have no intention of overpowering anybody. I am simply going to call up the police."

"You are?" said Johnson in tones of mild disbelief. His arms dropped and, as Innes's hand whitened on the trigger, sprang straight again.

"You think I won't tell the Trust all about it?" Innes said. "But I will. They'll hear all you've been up to. I'll tell them about the break-in at the Dome that was so cleverly hushed up. And they'll want to know what you are all doing here. I don't need to ask what this is. This is the hideout of the man who sold Ruth Russell and Digham that balloon."

There was a brief silence in honor of this earful of dazzling facts. Johnson was the first to recover. He said to Innes, "We're here because we managed to track down the balloon man and thought that we'd trapped him. Why are you here?"

Innes stood, the telephone still in one hand because he had not yet solved the problem of how to dial a number while keeping us all at his gun-end. He said, "Need you ask?"

"Darling, he needs," said Diana gently. "Go on, tell him."

Innes stared at us all. He said stiffly, "I was telephoned by a Fall Fair official. He referred to the misunderstanding which led to my accident and invited me to this address for a drink and an apology from the Organizer."

115

"And when you came, no one was here," Johnson said.

"I knew as soon as I opened the door," said Innes indignantly. "No one answered the bell, and when I found the door open I walked in. As you see, no one in their senses would take it for a fitting rendezvous for such a purpose. It is a street trader's lodging and workshop. And the street trader, I have no doubt, is the dubious one you encountered. Naturally, I feared for my life."

"Then you heard us come up the stairs," I said. "But didn't you guess who we were by our voices?"

"Of course," said Innes. "But surely it is obvious that the source of the whole trouble lies with someone connected with the observatory?"

"That's what we thought," Diana said.

Innes stared at her. The splendid certainty which had informed his every action to date ran out a little. His revolver hand slackened. Johnson said, still gently, "That's why we wondered, you see, what you were doing here. Do you usually carry a gun?"

Innes dropped his gaze and looked at it, and then at all of us. You could see the scientific brain assimilating the facts and then spewing out, with however much distaste, the deductions. He said, "You expected to find your balloon seller here?"

"That's right," said Johnson patiently. "We got a photograph of him the other day by a fluke and I checked it with the authorities. This is the address we were given. But he seems to have gone. Do you usually . . ."

"No, I didn't," said Innes irritably. He gazed at Johnson, and then at Di and then at me.

Di said, "You can't be the working man's Maigret, darling, unless you keep your revolver pointing at the thing you're shooting."

Innes looked down at it and said, "I got it off a card on the table."

"Super Bum-Bum," I said, trying not to burst into open hysteria. Innes threw me a look of dislike and dropped the hand with the gun in it. Then he slowly hung the telephone receiver back on the hook. It wasn't much of a vote of confidence, but it was better than nothing. Johnson said, "You really did get a message to come here?"

"Yes," said Innes. He made as if to move away from the telephone toward us, and then stopped. He said to Johnson, "If you expected to find one of the criminals living here, how come you dragged the girls into it?"

I said, "We dragged ourselves, Innes. I came to help because I don't want the Trust mixed up in a scandal."

"And I came for other reasons entirely," Diana said, and stared at Johnson with that peculiar sexless stare that model girls assume for the camera. Johnson blew her a kiss, and I swear she reddened. She said quickly, "I take it, by the way, that Mr. Paladrini-Susini *has* departed? You've checked the other room?"

We all looked at the inner door. High above our heads, as if triggered off by the action, there was a sudden violent movement. In a response totally automatic, Innes flung up his fist with the gun in it and squeezed the trigger.

There was a searing flame, an earsplitting explosion, and the glazed roof came down in a curtain of glass crystals and plaster, followed by the unimpeded weight of the whole drumming downpour. On the floor, twitching faintly on a bed of bright broken glass, lay a locust of monstrous proportions. A second one, emerald green and as large as a small bird, regarded us uneasily from an unbroken astragal and began cautiously to creep sideways, its tail quivering, its long wings vibrating with a dry crackling sound. "There's a plague of them," I said. "You should get a bullwhip."

Innes dropped his gun and was standing, breathing heavily over the insect. He said, "But it was a toy gun. From the table!"

"Then I hate to think," Johnson said from the table, "what you could manage with the Vampire Fingernails."

The rain beat on our heads, driving the plaster dust into our shoulders and soaking the showcards and beading the cards of toy sunglasses. Innes said, "It seems I owe you an apology. I can only say it was a genuine mistake. I was brought here under false pretenses, and it is necessary to be careful. I do assure you I had no idea that thing was loaded."

"None of the others are," Johnson said. "All genuine guaranteed kiddie-fodder." He bent down, broke and examined Innes's gun and handed it back to him. "There are still five bullets left. Why not hang on to it? You don't know what we'll find in the next room." And he walked to the inner door.

He and Innes kicked it open in the end while I hung back with Di, less to avoid a volley of gunfire than to avoid seeing my third corpse in five days. But there was no one dead or alive in the bedroom, merely Mr. Paladrini's wardrobe with a few clothes still hanging inside it, and his bed, recently slept in, and a table and one or two chairs, all covered with a litter of cheap toys and fancy balloon shapes. Beside the bed, presumably to segregate it from the room with the stove, was a gas cylinder with a nozzle for inflating them.

Everything was rather wet, as the skylight in this room had fallen in sympathy, and there were three dead locusts in various prayerful attitudes on the linoleum and another in the bathroom just off. Of Mr. Paladrini there was no other sign, unless you counted a blue faded overall hung on the back of an armchair.

Johnson lifted it up and began, not very enthusiastically, to search it. It was in one of the inside pockets that he found the cardboard fish, in a color different from mine, but otherwise identical in shape and material.

It had a message, too. It said, *S.M. Capri 20/- 1500*.

We all crowded around. We could hear people in the outer room, exclaiming over the hole in the ceiling, and a steady pounding of more feet up the staircase as the neighbors rushed in to see what crime passionel had taken place among the toy sunglasses. Innes, who had a social conscience, looked over his shoulder at intervals and said, "In a moment."

I said, "It's another appointment. Capri: it can't be the Isle of, surely. And S.M.? And twenty?"

"November twentieth?" Johnson suggested. "Yes, maybe. But think. This was going into a balloon. It wasn't an appointment that Paladrini was necessarily going to keep. It was one he was going to pass to someone else, inside one of his balloons. What we want to know is, who was he going to pass it to?"

I said, "You'll find out if you go to Capri at three P.M. on November twentieth and look for S.M., whoever that is."

"Shall I?" said Johnson. "We don't know where to go, or who to look for if we did. Mr. Paladrini may not be there this time: the appointment may be between two perfect strangers. No. There's only one way to be certain, and that is by watching who buys the balloon."

"Fine," said Innes, turning back from saying "In a moment" again to the neighbors. "If you think Mr. Paladrini is going to come back here, blow up a balloon and then proceed to the agreed place to sell it."

"Along with the mechanical mice," Diana said, a sign that her interest was dwindling.

"I feel," Johnson said, "that Mr. Paladrini has blown up his final balloon. But there seems no reason why we shouldn't do the job for him."

"Us?" Innes said.

I said, "We don't know when and where to take the cart. Assuming the cart is still there where he kept it."

"Yes, we do," Innes said. From among the litter of paper on the table he picked out a sheet from a notebook. On it, in rain-smeared Italian, was what appeared to be a rough timetable. He conned it. "Wednesday . . . ?"

"Nothing for today," said Johnson, looking over his shoulder. "But tomorrow . . . Tomorrow, my children, you have a full day ahead of you. Look at it. The Colosseum, the Piazza San Pietro, the Castel Sant' Angelo . . ."

I said, "Look at the Castel Sant' Angelo. There's a number against it. Twelve. Do you suppose . . . ?"

"That the cart was intended to be outside the Castel Sant' Angelo at midday tomorrow, with the balloon prepared to hand to its new owner? I do," Johnson said. He turned to face the oncoming prow of the lady who undoubtedly had been the absent Mr. Paladrini's landlady. "Signora," said Johnson, "we came, you understand, to celebrate a christening and regard! The effects of the opening of the champagne. Fear nothing. It will be repaired; it will be paid for. On my cousin's behalf, I guarantee it."

There was the slight change of air which results when many thousands of blanketlike lire float from one hand to another. "But of course!" the landlady said, while, like fading detergent, the neighbors receded behind her. "You assure me that no one was hurt? And the bambino?"

"With its little mother," said Johnson. "You understand. A young mother's health must not be risked. But you may congratulate the happy father. See!" And raising one implacable finger, he propelled Innes forward.

"Ah! So young!" said the landlady, and kissed him. "This is a great day, is it not? One you cannot celebrate here, in this rubbish. Since Marco is called away, why, I am your hostess. Follow."

We did, to the flat below, which was where all the neighbors had gone to, anyway. When we got out two hours later, weaving more than a little and with our pockets squeaking with blue sugared almonds, it took us two casts around the Piazza del

Popolo to find Johnson's car, and then a miracle to drive it to Velterra.

Diana was weeping with laughter and even Innes cracked a smile now and then, which wasn't surprising considering what I'd put in his squeezed lemon. Johnson sang all the way in between making up some obituaries which would have done Digham credit and some others which made Di begin to scream, so that we had to hammer her on the back.

And I sat in the back, with a bullwhip. And a paper bag full of string, and colored balloons, and a fish with an odd message on it.

CHAPTER 8

I ATE IN THE DOME that day, lunching off some of Innes's bread and salami with a mug of black coffee steaming among the jars of hypo while I developed the plates from my night's work. Johnson and Di had gone straight to Maurice's villa, where Di appeared to be staying, and Innes was in Mouse Hall, after entering the Dome briefly with me to demonstrate how to trip a Wyoming steer with my bullwhip. This he managed to do after unhooking both the flanking bay trees from their tubs outside the door and reducing a spare chair to batons; I had been more generous with my doctoring than I intended. Then he wandered off to give Poppy her bran and water and Cuddle.

It was then that I remembered the body in the meat safe and went off, not too steadily myself, to make the black coffee. If you have ever thought of working alone on an Italian hilltop with a corpse frozen hard in the meat safe, my counsel is not to. *Sadly missed along Life's way,/But quietly remembered every day.* Then Jacko came in, carrying sensational news from point to point like a concrete mixer.

Someone had pinched our frozen friend's film from Maurice's amphora, and Maurice was raising the roof about it. And someone, while Maurice was raising the roof, had been raking through all our belongings. My possessions and Charles's were scattered all over the digs, Jacko said, and his own room was a shambles. He'd just been fixing it and trying to stop our landlady from calling the police when Maurice had rung to report the film stolen.

"And I've just come from Innes's digs," said Jacko virtuously. "In case there was trouble, you know. And *his* room is a sensation as well. He'll blow his top when he sees it. *When* he sees it. Where have you types been spending the morning? Charles came in after breakfast to find you, and then came raging back this afternoon from the Villa Borghese in a froth because none of the models had turned up and you weren't to be found in Rome either. His face when he saw his paisley underwear all over the floor was quite something, I can tell you. *And* his precious film missing. He's going to have to take his shots all over again tomorrow morning."

"No, he isn't," I said. "Johnson and I have work for him tomorrow morning." And I sat him under the red light in the developing room while I finished off what I was doing and told him all that had happened.

What with that and the gin and the fact that the

thing that mixes the emulsion had retired for the season, the results from that batch of plates were never to my mind what you would call totally reliable, which just goes to show that you should never get your astral bodies mixed up with the two other kinds. At the end Jacko, who had interrupted all the way through, jumping up and down like another bloody locust, said, "And Innes. Do you believe him?"

I switched the light on and dried my hands. "Jacko, how do I know? I will admit, he gave me a few anxious moments. But his story rang absolutely true and he really did go sage green when the gun fired. Johnson thinks we should take him on the balloon truck expedition and just see what happens."

"Um. Ruth?" said Jacko. I had hung up my lab coat and was switching off to go down to the office. Jacko followed me thoughtfully. He said, "We know you're all right because you nearly got killed, and you know I'm all right because I was with you when it all happened—"

"And saved me," I said. I stopped and issued him a kiss of merit with my fingers under his chin and then went on downstairs.

"Well," he said, still following, talking. "But what do we know about Johnson?"

"I thought of that," I said. I had reached the ground floor. I turned. "But everything checks. For one thing, we shouldn't have traced the balloon man at all but for Johnson. And for another, he's far too well known. Just try and work out how an internationally famous portrait painter could get mixed up in something as petty as this. Or would need to. He must be loaded."

"A fair description," said Johnson's voice just behind me. I turned very slowly and said, "How did you get in?" and he smiled at me rather hazily and held up two keys for inspection.

"Innes has gone home to have a good sleep, and Maurice says he doesn't intend to be the only sober person at a portrait sitting. You promised that one day you would show me over the observatory."

I stared at those devious glasses. Then I got it. "Your room has been searched as well?" I asked.

"Right," said Johnson. "And *after* the signed film was stolen."

"And it occurs to you that perhaps the Dome has been turned over?"

"It seems to me," Johnson said, "that two people are after that film. One of them has it, and the other is still trying to find it. And if the person trying to find it is the man who broke in the other night, he has a key, or access to one, remember?"

"Wait a minute," Jacko said. He came down the last of the steps and stood frowning at Johnson. "If the film has gone from the vase, then one of us either took it or told about it."

"That's right," said Johnson placidly. "The same applies to this character who's now hunting it. He was too late in reaching the amphora . . . You're quite right, you know. Even Maurice has his suspicions. You can see him, if you like, in raccoon collar and cuffs and a Stetson, limping about the grounds looking for footprints. I thought I would come and look for footprints as well."

But although we scoured every inch of the Dome, we found no trace of disturbance which means there hadn't been one: whatever else we are not, Jacko and I are reasonably methodical. In any case, as we realized when we thought about it, Jacko had been in the Dome all the morning, and there had been the briefest of intervals between his departure and my fuddled arrival with Innes. At the end of the search, Johnson removed himself and his glasses from the fascinations of the developing room and said, "Right. That leaves only Mouse Hall."

I remembered the second key in his hand. I looked at Jacko and Jacko said, "Innes gave you the key to Mouse Hall?"

"Well . . ." said Johnson. We were eating Innes's biscuits in the kitchen, since work makes you hungry. Jacko said accusingly, "You stole that bloody key!"

"Well," said Johnson. "I *should* like to know what he's got in that building. After all, I've practically slept with his mouse."

Innes's pad is five minutes away, and, even with the wisteria off it, looks more fit for Giselle than Innes. But within the pillars it was once an observatory. Its corrugated roof moves on a long ratchet which slides back at the touch of a switch. If its own generator should fail, which Heaven forbid, the roof can be rolled back with a kind of starting handle. But since Innes created his Incubator the roof has never been rolled back and there have been no power failures, for the simple reason that Innes took everything to pieces and replaced it with British Imperial Standard, to the last twist of fuse wire and screw. We in the observatory envy Innes.

We envy him for more than that. While we congeal in the Dome, Innes works day and night at a comfortable 68° Fahrenheit, because that is what the Incubator fancies. Otherwise it would rust up like a tin can from humidity.

The gush of warm air greeted us the moment Johnson unlocked the door and we tiptoed in. I don't know why we tiptoed in, except that neither Jacko nor I had ever been in Mouse Hall on our own before. It felt like stealing more of Innes's biscuits. I shut the door fast behind us and walked up beside Johnson Johnson, who was looking as everybody looks when they first step into an electronic workshop. That is, blasé.

This is the fault of the S.F. kiddie shows on the telly. In Innes's workshop, two thirds of the walls, benches and floor space are covered with banks of dials filled with illuminated rows of running numbers. Disks of colored light flicker on and off all about you: rows of scarlet horseshoes shimmer and wink; machinery buzzes and drones and the air conditioning breathes at you heavily. Because electronic machinery doesn't like being switched on and off, Mouse Hall is always furtively busy as well as cozy. The total effect is pure Disney.

I knew exactly how Johnson's mind was working. If it looks spurious when it is real, it wouldn't be very hard to make it look real when it is spurious. He walked to the end of the room, where Poppy poked her white nose out of her cage, her eyes sparkling like garnets from the clinical orderliness of the work bench and tool-making area. A corrugated wall partition, running on tracks, could divide the room when the lathe was in action. The Incubator, along with Innes, didn't tolerate dust.

An oscilloscope, plugged into a faulty photon developer, displayed a jagged green line, trembling, on its rectangular screen. "He has a laser?" Johnson said. He was offering Poppy a sunflower seed. She sniffed it, twitching, and then drawing it from his fingers, ran with it into her medicated nest of white shredded Cuddle, from whence the sound of cracking emerged.

"She would stay longer if it was Innes," I said. "She isn't very tame . . . We all use the laser. To test new equipment, for example. Opticals come in from Switzerland, and we keep the truest and send the others all back. It's done by passing light through a half-silvered plate of very true glass, separating the beams and then marrying them on return."

"Then you need a good deal of power?" Johnson said.

Everyone always mentions the power because the wires are so obvious. Every workshop is hanging with wires, and this was no exception. Hanks of colored wire descended from almost everything visible. At the Dome, our main cable runs around an open pelmet just above arm's reach under the cupola. Innes's travels all over the ceiling and down one wall. We work on 500 volts and make do. "Innes has two thousand volts there," I said, "if he wants it. And it's connected to the Incubator. That's why we never remove the casing if Innes isn't here. No one would like telescope-flavored crisps."

"Ah, yes," said Johnson, and turned to the middle of the floor at long last. "Ah, yes. So this is the Incubator."

The Incubator was, of course, pure science fiction, bedded in concrete because of its weight, with a working surface built all around it. It was dazzling white like an igloo: another of Innes's precautions. No damp could get through the casing of foam plastic blocks which enclosed it. They were cut as with a jigsaw, fat and warm and solid with calculations scribbled all over them, and fringes of thin colored wires festooned below.

There were sheets and sheets of calculations on the work surface also, all neatly pinned to backing boards and numbered in Innes's writing: if Innes wasn't engaged in advanced scientific work of an experimental nature, he was giving a very good impression of it. Johnson walked all around it and said, "Should I understand what it does, if you told me?"

"We can't even tell you," Jacko said. "Innes would have to do that, or some buff at the Trust, and the chances are that you wouldn't understand, anyway. But you can take my word that he's a fully qualified scientist in his line, just as he's a fully qualified stuffed shirt in private life, the poor little bastard."

"You mean," said Johnson into a sudden silence, "he isn't a solo vibraphone player suborned by the Chinese for luncheon vouchers. But that's no secret; we know all about his career . . . The point is, what is he doing in Velterra?"

"The point is," I said, "what are you doing in Velterra? You've switched off the power."

"Christ!" said Jacko with more reverence than I have ever heard from him except in the developing room. He hurried over to where Johnson was standing in front of the switchboard. Johnson continued to stand in front of the switchboard and Jacko came to a halt. "The damage," said Johnson mildly, "is done. Why not make the most of it?"

With the power hum absent, the silence screamed at you. All around us the lights had gone out; the needles, shocked, were oscillating to a standstill. In her cage Poppy still cracked industriously over her seed. Whatever experiment or series of experiments had been ticking on inside the shed, everything had come to a halt. I said, "That was inexcusable. That was inexcusable even for a layman. Nobody does that, ever, to another man's work."

I know Jacko felt exactly the same. We both stared at Johnson and met nothing at all but the blank, icy flash of his spectacles. "As Timothy would say, silly me," Johnson said in a voice as hard as his bifocals and, walking forward, laid hands on blocks of foam plastic and proceeded methodically to remove them. Then, when it was all laid bare, he turned to me and Jacko and said curtly, "Well?"

I don't think even I had realized the delicacy and complexity of what Innes was doing before that. But for the network of fine colored wires that hung everywhere, the inside of the Incubator might have been a fantasia of pure abstract design; a garden of convoluted plastic as fine as paper sculpture, interlaced with silvery wafers of metal and stiffened, here and there, with arcs and rods of stuff more solid. There was a red laser fitted inside it. What else there was could hardly be distinguished in the gray light from the single small window. I leaned forward, holding my breath, and a little jet of light sprang from Johnson's hand into the central bank of the machine. He handed me the torch and I used it and then gave it to Jacko.

Jacko switched it off and looked at me. "I can't tell," he said. "It's more advanced than anything I've ever seen before. It seems to have to do with cosmic ray tracking, but that might be only the initial stage toward something much more important. It isn't a fake and it isn't a toy, which leaves us all out on a limb. However well we put all this back, Innes is bound to know from his records that his power's been switched off, and when."

"I see," Johnson said. He had a last look inside the Incubator himself and then, with great delicacy, began building the nest of white blocks around its contours again. "We can't fake it?"

"We can't fake it," I said with finality.

"And you wouldn't if you could," said Johnson, stepping back and pressing down again the handle of the power board. With a whine, the air conditioning came into action and the twinkling dials, roused to life, began presenting their hurrying messages. "But as it happens, it doesn't much matter. Since it seems Innes has nothing to hide, then it is unlikely that Innes will take issue over a checkup. Particularly as there is one matter that he hasn't yet explained to us fully himself."

"What?" said Jacko. I didn't say anything, because I was thinking.

"The revolver," said Johnson. "The one he said he got off a card, which proved so alarmingly genuine, was a Dardick. The toy guns on the card were seven-bullet Glisentis, and there wasn't one missing. Innes fired his own gun there this morning."

We left after that; Johnson to have a lush dinner

with Maurice and Timothy, and Jacko and I to return to the Dome. Jacko sat on the office desk and conducted a long telephone conversation full of heavy breathing with Di, at the end of which he put some new film in his camera and went off singing "Arrivederci Roma" in a passionate baritone.

I was on duty from seven, and it wasn't worth going home. I waited till the phone had cooled down from Jacko and then rang Charles and cheered him up. That is, I meant to; but instead of being mollified by the tale of how Johnson and Di and I had spent our lunchtime he turned out to be spitting with rage. After a while I realized that most of the four-letter words were being applied to my absent friend Johnson for having the bloody nerve to take two silly cows to hold his hand while he went and unfortunately oathing well failed to get himself drilled full of bullet holes. This was very nice and I spent a quarter of an hour soothing him before I went off upstairs and got the cupola opened. It revealed a splendid blanket of cloud which looked as if it was going to settle down for the night and, in fact, did. I waited dutifully till midnight, and then went off home to Charles.

He had put all the paper-covered novels back in the bottom of the drawers and otherwise cleared up the effects of the search, though unable to distinguish between bras and bikinis, and the tights with a few holes had become mingled forever with the tights with a lot of holes and the tights with no holes at all. He seemed glad to see me and proved it. I had to admit that Charles was really rather splendid. I was well aware that in the Stone Age there would have been a queue of fur-coated ladies at the cave mouth on a rotating basis. It was because I was sure I should have been one of them that I refrained from marrying Charles. I know I have the slave temperament, but there was no reason why he should find out.

Lying there in ergonomic total comfort, with our hair mixed together, I said, "There's a full moon coming up, as from Saturday." On Saturday, we were going to Naples together. That is, Jacko and I had business to do there, and Charles said he would come and chaperone us.

And after that, no more bloody night shifts, just paperwork. I don't know when I have felt more contented.

Next morning we all went to the Castel Sant' Angelo.

The behavior therapists have got it all taped: there is nothing like a good night in the hay for taking the edge off the verve next morning. At nine o'clock Charles and I reported to the gates of the villa to pick up Diana as directed, and proceeded in lackluster silence to Innes's digs. Innes was in sparkling form and sounded off on the trade figures for November for five solid minutes until Di told him very briefly what to do with them. Then we had a long, silent journey into Rome and over the Ponte Vittorio Emanuele to the garden just outside the castle, where Charles parked the Alfa and said a prayer over it. Then we all got out and walked in silence around the corner to the Castel Sant' Angelo and our rendezvous with Johnson Johnson.

The fortress of St. Angelo is an ancient papal funk hole connected to the Vatican by miles of covered passageway and built at the head of one of the bridges over the Tiber. There is a narrow road filled with frantic Roman traffic between the castle and the river. If you cross to the opposite pavement you can lean on the wall and look down on the water, which is yellow and sluggish and full of weeds with broken boats lying in them. The bridge is guarded by a couple of curly-haired angels and a chestnut vendor, who was sitting on his box glaring at the other side of the road, where stood a jolly little truck covered with colored balloons and the legend OCCHIALI GIOCATTOLI on the side of it. Johnson stood on the pavement beside it, a balloon in his hand.

"Christ!" said Charles, and skidded to an utter and invincible halt. "Not on your effing nelly."

Considering what he thought about Johnson, we were lucky to have got him so far. Di and I looked at one another. Di said, "Please yourself, lover. I thought you wanted to save us from the pistol-packing peasantry?"

I shoved my elbow into her side. No one had said anything about Innes's gun, least of all Innes. If he knew his power had been cut off the night before, he was getting nothing but kicks from it. He looked radiant. More or less. Charles said violently, "You're not going there either. Or Ruth."

"Yes, I am," I said. We had been over all that. It was the sight of Johnson and the Occhiali Giocattoli that did it. I added, "Look. I'll be perfectly safe Innes and I are on standby, knowledgeably examining the castle. Di will be draped on the wall, being photographed by you with the chestnut vendor. All we have to do is watch, and help if there's trouble. I ask you, love. If someone comes up and buys that balloon, you can't expect Johnson to idle along with a load of toy glasses, pursuing him. The girls look after the wagon. You and Innes and Johnson light out and follow him, in the car or on foot."

"I forgot to ask," said Innes, "how do we make sure that no one but the right person is given the balloon with the fish in it? . . . I'm sure," he added, "that our ingenious oil-painting acquaintance has thought of a method."

He bared his de-scaled incisors in a smile. So he did know, I thought, about Johnson's visit to Mouse Hall. I wondered if Poppy had told him, and then reckoned that if Johnson had left that extra sunflower seed in evidence she probably had. Di said, "The message is in a red balloon again, the only one on the stall. And it's firmly tied to the framework so that it has to be asked for. That's all we can do. That, and try and use the same exchange of words that you had with Mr. Paladrini when you bought Ruth's balloon."

I had dredged my memory for those, and now I recited them. Charles had said, "I'll take that one if it's got a fish in it." And Mr. Paladrini had said, "Only the red balloons have fish in them."

Charles stared at me as I repeated it. He then laughed wildly. "An intricately coded exchange of terrifying complexity. It struck me at once, I remember."

We had got him walking again and we were now level with Johnson who was wearing a lot of long clothes and a pair of dark glasses. He looked like Paul Muni in a very old feature movie and was coining money; he sold three clockwork mice and a gun while we were looking at him. Then Di strolled across and told him what Charles had said to the balloon man and then strolled back and, taking Charles's arm, led him across the road to the river wall.

In a moment she was arranged up it like Virginia creeper; it is a habit photographers' models seem to have when faced with any piece of rough masonry, and is one of the few occasions on which they do not require a gale-force wind. Innes and I had a brief conversation with Johnson about a jumping dog, which I bought, and then retired to the entrance arch of the castle to study Diana's Baedeker, lent us for the occasion. Having been already right through the villa and twice around the Dome, it had acquired a number of annotations which didn't date back to 1900, when it set out to render the traveler as independent as possible of guides and valets-de-place, to protect him against extortion and be the means of saving him from many a trial of temper, for there are few countries, as the editor pointed out, where the patience is more severely tried than in some parts of Italy.

Check. Lower down, someone had underlined the bit that said, *Where ladies are of the party, the expenses are generally greater;* and someone else, in a different color, had put a range of exclamation marks after *The fierce rays of the Italian sun seldom fail to sap the physical and mental energy.* Charles and I, as I recall, had puzzled briefly over *Lieux d'Aisace (10c)* and the ensuing list of addresses until we realized, with gentle awe, that we were looking at the birthplace of the loo.

I mentioned it to Innes, to see if he would be embarrassed, but he wasn't. One up for America.

We bought tickets into the castle and wandered devotedly up and down the courtyard, peering out on occasion, and watching the time creep on toward the hour of assignation at noon. Charles photographed Di for the eighteenth time and I began to get jealous. Noon arrived, and left.

At fifteen minutes past twelve, a man who had been reading a newspaper on the other side of the road folded it and began to cross, then nipped back as the traffic lights changed and five hundred Fiats moved forward like bath buns on a conveyor belt: *The ordinary Italian rarely walks if he can possibly drive, and how walking can afford pleasure is to him an inexplicable mystery.* A family of five, approaching from the pavement, began to converge on the toy wagon, the children squealing *"Questo?"* A chauffeur-driven limousine with Maurice in it drew up and stopped.

He put his head out of the window and said, "Poor creature," in English, and then called to Johnson in excruciating Italian, "And how is your wife, my dear fellow?"

On the other side of the road, Charles had stopped photographing Diana and had turned around with the words *The wicked old bastard!* as clear on his face as if he had spoken them. The family of five had arrived at the cart and were whistling to attract Johnson's attention. The children were all holding revolvers. The man with the newspaper arrived on the right side of the road and, standing with his hands in his pockets, was studying the contents of the wagon. Johnson, whose Italian, it seemed, was far from excruciating, turned a gaze like a pining jerboa upon the electrically operated windows of Maurice's limousine and informed him rapidly that his wife suffered, alas, in herself, but was all the better for his lordship's inquiry.

Maurice smiled kindly, bought a jumping dog, and let up the window. The limousine rolled away. Johnson accepted the money for the assorted purchases of the family of five and turned to the man with the newspaper. The man with the newspaper pointed at the red balloon tied to the canopy and said, "I'll take that one if it's got a fish in it."

Everything stopped. I saw Charles and Di, on the other side of the road, staring at the man and his raised finger, and at Johnson. Beside me, Innes gave a kind of shiver of excitement. I stood and looked, because I couldn't believe it. Then I thought of what was in the meat safe at the Dome, and I could believe it all right. Johnson said, "Only the red balloons have fish in them" and began to untie the one with the message. He fixed it on its stick and handed it over. There was an exchange of money and the man walked away, carrying the balloon head downward, like a rifle. Charles shut his camera and prepared, with Di, to rush over the road. Johnson pocketed the money and began, in a series of rapid movements, to close up the framework of the truck ready for travel. Innes strolled negligently forward, all set for pavement pursuit.

Except that the man didn't walk off along either pavement. He stopped, looked around, and then, brushing past Innes and me, stepped through the doorway and bought a ticket for the Castel Sant' Angelo.

Innes and I goggled at Johnson, and Johnson gave us a snap of his head which we couldn't have mistaken had we wanted to. We were the only ones in the party with tickets already purchased and usable. Holding the Baedeker, Innes and I hurried in and climbed the steps after our quarry.

CHAPTER 9

THE CASTEL SANT' ANGELO is cylindrical because it used to be Hadrian's tomb before it was remodeled as a citadel by the Early Middle-Aged Romans, the greatest repair and conversion men in the business. The man we were following, who was fortyish and bald and wearing a short navy overcoat and black gauntlets, was clearly zonked out of his crust by pal Hadrian. We overshot him in the vestibule in our enthusiasm and found him in the hole where Pope Leo's lift shaft used to be, gazing up at the bricks. We fell in behind him as he climbed the spiral ramp that corkscrews up inside the cylinder. He stopped everywhere the guidebook said to stop, and gazed up at the ventilator-prisons in the ceiling and down at the railed-off pieces of terrazzo on the pavement. We nearly cannoned into him so often that I took to consulting the early warning system in

Baedeker; then Innes got interested in Baedeker and we lost our man momentarily on the stairs at the top of the ramp and had to take the bridge over the sepulchral chamber at a faster clip than it looked safe for. The bottom was a long way under us and the only ashes in it were those of Players No. 1, the imperial sarcophagus having long ago been nicked for his own uses by Innocent II. (*A smile for all, a heart of gold/One of the best the world could hold./Never selfish, always kind,/ These are the mem'ries he left behind.*)

I kept on the other side of the bridge from Innes, just for safety; I wondered if he had his gun with him or not. Since the trick played on him in the Via Margutta he had displayed a dedicated interest in nabbing those who had tried to involve him: if Benvenuto Cellini won now and then, it was only because he was programmed to Baedeker, as you might say, rather than the Police Gazette. As we hammered into the open air and up some more steps into a courtyard I began to worry about what Innes would do if we found that our bald-headed villain was mad about Benvenuto Cellini as well. It is the sort of thing that has given lesser men asthma. There was no sign below of Johnson or Di or Charles catching up with us.

There was no sign either of the red balloon, and the courtyard turned out to have eleven doors and three sets of staircases in it. We scampered through four rooms of Arms and Armor 15–18th C. and in and out of the Halls of Justice and Apollo like two rutting rabbits. We shot through a dark passage into another courtyard, in the second room from the right of which Benvenuto Cellini was imprisoned during the first period of his captivity.

The bald-headed man wasn't there, but there was a flight of steps and a notice which said TO THE HISTORICAL PRISONS. "Christ!" I said, and, seizing Innes once more by the arm, I flew to the stairs and plunged down them.

All the historical prisoners were four feet five inches high, which made it easy to lock them up, in a row of pitch-black stone cubicles entered by a hole in the wall from an underground passage. Innes, who is shorter than I am, folded in three and poked personally into every cubicle while I stayed outside holding the Baedeker and listening for Johnson above the noise of my stomach, which was rumbling like a mechanical harvester. When Innes backed out for the eighth time without either Johnson or the bald-headed man materializing, I gave him his Baedeker and followed him like a squaw through the next bit, which was a chain of dark cellars filled with rows of Ali Baba oil jars and more prisons.

A gleam of daylight announced the staircase leading back up to the courtyard. We bolted up it and crashed into the bald-headed man, who was standing at the top with his balloon stick tucked under one arm and a printed diagram of the citadel held in both hands, which tore neatly down the center as we hit him.

Innes disappeared, sinking downstairs as into a slow-sand filter bed. I said, "I'm most terribly sorry. We were dying to get up to the loggia. We didn't look where we were going."

He gave me a single furious stare and emitted a

lot of chilly Italian, of a kind which indicated that if I had been of the other sex I should have been presented with one on the kisser. Then he stalked off. We waited until he had walked up the stairs to the loggia, and then crept carefully after.

An arcaded gallery runs right around the third floor of the Castel Sant' Angelo and gives a nice view of the Outer Ward and the gardens. On the other side of the gallery, if you hang over, you can see the broad yellow wheel of the Tiber, with the bridges like white spokes all spanning it.

Johnson was sitting on the river wall being embraced by Di. Charles, with his elbows pointing heavenward, was photographing them both. I opened my mouth to let the steam escape and Innes said, "Shut up," and, gripping me firmly in his turn, rushed me across to the Papal Apartments, into which the bald-headed balloon buyer had vanished.

The Papal Apartments are 15th C. and 16th C. and connect with one another. We came face to face with that man and his balloon five times as we went from salon to bedroom to library and up to the Room of the Treasure, where the current Pope on the run popped his valuables. The trinket box was seven feet high and wide open. The bald-headed man, keen to miss nothing, was perched on a flight of steps gazing into it, with his balloon arm idly dangling over the side. I had a theory that a dwarf from Bonnie Cashin was sitting inside deflating the balloon and reading the message, but he lifted the stick after a moment and went out.

Innes and I rose from the other box we had been subjecting to devoted study and rushed up to peer inside the casket, but there was nothing except some more relics of Players No. 1 and a piece of equipment for brave brave manicure dropped by an excited client. Then we followed the bald-headed man onto the roof.

All Baedeker says about the Platform of the Castel Sant' Angelo is that it commands a beautiful view of St. Peter's et cetera. It also commanded a howling gale and a telescope, which the bald-headed man was employing with difficulty, his balloon vibrating in the wind and one eye, I was sorry to see, screwed up in a manner which would undoubtedly cause him suffering if he were ever to think of astronomy as a career. The lens was focused on the river wall of the Tiber, and on the river wall of the Tiber were perched Charles and Di, gazing upward like two Jambu Fruit Pigeons who had lost their Jambu Fruit. Of Johnson there was no sign. The bald-headed man removed his eye from the telescope, cast upon us a glance of wholly unqualified dislike and disappeared down the small-bore spiral stairs from the platform like a draft of cold air down a straw.

By the time we got down those stairs after him, there was no room for any more doubt. The bald-headed man was fed up with us. He had finished his tour. He wasn't going to waste any more time looking at frescoes. He was getting the hell out of it, and fast.

I have no excuse for what happened next, and I have no intention of becoming the Bore of the Bastions. It is sufficient to say that we descended the interior of that cylindrical edifice, Innes and I, as if someone had pulled out the plug of the bath and

landed dismayed on the path halfway between the
Bastions of St. Luke and St. Mark with no trace of
the balloon buyer whatever. To the right, barred by
a grille, was the beginning of the covered way to
the Vatican. Behind us, a passage led out to the
green of the gardens. To the left, the paved way
plunged down to the Inner Ward and thence to the
main entrance.

We stopped. There was no sound of running footsteps. There was nothing at all to show which of the
three ways the bald-headed man might have chosen.
Innes said caustically, "All right. Run and ask
Johnson if he has the keys to the Vatican." He
shook the iron grille but nothing happened, except
that a custodian turned around and began to stroll
toward us. Innes said, "Ruth, you take the courtyard. I'll go through to the garden. Yell if you see
him."

I held out my hand for the Baedeker but he had
gone. I smiled at the custodian and walked off, very
fast, down the slope to the paved ward around the
castle.

The bald-headed man was there, and so close
that I couldn't have yelled or even muttered. I
looked back. Innes was out of sight. The bald-
headed man, who had been consulting his guide,
suddenly put it away and began walking fast to the
entrance. There was no time to do anything but follow.

He walked through the arch and into the road
while he was barely an arm's length ahead of me. I
saw Di straighten on the opposite pavement and begin to go into action. I saw the balloon truck prepared at its stance, with its sides and back slatted

146

up to the canopy, and Johnson and Charles standing outside it, chatting.

The man with the red balloon didn't give them a glance. He walked to the pavement and turned, and a long and magnificent Mercedes-Benz traveling along from the Piazza dei Tribunali drew across and stopped precisely beside him. A uniformed chauffeur got out and held the back door open while the bald-headed man got inside, closed the door, entered the driving seat and put the car smoothly into gear, his head turned to watch for a gap in the traffic.

Johnson jumped into the balloon truck and dragged Charles in head first beside him. I jumped up and down saying *"Your car!!!"* without anyone answering me. The truck gave a bound forward, the door swinging, and I ran forward and jumped in beside them, closing the door as Johnson spun the wheel and lurched into the traffic. The last thing I saw of the Castel Sant' Angelo as we left it was Diana, saying "Hey!" standing erect on the pavement beside the chestnut vendor. Of Innes there was no sign whatever.

Three people in the front of that truck was something that the makers of Occhiali Giocattoli had never planned for. Charles's arm and my ribs reduced each other like cheese on a grater. Behind us the stock, imprisoned by canvas, joggled and clattered as we heeled over to enter the Vittorio Emanuele bridge after the Mercedes, and a clockwork mouse, trembling, gave two leaps and hit me on the cranium. I yelled, "What about Charles's car?"

"It wouldn't start," shouted Johnson.

"It got b'd up by the bloody bambini!" shouted

Charles. Johnson screeched to a halt in the traffic and a balloon, jerked from its moorings, hit the underside of the canopy behind us and began bumping about among the toy spectacles. The traffic moved off, including the Mercedes, and Johnson let in the clutch again. The noise was awful.

We inched along the Corso Vittorio Emanuele, and I told them what had happened in the Castel Sant' Angelo, and how I had lost Innes. Johnson, his dark glasses trained through the windshield like a fly's head seen under a microscope, was driving with one hand on the wheel and the other elbow resting on his open window. At every halt he turned his head and exchanged a series of brief civilities, in Italian, with those drivers within earshot. The Mercedes remained, like a quail's egg in aspic, comfortably two cars in front of us. Rome has four rush hours a day, and this was one of them. I said, "What happens once we get out of town?"

"That," said Johnson, "is a possibility I am trying not to contemplate." Another balloon unhitched itself and the first one, nudged out of place, wandered over our shoulders and bobbed about in front of Johnson's face. Charles batted it back among the stock and stopped a landslide of nursing wolves with his elbow. The lights changed and the traffic poured forth in a controlled *Avanti* that interfered with all the Occhiali Giocattoli. Three more balloons stripped and came undulating into the driving cab and hung about, caressing us in a rubbery way. Johnson scraped somebody's fender, applied his brakes and swore as someone bumped us, mildly, in the rear. "Will one of you," said Johnson in impeccable if simplified English, "kindly burst or otherwise get rid of these effing balloons?"

It was the first time I had seen him lose his bland. I made a face at Charles and helped him propel two of the balloons back into the rear. The third I began to propel through the open window. A hand closed on my arm. "Stop!" said Charles.

Five more balloons drifted up to the windshield. A double-decker bus in front of us drew suddenly in to the curb. Johnson wrenched the wheel around with both hands and scraped past it into the mainstream, escorted by a chorus of hooters and a lot of advice. He said in a controlled voice, "I can't stop and I can't see either. Burst them. Just burst them."

Charles's hand wrung my wrist and I stopped trying to push the balloons out of the window. O.K. they might blind somebody else. Good citizenship and S.P.Q.R. before everything. I turned over my lapel and unlocked my emergency safety pin.

"No!" said Charles. "Ruth. No! Stop it!"

A balloon touched my hand and joggled away. The driving cabin was full of spherical rubber. The sky and the buildings around us appeared through the stretched skins as expanses of light and dark cobalt. It was quickly becoming impossible to see more than shifting glimpses of clear window space through the windshield. They were all blue balloons. I stabbed with my safety pin.

Charles hit my hand and the safety pin dropped down between us. He yelled, "They're all blue balloons!"

The truck stopped and started, the sound of Johnson swearing fluently under his breath in English providing the bass clef to the sound of all his fellow drivers swearing at the top of their voices in Italian. A balloon dropped back and the Mercedes-Benz, now three cars ahead, put on a sudden spurt and passed the next traffic lights ahead of us. Johnson put his foot down on the accelerator just as the lights changed and the balloons closed in again. He kept his foot on the accelerator and I closed my eyes and then opened them again to hunt like a terrier for my safety pin. Then it came to me what Charles had said. I straightened and said, "So what? Blue balloons?"

Charles said, "It was a blue balloon the man in the zoo toletta had."

I said, "Charles. We're going to crash. We must burst them." Ahead, wild as an anthill, lay the Piazza Venezia.

Charles said, "His head was blown off. He didn't have a gun, Ruth, but his head was blown off. The blue balloon did it."

I said, "Air can't—"

"It wasn't air," Charles said. *"Will you stop touching them?* It wasn't air because I found bits of the balloon in the loo and they smelled. They smelled of chemical. You said there was a cylinder of gas in Paladrini's flat. Well, what was in it?"

"Nitrogen," Johnson said curtly. He clawed half a dozen balloons off the windshield and beat them back into the body of the truck. I tried to do the same and Charles caught my arm again and hung on to it.

I wrenched myself free. "Look. Nitrogen couldn't blow anyone's head off. Not at that pressure. You're dotty."

"In any case," Johnson said, "I didn't fill these

balloons in Paladrini's flat. I filled them from the developing gas in the Dome. Jacko helped me."

There was a sharp silence. Then I said, "You couldn't. The nozzle's too large."

Something banged against the off door of the truck and we stopped and started. There was a lot more yelling. "It isn't," Johnson said. "It was just right. *For God's sake,* will you get rid of . . ."

He stopped talking. I withdrew both hands sharply from the bunch of balloons I was holding in check and let them collect where they wanted. I said, "Did the cylinder have a red and white label?"

And Johnson said, "No. It had no label at all."

A couple of balloons drifted onto my knees and I arched back and looked at them. I remembered the dead locusts in Paladrini's bedroom, where no shot had been fired. And the gas cylinder in that same bedroom, which had had a red and white label. And, I now remembered, a smeared instruction in green felt pen.

That hadn't been Mr. Paladrini's own gas cylinder which he used to fill his balloons. That had been the cylinder from the Dome. And the one now in the Dome, which Johnson had used to inflate these balloons for the Castel Sant' Angelo, had been filled . . . was almost certainly filled with the chemical which had killed the unfortunate man from the Villa Borghese in the zoo toletta.

I said, "How many did you sell?"

"None of the blue ones. Listen," said Johnson carefully. "I'm putting up my window. We don't want kids to get hold of them. Ruth, take your jacket off. Charles, keep her from squashing the balloons while she does it. Now turn and lay the jacket over the rest of the stock so that nothing can prick the balloons. Right. Now Charles, take off your coat and see if you can rig it between us and the back of the truck while Ruth pats the balloons to the back."

We did as he said. He drove with one hand through the Piazza di Venezia, parting balloons with the other and going so fast that at one point he nearly overshot the Mercedes-Benz. The chauffeur was sitting stoically negotiating the traffic jams and apparently oblivious to the drama going on behind him. The passenger in the back seat had not even turned. Occasionally you could glimpse through the back window the edge of a red balloon. The very word balloon was beginning to bring me out in a rash. I got my jacket off and Charles and I turned, overlapping like salmon in a fish ladder, and struggled to spread it over the sharp-edged display cards and ball-point pens and metallic badges.

A balloon slid down the inside of the seat and rested, bulging, between his knee and the bench back. You couldn't even push him off it because balloons were clinging to our hips and the backs of our legs; the floor was deep in them. I grabbed Charles's knee and eased it up with my fingers while he looked down to see what was the matter. In the blue light he looked like a rather sickly stained-glass window; I expect I looked the same. Johnson scooped away the balloons from the windshield; the traffic lights changed to green up above us and he put his foot down to get into gear.

There was a blue balloon just resting between his instep and the underside of the clutch pedal. I let Charles go and twisting around, dived for it. Johnson, pushed on by a surging comber of traffic, continued to press his foot down unnoticing. The balloon flattened, squeaked and popped sideways from under the petal as I hit the floor, parting three more balloons and compressing another in my middle. I felt the hard resilience of it as I folded onto it like a jackknife. Then Charles, with a gasp, was holding me back by the elbow and easing out the balloon with one shaking hand. I burst into tears.

I am not proud of that journey, and I don't suppose Charles was, either, unless there are any medals going for doing what you are told while vibrating like tuning forks. We never did get all the balloons in the back. We could only hold Charles's coat, and it wasn't big enough to cover all the space between us and the back of the truck. There was nothing to tie it to and nothing to tie it with, anyway. So Charles went on holding it, jerking to and fro as the truck stopped and started, while I persuaded the balloons to bob around behind it. Whatever I did, the moment Johnson stopped, which he did every forty seconds or so, the whole flock rose up and swam to the front of the cabin again. When he started again, they were apt to move backward. That is, they came drifting and clinging about me, and filled the floor space and bumped on the roof while I tried to pat them gently out of the cab, remembering to take a breath now and then. The Mercedes got to the Piazza dell'Esedra and began tooling around the fountain in a Wall of Death composed of Fiats and scooters.

Johnson said, "Ruth. It's up to you. If I stop, we'll be run into. If I draw in to the side, we'll attract the police, which you may or may not think is a good idea. There's no legitimate parking for miles. If we let the balloons loose we'll cause a lot of deaths, mostly to children. If we go on I can't guarantee that you won't either be killed in a car crash or blown up by one of these anyway. So—"

The Mercedes-Benz had pulled past the railway terminal (Bagagli in Arrivo), rolled through a tunnel by the post office and passed Lazio Station to halt on the diamond cobbles at another set of traffic lights. A blue and white single-deck trolley bus loomed up; its arms waving and another chorus of hoots and Charles's shout combined caused Johnson to break off and spend a few concentrated moments on scraping alongside and eventually sliding out of its way.

The windshield had jammed up with balloons again. I began knocking them back while dimly, through the rubber, we could see the lights changing from red to green. A string of brick viaduct arches loomed ahead, and a single-decker No. 12 trolley bus in two shades of green took an unexpected sweep toward us. The Mercedes disappeared under the arches and Johnson, veering away from the trolley bus, glanced against the side of a taxi and then accelerated after.

"—So at the first opportunity I am going to slow down and you will both jump out," he said.

"Leaving you to crash. Powerful solution," I said.

"Leaving me, I hope, to follow and hold a moderately gripping conversation with the bastard in front— There's a balloon under the gear lever . . ." said Johnson quickly.

Charles dropped his arms and then straightened them again as half a dozen balloons lipped over his coat and floated up to the windshield. I eased forward and cleared the gear lever and then began gently to clear the cab again, my hair in my eyes. The red brick viaduct had dropped behind and the stream of traffic, with us and the Mercedes-Benz still in it, flowed forward into the Via Appia Nuova, which is two-way, with a tree-lined tramway track fenced off in the middle. I said, "If we weren't here you couldn't drive at all, mate. We go on or we get out together." The windows kept steaming up. It hardly mattered because you couldn't see through them anyway, but I wiped a space in front of Johnson and said, "I'm staying if you are. He might stop. He might stop at any moment."

"Are you crazy?" Charles said. I could guess what his arms felt like, stretched out up there; he was speaking in a strangled kind of way over one shoulder. He said, "Do you think that bastard in front hasn't noticed there's a truck hanging with balloons panting after him? He's getting out of the city because he wants a clear stretch of road. And as soon as he's got a clear stretch of road, he'll open up and you've lost him."

We stopped and started again at some more lights. The Supermercati and tabaccherie and all the rest of the shops were closed for lunch; torn election posters flapped in the wind. The Mercedes turned left into the Via delle Cave and we followed. All Rome goes home to its wife for its midday canneloni. We were in the middle of all Rome going home to its wife. I said, gazing at the car in front

155

and all I could see of the passenger, "I bet he doesn't have a wife."

"He had a wife, but lost her. The circumstances," said Johnson, "were tragic."

We passed a flower market and some road-mending machinery. "She got caught," said Charles defiantly, "in a multicore cable factory. Am I to take it, then, that we're going on after him?"

Johnson said, "I'll stop if you want to." Ahead, there was sky and green fields. Soon the road would be opening out.

"No," said Charles. "But you have thought of what will happen if someone gives us the smallest knock and, for example, the window glass shatters?"

"Broken glass," said Johnson.

"Burst balloons," I added. My heart was going like one of the jumping dogs and I wanted to laugh and laugh. I said, "Why a multicore cable factory?" I put into place a bobbing shower of balloons and begged Charles, without words, for an obituary. He looked around at me and grinned, and I should have married him, then and there, if he had asked me.

"All right," he said.

> *"They dug her grave the other day.*
> *It stretched for twenty miles each way*
> *She carries gas to Beachy Head*
> *And lights up Brighton from her bed*
> *And transmits chat from Lewes to Hove*
> *My multicore departed Love."*

Then Johnson said, "Hold on to your hats, children," and put his foot down on the accelerator.

The following ten minutes I prefer not to remember. We got to the open road, or the sort of open road that lies around outside Rome. Grass, trees, filling stations, generating stations, henhouses, woodyards, villas, vineyards, tilled fields, small bars, sixteen warehouses for Venetian chandeliers and rows and rows of antico acquedottos on the horizon. The Mercedes moved very gently into the fast lane and, as Cassandra had predicted, got the hell out of it.

Johnson followed. What he did with that harmless little truck would have brought tears to Mr. Paladrini's eyes, if Mr. Paladrini had stayed around long enough to see it. The speedometer needle began to creep upward. Peering through the balloons Johnson moved into the fast lane and put his foot down still more, but this time you couldn't see what the speedometer needle was doing, it was vibrating so much. So were we. Our heads were nodding like pecking ducks and the balloons had stopped swaying backward and forward and stayed where they were, chattering.

They were also getting warm. The hood was steaming lightly and the noise from the engine was only bested by the noise from the exhaust when it kicked off its silencer. We vibrated on, hooting courteously and occasionally glancing lightly off the sides of accompanying traffic, but we didn't lose the Mercedes. There were a few times when the rise of the road may have hidden her from us, and once an angry cinquecenti threatening legal action momentarily held us up because he kept banging his fist on the driver's window as we traveled side by side and we thought he was going to drive it right through the glass. Fortunately there arrived a gap in the traffic at the right moment and Johnson drew away in a terrible cloud of burned cooking petrol, and there was the Mercedes on the horizon ahead, turning off to the left.

It was a miracle, for thirty seconds later we should have lost him. We juddered steaming along to the junction and turned off up a green country road after our quarry.

Turned off and screeched to a halt. For across that quiet country road was drawn up a blue van with CARABINIERI printed across it, and on either side of it were three or four white-helmeted policemen on motorbikes, with guns in their holsters.

We all looked at the wing mirror. On the wheel I could see Johnson's hands, twitching to swing around and make a dash back for it.

It was no good. Behind us, a couple of police cars and two more cyclists had followed us off the main road and were now strung across, blocking our exit with complete efficiency.

Our little train of accidents had not escaped the notice of the police. We were about to be slung into jail, and after all we had endured, the man in the Mercedes was escaping. Johnson whipped off his dark glasses and said, "I'll have to open a window. Clear it."

We pushed the balloons behind Charles's coat and held them. With the car still, they stayed. A man wearing a blue uniform with red stripes on his trousers had got out of a jeep and was coming toward us, swinging leather-gloved hands. He had a cased rifle slung at his right side. Johnson wound down the window as the policemen arrived and, bending down, looked at us all.

It was a long, steady look. Then he asked, politely, for our driving license, our passports and our papers. Since we didn't have a driving license and I knew for a certainty there weren't any papers I wondered what Johnson was handing him. Then I saw it was his visiting card, with a 100,000 lire note wrapped around it.

"A burglary has been committed on the property of Signor Maurice Frazer, with whom I am staying," Johnson said in exemplary Italian. "We are in pursuit of a Mercedes-Benz which we have reason to believe is involved in it. Our present vehicle is borrowed. If you will be so kind as to accompany us, I hope yet to overtake the other car and bring the scoundrel to justice. Any charges being preferred against us for damage caused during our journey I shall be only too happy to meet in full presently."

The officer didn't take the 100,000 lire note. He didn't take the rifle out and shoot us with it either. He said, "The black Mercedes-Benz which only this moment preceded you?"

"Yes," said Johnson quickly. "With a man with a red balloon seated inside it."

"Ah!" said the officer blankly. He bent a little farther and looked at me, and then at Charles and then back to Johnson again. He said, "But the Mercedes-Benz you speak of has halted. There is no difficulty about addressing the passenger. It was the passenger who asked us to stop you."

I thought of all the teleromanzos I had seen and said hoarsely to Johnson, "They're fakers! They're not carabinieri. They're going to take us all prisoner . . ."

The officer was smiling at me. Still smiling, he put his hand inside his jacket and producing a police identity card, held it so that we could read it. As a matter of fact, it was creeping upon me that in this day and age it was unlikely that five police motorcycles, a jeep, a truck and three cars could be rigged up out of plasticine. Then I saw the truck backing a little, to allow a glimpse of the black Mercedes-Benz standing docilely in the road just beyond it. And opening the door and strolling toward us was the man with the red balloon, without the red balloon, or a gun, or anything but a cold, satisfied smile on his face. "That's the man," I said quickly.

"That's the man," Johnson said, "who we believe broke into Signor Maurice Frazer's property."

"That," said the officer, turning to face the bald-headed man, saluting and turning back to Johnson again, "is the Chief Commissioner of our police, Signor Johnson."

CHAPTER 10

AND THAT, if you like, was the tragedy of Innes's life. A Chief of Police devoted to Benvenuto Cellini, and Innes wasn't there to make anything of it.

As it was, the bald-headed man stalked, hands clasped, before us; stopped; peered and said, in not unworthy English, "Ah. The young lady of the Castel Sant' Angelo."

"She doesn't know anything," Charles said easily, over his shoulder. "She came along for the ride."

Humphrey Bogart again. I didn't see why I had to be protected from the Commissioner of Police, but cinematic dialogue dies hard. "It seems to me," said the bald-headed man, smiling harshly, "that none of you gentlemen knows anything. I take it you have not seen the early editions of the newspaper?"

"No," said Johnson cautiously. Charles slackened

his grip on his coat and then lifted it again. The bald-headed man removed from his pocket the newspaper he had been reading outside the Castel Sant' Angelo and opened it so that we could read the headlines from inside the car. They said, "DRAMMATICO ED OSCURO EPISODIO. Un uomo di 38 anni, Marco Susini, giocattoli-vendolo, è morto precipitando dal sestro piano, all' interno della gabbia dell'ascensore in un palazzo di un quartiere centrale e moderno. Si esclude l'ipotesi dell'omicidio."

Mr. Paladrini had killed himself. He had gone to a block of central high-rise offices, and he had flung himself into the lift shaft. We all read it three times in silence. Then Johnson said, "How do you know it was suicide?"

"He left a note," the bald-headed man said. "They usually do. It informed us of the murder he had committed in the Gardens Zoological. It informed us of another crime even more dreadful, which I shall be sorry to relate in front of the signora. But it is necessary to inform you of these happenings and receive your corroboration for our records. But for the traffic, naturally, we should have stopped you much sooner."

"Naturally," Charles said. I could see an epitaph for Chiefs of Police forming behind his raised eyebrows. I said, "You mean we have been followed? All the way from the Castel Sant' Angelo?"

"And before. Naturally," said the bald-headed man once again. "You do not understand what has happened? Directly after the toy-seller's suicide yesterday—"

"*Yesterday?*" Johnson said.

"Ah, yes. We do not release every item of news

at once to the newspapers. Immediately after the suicide, we have searched and then watched his apartment in the Via Margutta. You and the two young ladies were seen to enter. The Signor Wye, we knew, was already inside the building. The accidental shooting we witnessed, and the removal afterward of the truck with the balloons. We also," said the bald-headed man prosaically, "had seen the fish and the chart with the route marked upon it. From the toy-seller's note, it seemed unlikely that he had an accomplice still alive. But stranger things have happened. We watched, therefore, to see whom you were all planning to meet at the Castel Sant' Angelo at noon today. No one else came. No one asked for the balloon, employing the formula we knew from the balloon-seller's note. Therefore I, myself, bought the balloon."

"We've been idiots," Johnson said.

"But innocent idiots," the bald-headed man said. "Instead of delivering your message and moving off, you made clumsy attempts to pursue me. In other words you were no friends of the unfortunate toy-seller. You were merely, like the police, attempting to trap a criminal in your amateur way. You must be extremely cramped. Would you not prefer to stretch your legs in the open air while we make our arrangements?"

I said, "We can't get out because of the balloons."

"They have been tied," said the bald-headed man, "extremely insecurely. It was fortunate that no serious accident occurred on your journey."

"They are also," I said sourly, "filled with gas."

"Prego?" said the Chief of Police a little wearily.

"They're filled with gas," Charles said clearly, in better Italian than I had ever heard him manage to dredge up before. "Explosive gas. Gas that will go *bang* if they are punctured."

"Or *Bum-bum*," I said. The idea of Johnson and the police setting traps for one another and Innes going in and out of all the Historical Prisons in the Castel Sant' Angelo was beginning to turn my head a little.

"We have a theory," Johnson said, "that this was how the man in the zoo toletta was killed."

"But that is so," said the bald-headed man. "You suggest that the toy-seller filled all these balloons also with explosive gas?"

"He didn't, I'm sure," Johnson said. "The balloons floating about are another matter. I filled those. And I think I've filled them with the toy-seller's gas."

The bald-headed man stared at Johnson. Then before we could stop him, he stepped forward smoothly and opened the near door of the cart. I fell out, and a dozen balloons trotted out with me and swam undulating over the roadway. I screeched and tried to gather them to my bosom. Charles, flinging himself from the same door, began to leap about like a pierrot, helping me. Johnson, a practical man, sat where he was and put his fingers in his ears. The Chief of Police nodded, and the carabiniere standing nearest took his revolver from its holster, aimed for the most distant balloon, at that moment soaring over the vineyards and about to blow the heads off a yard full of chickens, and shot it.

There was a pop. The balloon, deflated, sagged

to the ground. The policeman smiled, took aim, and casually shot a second balloon. It popped too. It popped so quietly you could hardly hear it over the traffic.

"Explosives, eh?" said the bald-headed man reflectively. Johnson removed his fingers from his ears and stared at him. I looked at Charles. Charles, who had been hugging an armful of balloons, let them go and they swirled into the air, which became full of a crossfire of bullets, intent on bursting them. The policeman with the rifle had it up to his ear, loosing off at the ones that got away. A bullet went through the flap of my handbag. "I think," said Johnson apologetically, drawing me off to the ditch where he had already laid his jacket, "that we should take cover."

Charles joined us there at that, but the bald-headed man stood stoically in the center of the mayhem, as his gunmen demolished the last of the floating escapees. As the last one popped, he strolled through the thick smoke toward us and said, "It seems likely, Signor, that you were mistaken. But the Roman police always like to make certain. You would like to take the last shots?"

There were four red balloons left still tied to the pole of the toy truck.

Johnson shook his head speechlessly. So did Charles. I was incapable of shaking anything except, perhaps, a very strong Bloody Mary. The bald man smiled again in a commiserating way, and, snapping his fingers, received and raised the police officer's rifle. He aimed at the pole of the toy truck and fired it.

I suppose we all hoped he'd miss, but he didn't. He hit the first red balloon plumb in the center.

There was a burst of white heat like Hiroshima, a sheet of red, an uprush of black smoke, and the sort of explosion they put on the sound track of war films. The toy cart rose in the air and dispersed in the direction of Pluto.

Johnson said, "Christ," very, very slowly.

The bald-headed man didn't say anything at all. He just turned, equally slowly, and looked at the Mercedes-Benz in a very considering fashion.

We spent a long time after that at the Questura, and had our statements taken down and read back to us, and we all signed them. No one could have been more helpful or cooperative than the Commissioner. We were in no way to blame. We were even excused responsibility for our collisions. The Commissioner was happy to have known us.

He was happy to have known Innes, too, when they pulled him in and got him to sign his statements. Innes, who hadn't known about the body in the meat safe, lent the right air of horrified disbelief when the Chief of Police arrived at that part of the late Mr. Paladrini's confession. Charles, by artistically refusing to believe it at all, went too far and nearly roused police suspicions. I sat beside Johnson and wished it was all over and I could go back to the Dome.

Then I remembered what else, besides a body, was back at the Dome. I siphoned in a breath that caused high tide at Ostia, and Johnson patted my hand. "It's all right," he said. "We phoned Jacko."

"The gas cylinder?" I said weakly. "Charles? The gas cylinder at the Dome?" It was Jacko's day to do his developing. INTERMITTENT GASEOUS BURST VALVE said the label on that cylinder. And when Jacko switched it into the fluid, it certainly would.

"I phoned Jacko," said Johnson again. "Ruth? I phoned him."

"The telephone rang," said the bald-headed man reassuringly. He was drinking a mild cup of coffee.

"And a girl answered," said Johnson, equally reassuringly.

"Di?" I ventured. We had left Di at the Castel Sant' Angelo saying *Hey*. I remembered Maurice passing by in his car, and the look on Di's face, and it wasn't very hard to conjecture just how Maurice came to pass in his car. Or indeed why Di hadn't been disturbed to come all the way to the police station to make her statement. She was Bernadette Mayflower's daughter and the heiress of Prince Minicucci. Di had gone straight to the Dome and to Jacko.

"How did she sound?" I said, as Johnson nodded.

He considered. "As if she'd made it with North, South, East and West and one of them had declared. You can relax. No intermittent gaseous burst valve has a dog's chance alongside your rutting photographers."

We all laughed, ha-ha, and Charles threw in an obituary.

> *"Her life was full of kindly deeds*
> *A helping hand to all in need*
> *A happy smile, a heart of gold*
> *The finest lay this world could hold."*

You would think our troubles were over.
You would. I knew that they weren't.

The next day, the Director of the Trust arrived from England to find out what exactly had been occurring in Maurice Frazer's Tibur Hill observatory, and Charles's flatmate Sassy Packer was arrested for illegal gambling. So Charles roared off to Rome to bail him out and protect his Sedan Chair Bar from the carabinieri while I remained in the Dome kitchen with Jacko, chain-drinking coffee and awaiting a summons from Maurice.

We knew the Director had gone straight to the villa, provided with a short, well-sharpened stiletto. Within limits, the Zodiac Trust would do anything to further the causes of astronomy. But allotting work to a group of shifty astronomers who established their dead in a meat safe was a different matter. A strong feeling that the Trust's sacred projects were in quite the wrong hands had brought Professor Hathaway to the Villa Sansavino that morning.

Innes, in solitary vigil, spent the morning in Mouse Hall grooming Poppy and listening to the names of all the quiz winners on "Rischia Tutto." At lunchtime he turned up at the Dome and we all three had some more coffee and a tin of crumble cookies from Innes's grandmother which Jacko had pushed to the front of the shelf. There was nothing else because no one had gone shopping. The gas cylinder had been taken away and so had the body but it wasn't like home. And Johnson, report said, had been sent for by the Vatican to continue the portrait of the Pontiff.

At least, we hoped that was why the Vatican had summoned him. I spent some time comforting Jacko, who had never been christened. Innes said he knew someone who would do a quick job and

Jacko was hilariously grateful but wrote the name down carefully in his diary. The 50-Inch got blessed every Candlemas.

Then the phone rang and it was Timothy, asking us all three to come to the villa and take after-lunch coffee with Maurice and the Director. With sober clothes and clean shirts and alimentary canals brimming with coffee, Jacko, Innes and I shuffled over.

The Director of the Zodiac Trust is a woman. Everyone in astronomy has worked at some time with Professor Lilian Hathaway, who is an experimental genius and right out of my field. She is, in fact, right out of the Trust's field too, if the truth be known. The Trust chugs along while Lilian Hathaway sits at her desk constructing original theories and occasionally propounding them at meetings with other top-level astronomers. The fact that the prime job at Herstmonceux had just been filled over her head by another female astronomer seemed to have escaped her notice. The occurrence of a suicide, two murders and a near-fatal accident in or around the Frazer Observatory might have escaped her notice as well, if our luck had held.

We walked across the marble halls of the villa and up the marble staircase and were welcomed in whispers by Timothy, in a black suit with a stunning lace cravat, chastely pinned with a diamond. Jacko said, "Who's winning?"

"Darlings, you can't be worried," said Timothy. "Maurice is devoted to you. You know he is, and look how he's aching to be painted by Johnson."

"Ah!" said Jacko. "Do I understand that Maurice and friend Johnson have had a heart-to-heart?"

"You can take it from me," said Timothy, "that

they understand one another *perfectly*." He didn't look at Innes and his eyes glided over me as well. It took me one minute, and then I got it. Timothy was on standby this morning. Timothy wanted one thing for Christmas and Timothy thought he was going to get it. Timothy wanted Charles.

Maurice kept us waiting five minutes, and then he and Professor Hathaway received us in the Charles Stuart Room. Scotsmen have been known to burst into tears on entering this chamber, which is carpeted in Royal Stuart tartan and laddered with crossed swords all over the paneling, and targes above them like kneecaps. The rest of the space is occupied by portraits of Bonnie Prince Charlie and his brother in full length and miniature, together with an oval oil of their father in a cloud of shoulder-length iron curls and half armor. He had large, mild eyes and a mouth pursed and rose-pink like Poppy's. There were marble busts all over the tables.

Some of them were originals. In the heyday of his hang-up Maurice used to travel about every anniversary laying wreaths in the cathedral at Parassio and the Villa Stuart and below all the monuments in St. Peter's. He had since moved on to worship Neil Armstrong. It was, in fact, a subtle sign of belligerence on Maurice's part to receive anyone in the Stuart room. I wondered if Professor Hathaway knew it.

Beside the white mink and Famille Rose beauties of Maurice, Lilian Hathaway looked like an advertisement in *Field and Stream* for budget hairdressing. She was lean and sloped like an unpadded clothes hanger. Her glasses, which were strong, divided a long, adenoidal face with a top feathering of fluffy gray hair under which her sugar-pink scalp showed all over. She had on a jersey suit and was sitting in a silk brocade armchair talking about Red-shift Discrepancies. While we watched her she moved on to recent developments in the theory of Degenerate Dwarfs. I could see Timothy hanging on every word.

Maurice said, "Ah, children. The Director is *agog* about our little Orgia di Cadàveri: come and tell her all about it. Ruth darling, you look like a cover girl. Innes, how is Poppy? Jacko, you appear exhausted. You must not give so much, dear boy, to your work."

Maurice, doing the wicked sophisticate. Innes threw him a glare of active dislike and sat down. Jacko lowered himself into a straight-backed chair with a royal coat of arms in the back. His mustache made it difficult to tell what he was thinking but he looked at a guess as if he wanted to lie down flat in the men's room. I said, "Good morning, Professor Hathaway. I'm sorry you had to be dragged over. We all did our best to keep the Trust out of it."

"You're mad, quite mad, darling," said Maurice cheerfully, indicating a chair between himself and Professor Hathaway and waiting while I sat on the edge of it. "Chasing miscreants up and down the Corso, breaking into flats and firing off guns on the premises; stealing a toy-vendor's truck and chasing the Chief of Police half through Rome in it. Not to mention selling him a balloon filled with highly volatile explosive."

Maurice was a bastard who had gone over to the

171

enemy. I said icily, "You knew as much about it all as we did."

"My dear child, I observe," said Maurice, sitting down airily. "I do not report, like you; my reporting role in the world is now over. I do not advise. I do not interfere. I merely watch the antics of my fellow men and now and then stretch out a willing hand to help them. Coffee?"

"No, thank you," I said. Jacko also refused. Innes accepted and then sat with his cup rattling like a tin lid on a spin-drying machine; after a while he put it down. The Director's pebble glasses, which had been glinting obediently at each of us as we spoke, settled on Maurice.

"Dear Mr. Frazer," she said. "Alarming though you contrive to make it all sound, we are not yet off-off Broadway, or even on it. You will help us, indeed, by remaining quite calm. Ruth, my child. You appear to be having environmental problems. Suppose you tell me how it all happened."

Good Old Lilian. Everyone always said Good Old Lilian. You could see it written all over Jacko's face, and even Innes's. It didn't do to forget that once the mirrors were all in alignment and you had her attention, Good Old Lilian was a very sharp cookie indeed. Unhappily, I embarked on a full account of my environmental problems. I.e., the murders.

It sounded just great, every word of it. How Charles and I had lit out after finding the corpse in the zoo toletta. How we had kept to ourselves the break-in which ended in the trussing of Jacko and the smashing of Charles's camera. How we had gone sleuthing around after the Fall Fair as Maurice had said, pursuing the balloon man and taking his place when we found his flat empty. Maurice said, "And don't forget the night you found the body in the meat safe."

He was not only a bastard, he was a rat. I said, "We didn't tell the police about that. You wanted to bury the man in the garden. Remember?"

Maurice smiled. He spread his pink hands toward Professor Hathaway and lifted one shoulder of his embroidered smoking jacket. "If they had only listened," he said.

Jacko sat up slightly. "Well, listening to you wouldn't have saved Ruth from falling through the floor of the dome," he said. He had strong feelings about what happened that night. "You didn't hear about it till afterward." He turned to Professor Hathaway. "We knew about the meat safe because Paladrini broke into the Dome one night Ruth and I were both there and tried to get to the freezer to remove it. We chased him. He lifted the cupola trapdoor and Ruth almost fell through." He paused. "We didn't tell the police either that we found Charles's film on the body. Maurice kept it here, in his room, but it was pinched back. By Paladrini, I suppose." He said to me, "Did Charles get it back? The police must have found it."

I shook my head from side to side, glaring at him. He winced. He didn't mean any harm. But I was trying, Jacko . . . I was trying to keep Charles's affairs out of it. The Prof wrinkled up her short nose under her spectacles and then looked at me through them. "I am sorry, of course," she said, "for Lord Digham's difficulties with his film. I am rather more sorry, my dear, that the Trust's name had to become involved with them."

And here it came. I said, "You can't be more sorry than we are. It was the purest accident that the two cameras got mixed up in the Dome in the first place. It might have happened anywhere."

Lilian Hathaway put her two sets of fingers together and smiled, as if I were at the wrong end of a telescope. "But it was perhaps a little more liable to happen since Lord Digham was a frequent visitor, I imagine, to the observatory," she remarked. "He may perhaps even have developed some of his pictures there. Using, I am sure, his own materials and taking every care not to inconvenience you or Jacko . . . You are about to tell me, of course, that it is quite customary in astronomy for husbands and wives to stay on duty together, and that we must all move with the times."

I had been about to tell her exactly that. Well, not perhaps exactly that, but near enough. Jacko's mustache moved convulsively, heralding an impulse to tell Professor Hathaway, I imagined, that he had it off with Di regularly on Tuesdays and Thursdays in the developing tank, and she could announce it in the trade press if she felt like it. Innes took a rattling drink of his coffee, and I could tell he was thinking of Poppy. I said quickly, "I suppose, Professor Hathaway, the quality of our work is what we hope you will judge us by."

"I shall certainly do that," she said, smiling. "I shall take the plates back with me this weekend. Nor are we so unfeeling, Ruth, that we expect to disipline the private lives of any scientists outside their work program. But I don't need to tell you

174

intelligent people that while you are in Italy, you are ambassadors not only of the Trust and of your profession, but of England. The conventions for unmarried women are different in Italy, and there is a strong case for not openly flouting them. As for any irregularities involving the criminal classes, the Embassy is there to advise you. This time the authorities were lenient . . . Next time, you may not be so fortunate."

"My dear lady," said Maurice. He had lit another eleven-inch cigar, ejecting the flame from a Ronson encased in a replica of one of Prince Charlie's dress pistols. "I can tell you this much. If this sweet child hadn't been sharing a bed with Charles Digham, I should have had half the eligible bachelors in Rome breaking down the doors of the observatory to get at her. The Frazer Observatories have drawn loyalty and devotion from this stable and happy household of two loving young people, and, but for an unhappy accident, would have continued so to draw it. Compare Ruth with that sexstarved neurotic, Jacko Middleton, whom you see before you. And poor Innes, who has to transfer his fixations to the animal kingdom. The life I have led," said Maurice, shading his tone toward a faint melancholy, "has taught me a little of these things."

"Indeed," said Professor Hathaway mildly. She opened a handbag and taking therefrom a square case, extracted from it and lit a seven-inch black cigar, whose aroma, curling toward the smokeblackened targes, immediately overwhelmed and extinguished that of Maurice's. She peered at him over her glasses. "You have the look, now I come to see you, of a strong family man. I'm glad to see it. I

175

came over from England, Mr. Frazer, thinking that my nominees had been taking unpardonable liberties with your property. It now appears that a good deal of it was at your instigation."

"Mine!" said Maurice. "My dear lady, you flatter me. An old man of sixty, hardly able to move from my bed to my chair. The theater takes its toll, takes its toll. Astronomy, it is well seen, is kinder."

He was seventy, if he was a day. I saw Jacko's face turn a bright scarlet. Professor Hathaway, blowing an unperturbed cloud of brown smoke, said, "It makes calls on the intellect, certainly, which in quite mature years may still hope to be answered. I trust the young people were helpful. I should prefer, however, to consider the scenario ended."

"With the chief actor so newly arrived?" said Maurice, and extended a gallant pink hand, his eyebrows rising into the mink. I stared at them both with my mouth slightly open. I could hear Jacko breathing, and Innes was sitting with his hands clasped so tightly together that his nails had gone white. As a dialogue, one had to admit, it had a certain paralyzing quality. Professor Hathaway, it was abundantly clear, hadn't nipped over from England wholly because of our unworthy conduct. She had come over because she knew Maurice Frazer's little habits and thought it was high time to check them.

And Maurice, damn him, was enjoying it. He leaned back in his chair and stretched out a hand. Timothy, gliding noiselessly forward, caught an inch and a half of Corona ash in a Prince Charlie snuffbox and retreated. Maurice said throatily, "Tell me, Professor Hathaway. Are there not times when you find the study of the stars a little too cold and distant? A little inhuman?"

You could hardly see her for smoke. I could see Timothy trying hard not to cough. Even Maurice's nostrils were flaring. Lilian Hathaway looked at him thoughtfully. "You have a novel idea, there. No."

"It suits you precisely?" said Maurice. Smiling.

"As the theater is the chosen field for your temperament. If you had made a mistake, I imagine," said Professor Hathaway, "you would have changed your profession rather earlier?"

"Perhaps I did make a mistake," Maurice said. "Perhaps in the pure, detached study of astronomy I should have found my true self. I have enjoyed watching my Dome being put to its true purpose. I have found an inner peace, some nights, standing in the darkness under the stars, looking at the round, dry whiteness of that terrible moon. You know this. You feel this. The infinite smallness of man, compared with the unmeasured stretch of the universe."

"Naturally," said Professor Hathaway. A smile, like a rabbit, appeared on her lips and then hopped it. "Women, of course, are a different matter."

Maurice laughed. He had to, having underestimated her to quite a marked degree. I wondered why he hadn't got her taped in previous interviews, and then recalled that they had only met once, to my knowledge, and that the occasion was probably formal. He laughed in any case most splendidly, with a sort of effervescence of liquid espresso, and then, leaning forward, lifted his cigar case and held it out fondly. "I propose," he said, "to call you Lilian. I

177

also propose to introduce you to the other actor in my little comedy. You haven't met Johnson Johnson. He's painting the Pope."

"He's back," said Timothy, dividing his smile between Maurice and Professor Hathaway and standing with one wrist bent, to show he hadn't stopped speaking. "Just rushed off to scrub off the incense. Would anyone like a teeny liqueur, Maurice? A port? A little splash of Marsala?" Timothy, with his infallible intuition, had divined that the scalping was over. Maurice nodded and Jacko excused himself with the first note of hope in his voice since Wednesday. A silver drinks tray made its appearance followed by my portrait-painting friend, Johnson Johnson.

He looked the same, except that today he had on a blue baggy sweater by his uncle in Brighton and was carrying a *Honk for Jesus* rear window sticker and a lapel button with PONT MAX printed on it which he gave to Innes with a sincere shake of the hand. He said that a large part of the morning's conversation had been about Filippo d'Edimburgo and could he have a brandy but not in a balloon glass if it could be avoided. The thought crossed my mind that if Johnson Johnson had been ten years younger and maybe two inches taller and had worn wolfskin coats instead of raveling jerseys I might have met and settled down with him instead of Charles. Except that Johnson looked the marrying kind, and I didn't want to take the place of his uncle in Margate.

He looked around for somewhere to sit and only then appeared to notice the pebble glasses and angular figure behind the heavy curtain of Corona

Corona. He fanned it away with one hand and said, "Lilian!"

Jacko, coming back just in time to catch it, blanched again. Our work-mate was a friend of the management.

The rabbit appeared and vanished. The Professor had smiled. Johnson craned forward and kissed her, and then groping about, found a love seat and dropped there beside her. He said, "You got the whole story, I assume, from the police. We did our best to keep you out of the papers."

"So Ruth and the others have been telling me," said Professor Hathaway. I had remembered something. I had remembered that when she left Mount Hamilton to come to the Zodiac Trust, she had had her portrait painted. I had seen it once, reproduced in a newspaper.

It had been a good, lively likeness, which was just as well; she would take a bloody awful photograph. And painted by, of course, who else but Johnson. The pebble glasses turned on the bifocal spectacles in a dazzling encounter of vitrines and Lilian Hathaway said, "And you are about to suggest, I suppose, that I should be lenient with them?"

"Do what you like with them," said Johnson callously. "They'll all get jobs with somebody." He pointed a finger at me. "I want that one for a mascot."

Innes stood up and started to speak. His voice cracked, and he had to begin again. "You will excuse me, Professor Hathaway," said Innes stubbornly. "But these are matters that I and my colleagues would like to discuss with you in the privacy of the observatory. If you please."

You could tell he had had all his brandy. He remained standing while the Professor considered him. Then she said, "Sit down, Innes. Unless your girl friend has been developing photographs in the observatory, there is nothing to discuss. You have all been foolish, but it was an attempt, I realize, to keep the observatory out of the public eye. Luckily, thanks to the police, if not to Mr. Frazer here, it has succeeded. The matter is closed. Ruth, I shall come with you to Naples tomorrow."

I caught the whites of Jacko's eyes through the smoke: we had expected to go there together. Before we came out, Lilian had asked us to check on the Trust's training station. It isn't a school, but a practice post high in the hills by the city. Charles had planned to come too. Johnson said softly, "Lilian!"

"Ah," said Professor Hathaway, to no one in particular. "Ruth. What remains to be done at the Dome?"

There was two days' work left in the Dome, and I said so. Our contract with Maurice had a full week to run after that. But if she wanted him to send us home now, you couldn't blame her.

Instead she said, "I see. The police tell me that they require you to stay in Italy for at least ten days while they clear all formalities."

It was the first I had heard of it. A telephone began to ring somewhere persistently, and while Timothy went off to answer it I exchanged a fleeting twitch of the eyebrow with Jacko. "In Rome?" I said. So much for our expedition to Naples next morning. Naples with Jacko and Charles was a pipe dream.

It wasn't a pipe dream. "Anywhere on Italian soil," the Professor said briskly. "You may proceed therefore, James and Ruth, with your planned visit tomorrow to Naples. I shall accompany you."

She paused, while Jacko and I continued waxily smiling, and puffed a cloud of cheroot smoke in Innes's direction. Innes winced.

"I do not believe," said Lilian Hathaway briskly, "in keeping idle staff in working quarters when there is no useful employment for them to do. I suggest therefore that you treat the rest of your legal quarantine as a holiday. Naturally, at your own cost entirely. If you wish to remain in the Naples area, I shall leave you there. Innes, you have no business in Naples, but I can offer you a seat in the car should you wish it. I should in fact appreciate a long talk with you during the journey."

I looked at Jacko and Jacko looked at me. That was Innes booked for Naples whether he wanted to leave Poppy or not, but Jacko and I didn't mind. We had our trip to Naples endorsed, transport free, and we needn't go back to Maurice afterward. Not for ten days, if we didn't feel like it.

Good Old Lilian. I let Jacko express our joint gratitude. I was figuring out how to get Charles to Naples immediately Professor Hathaway had gone back to England. I was still figuring it out when Timothy came into the room, rather wan round the petals. He made a short keening sound in the direction of Maurice and then, bending over me cozily, said, "Ruth? I've had a call from a friend at the Embassy. Charles Digham has just been arrested."

CHAPTER 11

He had, too, for illegal gambling with Sassy
Packer, which might have been true but actually
wasn't. I went to see him straight from the villa, and
I must say, the jail was quite passable. Sassy was
in the next cell, and they had had pizza for supper, Charles said.

I took in his clothes and some cigarettes, but
they weren't the kind Sassy smoked, and after looking at him more closely I thought it was just as
well. The trouble with having a lot of friends as
Charles does is that your friends have a number of
variable habits. Sassy, for example, was wearing a
Bosnian peasant blouse with a fringed sash and
looked the entire bit that the Afghanistan authorities
keep trying to deport. Charles, who was again wearing his pajama top under a sage green quilted cotton suit and hadn't shaved since last night, looked

hardly better. He said it was a piece of bloody nonsense and he would take the Rome police apart and feed them to the newspapers limb by limb, and his mother was coming over on the evening plane.

That meant business in a big way, particularly for the Rome police. The Teddingtons may not approve of their only son's every action, but they will back him against any unfortunate foreigner who might consider Digham had taken one picture too many. I remembered an unfortunate incident in Chile. I said, "Aren't you *worried?*"

"No," said Charles, looking astonished. "Look, I don't know anything about his bloody club. I haven't been on any trips. I haven't even been in the flat so's you'd notice. I've got a bird somewhere else."

We grinned at each other. He really did look unconcerned. It is not, after all, the first time he has been in clink. He said, "You go on to Naples, angel. It'll all be over before you get back," and threw in one from the book, somewhat perfunctorily:

> *"At night when all is silent*
> *And sleep forsakes your eyes*
> *Your lonely thoughts dwell on the jail*
> *Where your poor Charlie lies."*

I had told him, in the past tense, about the proposed joint excursion to Napoli. I stared at him. "Don't be mad, darling. Of course I'm not going. You might not get pizza every meal. I shall bring you your crusts and the *Daily American* and have long conferences with your defense lawyer."

"Don't think I wouldn't settle for that," Charles said, and pulled a violent face. "But Mother will be doing just that, with the combined British Press

183

at her elbow. On the other hand we could announce our engagement. Ruthie, will you marry a junkie photographer?"

He was grinning behind his hair, but it was rather an intent grin. My stomach turned over and I wanted to cry, and be comforted and, if possible, go to bed. "No," I said rather shakily. "I won't even marry you."

I could see his Adam's apple move as he swallowed, but he went on smiling. "You are a bitch, darling," he said. "Go on and enjoy your holiday. It's all right, I promise you. I should tell you if it weren't."

There was a bit more, but it was off the record. I went outside and got into the souped-up Fiat beside Johnson, who had driven me into Rome, and blew my nose all the way through the traffic jams.

Johnson didn't say a thing. He didn't take me right home to Velterra either. When we got to the Piazza dell'Esedra he hooted three times and an old Alfa Romeo Z600 that had been parked among the other five million cars revved up and backed slowly out, allowing Johnson to back slowly in and park in its place. Then he switched off the engine and said, "Before we go any farther, you are to have a Whisky Black e White and a lecture. Pontiff's orders."

I don't remember making any protest. I powdered my nose and noticed that my eyes looked like workingmen's oysters. Then Johnson switched off the car lights and it didn't matter, because the power lines had failed once again and there was no lighting outside whatever. He took me to the Hotel Quirinale and the walk there was a vivid experience as the traffic lights weren't functioning either and every crossing was full once more of Fiats steaming eyeball to eyeball. We picked our way across the marble floors of the Hotel Quirinale by the aid of some candle in saucers and seated ourselves in a dim corner under a tapestry. In a moment a waiter brought us a candle and then two double whiskies. Johnson blew out the candle and then, groping, clinked his glass against mine and said, "Here's to crime," rather vaguely. Over on a far corner another couple were giggling in complete darkness. Apart from that, the only other people in the salon appeared to be a group of twenty Indian women in saris who were standing about in the middle, talking sharply to one another. I don't suppose the power supply in Delhi is all that hot either. I drank half my whisky and hiccupped.

"I wanted to talk to you about Charles," Johnson said.

I said, "He hasn't done anything." My voice sounded sharp, too.

I could hear the grin in Johnson's voice. "He hasn't embarked on illegal gambling with Sassy Parker, if that's what you mean," Johnson said. The grin disappeared from his voice. He said, "Ruth. The police aren't holding him over Sassy's misdemeanors, although that's the excuse at the moment. That's what they'll tell Lady Teddington and that's the charge on which they'll keep him in prison until it suits them to change it for a worse one."

"A worse one? What? The idiots," I said. "What will they charge him with?"

"Murder and espionage," said Johnson briefly.

A match, struck a long way away, gleamed for

a moment in the depths of the drink in his glass; otherwise he was a bodiless voice speaking from blackness, and I suppose I was the same. After a moment I said, "What murder? What espionage?"

His voice remained impersonal, damn him. "Mr. Paladrini's," said Johnson. "And possibly the man in the meat safe as well. The suicidal note was a forgery. The police haven't much proof they agree, so far. But, you see, the confusing of the two cameras was suspicious. They say Charles had something of importance in his own camera and meant to conceal it. You and I know he didn't, but we must show them evidence. The time has come, Ruth, to dig out Charlies's girlie pictures, wherever you've hidden them." His voice softened. "Don't worry. We'll tell Charles the police found and developed them."

I didn't enjoy being humored. I stared straight out into the darkness and said, "I can't dig them out. I haven't got them. I took the roll out of hiding and burned it."

"Oh," said Johnson, and then I got angry.

"You know it's nonsense," I said. "Even without the film, it must be perfectly obvious. Why on earth should Charles risk his career for the sake of selling a few couture secrets? He would be the first person suspicion would fall on. And no fashion house would ever employ him then, ever."

"It seems," said Johnson, "that it isn't only a matter of skirt lengths. The traffic Mr. Paladrini was helping to direct from his balloon cart was a traffic in real, old-fashioned espionage."

The Indians were filing out. I said, after a while,

"Then the two men from the Villa Borghese? How did they come into the picture?"

"They were security agents," Johnson said. "Large firms employ them. Also governments. Some marketable photographs were on their way to a vendor, and the agents thought, quite wrongly, these were in the camera Charles was carrying. They also thought they knew the interested parties. That was why they were killed. The first one, if you remember, was sold the gas-filled baloon by Paladrini."

"And," I said, "they think Charles killed the second security agent? And then slaughtered Mr. Paladrini, who himself murdered the first?" I remember giving a bray of cross laughter, dismissively. "They can't believe that. It's too bloody silly."

"Oh, Mr. Paladrini was killed by his own side," Johnson said. "After his photograph was taken, he had to be. And the suicide note might have closed the police inquiry into the murders. As it was, the police think the man in the meat safe was shot by the intruder who twice found his way into the Dome. The man who knew where the trapdoor was, among other things. And who pinched the signed film, of course, from the vase in Maurice's bedroom."

"Then," I said, "that couldn't have been Charles, because of the Mouse Alarm."

My voice shook as I finished saying it and Johnson must have heard it because he said briskly, "Yes. That's it, of course. The police know in theory that Charles cannot tolerate ultrasonic emissions, but only you and I know that it would be truly impossible for Charles to remain in the room while the alarm was transmitting.

"No one could have faked that amount of dis-

187

tress, or even have known when to show it. Only Maurice and Timothy know when the alarm is switched on, and not even they know whether it is transmitting properly. But that morning it was guaranteed to be in perfect condition. Because I blew the fuse, if you remember. And within five minutes, Maurice's electrician had repaired and tested it. During those five minutes we know that Charles was out of the chamber. We know that if he had come back he would have found the signal transmitting continuously. We know that there are no accomplices among the servants: they have been in Maurice's employment for anything from twenty years upward. And we know that the servants admitted no strangers to the villa that morning, and that Di and Innes, who both came to see Maurice, called *after* the film had been stolen. I have told the police all this," Johnson said. "But, you know, it isn't enough."

I said, my voice breaking out of its whisper, "What would be enough?"

"Your film, but that's burned," said Johnson mildly. "Proof then, that others are guilty. Evidence that while Charles is in prison, the real villain is still out there, operating. You've forgotten the fish."

"S.M. Capri twenty/fifteen hundred?" I quoted. My heart was going like a pinball machine.

"That's what it said," Johnson acknowledged. A candle flame appeared in the darkness, moved across one lens of his glasses and disappeared as the waiter carrying it moved up the stairs. Johnson said, "The other paper I found in Paladrini's flat was much more explicit. I didn't tell you about that and I didn't mention it to the Rome policemen either. It said *San Michele, three* P.M. *twentieth Nov.* It also said, *Ischia, twelfth. Lipari, fifteenth. Taormina, seventeenth.* Two of these are islands off the Italian coast, and the last is a small town in Sicily. No times or places were specified, but it seemed fairly clear to me what they were. These were the next trading points which Paladrini was to mark on his balloon fish. Each of these was a rendezvous between buyer and seller. The question is, did he manage to tell any buyers or sellers of these meeting points?"

"He might have done," I said. "Or they might have called as we did, and found the notes in his room after his death. Or if he was working for the selling side, his own people would have seen to it that the buyers were advised of the dates."

I paused. "But if his own side killed him, they must know the list was in his room and the police were likely to see it. Won't they change all the dates?"

"Perhaps," Johnson said. "Perhaps they can't. And this paper wasn't in the man's overalls. It was extremely well hidden. Suppose, while Charles is in prison we keep those dates. And suppose we come across one of these transactions and find out who the principals are. Or, better still, who is running the exchange market. For that, dear Ruth, is what I think we have stumbled on. An international auction house. A broker in espionage, one of whose agents was Paladrini."

I thought of Charles, and Lady Teddington, and all my jokes about pizzas and lawyers. I thought of the sanity of the star charts and the holiday I had been going to have in Naples and the plans Charles and I had made for Christmas and the look in Professor Hathaways's eyes when Maurice sat in his giltwood armchair airily fantasticating. I knew Johnson was asking me to go with him to all these places and I wondered blearily how he expected to reach them until, a moment later, I remembered. The *Dolly,* she was called, Charles had said. Johnson had a yacht called the *Dolly* in Naples. I said, "Professor Hathaway's given us extra leave. The police said we all have to stay ten days in Italy."

"I know," Johnson said. "I told them to say it."

"Told them?" I repeated. I remembered the Chief Commissioner and the 100,000 lire note around the visiting card. Whoever did the telling that time, it wasn't Johnson.

"Yes," said Johnson. "I wanted ten days to back my own fancy. Did you know Maurice has a yacht called the *Sappho* in Lipari? He uses her when he goes to Vulcano."

I knew about Maurice's autumn trips to Vulcano, though not from Maurice. He steamed his arthritis in the sulphuric hot springs of Vulcano, and Timothy managed his yacht—"With a friend, dear, and of course a little man full-time greasing the engines. Day and night, I promise you, he sits there turning them over and singing to them." I said, "Will they be there while we are at Lipari?"

"I should think," Johnson said, "it's amazingly likely. And who knows whom else we shall meet? I'm sure Jacko likes sailing. Innes will want to see the Greek theater at Taormina. You have been instructed to remain for ten days in Italy. Professor Hathaway can hardly object."

I didn't get it. I was still staring at him, not getting it, when the lights came on. I stared at him with my eyes screwed up against the brilliance, remembering Jacko's hurried consultation of *Who's Who* in Maurice's library. Johnson Johnson had been in it all right. His people came from Surrey and he had been to all the right schools and belonged to all the right clubs, with a formidable painting career and a spell in the Royal Navy for good measure. He was who he said he was. The twenty people who had recognized him at Maurice's party testified to that.

I had taken such trouble to prove to myself that he was harmless that I might never have found out otherwise. Until I saw him suddenly, in all the hard clarity of that new-restored lighting, and knew that when he said he instructed anyone to do anything, he meant exactly that. And whatever had happened over the balloon cart had no bearing at all on the present attitude of the polizia toward him. Because he knew so many things that a nice portrait painter from Surrey couldn't have known. He knew that the two men from the Villa Borghese were security men. He knew that Paladrini's death wasn't suicide. He had had time—when?—to search for the note from Paladrini's flat he had just read me. The police had been watching the flat and certainly would not have let a member of the public return there without question. In short—

I opened my mouth.

"Well," said Johnson pleasantly, "we certainly took a long time getting there. Don't look so harassed. I'm working with the Rome police but I'm paid out of your taxes. And come to think of it, not even the Rome police knew about it till yesterday. You can tell Charles but not, I beg you, *not* anyone else."

I had dropped over the zoo wall, and Johnson had caught me. I said, "But you were here at the beginning!"

"Painting the Pope," he agreed. "That's what happens. I'm sitting comfortably somewhere minding my own business and someone asks me to check the ignition of two security agents. Would you mind very much if we sail in rough weather?"

I thought frantically, Ischia, Lipari, Taormina and Capri, in November. With a British agent on board and a mugging in every port, I shouldn't wonder . . . I was damned if I'd do it.

But if I didn't do it, Johnson would think I didn't want to help spring Charles from clink, and I did. I wanted Charles in my scene, taking photographs and delivering obituary verses, carefree as a bird. I wanted Charles.

I said, "I don't mind rough weather," but it didn't ring as true as I would have liked. The fact is, I was afraid of rough weather and nastiness, but there seemed little object in saying so. Everyone is, and you just have to get on with it, and make up obit verses and laugh at them.

Back in Velterra, Johnson dropped me off at my digs and I brought him in to tell Jacko that I was sailing on *Dolly* from Naples. "Ischia," I said airily. "And, of course, Lipari and Taormina. And Capri on the twentieth, to end with."

"You lucky bitch," said J. Middleton enviously. "And if they spring Charles, I suppose you'll do it together."

"I suppose so," I answered. I didn't tell him they

weren't going to spring Charles: not for ten days at least, if ever. I didn't tell him the reason for the itinerary either, but he hit on part of it.

"Hey," said Jacko. "You'll be at Capri on the date of the meeting. The date on the fish in that balloon-vendor's flat? You sneaky blighters!"

"Want to come?" said Johnson lightly.

He had Jacko around his neck before he got quite through speaking. We went through the same thing with Innes. Innes remembered the date in Capri as well, and we didn't tell him about the others in between. We didn't tell Innes any more than we told Jacko, but he fairly jumped at the invitation when Johnson made it. I said crossly, "What about Poppy?" and Innes said his landlady would look after her he was sure, and he had a very strong stomach. Then I thought that maybe I was denying Innes his first anthropological experience, and felt ashamed of myself.

But it was uncanny how all Johnson's predictions came true. Even to the interview in Maurice's villa when we related our plans to Professor Hathaway, and she gave her rabbity smile and said that she was hoping the invitation included herself.

There was the very beginning of a silence, swept away by Maurice's most delicious cries. Of course she must go. And he and Timothy would fly south to meet her. "I have a yacht there," said Maurice. "A little thing called the *Sappho,* so appropriate, although I warn you, the heads are too tiny. You will dine on her. They will dine on her, Timothy. If the weather isn't too dreadful, you may sail on her . . . Such nights. You will see stars on *Sappho,* I promise you, Lilian, such as your dull telescopes have never shown you before. You may never come back . . ."

If the film had gone from Maurice's vase, Johnson had once agreed, then one of us must have taken it. Mr. Paladrini was dead, but we—all of us—were still living. And we—all of us—for one reason or another, it seemed, were to share in some part of *Dolly*'s voyage.

We left for Naples the following morning, Saturday, November 11, in a rainstorm. I had been warned that Charles couldn't have phone calls. But before we set out I posted him a long letter with SWALK on it to make him laugh, telling him everything and ending

> *Silent thoughts and tears unseen,*
> *Wishing your absence was only a dream.*

It crossed with one of his to me which came with another obituary:

> *We said farewell that autumn day*
> *My heartstrings felt the tug*
> *You laid your hair down far away*
> *And left your heart in jug.*

It takes four hours to drive to Naples and it rained all the way. Sheets of water sprayed up on each side of the Fiat, in which I was cravenly sitting with Jacko. Maurice's chauffeur-driven limousine rolled majestically behind, bearing Innes and Professor Hathaway, talking.

The Fiat did a hundred and twenty on the autostrada and got to Naples ahead of the Maserati, with Jacko slumbering heavily in the back, on the way to rehabilitation after a brisk farewell warm-up of pages one to six of his address book. The yachting haven is on the north side of the bay. Johnson wove past all the stalls selling varnished shell ashtrays and splashed over a long concrete jetty lined with covered boats.

There was only one with the cockpit canvas stripped off and she was a gas: a big, snow-white ketch with two tall pitch-pine masts, glittering with naval brass and expensive teak and fine paintwork. A man in a peaked cap standing under the waterproof awning nipped up to the aft deck as the Fiat drew up and, hopping ashore, sprinted up to us with a broad grin on his face. He was a short, powerful man with large ears and the gold lettering around his capband said *Dolly*. His name, it turned out, was Lenny Milligan, and his accent, greeting us all, was ripe Cockney. He helped haul out the luggage, and we walked toward the lushest seagoing pad in the harbor.

I don't know why it surprised me. Next to *Who's Who*, Maurice kept an up-to-date Lloyd's Register in his library. We all knew the *Dolly* was a gaff-rigged auxiliary ketch of 59 tons with a 60 BHP auxiliary engine. What's more, the owner's name in the list bore an asterisk, which meant that Johnson Johnson held a Board of Trade Master's Certificate.

I was glad of it. The Tyrrhenian Sea in November is no place to be without the Board of Trade Master's Certificate, and perhaps even with it.

Below decks, Johnson's yacht was deep-carpeted and warm and candidly comfortable. In the desperate silence of ignorance, Jacko traversed with me the cushioned saloon whose paneled walls contained all the civilized comforts. Johnson had a television set and a stereo record player and a radio and a fridge and a full-scale bar within which Lenny, in a white jacket, was already making himself busy. We passed through a door at the forward end and into a passage which contained the door of the galley on its right and that of a single-berth cabin on its left.

"Mine," said Johnson, indicating the last. He opened a third door facing us at the end of the short passage and ushered Jacko gently in. "The forward stateroom. You'll share this with Innes. Lenny sleeps in the fo'c'sle beyond it, but he won't disturb you if he can help it. He comes and goes by a hatch to the deck."

There were two single bunks in the stateroom and the covers and curtains and cushions were Swiss and patterned in pure fadeless dyes of bright color. What Johnson didn't put on his person, he put, it seemed, onto his ship and his palette. I said, "I can't wait to see where the Professor will doss."

Jacko was trying the bed. Johnson led the way back to the saloon. He said, "She's not a very large yacht, remember."

I stopped where I was, which was in front of a bookcase. I said, "You wouldn't dare."

"I don't know what you mean," said Johnson, his bifocals perfectly limpid. "Very few boats have double beds. Double feather beds with monogrammed sheets and four pillows."

I sat down. Jacko, emerging behind me, said, "Oh, my Gawd," and started to cackle. The cackle became a shriek. "You can put each other's rollers in, Ruthie."

I said, "I am not sharing a bed with Professor Hathaway."

"No, you're not," said Johnson comfortably. "Although it was an enticing vision of splendor, I must confess. You are, however, sharing a stateroom. Come and see."

I glared at him, smacked Jacko's head, and tramped out of the saloon and up into the cockpit. There, he opened a door leading aft.

He had given us his own master stateroom. It didn't contain a double bed, but it did have every other amenity known to man, including two quilted bunks and a bathroom. I wondered who occupied the other bed when he had the boat to himself. He brought in my case and said, "She's a nice old stick. I hope you won't find it too awful."

I said, "Who was Dolly?"

Jacko was unpacking. Behind me, Lenny was laying glasses out on a tray. Johnson put his hands in his pockets and leaned against the stateroom door and just grinned. "A one-eyed colored Gay Power bus driver in Peckham," he said sweetly. "Why do *you* come to the clinic?"

"Sorry," I said.

"Granted," he said.

Then we all went into the saloon and drank gin until the Maserati arrived. We'd got the Professor but we hadn't, thank God, brought the telescope.

After lunch, the Director left to make her statutory call on Bob and Eddie in the training post, taking the three of us with her. The trip to the hills was uneventful, if you discount a series of mid-brown torrents which poured down the mountain on top of us, and the hideous discomfort of the student establishment, which had been shipped out piece-meal from England and erected by none other than Bob and Eddie, who would never add a touch of distinction to your rock garden.

They were birds of passage, in any case, creating a center for others to live in. Professor Hathaway complimented them on their log book, and they became even more cheerful when they heard that they were to drive down to *Dolly* for dinner. Jacko, Innes and I hung about adding the light relief till it was over. Then we all piled into two cars and slid down the hill to the harbor.

Lenny did the dinner. We had baby clam soup poured over toast squares, and breaded veal escallopes with frail bones like thrushes and fried slices of salty, crumbled artichokes, frilly green inside their brown coatings. And sweet pastry rings made with brandy, and served red hot and with a sifting of sugar and cinnamon. And coffee.

I ate my way through it all, and Johnson filled my glass from a tinseled Murano glass wine jar and I didn't stop him. I had a liqueur called centerbe, and maybe another one.

So did Bob and Eddie, who were wearing collars and ties in honor of Professor Hathaway, and red satiny faces in tribute to Johnson's centerbe. Eddie, enunciating like an elocution teacher, said "You'll never guess who we met the day Charles came to Naples. Sophia Ow."

The *Ow* was because Bob had kicked him. It was no news that they had had a drink with Charles during his visit to Naples. Anyone who knew me in England also knew Charles. Eddie had been loud in his indignation over the jailing and I had explained how it was all a mistake because of Charles's flatmate. They told me a few stories about Sassy that had been going round the network that not even I knew.

But I didn't know about Sophia. Sophia Lindrop was a sharp little blonde who had been educated at Roedean and Zermatt and three foreign universities, including Hamburg. She was in the same circuit as Charles. She was engaged to Charles when I first met him.

There was no point in embarrassing anybody, so when Bob launched into a desperate account of some Italian pop concert, I let him get on with it. I didn't have any more centerbe. In fact, to be candid, I excused myself pretty soon and got rid of the centerbe I'd had already, as well as the clams and most of the veal cutlets. It was a terrible waste.

I was standing up on deck after, feeling low and looking at the lights over the water when the saloon door opened and shut on the chatter and Johnson vaulted up and strolled over beside me. He had left his pipe behind. He was altogether too damned perceptive. After a moment he said, "A little fair girl, isn't she? Lenny saw them together, as it happens. Not, I should have thought, very disturbing competition."

It was none of his bloody business. I wasn't going to go through life spending every second day crying on Johnson. I didn't answer. He waited and then put his arms on the rail and said thoughtfully, "So. Disturbing competition. Perhaps even the someone else he was engaged to, who was so furious."

I had forgotten I had ever told him that. I talk too much. I blew my nose and glared at Vesuvius.

Johnson said, "I wonder just how much she dislikes you. Enough, would you say, to have your cabin searched?"

I ran away from him. I got down to the loo just in time to part company with the rest of the veal cutlets. I heard the saloon door open and shut, and then open and shut once again. When I came to the door of the stateroom Johnson was standing there, with a bottle of mineral water in one hand and a glass in the other. He said, "I think this might help. May I come in?"

He came in anyway and I backed and sat on the bed. When you came to look at it, the cabin was perfectly neat. I took the glass and held it chattering against the neck of the bottle as he poured. I said, "You said our things had been searched."

He put down the bottle. "The whole ship had been searched. I called in the carabinieri but there was no trace of the intruders. It had been done very neatly. And nothing that we know of had been taken."

There was the least firmness in the words *that we know of*. I said, "I burned the negatives from the meat safe. I told you."

"I know you did," Johnson said. "But the character who pinched the dud film from Maurice's vase doesn't know it. He's developed that roll, and *he* thinks the blank pictures were planted. Now he means to find out which of us has the real film."

There was a long silence. I found I was still holding the glass of mineral water. I drank it off and put it beside a guidebook lying beside the Prof's bed. It said, "STROMBOLI—*an unimaginable and stupendous reality in a painting of both*

200

exultant and terrifying eurhythmy. The Exhaust Pipe of the Thyrrhenian Sea." I said, "So now he knows we haven't got it. Maybe he'll try Di and Maurice and Timothy. And when he finds they haven't got it either, he'll give up. After a while, even couture pictures, surely, lose their value."

My hands were cold and I gripped them together. "Look. It's Charles's film he seems to be hunting, and I've seen it. Girls and fashion shots. No desperate international espionage, only skirt lengths."

"You'd be surprised," Johnson said, "what you can get into a skirt length. That's why I wish you'd kept Charles's pictures. There are some ingenious men about in this business. Men who'd print a formula on a model's hatband and persaude an innocent photographer, say, to take a shot of her. Charles himself may not have known what was in his roll of pictures."

There was another silence. Then I said, "in that case, you think the hunt for the film will continue?"

"My dear, I hope so," said Johnson patiently. "Because, don't you see, we must try and catch him? The man who is hunting that film is the man who can vindicate Digham."

I said, "Of course," but I found it hard to be cheered by the prospect. Then he asked about Sophia Lindrop, and I told him.

We went back to the saloon after that, and in due course saw off Bob and Eddie, who had some trouble getting from deck to jetty. The night with the Prof in the stateroom went off rather better than I had feared. She retired just after we speeded our dinner guests, and when I eventually got to the cabin, primed with two pale blue liqueurs and a lot of juvenile exhortations from Jacko, I found her already in bed, buttoned up to the chin in Viyella pajamas and deep in her paperback guide-book with the chapter headed VULCANO: Rich of Fenomena. The stateroom was foggy with Mani-kins.

She continued to smoke and flip the pages while I undressed. I was in my nightdress and sitting down oiling off eyeliner when she laid the book down and said, "You don't quite fit your clothes, do you? What is it? Nibbling for comfort? Too many patisseries at Donay's and Aragno's?"

I was so taken aback I looked at her in the mir-ror with my mouth open and the smudgy black pad in my hand. It was perfectly true. In the first six months of living with Charles I had been about fourteen pounds underweight: edgy but interesting. In the last few weeks, on the other hand, I had found it hard to avoid those small nighttime visits to Innes's grandmother's cookies. I wasn't fat. I wasn't feeble-minded enough to be pregnant. But the hook and eye above the zip didn't get done up so often anymore.

Lilian Hathaway said, "I've got some sewing of my own to look after. If you leave your things out, I'll fix them once we are sailing."

It had never occurred to me that the professors of this world would ever know what to do with a needle unless it was oscillating. I looked at her and said defensively, "It's all right, you know. I can manage."

Professor Hathaway stubbed out her cigar, switched off her bed light and plumping her pillow prepared to lay herself down for some slumber. "I am not proposing," said the Director of the Trust with some resignation, "to psychoanalyze you. I think, however, you should adhere to some sort of diet. Otherwise we should both have our work wasted, shouldn't we?"

I said something. Her eyes were closed already. The pebble glasses lay at her bedside, long-legged and lifeless as locusts. She went to sleep right away, with a quiet, bubbling snore which you could almost call comforting.

CHAPTER 12

THE NEXT MORNING I dashed out to a newsstand while Lenny was cooking breakfast. The papers were full of ARRESTATO A ROMA: FIGLIO DI MARCHESE INGLESE. His madre, I noticed, had flown in, and good luck to her. I bought a diet sheet and went back and helped Lenny fry eggs while we discussed it. Breakfast for lunedi, we worked out between us, was going to be latte gr. 200 and un uovo sodo o alla coque.

I thought, as we prepared to set sail for Ischia, that milk and one boiled egg was my bloody level exactly.

The Island of Ischia lies eighteen miles out of the Bay of Naples and it takes an hour and a half of Mercedes-Benz chugging to get there. No one tried to put up *Dolly*'s sails, although both Johnson and Lenny wore navy sweaters and baggy blue trousers and moved about gently like hospital orderlies in trim canvas sandshoes.

There was a lot of movement, which is the correct seagoing term for a lousy pitching, and Jacko stayed below admiring the cabin ceiling.

Professor Hathaway, wearing an anorak over elderly trousers, was on deck, to no one's surprise, with her fingers in the guidebook where it said, *In this natural aquarium of warm sea everything from bream to swordfish can be knifed or shot.* Beside her, his face full of natural color, was Innes. I must say I had never realized before what an effect antiquarian interests can have on the stomach.

The seabed under the Bay of Naples is a slagheap of extinct volcanoes, not excluding Ischia which is still gushing with curative springs and where you can cook an uovo sodo, if you have to, on one of the beaches. The harbor of Ischia Porto turned out to be the perfectly circular crater of an extinct volcano with a ferry-boat in it, and three hovercraft and a few yachts and two gray naval frigates with red life belts and a lot of Italian sailors who hung over the rail whistling until they saw Professor Hathaway.

A broad white roadway lined with tavernas and trattorias ran all around the harbor, interspersed with palms and lemon and persimmon trees; and behind it all were crowds of volcanic mountains, lushly coated in tropicana.

The yachts were all tied up to bollards in the main street. Leaning overboard with his hand on the tiller, Johnson reversed us deftly up the quay between two floating palaces, and Lenny tied up, after shifting a Birra Löwenbräu van parked in front of our bollard. The ristorante on the other side of the road sent over its menu.

We sat on the afterdeck drinking gin and sunning and studying it. The sun wasn't quite as strong as the martinis, and the square paving stones of the quayside were still puddled here and there with wet, but a sense of gaiety, if not outright relief, had undoubtedly crept into the proceedings.

I knew, all too well, how Jacko and Innes were feeling. They had made their first sea expedition, without loss of life or of limb. Work lay behind them, and a succession of boozy islands and meals cooked by Lenny queued up enticingly ahead.

They didn't have to worry about Sophia. It didn't matter to them that this was Sunday, the twelfth of November, and we were here, on time, in Ischia. "All we can do," Johnson had said to me that morning, "is go there. The island has thirty-five thousand inhabitants and is thirty miles in circumference. If you have a hunch where our buyer and seller are meeting and what they might look like, don't fail to tell me. Otherwise we have to leave it to fortune. Will the Professor, for example, want to go to the Geophysical Observatory?"

The Professor, as it turned out, didn't want to go to the Geophysical Observatory but was a pushover for the Aragonese Castle, which is a conglomeration of ancient buildings erected on an offshore rock to the north of the island. She told us all about it while we sat there drinking gin and agreeing. I could see Jacko scowl at his camera and knew he was renouncing, for the sake of his career, all those ripe Ischia friendships he had been hoping to develop. Di had disappeared before we took off for Naples and hadn't even asked him to write to her.

Innes, of course, was keener on ruins than the Professor was, and we were all fixed up to go there in a twinkling. Johnson didn't object. Lenny fed us and after lunch we all got into the speedboat leaving him on guard below, washing up the lunch dishes. I had had juice di 2 limoni and pane tostato, gr. 10. All he had to do with my plate was breathe on it.

There is a causeway, if you want to be a sissy, but the trip by sea to the castle is better. We rocketed out over the harbor and between the jaws of the boatyard and lighthouse. A hovercraft got up on its haunches and honked at us, and Johnson raised his hand, and then opened the throttle. We zipped past a succession of gray beaches backed by pale-tinted beach hotels and villas and gardens and I felt as if I were being dry-cleaned and enjoyed it. Jacko, behind me, was standing with his eyes in slits and his hair blown out and flapping behind him. Jacko and Johnson had had a long talk before lunchtime, all about souped-up Fiats. I hadn't known that Jacko was a world expert on motor engineering, but it had begun to seem like it. He hadn't mentioned girls once the whole time, even when the Professor was absent.

I looked at Johnson to see if he was studying anyone else in depth, but he was only talking to Lilian, who was sitting beside him, her scalp covered with a low knitted cap and her spotted hand on the rail. Innes was sitting also, frowning into the communal Baedeker and trying to stop the pages from flapping. It struck me that if I knew my onions,

I was the one to get Innes talking, but it seemed too much trouble. Then we arrived, and tied up to a ring off the causeway.

It was slippery scrambling ashore. We all did it like ballet school candidates, with the exception of Johnson and Professor Hathaway, who stepped out and walked off like hitchhikers. Professor Hathaway, it was now apparent, had been on boats a few times before.

The rock darkened the sky above us: a high mound plastered with walls and with arches, and topped by a cupola. In it were the fortress and palace and cathedral as strengthened by Alfonso of Aragon. The Professor led the way up the steep slatted stone passage which led into the citadel and up past small houses and gardens, crumbling buttresses and walls covered with creeper and rose trees. On a plateau the cathedral reared its three roofless sides like a kind of dismembered Versailles, white and flaking; the walls furnished with crumbling cherubs and statues, with rococo arches and pillars and architraves. Steps on the left led us down to a crypt with a long vaulted roof, dimly lit and damply chilly, off which one could detect niches containing painted (13th C.) fragments of mystics with vague incised halos.

We pried Innes loose, with some trouble, from the crypt and continued up the steep path where Jacko's instinct told him, with justice, there would be a terrace with a view, and some birra.

He was right, and by the time we had got there, we needed it. On the terrace there were tables and chairs and a citizen of Munich sitting reading a guidebook in German. Professor Hathaway looked at him as the three men went off to buy their beer and my succo di arancia. "Ruth?" she said. "Have you got our own guidebook?"

I hadn't, but I remembered where I'd last seen it. Innes had laid it down in the crypt while kneeling to inspect a genuine 13th C. painted toenail. I told her, and set off downhill to get it.

O.K. I trusted people. I was new to the business.

Apart from braking at corners, I took the gradient at a trot. There wasn't a soul on the path to divert me. I lost an ounce and a half skipping through a waste garden and climbing a wall for a shortcut, and I thought of all the further ounces I was going to lose pegging back up again. I galloped into the precincts of the ruined cathedral like an Olympic runner taking the sacred flame to Holborn Viaduct and shot down the steps to the crypt.

A man jumped at me.

I ducked, with my mouth stretched wide open to yell with.

I didn't. I was grabbed instead by another man who had been standing behind me. He caught my wrist and rammed my head into his diaphragm. Then he held it there while the first man tore the bag from my shoulder and up-ended it.

My dark glasses cracked on the pavement. My compact rolled into the darkness, my keys jangled; my lipstick separated and took off in two stages for different parts of the building. Two handkerchiefs fell, and a purseful of tinny lire, and a billfold full of dirty Italian banknotes and a comb I meant to wash that morning but hadn't, and a shower of plastic shop credit cards, and a tube of cleansing cream and a small pack of tissues. There were also two used bus tickets and some safety pins. A handbag atomizer, tightly squeezed in a pocket, fell last of all, and splitting, voided four pounds' worth of Hermès scent over the bloody 13th C. paving.

I lost my cool. I hacked the shins of the fellow gripping me and butted him hard in the stomach. I landed the heel of my sandal on the chin of the man bending over my handbag before he gripped me around the ankle and threw me. The man behind struck me on the cheek with his fist at the same time.

I went down. I struck the paving and rolled over in a patch of watery sunlight. Through the ringing in my head I could see them both on their knees groveling about after the stuff from my handbag. One of them ground his heel in my compact and then did the same with the aerosol. They shredded the tissues and emptied my billfold so that the lire lay like old potato crisps everywhere. They squeezed the cleansing cream tube to the end, so that it lay like birthday-cake icing all over the wreckage, and then they tore the lining out of my handbag.

I said, "What do you want? I haven't got anything." And they both turned and came stalking toward me.

I remember thinking that they were neither of them English. They smelled of Italian food and Italian cigarettes, and they had stocking masks which covered dark Italian hair. The bigger of the two bent over me now and with the flat of his hand hit my face, first on one side and then the other. "Where is it?" he said. And he spoke an Italian's English.

I said, "If it's the film you want, I've burned it."

Afterward, I realized I had made a mistake, but I didn't think of that at the time. I only wanted to stop them manhandling me. And to induce them to say something—anything—which would prove to the police Charles was innocent.

It didn't work, because they didn't believe me. The first man held me by the chin and the second one laughed and said, "Yes, it is the film we want, little darling. Where is it?" He was getting ready to sock me again when he looked up, and so did the other man.

What they had heard was the pounding feet of men running toward us. I screeched *"Johnson!"* before they could stop me, and heard the feet change direction and come straight toward us. The first man swore and started toward the doorway, and the crypt seemed to be full of struggling men.

You would think that it would be the skipper of the expedition who had come to the rescue but it wasn't. It was Innes Wye who burst through that doorway, with Johnson behind on the staircase. I rather hoped, when I saw him, that Innes had brought his revolver but he hadn't. He just aimed a blow at the first of the men that all but stopped him dead in his tracks and then threw himself down beside me, both his clean, manicured hands seizing mine. "Ruth! What's happened!"

I heard Johnson, ducking expertly behind me, yell, "Is she all right?" Innes, recalled by the cry of the jungle, shouted heartily, "Yes!" and, dropping my hands, did a swallow dive into the melée. The fighting hurtled out of the doorway and receded across the worn paving. There was a running of feet.

I got up. My sandals ground into glass, as they had in Mr. Paladrini's devastated studio. My money, dispersed all over the crypt, stirred lazily in the draft from the doorway. A trail of ants, proceeding out of the stonework, had begun to investigate the scented evacuation of cleansing cream. The place reeked to high heaven of Calèche.

My face hurt and the painted worthies with their well-deserved halos wavered up and down in a way that had nothing to do with the primitive wattage that lit them. Jacko, arriving late and pale as a stick of self-blanching celery, was the only one who actively helped me. He said, "Hold on, mate. Astronomers on the job never snuff it." And made me sit on his coat and recover, while he fixed all the holes in my clothing with safety pins.

Five minutes later Innes and Johnson came back, grazed and cursing, and coinciding with the arrival of Professor Hathaway, strongly treading, with the proprietor of the café, and a bottle of brandy held by the neck in her fingers.

Johnson, it turned out, had a corkscrew at the end of his pen-knife. We all sat on the floor of the crypt and drank out of the bottle in turns, while we discussed filing a complaint of assault and also the likelihood of the Ischia polizia ever tracing a hired launch with two bleeding men in it. It had been tied up at the top of the causeway. They had almost stopped them, said Innes, and Johnson, but a third man had appeared on the jetty. Innes, I saw, was going to have a black eye and Johnson had two sets of skinned knuckles and a rip in his jersey.

As I stared at him, he delved in his pocket and took out and resumed his bifocals.

I wondered if they had been knocked off, or if at some stage in the fight he had paused in order to file them. I wondered why it had been Innes and not Johnson who had first found me gone and come after me. It was because of Johnson I was here at all, sticking my neck out. "We must try and catch them," said Johnson, and a fine bloody agent Johnson had turned out to be. I glared at him, and he looked back at me blandly. I bet his oil painting of the Pope was a shambles.

We didn't file a complaint of assault since, as Professor Hathaway pointed out, the men had clearly escaped, and we should merely be asked to devote all our free time to formalities. We left the castle and zipped back to *Dolly,* having silenced the dazed café properitor with lire.

I thought, on the journey back, that all I wanted was to take my angst to bed with a barbiturate and a hot-water bottle. But, as the sun sank and the lights came on all around the haven and my fighter escort, laying me tenderly down in *Dolly*'s saloon, proceeded to salve my grazes and their own from *Dolly*'s medicine chest, I began to feel life held something yet.

We had dinner in the trattoria over the road which had sent us its menu, selecting our supper from a vast mesmeric fish tank undulating with frilled fish and lobsters and green misty columns clinging with mussels. We had negronis and crusty bread and butter and antipastos of salami and olives and anchovies and I sat on my diet sheet, which said, Sunday, 8 P.M.: Riso e rape *(riso gr. 25, olio crudo, 1 cucchiaino).*

I ate lobster, and I wasn't complaining. I might have missed out on the riso but I was nearly hell of a strong on the rape.

Then the management stood us free cognacs, and the guitarist in a flowered voile shirt and a locket came up and sang "Santa Lucia" and the light rippled on the pool of the harbor and Johnson said, "Now let's plumb the collective unconscious and talk about Ruth's little troubles."

Professor Hathaway leaned back and inspected him. Her spotted arms protruded from a sagging jersey dress of impeccable quality, and her face wore a nimbus of Manikins. She said, tapping her ash into a dish, "Someone is looking for something. Does Ruth carry about any of her inamorato's more valuable photographs?"

"No," I said.

"Well . . ." said Johnson. "You know, Ruth, Professor Hathaway is quite right. It is the missing couture photographs that someone is looking for." And he explained, cheerfully, about the burned photographs.

Everyone listened respectfully. Even I listened respectfully in view of the amount of information he was brazenly withholding. Apparently I destroyed Charles's film after developing it, on account of some indelicate pictures. Thus destroying, as well, the fashion shots the marauder was after.

So far as it went, it was gospel. It was soothing as well, since he went on to describe the extremely short-term value of fashion shots. It was my point, and he looked me straight in the eye as he made it. Therefore, he explained, there was little fear of any recurrence. The thieves would discover the film was untraceable. And soon the prints would have no market price anyway. No word, note, of any leak but a couture one.

They heard him, and then sat and thought about it. The guitarist had switched to "O Sole Mio." "Should we inform the police," said Professor Hathaway thoughtfully, "that Mr. Paladrini has left an associate?"

"Do we want police on our cruise?" remarked Johnson.

"Yes," said Jacko sourly. His face had turned red and satiny like Eddie's and Bob's back in Naples. Being deprived of alcohol during working hours seems to have a fatal effect on astronomers.

"Or," said Innes, "do we want to trap the bastards ourselves?"

It was the most surprising thing since the Declaration of Independence. "If you like," Johnson said. He appeared more astonished than any of us.

"That is," said Innes, "unless you consider it's none of my business. Like I would consider some things none of your business. Like forcing your attentions on this lovely girl. And feeding other men's mouses."

His face was red and satiny too. I gazed at it in utter fascination. "Mice," said Jacko uneasily.

"I found," said Innes tragically, "the husk in her cage."

There was an embarrassed silence, during which it came to everyone except, apparently, Professor Hathaway that Innes was tiddly. Professor Hathaway said, "That is correct. Poor Innes told me about

215

this, and I have witnessed the proof of his workshop."

Pebble glasses met bifocal lenses in a reciprocal explosion of light. She said, "You disconnected Innes's power. You switched off and examined his machinery."

"We all did it," said Jacko unexpectedly. I didn't think he had it in him; it must have been that long talk with Johnson. Live with wool and feel that little bit richer.

"Yes, I'm afraid we all did it," I said. "I'm sorry, Innes, but we weren't sure if you just kept your lunch in it."

"McVitie's biscuits," said Jacko.

"And it was suspicious, you know it was," I said earnestly, "firing that revolver."

Innes controlled himself with an effort. "As the only scientist among you," he said, "I resent that. Who is James Middleton? A limey with a second-class mental capacity and the sexual application of a woodpecker. Ruth? A fine, intelligent person ruined and exploited by her lovers." He turned his face, with what might have been a sob, to Professor Hathaway. "Have *you* ever seen an observatory with a bullwhip in it?"

"Have you ever seen an electronic workshop with a mouse in it?" said Johnson dryly.

It wasn't fair. You could see Innes's brain trying to function, and then outrage and booze overcame him together. "What," he said, "would you know of a scientific workshop? A parasite. A playboy. A man who lives off other men's inventions and then turns off the amps of their Incubators? Are you on the level? Who pays you?"

216

"The Pope," put in Jacko.

"And Maurice," said Johnson, considering. "Is that why you have a gun, Innes? To keep snoopers away from the Incubator?"

"Sure it is!" said Innes, suddenly focusing. "You don't know what that is. That's my life work. You don't know what to make of it, but I'll tell you. There are people not a thousand miles away from the Kremlin who'd give me the earth for that mechanism."

The guitarist hit a sour note and slogged on gallantly. The echoes of Innes's voice sank and died among the riveted tables. There was no doubt about it. In terms of asking to be slugged by two foul Italians in stocking masks, Innes had just won the Dracula challenge trophy. "Don't be silly, Innes," said Lilian Hathaway, puffing peacefully at a fresh Manikin. "You could exhibit the whole thing in Hanley's and no one would be any the wiser." She turned to me. "You saw the machine. Did you or Jacko make anything of it?"

I shook my head.

"Quite. Because there is nothing at this point to make," said Lilian Hathaway. "In any case, I understood we were talking about couture thieves, not espionage by enemy aliens. Mr. Johnson made a profound miscalculation in severing the power supply to your workshop, and for that he will make a donation of five thousand pounds to the Zodiac Trust Fund. On the other matter I am not perfectly clear. Is the miscreant, in your view, still hoping to trace the photographs from Lord Digham's camera?"

Innes was sitting looking at the Director like a

217

White Russian receiving word of Biological Ajax. Jacko looked horror-struck. Johnson himself, quite unaltered, did not appear to notice that he had just lost five thousand pounds. "It seems possible. For a time," he said, meditating.

"Then," said Professor Hathaway, "I suggest you accept Innes's suggestion and attempt, as he suggests, to capture the bastards."

She did know that Innes was sozzled. "Especially," added the Director, "if he has a revolver. *Do* you possess firearms still, Innes?"

"Yesh," said Innes, and made an untidy clutch at his armpit. Then his fist semaphored out with a Dardick in it.

He took a moment, narrow-eyed, to consider it. Jacko squeaked. At a nearby table someone, of indeterminate gender, let out a bellow.

Innes didn't hesitate after that for a moment. He wheeled his arm carefully around, took aim, adjusted professionally and fired fifteen bullets into the fish tank.

In this natural aquarium of warm sea everything from bream to swordfish can be knifed or shot. I had had my reservations about Innes, but that moment when I saw him, gun smoking, standing there knee deep in lobster and octopus was a watershed. I was sure the Supreme Soviet would like to see Innes's Incubator. But one look at Innes and they'd all send him straight to a funny farm.

CHAPTER 13

WE LEFT ISCHIA, as I remember, next daybreak.
Innes didn't put in an appearance at breakfast and
neither, to be candid, did Ruth Russell.

The weather broke down, and only the integrated
optics of Johnson and Hathaway, that spanking
comedy team, kept the action going as we heaved
south to our next date at Lipari.

They say we called at Amalfi, but I can't vouch
for it. I remember mountains plunging down to the
water's edge, with colored cube houses spilled
everywhere, and the tunnels and viaducts of a motorway.

I remember a square with a small mossy fountain and five million steps to a cathedral. Innes and
Professor Hathaway went inside and met the Apos-
tle St. Andrew, to Innes's benefit, while Jacko,
Johnson and I walked about in the rain in a huddle

like a self-reproducing tiddlywinks cluster and helped Lenny to shop.

No one attacked us. At midday I decided I wanted my sickbed. We walked back to the boat in the same cohesive cluster and got into our bunks for the journey. Professor Hathaway's guidebook was open at Lipari. *The air is pure, so pure and warm,* it said, *that our souls want to be a wing, to glide around, our hand would like to rest softly on another, and our eyes would like to meet those of a known person, whose nearness we deeply love.*

It didn't mention how to spring him from jug.

Johnson and Lenny sailed out of Amalfi, in a pure, warm air blowing about eight on the bloody Beaufort scale, and the rain lashing down. After becoming exceedingly well acquainted with the water filling the Gulf of Salerno, we fled into a fishing harbor called San Marco and spent the night offshore in a cat's cradle of other boats' cables.

Nothing happened next day, except that you could see the spray coming over the sea wall without ever leaving your cabin.

In the afternoon we climbed up through orchards of lemon and almond and cherry trees to the mountain town of Castellabate and found a cozy crumbling taverna and a paper shop.

My newspaper said that the English playboy photographer was still in prison, and that representations for his release were being made by the British Ambassador. There was also a small paragraph on another page to the effect that the famous English playwright Maurice Frazer, who had now made his permanent home outside Palassio, was paying a short visit to the Aeolian Isles for health reasons.

His companion, Mr. Timothy Harrogate, said that they hoped to make their usual visit to Taormina.

That meant that Maurice had flown down already. And that *Sappho* was in Lipari, where our souls wanted to be a wing. I didn't know that Timothy's second name was Harrogate and I doubted it even then. "The wind is dropping," said Johnson at that moment, looking over his spectacles.

It was. While Lenny was making supper the fishing boats began to move out of the harbor and Innes and I went to watch them.

I was beginning to have hopes of Innes. I had felt more warmly about him since that Sunday at the Aragonese Castle and Professor Hathaway's faith had never been shaken, even after the saturation attack on the fish tank. She had paid, with perfect dignity, for the damage and recouped from Innes next morning, putting the whole thing down to an infusion of Chianti and seasick pills.

Ever since, she had tucked him under her wing and he hadn't had a drop. It did occur to me, looking at him with his old-fashioned face and trendy tie and tidy American socks, that if a killer did come aboard, all he would have to do to dispose of Innes was feed him a liqueur chocolate. I said, following a train of thought, "I wonder if Poppy is pining. Innes, why don't you get her a boy friend?"

"Can't afford a big family," Innes said. It was the first joke I had ever heard him make. He added, "Are you all right now?"

He asked me that every time he saw me, even waiting in a queue at the heads in his Happy Coat. I nearly said I was, because I couldn't afford a large family and then decided not to rib him. Instead I started talking shop, a hoot for Jacko, if he had heard me. I thought at the time it was to draw out Innes, but it was probably because I was beginning to want comforting too. Astronomy, they say, is the safest of all the professions.

Innes is a Steady-State man, having done a sabbatical on radio astronomy at Cambridge. He is usually apt to hold forth about quasars and pulsars and has been known to devote whole lunchtimes to black holes, which according to theory are nonluminous stars which have exhausted their thermonuclear energy and are lurking about, concealing whole galaxies, for all anyone knows, to the satisfaction of all the Steady-Staters.

I have nothing against professional argument: if, for God's sake, you are going to sit for hours at the end of a telescope without thinking about it, you might as well work in a clock factory. I just believe that lunchtimes are for lunch and that theorizing goes with beer and short-sleeves and lying about in other friends' flats after midnight. This time I got off to a good responsible start: all about, as I remember, what we were going to do once we knew whether Maurice wanted us back after Christmas. I didn't say a derogatory word about a science research body—any of them. I avoided the subject of the food at the Trust, and the bloody air conditioning and the man from Kitt Peak who thought the universities ought to run all the observatories.

It was Innes who picked all those subjects. While I stood with my jaw dropped, he began to let off steam about the Zodiac. I tried to introduce Wobble Excitation and he sidetracked into the bloody incompetence of the computer room. He then told me who was sleeping with whom in the typing pool. I knew it all, but I was so shocked I could hardly look at him.

Finally he asked if Charles was a drug addict, and I said No more than anyone else, and saw at last from his face what he was on about. It was so surprising that I turned my back on all the wolf whistles. "Innes!" I said. "You don't think I am Under Another Man's Influence? May I tell Charles?"

"Charles is in prison," Innes said. I was right. His nostrils bulged and went in again.

"Innes," I said. "I love my Charles. I love Johnson, too. I loved three boys at school and eight at university and several more subsequently. I also adore Lilian Hathaway and I think Jacko is priceless and I don't mind you, at that, when you aren't being stuffy. But I don't let anyone run my life, even the person I'm going to bed with, which happens to be Charles and no one else, dearest Innes. Do I *look*," I said rather crankily, "like a weakminded female?"

And, heaven help me, Innes said, "No." Then he said, "I had a theory."

"About me?" I said.

"About the guy who was hunting those photographs. Anyone as persistent as that, I figured, must think the photographs are still in existence."

"They're not," I said.

"Johnson seemed to have doubts about that," Innes said.

"And that's another man with a galloping neurosis," I said. I was sorry afterward, but I was outraged. An entire conversation conducted with the sole purpose of psychoanalyzing my relationships.

First Johnson, then Lilian, and now Innes. I ask you. Am I a nymphomaniac?

The conversation died, and I helped to kill it. But there was, I thought, a gleam in Innes's eye when I left him that had something almost wistful in it.

He had certainly wanted to pump me. But he had wanted, I thought, something else maybe as well. Perhaps Innes was tiring of Poppy. Perhaps he was beginning to wonder if he could afford a family. Every mammal, they tell you, has its own display patterns and mating habits. Pigs, for example, chew their sows' ears during sex.

No kidding. We all have the same lousy problems.

The next rendezvous, Johnson had said, was tomorrow on the island of Lipari. The island of Lipari was a long, long way south and Johnson and Lenny took us there, thank God, while we were sleeping.

Or while I was sleeping.

I didn't know each of the others got up in turn through the night to help him, even Professor Hathaway. I didn't know either until the next morning that she had put a phenobarbitone in my cappuccino to make sure I shouldn't. The general impression seemed to be that for failing to stand up to life's little buffets, I had to be cosseted. I got up, very cross, at first light and plunged into the cockpit to find Johnson and Stromboli, smoking together.

"Hullo," said Johnson. "Did Innes wake you? We found him downstairs, trying to shake you out of a dying coma. I had to explain that you'd been zonked by the Director."

224

Behind his head, Stromboli rose from the sea like a pyramid bottle with smoke rising from the neck. It was olive green, with spillings of lilac and brown and gray down its sides. A lot of little white blockish houses lay scattered at its foot. Johnson's bifocals, dividing their attention between the burgee and me, were noncommittal as ever. The sails were up, and there was no sound at all from the engine.

I had a faint, nightmarish recollection of being grabbed by somebody and rolled backward and forward. It was the most interesting piece of information I had received on the voyage. I said, "If it wasn't for Innes, I suppose I should have missed the whole of my bloating morning feast? Where is my tè and pane, twenty grams?" A pale, steamy cloud was rising slowly from the volcano, while new whiter plumes began to appear at the brim of the crater like lace, and blossom upward in their turn.

"If you go in," said Johnson calmly, "you'll find Lenny with his running spikes on. We're going to circumnavigate the volcano on the recommendation of Professor Hathaway's guidebook. It says Stromboli should be seen just before dawn, shaded in the morning haze, hollering lowly."

"What?" I said. I could hear it.

"Not that," Johnson said. "That's a joke Jacko has discovered in his paperback." He added, without changing his tone, "Don't play with Innes. He doesn't understand obituary doggerel."

"I wasn't going to ask him to invent any," I said irritably, and went in to have my miserable breakfast. Innes was up on the foredeck with the Professor, timing the eruptions which came every twenty minutes in a sort of creaming cauliflower shape in a

225

nice tint of café au lait, rising to a burgeoning mush-room and dispersing in transparent apricot. A long lilac streamer hung behind when it had vanished. Close to, the old lava was layered like oyster shells, and the new falls were gray and turgid like mud, with the green and yellow of whin at their edges. Jacko, having failed to witness either Ingrid Berg-man or a major natural disaster, continued to stay below with his paperback and Johnson finally took down the sails and, starting the engine, turned *Dolly*'s head south for Lipari.

I said to Innes, "I'm sorry you were worried this morning. They made up their minds to keep me out of trouble."

"Is that what they told you?" said Innes.

"That's what the Professor told me," I said. I was surprised. Innes and the Professor were as thick as thieves.

"I'm sure she meant it," said Innes enigmatically. Lenny was out of sight and Professor Hathaway had wandered to the other end of the boat. He turned and, putting his hand on mine, looked into my eyes. Really looked, as if he wanted to get a formula across and wasn't sure what grade the stu-dent belonged to. "You took phenobarbitone," said Innes tensely, "but it might have been anything. Watch what you eat. Watch what you drink. And if you take my advice, don't trust anyone."

I nodded. There seemed nothing constructive I could add to it. And I had one consolation as the yacht breasted the waters and the Exhaust Pipe of the Thyrrhenian Sea dropped behind us on the ho-rizon.

No one was watching their food more carefully, damn it to hell, than I was.

We reached Lipari just before lunchtime, and the first thing we saw was the *Sappho*.

The next was Di Minicucci, hanging over the rail in denim pants and a jersey slit to the navel. There were about five other heads with her, all plentifully covered with hair. Innes gazed at them all with an expression of impenetrable scorn, but you could have heard Jacko breathing in Jugoslavia.

Johnson began to gentle *Dolly* to lie in beside her, and Di came and hung over the other rail like a popped pod all ready for Birdseye. She had a book in her drooping left fingers. "Hullo, darling," she said. "We've all found the most super guidebook."

"So have we," I said with resignation. *"There is a big talking about the isle of Lipari: some people are convinced that Lipari does not outstand in character as the other islands do?"*

The pod popped further and Di did nothing about it. Jacko moved up the rail, as if trying to get back to his reservoir. She said, "Have you seen the bit about George Sand?"

The engine cut out. Under a large notice saying BENVENUTO A LIPARI large numbers of workmen were congregated, listening to every shrieked word. I had seen the bit about George Sand. I thought, for a hysterical moment, Di was going to read it all out: *George Sand was much impressed by these islands. He was struck by the beauty of the sea and the sky. Perhaps Sand had found here a new valley of Eden? That is how these islands appeared to him.*

227

"We've read that bit too," remarked Johnson. "It must have been the hell of a shock for poor Chopin. You haven't met Professor Hathaway. Professor, this is Diana Minicucci."

Diana Minicucci leaned on the rail, looking at the knitted cap and the blue baggy trousers, and the Professor looked at Di Minicucci.

"Very charming," said Professor Hathaway with pleasure. "You will have no recollection of it, but I spent a short period many years ago working for one of your father's laboratories. Is Mr. Frazer on board?"

"We dropped Maurice and Timothy at Messina. They're in Taormina now," Diana said. "They got bored with Vulcano. Too awful."

The beautiful person on her right, in a masculine voice, added, "They got bored with Diana. Poor Maurice was sitting about in his mud baths, and Di kept lighting pieces of paper and erupting them. She sent the volcano up once. It was rather a pity, poor elderly Maurice, hopping out of his hole like lychees in neat whisky flambées." As he said this he grinned at Diana, who kicked him expertly in the groin but lightly, I couldn't help noticing. He slid back, protesting, and Diana, turning back to Professor Hathaway, said, "Why not come aboard, all of you? We're just going to have drinks."

If the idea was to indicate that they hadn't just been having drinks all the morning it was a dead loss, because the icebox was empty and there were unwashed glasses on every available horizontal space including the loos. I collected the glasses and took them all back to the galley for washing. No one was there; even the little man who sat and sang

228

to the engines. I said to someone else of indeterminate sex who came in to dry for me, "Who's running the boat?"

"We are," said the dryer, who proved to be a
female called Charlotte. "That is, Di's little man
works the engine and sails her and we do the rest."

I didn't say "What rest" although I had caught a
glimpse of the cabins, which were three feet deep
in towels and ragged handmade underwear and
screwed-up sheets with coffee stains on them. Since
anything Timothy lived in always looked as if it had
come fresh from Asprey's, I wondered why Maurice had let Di and her crew come aboard *Sappho*.
Then I realized what Charlotte had said. I said,
"Doesn't *Sappho* belong to *Maurice?*"

"He likes to think so, doesn't he?" Charlotte said.
"No, darling, it's on permanent loan from Prince
Minicucci, doing his Renaissance patronage bit. Not
that Maurice couldn't buy a yacht if he wanted to,
but it's so much less trouble this way. And it brings
Di around. You know how Maurice adores being
grand seigneur with all us golden children devotedly
draped around his kneecaps."

One of the hallmarks of Di's personality is the
number of extremely shrewd golden children she is
able to gather around her. I said, "So Maurice and
Timothy are alone at the moment in Sicily?"

"Darling, how romantic it sounds," said Charlotte, breaking a glass and throwing it gracefully
through the porthole. "But I expect you're right. In
any case, we've all to get off before you join him in
Taormina, Timothy's orders. I expect eighteen
charwomen will come on board tomorrow and make

229

everything simply gorgeous for everybody. Do you smoke?"

"No," I said. I wasn't thinking. "Professor Hathaway does."

"Does she?" said Charlotte, looking astonished. "I must say, she looks a sporting old horse. Well, you'll find it behind the netting on the second shelf of the cold store, but Timothy says don't use it all. His little man with a rowboat was picked up last week and he says the rising profits trajectory could accelerate any moment . . . I think that's enough glasses."

I had been going to wash them all, to preserve the *Sappho*'s passengers from more cross-infection, but their microbes were already probably mixed more than anyone else would ever know. We carried a trayful up the galley steps and into *Sappho*'s palatial saloon, where we proceeded, with some justification, to dirty them again. Innes came and sat beside me.

Jacko, it was clear, was having a lovely time and all the other extroverts were lounging over beside Johnson with their best profiles elaborately displayed. I suppose they thought he was going to be like Maurice except that instead of putting them on the stage he would say, "My dear, you must let me paint you." Then some of them began to giggle and the next time I looked they were all sitting anyhow and laughing. He appeared to be talking about revolving bookcases, but you never know with Johnson.

Professor Hathaway was having a long talk with Di Minicucci and enjoying herself so much that it was quite hard to get her away for lunch. We arranged to gather for dinner that evening. There was a restaurant on the shore just beside us, standing on stilts overhanging the water. Then we went back to Lenny for lunch, and in the afternoon emerged en masse with guidebooks for a scientific exploration of Lipari.

" 'Somerset Maugham once said,' " said Innes, reading from our favorite literature, " 'No word/ can do justice to this paradise.' "

"Did she?" said Jacko.

I tell you, we shall make a scholar of J. Middleton yet.

Like them all, Lipari is a green and mountainous island, with the flat-topped white houses piled up around the harbor and topped by more ancient ruins and a cathedral and a wide flowery terrace with trees. We walked to the edge of the piazza and looked down on the white curve of the quay, lined with shops and with parked cars and shelving down at the end into a strip of coarse pebble beach with boats on it. Nearer was the blue roof of the Ristorante Mistral, and the long thrusting strip of the jetty, with *Sappho* moored on its far side, next to *Dolly*.

From above you could see the enormous beam of Maurice's boat compared to the long slender lines of the *Dolly*. *Sappho* was all motor cruiser, with a canopied wheel house and afterdeck big enough to hold a dinner-dance on.

I didn't spot anybody meeting anybody and handing an atomic warhead to him or her. Johnson didn't even come over and speak to me. I thought again what a dim idea it had been to come here, and then considered *Sappho* and thought maybe it wasn't so dim.

The entire payload of *Sappho* could be trading Plans like a roll-on roll-off ferry service, for all Johnson and I should know about it. But if, for example, they were still doing it in Taormina on Friday, and on Capri come Monday, there was a chance we might catch them at it.

Except that we hadn't caught them at it on Ischia. And they were getting rather good at catching us.

Seeing it was Di's party, I spent an hour and a half on the bodywork for that evening's dinner and subsequently climbed onto the jetty and walked around to the Mistral with the rest with some sort of restored confidence. In fact, when we climbed the stairs and found our way to the table, it became quite easy to sort out Di's males from Di's females from the way their eyes glinted above all the necklaces. Di said, "You rotten cow, I saw that in Fratini's and I was going to buy it. I hope you freeze to death."

The black velvet top was joined to the black velvet slacks by a lot of loose satin ribbons. I must say, I do take to Di. She has a gift for saying all the right things. Then we sat down, thirteen of us.

I stuck to my diet and had orange juice to drink, instead of buckets of Val di Lupo, which explains why I was still sitting opposite the disapproving presence of Innes listening to Johnson giving an excruciating performance in Englishman's German of a complete bowdlerized version of *Hamlet* with all the speaking parts and most of the action, when the passengers from *Sappho* began splashing wine and throwing cassata ice cream at one another.

Professor Hathaway, who had been holding a very lively conversation herself with three or four surprised young men at her end of the table, immediately got up, bent over Di and said, "You will excuse an elderly scientist, my child, but I think the night, outside the Dome, is for the young. Thank you." She kissed her. "I have enjoyed myself."

What with paying for the damage and arguing about the bill and compensating fellow diners for the splotches of ice cream on their priceless jackets and blusas, the last chance of making a quintet of graceful farewells vanished when the Professor did. In any case, we couldn't leave without Jacko, who had a girl on each buttock and appeared to be trying to throw them into the cassata-granita, or perhaps they were throwing him. Somewhat hampered by Innes, who kept attampting to hustle downstairs, dragging me with him, to the scornful delight of the mob, Johnson finally managed, with incredible calm, to find a guitarist to play for us. He then contrived, after two sets of Lancers and an Italian version of Strip the Willow which rocked the place on its piles, to charm the guitarist into playing down the stairs and along the long, sloping landing plank which joined the Mistral to the quayside.

It was bound to happen, and it did. Someone pushed someone and he fell into the water. Someone else jumped in beside him. Two other people thought a swimming party had developed and, diving in, began to splash about, ducking bodies and sitting on heads. Someone hit me a swinging punch between the shoulder blades and I went in as well, head first, with my black ribbons flying.

The first person to jump in after me was Innes, and the second, Diana. I hardly got my eye make-up wet, they were so quick to retrieve me. Charlotte, squealing, came by doing a moderate butterfly, followed by one of the boy friends, his hair streaming and his teeth shining.

The bow wave they created washed over us and I did get my make-up wet but not for long. I shot up with Innes's hand under one arm like the prong of a fork-lift tractor while Di's hand sought anxiously to heave my chin out of the water. I shook my head and said, "For God's sake, Innes. I'm *standing*."

"Oh," said Innes. He took his hand away. The water was all of three feet deep.

"And in any case," I said aggressively, "I *like* being in water."

I suppose it was a back-kick from being too sober. I wanted to show that I could be crazy too, man, on straight old orange juice. I kicked off my sandals, and turned, and launched into a good strong racing crawl, pointing straight out to Sardinia.

Sardinia turned out to be nearer than I had thought, and to have an iron stomach and a pair of uncompromising hands which closed on my arms, arrested me, and then turned me about to face the way I had come. "Oh, no," said Johnson. "I have a consistent dividend record, and you're not going to spoil it. Are you decent?"

I didn't know he'd jumped in. He must have gone in ahead of me. He must have swum faster than I had, if he hadn't. I felt about. "I've lost my trousers," I reported. I had my pants on, and a bra. I was decent. My God, I was more decent than Di when she was dressed for the Via Veneto.

As I was thinking this, Di came up with Innes not far behind her. There was a discussion, growing steadily chillier, over whether I should attempt to swim to the boat, or go back to the Mistral with Diana, where at least I could borrow a tablecloth. Innes, in the most fluent speech I have ever heard him make, pointed out that the two swims were equally lengthy, and to expose my condition to the already upset diners in the Mistral would be tantamount to having me arrested.

I must say he seemed to have a point there, or at least Johnson thought so. In the end I swam to *Dolly* with Johnson, Innes and Di around in convoy and waited, hanging on to the side, until Lenny came and let down the ladder.

Di came aboard too, which did nothing for the saloon carpeting, followed shortly by Jacko, bone dry and confused. Di said, "My God, darling, I am sorry. I'll get you another Frantini. And your poor bloody watch."

"I can maybe save it," Innes said. We were all standing wrapped in towels. "It needs to be plunged in pure alcohol."

Di bent upon him the gaze of the daughter of Prince Minicucci and the top earner in Gene Kelly musicals. "Why bother?" she said pityingly. "Hand over what's wrecked, Ruth, and I'll have it replaced for you, gratis. Unless you're too bloody coy to take presents?"

"No," I said with real gratitude and, wriggling under the towel, detached and held out the top half of the Fratini pants suit. "Another of the same, and I'll love you forever. The underpinning will wash. And the watch doesn't matter, it's waterproof."

"And the sandals?" said Diana briskly.

"They were Samo's," I said readily. "Handmade with foiled vamps at thirty-five thousand lire."

I was afraid she had noticed them, and she had. "You lying rat," said Diana comfortably. "They were Marks and Sparks; I saw them. Good night, alcoholics."

She blew me a kiss, and went and gave one to Johnson, and patted Innes, a little patronizingly, on the shoulder. Jacko, standing still by the door, continued to look at us all as if he were thinking in very simple phonetics. Di came up to him, placed her two hands in two very strategic pressure areas, and arching him slowly backward, sank a kiss full in the primary foliage of his Zapata mustache.

When she left and went out the door he was still laid on the bench seat, crepitating.

"The more we walk around," said Johnson, toweling himself slowly with an expression of ineffable smugness behind the steamed glasses, "the more we are amazed by this multicolored stage on which Nature likes to chisel and shape things following a skillful game and a genial whim. Every dawn, a new painting, an unexhaustible source of life, of love, of beauty, of peace . . . The too-marvelous-for-words beauty of this happy piece of earth smiling under ever-blue skies and subsiding into iridescent waters, harmoniously smiling, in an atmosphere of dream, life and beauty . . . Lipari!!!"

I went to bed.

CHAPTER 14

WE SAILED out of Lipari next morning leaving *Sappho* behind, the curtains still closed over her portholes. Five hours later we were in Messina, Sicily, Johnson having won the argument over whether to press on to Taormina by mentioning casually that both water tanks were empty and unless we called at Messina we shouldn't have any ice for the gin.

We tied up to a vast concrete waterfront filled with sightseers, whose feet were the first thing we saw through the portholes next morning. Then Lenny started up the engines, and we got going again for Taormina. On the way there we lost Italy, which receded gently into a long, light blue shadow and ceased altogether in a pale apricot scar.

I didn't like losing Italy. I felt cut off, somehow, in a way I hadn't before. In Sicily, people said, anything could happen, and people, as it turned out, had it right on the button. The first thing we saw, entering the bay below Taormina, was *Sappho,* sitting shining, smug and clearly deserted.

The next was Sophia Ow, alias Lindrop, decorating the Atlantis Bay Hotel's sunbathing piazza alongside Di Minicucci.

We all went ashore in two goes of the rubber dinghy, admiring the scrubbed flanks of *Sappho,* which had clearly lost its passengers and gained a number of charwomen. Bodies littered the beach and the lounge chairs around the waterfront bar, indicating that the wind had dropped, and the sun, shining mildly, was doing its best to remind everyone that they were in Sicily.

Di, nearest the bar, was reclining face down in a bikini, of which the top half was patently unfastened. Lying beside her, as I have said, in a gorgeous one-piece black bathing suit which showed off her last summer's tan, and her this atummn's figure and all that spectacular Finnish blond hair was Sophia Lindrop, the dish Bob and Eddie had seen with Charles in Naples. The girl Charles was once engaged to.

Di saw us and sat up, and the top half of her bikini fell off, and Jacko leaped forward to fix it. My blond friend preferred to phase her delivery. She turned her head. Her white-lidded eyes fell on Jacko, whom of course she had known through the Trust. She smiled at him and at Lilian Hathaway, cast a long, studied glance at J. Johnson and then discovered the enemy: me.

Of course, she knew we were coming. She was in Di Minicucci's company. She knew about Johnson and *Dolly.* She would know Charles was in clink and she probably knew all about the row we had had in Velterra. That didn't prevent her from studying me with vivid astonishment.

"Ah. The cradle-snatcher," said Sophia, and giggled at Jacko.

I am the same age as Charles; she is three years younger. With the others looking on I was damned if I was going to be childish. I grinned and said, "Hullo, Sophia. I've got a holiday pass from the geriatric unit."

Professor Hathaway smiled and shook Sophia by the hand. "You will be fascinated to hear what developments we have been making in your field, Ruth and I. How nice it is to see you. Are you on holiday?"

"I am here with friends," Sophia said. "I have to be back at the observatory on the twentieth. Old Mr. Frazer has so kindly offered to take me on *Sappho*."

Old Mr. Frazer, damn his eyes. She wouldn't call him that, I can tell you, when she asked him. Or when he offered. Maurice has grown into the sort of dramatist who doesn't need a stage anymore. He winds up people, and then lays them down and starts watching them. Innes arrived rather late, blushing, and was introduced, along with Johnson. Innes said, "What observatory are you with now, Miss Lindrop?"

I didn't know who she was with. I reckoned Bob and Eddie must have known, but they got off the subject so fast in Naples that I never discovered, and I didn't choose to ask anyone else afterward. I didn't know that Johnson had asked them. I didn't know how much he knew about Sophia Lindrop when he asked me so disarmingly that night to tell him about her. He was looking at her now, admiration printed all over his face around the bifocals, while Innes asked his gentlemanly question and Sophia opened her lips to reply to him.

Johnson forestalled her. "Miss Lindrop is with the Finnish Observatory. The Finnish Observatory on Capri, isn't that so?"

I could feel veins standing out all over my eyeballs. Capri. We had to be in Capri on Monday. And so, it appeared, had Sophia. Sophia, who had been made out of tungsten steel in a doll factory. "You may not be so pre-Columbian in bed, darling," had said Charles to me, "but my God, at least you're human."

So Sophia, who used to be engaged to Charles, was working on Capri, where the fourth and last meeting arranged by the late Mr. Paladrini was to have been held. And Sophia, according to Bob and Eddie, had been meeting Charles a fortnight previously in Naples. And Johnson, the rat, had said nothing to me.

I glared at him and he said to Sophia, without ever glancing in my direction, "We're sailing for Capri on Sunday. Maybe we'll see you there."

"Perhaps," said Sophia. "But you will be on holiday and I shall be working. It is possible, you know, for a woman to be serious about her career."

This aimed at me. She had a dimple in her chin and she took size 34C-cup brassières when she wore brassières. I knew because I found one in the laundry the week after Charles and I first shacked up together. Johnson stood there in his wrinkled bags with a hank of string hanging out of one

240

pocket and his pipe bulging out of the other and said winningly, "But there should, I hope, at least be time for a drink?"

"Of course there will," said Professor Hathaway heartily. I let her get on with finding out how Sophia was spending her weekend and dropped down beside Diana, who had flopped to the horizontal again and was being oiled with some enthusiasm by Jacko. The fact that she was watching Johnson all the time under her lashes escaped Jacko but not, I thought, either Sophia or Johnson, who was getting on like a house on fire with Sophia now I wasn't there. I hoped his interest was professional but it was a weak hope. Sophia deciding to move in on somebody was a sight worth selling tickets for.

Jacko went on oiling Di's sun-kissed areas and asking leading questions about the frolic on Lipari, which was probably still going on but without *Sappho,* which had sailed empty with her working skipper and Di down to Taormina, passing us while we were tied up in Messina. I was making my contribution to the dialogue and dripping Ambre Solaire onto a Sicilian ant queue when the sudden silence told me that my party had retreated Maurice-ward into the hotel. I got to my knees ready to follow them, and found Sophia standing over me.

It was an exciting sight. Her two eyelids were arcs of white paint where she was staring down at me, and her lipstick had disappeared altogether, because her mouth was pressed shut so purposefully. Then her lips came apart, blurred, and she said, "Your rich friends, your stupid friends, have gone away. And now I will have my property, please."

I looked around. "Jacko?" I said.

241

"Jacko," said Di firmly, "is out on charter already." She was lying on her face and Jacko was still preparing her deftly for fondue. Sophia continued to stare at me without moving. A few people on nearby towels lifted their heads, interested.

"Charles?" I ventured.

"I have him already," said Sophia. "Whenever I want him. I am talking of *that*."

It was getting interesting, if a trifle public. Di heaved around to look and even Jacko glanced up from his brave massage. Sophia was pointing to my left hand.

I looked at it, and so did Jacko and Diana. It was ringless. Part of the row Charles and I had had in Velterra had been over the fact that I won't accept any rings from him. Our blank faces maddened Sophia.

"*That!*" she said, raising her voice considerably, and bending, seized my wrist and jerked my watch strap painfully forward.

It didn't come far, being a man's leather strap and firmly buckled. I hauled my wrist back and gazed at Diana. Diana lifted her eyebrows, shrugged and flopped down again, abdicating. "Christ!" I said incredulously, chafing my wrist, and then, as more heads began to turn in our direction, lowered my voice. I said to Sophia, "Come on. Sit down. It isn't a play group. I'm wearing Charles's watch and you want it. Is that it?"

She didn't sit down. Nor did she lower her voice. "I not only want it, I am having it. Together with anything else I have paid for that Charles has given you. Why do you need it?" Sophia said.

242

"Charles is in prison and your new lover is richer. Ask him for a wristwatch. I want mine back."

"Listen! Pipe down!" said Jacko. He rose to his feet, a reasonable male, dealing reasonably with an unpleasant occurrence. "O.K., she's got Charles's watch on but you can't demand it back and expect to get it, just like that. If you want to talk about it, for the Lord's sake go inside."

The white-lidded eyes barely glanced at him. "Is it your affair?" said Sophia Lindrop. "If you are frightened, run after your party." She said coolly to me, "Do you wish me to show you the invoice?"

"Do you keep them?" I said, fascinated. "Sophia, do you want it back for the money, or are you really still sold on Charles? He won't come back. He really won't." I was thinking of all the other things he had told me about her. I hadn't forgotten the so-called meeting in Naples. But I was becoming surer and surer how it had happened.

"Won't come back?" said Sophia, and smiled. She smiled all around, at Jacko and Diana and even had a little to spare for the audience. "He *is* back, darling Ruth. Didn't you know? Where do you think he goes, when he must fly to those assignments in Livorno and Firenze? He goes there, yes, of course. You know it; you see the photographs. But he does not show you the photographs of what we do when we meet—in Capri, in Naples, in Ischia. I gave him that watch after the first twenty-four hours we spent together, and you will not have it, you stupid horse."

"Look here!" Jacko said angrily. He turned to me. "Ruth, go in. There's no need for you to listen to this."

It was good advice. I got off my knees, straightening my shift and trying to hang on to my dignity. I said quickly, "Look. If the watch means something special, Sophia, I'm sorry. But Charles only lent it to me, because the glass of my own one got broken. I'll tell him you're worried about it. You can ask him yourself for the thing, when they spring him. But I can't hand over someone's property to you, not just like that. No one would. Leave it, and we'll sort it out later."

I was proud of that speech. I had the feeling that the whole sunbathing piazza was proud of it also. It came to Sophia that she had lost the sympathy of her audience. She took one step toward me and at the look in her eye, I retreated. Then I remembered the pool and stepped sideways beside Di's gungy flask of sun lotion.

Di stretched out a languid arm to protect it just as Sophia rushed forward. Sophia's shins and Di's forearm collided and Sophia hurtled on, straight for the water.

Di and Jacko and I watched her disappear, head first, in her smart swimsuit. Then I went in to find Maurice's suite and join the rest of my party. I don't know when I've felt more justifiably cheerful.

> *The parting was so sudden*
> *We often wonder why*
> *But the saddest part of all, dear,*
> *You never said goodbye.*

We dined that evening with Maurice and Timothy, by which time Di and Jacko had spread the glad tidings and Maurice, who liked little Finnish birds in his entourage as well as great helpings of portrait artists and astronomers, was clearly devising how to maintain his offer of a sail north for Sophia without putting out Di or the rest of us.

He needn't have worried. Di's greatest enemy was boredom. She had already let herself be used by Sophia as a means of an introduction to Maurice. There was nothing Di would enjoy more than a couple of days pumping Sophia about her love life.

And so long as Sophia was on *Sappho,* I can't say I minded all that much now either. I had been worried about Sophia before I met her, but I wasn't worried now—not in the slightest. If I am sure of my boy friend, I don't make dramas over possessing mementos. I had Charles. I didn't care if she had his bloody wristwatch or not. But until Charles said she could have it, I wasn't handing it over.

We had a sparkling evening during which Maurice received fifteen people at his table and was photographed twice. We didn't even glimpse my late colleague, Sophia.

I cornered Johnson on the way downstairs to the rubber dinghy and he confessed that he had known she worked in Capri but hadn't told me in case I jumped to conclusions. "If it pleases you to know it," said Johnson, "I have had her investigated. Her career is impeccable; her life is an open book. It would be interesting to know however whether Sophia or Charles arranged that meeting in Naples—"

"Wasn't it obvious?" I asked sarcastically. *Dolly* and Lenny had been in Naples while Charles was there. Watching, I made no doubt, his every movement.

Johnson was unperturbed. "All that was obvious was that they met by prearrangement. It was a short meeting, in the bar of the hotel where Charles had been visiting a client in connection with a photographic assignment. They separated half an hour later. Much of the time, I am told, they seemed to be arguing." We had emerged from the hotel and were walking down the tiled steps past the swimming pool. "I notice," said Johnson, "that the situation doesn't disturb you. Do you think therefore that Sophia sought that meeting? Is she still in love with him?"

I said, "I don't think she's in love with anybody. I think she wants him back because her pride is hurt." I thought and—since there didn't seem any point, as Di would have said, about being coy over it—I added, "According to Charles, she is very Scandinavian in bed."

"And Finnish-type partners are hard to come by? I shouldn't have thought she had far to look, on Capri. I should tell you," said Johnson, "that the Rome police have not yet been told about Sophia. We know she works on Capri. We know that Mr. Paladrini was arranging for some exchange of what was possibly classified information on the twentieth in San Michele, Capri. We know Sophia has been meeting Charles. But we also know that from the outset Charles's movements have been made to look suspicious. Sophia is scornful of Charles in jail on a gambling charge. How would she react to Charles in jail for something more serious? Would that salve her pride?"

This was playing the field with a vengeance. I stared at him. Below, Lenny had brought the dinghy

246

to the water's edge and was steadying it, while I could hear Innes and Jacko and Professor Hathaway stepping out of the lift doors above us. Di was sleeping, or something, in the hotel.

"You mean," I said, "is Sophia framing Charles somehow? I don't know. She's certainly inviting publicity: that little scene by the swimming pool will have flown all over Taormina by this time. The payoff, I suppose, would be Charles turning up at San Michele, all set apparently for the appointment. You've saved him from that, anyway."

For the first time, I was grateful that the Rome police had put Charles in clink and Johnson hadn't done anything to rescue him. He had wanted ten days, Johnson said, to back his fancy. Six of the ten days had gone, and with Charles still in jail the yacht had been searched and I had been attacked and searched also. We had not, as we had hoped, surprised two of Mr. Paladrini's clients in the act of trading secrets but the more I thought about that, the more it surprised me that, without time and place, Johnson ever thought we should.

Capri, of course, was another matter. San Michele meant the most famous villa on Capri, now a monument and a museum. And 1500 meant 3 P.M. One was still left wondering who, after all the police intervention after Mr. Paladrini's death, would be fool enough to meet there.

Unless they had no alternative. Unless they had been advised well in advance and didn't even know Mr. Paladrini's death had a bearing on the matter. Unless someone trying to frame Charles had invented the whole rendezvous with the intention of enticing Charles there from Naples, and then blowing the whole thing to the police.

But you would have to be very deeply involved yourself, and very scared, to need to unload the blame like that on an innocent person. And Sophia's life, Johnson had just said, was blameless. Nothing might now happen on Capri, which would be a pity. For everything that happened, every act of violence, every interference with us or our liberty, was a step toward finding the truth and freeing Charles.

And that was a laugh. For the next act of violence did neither. It happened the next day in Taormina, the old, picturesque town on the mountain behind us.

I explored Taormina with Innes and Professor Hathaway, having swooped up the hillside by cable car. We saw Johnson once through the arch of the clock tower and again hopping down one of the little steep streets with pink houses and wrought-iron balconies and colored shutters and great earthenware pots of cacti and flowers and creepers streaming everywhere. Every time we came out of another old church we spotted Di going into another boutique, generally with Jacko protesting behind her. She was got up as Ariadne with a long floating caftan thing trailing behind her and dark glasses, which would have blown Theseus and made even Bacchus think twice, I shouldn't wonder.

Maurice and Timothy were easiest of all to find. They spent the day sitting on the paved edge of the Corso Umberto having coffee and diet pills and being universally admired. It wasn't that the place was full of raven-haired bandits. In fact, there seemed no middle course between fat Sicilians with black berets and boleros and lissom Sicilians in long sprigged shirts and shrink-wrapped trousers who smiled at Timothy.

Timothy, who was used to his reputation having preceded him, sat very correctly in his chair beside Maurice and played with a long, thin gold-plated ball-point from Gucci which Maurice had given him for his birthday. The boys' eyes followed it to such purpose that a kind of Inner Ring Road developed in the region and they had to rise periodically and change stations. At two o'clock, by prior arrangement, we all met to allow Professor Hathaway to feed us, which took, agreeably, most of the afternoon. At the end of it, Maurice announced that we were all going to the ruined Greek theater.

When Maurice mentions the word theater, no one contradicts him. We all, dammit, went.

The ruined theater crowns the ridge at Taormina and commands, I suppose, one of the six most beautiful views in the world. No one told me. I plugged up a road behind Timothy. All the shops were selling Greek masks and Maurice walked past them with grace, faintly smiling. No one recognized him. At the top we paid at a ticket office and filed through a boulder-strewn yard to the monument. Bits of building loomed over us, patched together from thin, oblong red Roman bricks and dove-gray Greek marble. With all his Player King instincts Maurice plunged through a high arching hall lined with fragments of marble which proved to be the fastest way onto the stage.

I was about to follow him when I noticed Johnson. With Professor Hathaway and Innes in close attendance, he had turned away from the arch and was climbing the steep flight of steps to the amphitheater. I cast a glance after Maurice, who was swimming gently along with Di on one side and Jacko on the other, while Timothy ran with little cries from sculpture to sculpture. Then I too turned, and climbed the wide, shallow steps leading upward.

We had, of course, like dried-out alcoholics, become overconfident. Nothing had happened to us since Ischia. Lipari had been devoid of incident, unless you counted my involuntary swim. Taormina so far had been equally devoid of incident, unless you counted Sophia's involuntary swim. From the top of an ancient Greek amphitheater, at least none of us could fall into water.

So no one stopped me when I hopped up the steps after Johnson, although at the top Johnson and his little party were nowhere to be seen, and I came to a dead halt myself from simple astonishment.

I had stepped from the stairs onto the outer rim of the shelving amphitheater, which plunged down to the ruined orchestra where I could see Maurice and his three companions picking their way, small among the blocks of pale gray and red fallen marble. Behind them towered the crumbling arches and walls of the scaena, the cracked white Corinthian columns shining against the wooded slopes of the mountains, spiked with poplars and dark green with orange groves, dropping through village and town to the scalloped blue rim of the sea. There was no horizon. Sea and sky met in a china blue haze in the sunshine and behind it all, glittering and magical, rose the snow-covered cone of Mount Etna.

A bloody, stupid voice somewhere said, "You will now give me that watch."

I don't think I was even frightened. I had been wrenched away from a private experience and I was angry. Irritated, exasperated, and this time, unforgiving. I looked about me.

The terrace on which I stood was empty, and so were all the wooden benches below me. Farther down, the original marble seats were still there, the Greek names of their owners carved on the backs. Farther down still, on the municipal stage which filled part of the orchestra, Maurice had raised his stick and appeared to be lecturing. Everything he said floated with terrible clarity to where I was standing and beyond. He had just begun to realize this, and, as I stood there, tossed off a couple of accurate epigrams and a clerihew. The voice said, "My watch."

Sophia, of course. I looked around again. I had seen, a moment after I came in, Professor Hathaway appear far below and vanish into a ruined corner of the Parascaenium, Innes beside her. There was still no sign of Johnson. A low broken wall lay between me and the seats. Between this and the outer wall, also broken, were a number of odd tumbled buildings with weeds and bushes growing beside them. I began to walk very slowly from one horn of the terrace around to the other. I wasn't afraid of Sophia. Or at least I wasn't afraid of a private discussion, however nasty, with Sophia. I didn't want another public battle, if I could help it. The voice of Maurice, quoting Sappho, intoned:

"This is the dust of Timas, who died before she
  was married
and whom Persephone's dark chamber
  accepted instead.
After her death the maidens who were her
  friends, with sharp iron
cutting their lovely hair, laid it upon her
  tomb."

I ask you. If ever there was a moment when I
didn't want to hear an obituary, that was it. Good
for Timas. If Sophia cut my throat in the next two
minutes, Di wouldn't so much as chuck me an Asi-
atic bang from Elena's.

However, I have never yet heard of trained astronomers giving way to crimes passionels over a
wristwatch, so I soldiered on. I got halfway along,
too, and was just circumventing a low Roman
blockhouse, or perhaps ticket office and candy stall,
when someone came up and grabbed me.

It was Sophia, with her long yellow hair coming
out of its ribbon and her face livid under the sun-
tan. I tried to drag my arm out of her grip but she
had such a tight hold of me that I couldn't do it. I
said, "You silly twit; I don't care whether you have
it or not, but it isn't mine to hand over. Ask Charles
for it, if you're so thick with him."

It made sense to me, but it didn't seem to reach
Sophia. She not only continued to hang on, but
struck my free hand out of the way with a blow
that made my eyes water and proceeded to scrabble
with my watch buckle, her hair hanging all over the
place. My wrist sawed up and down as I hauled it
away from her and she dragged it back, still unfas-

252

tening it. I continued to reason with her until I saw that she really had got the leather half out of the buckle and then I did what I should have done in the first place: swung my elbow around sharply.

It caught her just under the chin. As her jaws snapped shut, I kicked her legs backward from under her and she went down, dragging me half on top of her. I could tell she'd never played hockey at school. Down below, Maurice, pleased with the sonority of his vowels, had begun on Pindar, of which he seemed to know a great quantity. He had started to throw in some gestures. I scrambled to my knees whipped my hand at last from Sophia's slackened grip and got to my feet quickly.

I had got two paces away from her when her hand around my ankle brought me down again. I no sooner hit the ground than she was over me grimly, one hand grasping my forearm and the other attempting to drag off the wristwatch. Her teeth were sunk in her lip, and covered with Waikiki Coral Ultracreme lipstick. I foiled her that time by dragging my hand to my waist and folding over it, so that she couldn't get at it properly. I said, gasping, "Sophia, I'm *not* giving it to you. Why on earth do you want it?"

She was so excited that she answered in Finnish. Then she said, "Because you stole Charles from me. You shall not have my present. You have taken him and spoiled him and dragged him down. Look at what you have done to him! He cannot marry. You will not let him meet other girls. What can he do, but have sordid, illicit affairs and then come home to you, like a fat German hausfrau, always there, always waiting. He worries about his parents, his family. His friends are married; there is nowhere he is not invited. What does he say? *I have no wife because I have an old mistress who will not go away and I am sorry for her. May I bring her? Her manners are quite good."*

It hurt all right. It hurt a lot, as a matter of fact. But you had to allow for the Northern sense of drama. There wouldn't be any Ingmar Bergman films, for God's sake, if Nordics didn't go on like this as a hobby. I said, "Well, this bloody hausfrau is going to hang on to her gigolo's wristwatch, Sophia. And if it gets into the papers, it will all be too bad. Because the person it will damage most is your precious Charles. Think of it," I said, hissing at her. "He might even be forced to ask me to marry him. And I might even have to accept him."

Which was a mistake, and it was too long since I had seen any Scandinavian movies at that. Sophia leaned forward and sank her teeth in my left ear, and as I yelped and flung up my left hand to stop her, she whipped off the watch and raced off with it.

I staggered onto my feet and zigzagged after her Through the fingers clapped over my ear, I could feel the blood pouring down inside my collar. It didn't stop me from running. Sheer blazing fury, quite apart from the pain, kept me belting after that Finnish maniac until our pounding feet drew even the attention of Maurice. He broke off in the middle of saying, "I wonder, Timothy. A little rebuilding, dear boy, and I think my old *Mistress in China* might do here . . ." and looked up, put out, at the terracing. Innes turned, guidebook in hand, and Jacko shouted "Yoo-hoo!" smiling and waving.

I suppose he thought we were playing catch-as-catch-can. Di, who was wearing a crochet cap with swinging bead drops and her Ariadne outfit, stared up at us without moving but without shouting "Yoo-hoo" at us either. Professor Hathaway and Johnson and Timothy were nowhere visible.

Sophia didn't know the geography of the place. She probably didn't know what to expect at the sides of the amphitheater, and it was on the cards, of course, that any exit there might once have been would have collapsed long ago into a low stack of stones, or a hole. It was because she slowed up, looking about her, that I caught up. That, and the fact that, before or since, I have never run so fast in my life. I got my hand out to grip her just as she hesitated at the end of the terrace. In front of her was a platform with a choice of two possible exits. Beside her was a sheer drop of about thirty feet. At the bottom, looking upward, was the author of *Mistress in China,* the next lot of Pindar struck from him.

She heard me coming behind her. She stopped dead and turned, and I thought she was going to scratch me. She didn't. She put out both arms and came at me, her hair flying, her aim perfectly plain. She was going to push me over the terrace.

She struck me before I could stop her. I felt myself thrown staggering backward. I was thinking of Maurice's poor white mink scalp when a hand gripped my arm over the elbow and, swinging me around like a rotary blade, dragged both my feet onto paving again.

It was Johnson. I think Sophia saw him. I think only then, probably, did she realize what she was doing, because I saw her eyes go suddenly all white, as if the blue bit had vanished under her lids. She was running strongly herself, with her own impetus, but I think she could have stopped herself if she had wanted to.

I saw her decide suddenly not to want to. She went plunging right on to the edge and Johnson, releasing my arm, made one stride after her, found her hair flying past him, and grabbed it.

It was, if you thought of it, a comic tableau. For a moment she looked like a figurehead, bosom forward, chin up and hair straining back in the sea breeze. He had a good grip of it; the full hank with his two hands tight around it. It must have hurt like the devil and she screeched, I was delighted to discover, a damned sight louder than I had. Then she turned her head and came lurching backward, and slithering down at his feet, sat on the paving and had screaming hysterics.

"Silly girl," said Johnson.

He wasn't talking to me, but I yelled at him. "Did you see all that?"

"Yes," said Johnson.

"Then why didn't you stop it?"

"I did," said Johnson. He had taken off the jersey and was wearing a very old cellular shirt with a scarf in it. His bifocals stared at me glassily.

I breathed gustily. "Why didn't you stop it," I said, "before she bit my bloody ear off?"

I took my hand away. Blood still poured from my lacerated earlobe. Sophia, still howling helplessly, continued to sit on the pavement. Johnson looked down at her consideringly. "Should we slap her face?" he said mildly.

"Yes," I said with some venom. "After you've looked at my ear."

Johnson peered at my ear, and then, taking out and folding a handkerchief, proceeded to tie it around my head and neck with the aid of another. It hurt like hell but he did it so carefully that I began to feel, despite everything, faintly mollified. Then I caught the look in his eye behind the glasses.

"I once read something—" said Johnson conversationally, "I'm sure I read something about a sow's ears during sex. It makes you think. I take it the sow finds it's worth it." He slapped Sophia's face lightly on either cheek and she stopped screaming and continued merely to whimper.

"Dear me," said Professor Hathaway, emerging from the staircase and picking her way to the scene. Behind her and pulling out eagerly to overtake were Di and Jacko and Timothy. Maurice, leaning on his stick, was staring upward with some disapproval. Innes was reading his guidebook. With mice, these untidy events just don't happen.

Sophia cried into Professor Hathaway's shoulder and Jacko sat me down on his cardigan on a nice block of marble and Di said, "Good God," rather blankly, and removing her eyes from my bloodstains, added, "Don't tell me it was all because of Charles's stupid watch."

"Yes," I said rather curtly. "Thank God he hadn't lent me his diamond earrings."

"Who has it?" said Johnson. "The watch, I mean. Did Sophia take it?"

"She did," I said. "But I got it back." It was the first thing I did when she sat down. I had

257

it stuffed in my bra, and it was going to stay there.

"I wonder," said Johnson mildly, "if that was sensible."

We all looked at him. Even Sophia's head suddenly lifted and her bunged-up eyes peered through the hair at my friend the portrait painter.

"I think it was very sensible," I said with great distinctness. "In fact, I can think of no possible alternative."

"Of course, keepsakes are special," said Timothy. You could tell that, like Maurice, he didn't hold with untidiness, but his curiosity was absolutely overpowering.

"Yes. Well, this was Sophia's keepsake, not Ruth's," said Johnson kindly. "Ruth, hand it back to Sophia."

"What?" I said. I quacked. I barely, in fact, made myself audible.

"Do you want," said Johnson, "Sophia to have a nervous breakdown? Do you want Charles's name smeared all over the papers? Do you want your other ear bitten?"

I sat, stunned. Stunned and betrayed. "Yes, no, no," I answered.

"Then," said Johnson, "give the watch back."

I stared at him. My ear throbbed. My throat felt tight and tears began to work their way into my eyes. I said, "I won't. It belongs to Charles. He lent it to me. If she wants it back, she can go and ask Charles for it. You don't even know that she gave it to him."

"Don't you?" said Johnson, and stared at me with those impersonal, indecent glass eyes, and I knew what he was going to say before he said it. "Then why else should she want it back?"

For a soft, woolly, indeterminate, badly dressed Englishman, he was the hardest man I ever met in my life. I knew it wasn't any use for me to argue. I knew, and he knew, that he was going to get his own way.

I fished inside my sticky bra and brought out the watch and held it out, hot and filthy and covered with blood, to Sophia.

For a moment, I thought she was going to snatch it and fling it into the orchestra. She took it and clutched it for a moment, her nose running and her lips pressed together. Then she got to her feet and walked off, her head turned aside, her clenched hand still pressed to her bosom.

We watched her go. Then everyone looked down at me and began cooing.

I said a very, very bad word and stalked down the stairs and out of the Taormina Greek theater. *Mistress in China* might do all right, as Maurice said. But Mistress in Rome had been a hell of a failure.

CHAPTER 15

AND THAT, no one will be surprised to learn, was the moment I decided I was going back to Rome. The too-marvelous-for-words beauty of this happy piece of earth had had it, so far as this scientific observer was concerned, and so had whatever non-event was awaiting us all in the Villa San Michele, Capri. I wanted to take my ear back to safety and Charles.

Everyone agreed this was reasonable. It should have made me suspicious. Even Johnson, on whom I was running out, listened to me with patience as we walked two-by-two along the half-made highway from the cable car and said only, "It's up to you. But you know Capri may be our last chance of finding evidence which will indicate Charles absolutely?"

"I know," I said. "And I hereby invest you with

full plenipotentiary powers to deal with it. You might have better luck than you had at the Argonese Castle."

The bifocals turned on me reproachfully. "I wasn't expecting an outside attack on you."

I said, "I wonder what you *were* expecting?"

"Sparks," said Johnson. "We got those. Just enough to show, perhaps, where the fire is."

All good, enigmatic stuff but it didn't make me burst into tears and beg to be landed on Capri. I left Johnson and, moving up to Maurice, requested a passage on *Sappho* to Naples. Maurice, putting a gentle ringed hand on my shoulder, said he would adore to have me on *Sappho,* and he and Timothy and Lilian Hathaway were coming too. Professor Hathaway, drawing abreast of us, remarked that she also would be happy to get back and see what Bob and Eddie were up to in Naples. And that she would give the girl Lindrop a talking to.

My mouth dropped open, which drew a pang from my ear. The ear is one of the most difficult parts of the anatomy to bandage. That is, if you don't mind a bandage tied right around your head, including your nose and your mouth, it is easy. I said, "Is Sophia Lindrop still sailing on *Sappho?*"

Professor Hathaway said, "I had forgotten. It would be rather bad psychology, wouldn't it, to place you two together? But you know, Ruth, that Lindrop child does need help. She feels rejected. She had seen her fiancé throw her over for another woman. I won't say Lord Digham was wrong, but it has damaged her view of herself as a person. She needs her ego re-established."

"Well," I said. "They're your ears." And, "Johnson," I said, as soon as we had boarded *Dolly,* "please, Johnson, will you take me straight to Naples?"

He wouldn't, the rat. He was still fixated on that bloody fish and the probably nonexistent appointment on Capri.

"Johnson," I said. "Dear Johnson, will you take Sophia Lindrop then, instead?"

Those chilly, twin-arched bifocals inspected me. "You look after your life cycle," Johnson said, "and I'll look after mine. Sophia Lindrop is traveling on *Sappho.*"

"In that case," I said, "I am spending the night at the hotel. And tomorrow I am flying to Naples. Kindly ask Lenny to load my case into the speedboat."

At the hotel landing quay a page was waiting, asking me what my name was. A Lord Digham was calling from Naples.

It was Charles. The lawyers had sprung him. He was in Naples, he said, crackling furiously over all the Italian wiring, because I had said I was bloody well going to be there with Jacko and the others. He had had to telephone Maurice's villa to find out where to find me.

You cannot dispatch waves of deathless emotion across a communications system that sounds like an earthquake. In any case I could hardly speak from bewilderment and excitement. The case against Charles had been dropped, and there was no hint, as Johnson had warned, of a worse one. Charles was free. The laborious circuit on which *Dolly* was launched didn't matter. Someone else had committed those murders; someone else was involved in international spying but as far as I was concerned they could get on with it. Or perhaps the police had caught the real culprits already.

I didn't try to ask any questions; the line was too terrible. I yelled that I would catch the next plane to Naples, if he would meet me. And in a fit of madness I added that Sophia had taken his wristwatch, and was sailing to Capri with Maurice.

I hoped he would be reassuringly upset, but I wasn't prepared for a stunned silence. Charles said, *"What?"*

"Here in Taormina," I said. "Sophia. Fought me for your watch. Became friendly with Maurice. He's dropping her on Capri on Monday."

"It was your watch," said Charles. It came over very plainly, and sounded just beautiful. "What the hell does that bloody bitch want with your watch?"

"She says she loves you!" I yelled. An elderly Italian couple, walking slowly past, turned and gave me a stare.

A lot of swearing came over the line, followed by an inquiry. I said, reassuringly, "Capri on Monday, but it doesn't matter. Let it go. It doesn't matter. I'll see you tomorrow in Naples."

It transpired that he didn't want to see me tomorrow in Naples. He wanted to get to Capri tomorrow to tear the guts out of Sophia when she landed on Monday.

I didn't want Charles on Capri on Monday. Even if he were now free as air I didn't want Charles anywhere near anything that might happen on Capri on Monday. But if it was a toil blowing kisses over that god-awful telephone, it was a mind-blowing flop trying to argue. I shrieked that I would see him in Naples and he shrieked that he was going to Capri. I finally shrieked that I would go to Capri therefore on *Dolly,* and he could look out for me also on Monday. I wasn't going to leave him alone with Sophia, even for the purpose of mincing her.

I canceled my room and semaphored for *Dolly*'s speedboat. It was Johnson himself who came in it. Before he tied up I'd told him the story and he agreed, reloading my suitcase, that I might as well go to Capri on *Dolly*. He didn't seem either surprised or apprehensive, just cooperative. I said, "I didn't want him on Capri, but he insisted. He was furious. Furious with Sophia. If you hadn't given her the watch he wouldn't have wanted to go. But if the police have freed him, they can't be suspicious. Does it matter?"

I didn't mean to sound anxious. I did mean Johnson to clasp me by the hand and say, richly laughing, that it didn't matter. Instead he said, eyeing the shallows, that it probably didn't, provided that Charles wasn't caught in the Villa Michele handing over a submarine to a masked man in knee boots. Then he got the engine going and we wheeled out in an arc toward *Dolly*.

He didn't talk, and I wondered how I had offended him. Perhaps he was cross because I wouldn't come to Capri when he needed me, but would change all my plans to meet Charles there. Or was it possible that he had thought all along that Charles was guilty, and that he was annoyed that the Rome police had freed him?

Surely not. He was a clever man. And he had been honest with me.

It was a wonderful night; warm and bright with *Dolly* and *Sappho* resting each on a gloss of lit water. Farther out, the big fishing boats moved about, no longer gaudy blue and orange but graceful as gondolas with the lanterns hung bright in their prows.

On the land, the frantic traffic had slowed down at last: the khaki trains had ceased to hurtle past, blaring into the bowels of the next hill, their interminable trucks snaking after them. The steams of pale cars and lorries of incredible color and length crossing the straddling bright orange viaducts no longer filled the air with chirps and burbles and chortles, or the single, embittered cry with which they raced from tunnel to tunnel.

All had died away. Only by the constellations pricking the hills could you tell where the villages lay, and only when you looked at them long enough did you see how the hill lights were mixed with the tears.

The hill lights looked the more friendly. Perhaps I had chosen to turn my eyes in quite the wrong direction.

When we reached and climbed aboard *Dolly,* Jacko and Innes were there at the rail to help bring in my suitcase. Professor Hathaway had already left, they said, to become Maurice's guest on the *Sappho*.

Innocent that I am, I thought this left me the use of the master cabin. Then I saw the litter of striped velvet luggage and met six pairs of disgusted blue eyelashes, as Di emerged nude from my loo and surveyed me.

"*Christ!*" said Di. "It's like having a continuous

ink-flow ear tattooing machine for my bloody birthday. Why aren't you flying to Naples?"

"I'm sorry," I said, "if I'm spoiling anything. Charles is out. He's meeting us all on Capri."

"In that case," said Di, picking up ·a lit cigarette and heeling her clothes, with some effect, onto one of the bunks, "can we poor groaning bitches hope that you will settle down to *one* of your men and fling the other one out for retexturing?"

I said, "I thought you were pairing with Jacko." I was sorry for Jacko. Even after seeing what he had got hold of in Lipari, I was sorry for him.

"Ruth darling. A Minicucci," said Di, "always has the master bedroom. But not usually, I may say, with a bloody girl in it."

There was a brief silence. "Well," I said finally, *"I'm* not pairing with Jacko. Hard luck, Minicucci. If you don't like the henrun, you'll have—"

". . . to make do with the cockpit," said Di bitterly, echoing me. The thing she put on for dinner was, I swear, infrared as well as transparent and I sat back and watched Jacko squirming. I ate insalata mista (1 sardina; patate gr. 100). Innes got lightly squiffed and Johnson talked, as I remember, about Samurai body-painting, while sketching Di's trunk on the cloth in French mustard.

That man is an intellectual snob, a pouff and a traitor.

Charles was waiting for us on the strip of quay under the rock face at Capri playing football with the local kids when *Dolly* sailed into the harbor on Monday. He lobbed the ball and turned to catch the rope Lenny chucked him. It was morning and the sun was shining and he was wearing his hair brushed sideways and a chain belt and a Renaissance gold locket I'd given him and a grin with Entrapped Butter Flavor that would have warmed Timothy's cockles.

Sappho, which had sailed with us all the way from Taormina, was just coming in behind us to drop Sophia, but Charles didn't give her a glance. He vaulted aboard *Dolly* before Johnson had laid down the gangplank and collected me in a very satisfactory fashion. After a long, suffocating interval he let me go and kissed Di, who was wearing a scowl and a large cotton Stetson.

He mentioned, with a considering expression, that I had grown a few bones since he left me. I didn't mention the diet. But I felt I had arrived at the great crossroads of my pilgrimage: the moment of transfer from Dieta Dimagrante to Dieta Mantenimento.

He didn't comment on my blighted ear because I wore a silk head scarf tied pirate-style over it. The effect was rakish. *Sappho,* whose little man had the disadvantage of having Maurice and Timothy to tell him what to do, arrived rather unhandily and began to back into position beside us. In a moment, a lot of luggage was going to come off, followed by Sophia Lindrop. Charles was saying, ". . . So Sassy got three months, the absolute idiot, and they let me go free with a talking-to. Mother asked where you were. She wants a chat with you." He added, without changing his tone,

"You loved me mother, when I was small
And I won't forget you now I've grown tall."

"Still no sale," I said calmly. "My family wouldn't let me tie myself to a jailbird."

He cuffed my ear, and I let out a yell that would have made all the Valkyries drop their spears and Wotan go pretty spare into the bargain. Charles snatched back his fingers.

"Her ear," Johnson explained. "Sophia bit it, trying to get your watch back."

Charles said, *"Bit it!"* over a drop of eight semitones just as *Sappho's* companionway thudded into position and Maurice and Professor Hathaway and Timothy appeared at the head of it, all taking turns at kissing Sophia. Then she began to walk down it followed by Timothy, a steel-banded leather case in each hand. She was wearing white knee socks with a camel-hair jacket and Bermudas, and her smooth hair was bound with a bandeau. Below her dark glasses her face looked pale and pure and pathetically vulnerable.

She knew I was on *Dolly,* having seen me. But she didn't know our jailbird was at liberty. She stalked down to the quay and pulled up short, to find Charles looming over her. The rest of us, hesitating on the plank, stepped onto the quay and stood doubtfully watching them. Charles rested one hand on his hip and stared down at Sophia's upturned glasses.

"Charles! You're free! I'm so glad!" said Sophia quickly. She lifted both hands and held them toward him. The inside of her mouth, even, looked pallid.

He smiled. It was a deep, groovy smile and anyone might have been thrilled with it, except that he still didn't say anything. He didn't take her hands either. Sophia's eyes behind her dark glasses turned slightly in my direction and then back to Charles. She said, "Darling? I have so much to say to you. Come. Maurice will let us sit down and talk. You are not looking well."

I moved around and looked at him. He was looking well. He just didn't look sent over Sophia. She said, "Or in the town? Let me put my bags in the observatory, and we shall meet somewhere and talk. You do not know what has been happening, Charles. You must listen to me while I tell you."

"Oh, I know what's been happening," said Charles mildly. "You attacked a scientific worker from a private observatory and made off with her personal property. Ruth hasn't gone to the police, but I shall."

"She told you that?" said Sophia. "But do you really think, knowing me, that I would want anyone else's belongings? What I wished back was yours, the watch I had given you." She lifted her hands nervously to her glasses and, taking them off, stood looking down into them. She said, whispering, "It broke my heart to see her wearing it."

There was a tear, actually, on her cheek. It glistened in the sunshine and Timothy's eyes became misty. He put down the suitcases. "I expect it did, darling," said Charles callously. He was still standing squarely in front of her, his hand on his hip. "But it still wasn't your property. I worked for that bloody watch on a standard wage scale with guaranteed overtime rates and workers' grievance procedures and if you want it back you'll have to apply to the union. If I chose to hand it to a one-eyed Singhalese elephant-driver, it'd still be none of your bloody business. Hand it over."

I stood there like a one-eyed Singhalese elephant-driver and wondered what line Sophia could possibly take. She said abruptly, "I wanted something of yours. Something to keep when you are not with me. Something to remember you by."

Charles held his stomach and slid the hand from his hip into his pocket. It came out with a fiver, English money, which he slapped into Sophia's palm and abandoned there. "Something of mine," said Charles lucidly. "You've laid your oversexed little claws on my girl, darling Sophia, and if I weren't a gentleman you would be hitting that water, with a fat jaw to show just what I think of you. I want that watch, and I am not waiting, really, any longer. My watch. Or the police, Sophia. Or if you'd like it better I'll strip you here and now, till I find it."

He had the right idea, even if his enthusiasm now and then ran away with him. Timothy was sitting on one of the suitcases and Johnson on the other while Innes fidgeted, red-faced and aghast, just behind them. The complement of *Sappho* were not quite visible but definitely, I thought, within earshot; Jacko and Diana appeared to be neither. It came to me that while the cameras were rolling, Jacko was probably having it off in my cabin. Excitement takes some people that way. Everything takes Jacko that way, and Di quicker than anybody. Then Charles lifted his hand and Sophia screamed, "She shan't have it!"

"Give it!" Charles commanded. He had her by the elbow.

"She shan't! The jackal! The whore! The hag, she shan't have my watch that I gave you. The promises you made me!" She was crying now, her arm wrenched back from Charles's grip; the glasses jerking as she flung her hands upward. "What else is she wearing of mine?"

"A bloody ear. Would you like one to match it?" Charles added. The children had stopped playing football and were staring at him.

Sophia turned her head, breathing heavily. Timothy, transfixed by her gaze, stood up slowly. Johnson, with interest, rose to his feet smoothly also. "Timothy. Shall we go on?" said Sophia abruptly. Timothy hesitated.

Sophia sidestepped and walked sharply past Charles. Charles instantly moved just as quickly and planted himself in her path once again. "Not before I have the watch back," he said baldly. Timothy, lifting the cases, wandered up and stood helpfully behind them.

"No," said Sophia. She moved to the right.

Charles moved to the right.

She moved to the left.

He stepped sideways and blocked her.

She walked six paces, very fast, to the rock wall and, as he made to follow her, she bent and seized the children's ball which had dropped to her feet.

She might not have played all that much hockey, but she would have been a sensation at rounders. She chucked the ball straight at Charles's chest and if he hadn't fielded it with a snatch, he might well have been carried right over the quayside.

She had already started to run when he caught it. He whirled with the ball in his hands and, lifting it, hurled it straight after her. It hit her behind the Bermudas. She went full length on the path, with Timothy, uttering little cries, jettisoning the suitcases and charging after her. The rest of us followed more slowly.

Timothy was helping her up when Charles arrived. Her glasses were cracked and the look on her face as she flung them off almost made up for what happened in Taormina. Charles said, "The watch, please, Sophia."

I didn't know why the hell it mattered, but it seemed that it did. Perhaps it was symbolic or something. I know by that time I couldn't have cared if I had been offered Big Ben next to take home on castors. At any rate, Sophia knew when she was beaten. She put her hand into her bag and drew out Charles's beautiful watch. She held it out, and he reached out to take it. Then she dropped it on the path and ground it under her stout heel to powder.

We all looked at Charles, including Johnson, who now strolled forward, his bifocals glistening. He said, "Go on. Sock her one and then throw her over the quayside."

Charles, who had both his fists up, pulled himself together. "What?" he said.

"Decadent product of a Victorian educational system," Johnson said. He footed the ball in the direction of the children, who trapped it without moving and continued to stand in a trance, staring. Sophia kicked the remains of the wristwatch.

"There!" she said. "So much for your token of love. It is no use your coming to me when you are tired of her. I never want to see you again."

"Charles," I murmured. I was afraid he would cease to be a decadent product of a Victorian system and actually sock it to her. "You have to concede a ruff and discard. Goodbye, Sophia."

"Goodbye, Sophia," everyone said, eventually, in varying cadences. Timothy picked up the bags. After a moment, she turned on her heel and walked off, followed gently by Timothy. I said, "Charles. Now you won't be able to go to her when you're tired of me. She said she met you in Naples."

"She certainly did," said Charles with some feeling. "She wanted all her presents back. I told her she could have them when I got back the price of her engagement ring."

"She didn't offer you a bed," I suggested happily, "whenever you felt like a little variety?"

"Come off it," said Charles. "Of course she did. Do you think I'm losing my first bloom or something? She offered, and I fancy I kept her hoping. It's supposed to be kinder.

> *"Memories are like threads of gold,*
>   *Never tarnish or grow old."*

"It is not kinder," I said firmly, "to the older, permanent work force. Please be realistic in your dealings in future."

"Come on," said Johnson. "The ball's at your feet, Digham's Jackal."

It was, too. I even kicked a couple of goals, as I remember. Then I recalled it was the morning of Monday, November 20, and the day of the late Mr. Paladrini's last assignment and my footwork went off.

CHAPTER 16

I TOLD CHARLES after that who Johnson was. He took a long time to believe it and even when I brought Johnson in to confirm it, he couldn't quite keep his face straight. I was glad I had mentioned it. The letter I wrote to Charles in prison had never reached him and he had begun to wonder, who wouldn't, what the hell I was up to, wandering about the Tyrrhenian in Johnson's yacht in November.

So I told him about the list of dates, and what had happened on all the islands, which was a complete mistake because his chromosomes all began waving flags and he settled down nose to nose with Johnson in my stateroom masterminding the afternoon's visit to the Villa San Michele.

I squeezed up and down, passing them gins and pointing out that now it didn't matter a damn. Nobody was assaulting us, so the criminal element must have come to realize that Charles's pictures were truly disposed of. Charles wasn't implicated any longer. The idea that anyone in authority might have suspected him of complicity in the murders was so novel that we couldn't get him to take that seriously either and stopped trying. The final stupid outcome of that masculine conference was that both twits were hellbent on going to the Villa San Michele that afternoon and neither appeared to think it necessary, as I kept pointing out, for Charles to get the hell out of it. The other natural disaster was that I had to tell Charles I had developed his photographs.

I kept my cool, telling him because I'd had twenty-four hours to rehearse it in. Johnson lit his pipe. Charles went rather red and then said, reasonably, "Why?"

I wished Johnson wasn't there. I wished I had had two minutes alone with Charles since Sophia departed and we had all come back on board *Dolly*. I said, and could feel my own face growing hot, "I thought you knew they'd pinched the wrong camera. I thought you'd been using the other one perhaps for pictures of Sophia."

I could feel Johnson looking at me and I didn't care. I've never met a man yet who minded his girl friend being jealous of someone else. But I wasn't going to let Charles know my faith in him had dimmed, even for the space of an evening. I said, "I was an ass. And I'm sorry I burned them. Johnson says if I hadn't, it would have cleared you of suspicion immediately."

I added, tentatively,

"The kindness of his nature
The sunshine of his smile
Are things I shall remember
and treasure all the while?"

"I'm not sorry," Charles said. He took my hand and pulling me suddenly down to sit beside him continued to hold it so tightly that it hurt. He said rather thickly, "They were rotten pictures anyway," and at that moment, thank God, Johnson remembered something he had to do, and took himself off.

When we both emerged, to let a sarcastic Diana have access at last to her stateroom, it was to find that the spy fever had spread like foot-and-mouth disease through both yachts, embracing even the worldly sybarites of the *Sappho,* who had come on board *Dolly* to lunch with us. At three o'clock that afternoon, I could see, the Villa San Michele was liable to be thronged by excited astronomers calling to one another the now classic phrase, *Let's capture the bastards.*

Johnson did what he could to defuse us. "Do remember," he said, uncorking bottles. "Unless the message in Paladrini's flat has been seen and understood by the two parties concerned—the seller of information and the purchaser—nothing will happen today whatsoever."

Innes recrossed his legs irritably. He said, "Anyone looking for information about his next rendezvous wouldn't find Paladrini's flat, surely, hard to get into. Relatives, to remove the effects. Workmen, to repair the ceiling."

"It seems mad to me," Jacko said. "Why smuggle

over the date of an appointment when you might as well hand over the loot on the spot?"

The Professor's pebble glasses inclined toward this evidence of superficial thinking and Jacko wilted faintly in his folding chair. "I can think of several reasons," said Lilian Hathaway. "The material may not always be of convenient size to hand over in public. Provided the amount of contact is kept to a minimum, a mobile liaison office such as the balloon cart could be used over and over again, and doubtless has been. And lastly, it argues, does it not, that an appointment for the future is made because at the time of contact the merchandise itself is not yet available?

"Had the missing couture photographs been in Ruth's possession at the time of the attack on her in Ischia, no doubt they would have figured in the next meeting. Perhaps this was why the San Michele arrangement was made; in which case the seller has still to explain to the purchaser that he has nothing to give him. And I doubt if anywhere on the island you would find a house and garden with more secret corners for such an encounter than San Michele. Axel Munthe, of course, was a most unusual gentleman."

"You know the villa?" said Johnson.

"I have had cause to visit it," said Professor Hathaway calmly.

She had been to the Grotta Azzurra as well, so it transpired, and gave us a lucid account of the refractive effects of the sun's rays filtered through cavern water. I could see Jacko's illusions all wilting. Then she said that she would be glad to conduct us on a tour of the San Michele pre-

278

cincts and who else wished to be of the party? Too
many Chiefs, as well, and not enough unfortunate
Indians.

It appeared that everyone but Maurice and Di,
who wanted to get her hair done, wished to be of
the party; and Maurice only opted out because any
party Maurice is in has to be Maurice's party, and
this wasn't. In all, six of us fell into line behind
Johnson when he left the boat at 1300 that afternoon: Charles and I and Professor Hathaway, together with Jacko and Innes and Timothy.

We were, it is fair to say, inclinged to giggle. It
seemed enough, on the face of it, to frighten off
the toughest conspirators, but Johnson did nothing to stop it. He probably couldn't. Only Charles
and I, after all, knew his curiosity had official endorsement. All I could do was resolve not to let
Charles Digham leave my sight until the visit to
Capri was over, and a fat lot of good that was to
do me.

It was rather warm, I remember, and Jacko wore
moss green shorts with laced flies which the natives of Capri in their winter wool thought dead
dishy. Charles had on a needlecord shirt with a
flower pattern and a jeweled belt around his pants.
Johnson wore a white keyhole sweater and flannels:
L'Escalade de l'Erotisme. "Dear boy," said Maurice, "you look like a veteran seed with no balls
left. Do look after the children. I trust you."

Someone said that Capri was shaped like a slip-
per. From where we were floating, it was like two
mountainous knobs with a saddle between them.
At the bottom of the saddle is the big harbor with
a half circle of houses and shops and trattorias

279

swarming with traffic and tenders and cruise ships in season. The quickest way to Capri proper, which is the top of the saddle, is by funicular. From there, San Michele is reached by taking a winding hill road to the right-hand cliff, on which sits the little town of Anacapri.

'We all got into the scarlet carriage of the funicular and allowed Timothy to describe to us the orgies of the Emperor Hadrian while the fig and orange and lemon trees and the tops of the villas disappeared slowly down by our feet. A notice on the wall said, SEGNALE D'ALLARME: *In caso di pericolo, tirare la maniglia.* I thought if anything happened to this carriage, the Pope wouldn't get his picture and the Trust would need a new director, so why should I worry.

Then we got to the top, and walked around to the Umberto I Square, which is pure, living Kodak, with white buildings and greenery and café chairs and tables and a little square tower containing a blue and yellow clock with Roman digits just like my telescope.

It reminded Charles of something else altogether.

> *"Like falling leaves the years slip by*
> *But memories will never die*
> *Time may pass and fade away*
> *But thoughts of you will always stay."*

A sad thing happens with Charles and myself. If the setting becomes too romantic, he tips over into obituary verses. I suppose this is why I weep all the way through teleromanzi. I know moments of high romance will never come my way with wine and moonlight and soft violins playing. If Charles didn't break down and cackle, then I should.

We piled into two taxis for Anacapri.

With seven of us up, the taxis nearly didn't make it, and the steam was rising to the pine trees as we finally wheezed into the little square and tumbled out at our destination.

We were too early. There was no one standing about the sunken park with a Gents in the middle, or the hotels and houses and shops built around it. In front of us, a notice said TO THE VILLA SAN MICHELE. Behind that rose a large modern hotel with a submarine window let into its swimming pool. The only natives in sight were grouped before that green aqueous rectangle through which moved the stomach of a stout woman performing the breast stroke.

It was like the fish tank in the Ischia restaurant. Johnson said, "Let's go up in the chair lift."

One of Johnson's larky ideas, and very funny until it turned out that he meant it. Jacko, told there was a terrace with beer at the top, became instantly enthusiastic. I thought of the stiff in the meat safe. Some people never learn from life's lessons.

Innes was made of different stuff. "You bent on living dangerously?" he inquired of Johnson with sarcasm. "The view?" offered Timothy placatingly. He was anxious for Johnson to be pleased.

"Ah. The view," said Professor Hathaway, and we all turned and looked at her.

Charles got her point in fact before I did. "The view of San Michele," he said, looking at Johnson. "Granted. But if we can watch the approach

281

path, won't our quarry be aware of seven high-level spectators? Two taxiloads of yachtsmen in November can hardly have escaped anyone's notice. We must be notorious."

He was right. As far as public argument went, we must have the Runners-up Art Deco Cufflinks already. Johnson said patiently, "Ponder this. If this meeting hasn't already been canceled it's only because the two people concerned haven't been warned about us. And if they haven't been warned, two taxi-loads of bent foreign yachtsmen won't worry them."

"Well said," said Lilian Hathaway. "Likewise, what man of sense would attempt to dispose of seven people? Where is the chair lift?"

At Anacapri, the chair lift is like any other. You place your feet on a pair of red footprints, then the chair steals upon you from behind and sweeps you into the air, while a safety bar clips at your middle. Professor Hathaway was lifted first; then Charles and Timothy and Innes and Jacko. Johnson put me in the next chair and then seated himself in the last one. We rocketed heavenward.

I don't mind heights. I like, Charles maintains, being above people. I enjoyed looking down into their gardens and their vegetable patches, and passing their lanes and their roofs and their henhouses. The chairs were very close, in Anacapri, to the chimney tops. You could kick the tallest vine stakes with your sandals. You brushed the tops of their greenery: lilac bushes and olives and almonds, little poplars and oak trees growing densely below you in silence.

That was the main surprise: the lushness, the

mild air and the quietness. Sometimes a bird would twitter in the pine trees. Sometimes, far off among the dipping white houses, you heard the snore of a motorbike or the beat of a tool, distantly hammering. But up here in space there was silence, save for the four hissing wheels of each pylon as the chairs swung from tower to tower.

Ahead, depending from its single rod, I could see the chair with Jacko in it, his camera appearing first on one side and then on the other. The others, dark figures against the sky, were crossing the next chasm, beyond which the terrain seemed much wilder, with grass and bushes and slabs of crumpled gray rock underneath.

I wondered how high exactly was the mountain we were thus ascending. Parallel with us the empty chairs came swooping down on the other side of the pylons, their worn seats bearing the imprint of God knows how many thousands of summertime tourist bottoms.

Our seats were facing away from the villa. I turned around, my eyes searching for bearings. Behind me, Johnson was doing the same, standing embracing the bucketing rod, his binoculars pressed to his glasses.

If anything was manic stupid, that was. I made to call him, and decided against it. I sat fuming while we swept up to a tower. The ripped-silk noise of the wheels sang out and diminished. We began descending the arc to the next one. Johnson changed his stance as he too passed the tower. For a moment he released the rod while he focused his binoculars. I swore, and bumped around, glaring, to see if Jacko had noticed.

He hadn't. He was still taking photographs. After a moment, his elbows went down and he looked around, like a man who is expecting a shower. It was so quiet that you could hear the sparrows rustle below us. It was perfectly quiet. It was perfectly quiet because the wheels had stopped running.

My chair slid slowly to the bottom of its arc and remained there, rocking gently above the tiled and tumbledown roof of a very small cabin. A number of hens pecked about in a dirt yard. A dog, running out of a shed, began to set up a high, monotonous yapping. I twisted around to yell out to Johnson.

Johnson wasn't there. The chair seat behind me was empty.

He had therefore toppled out. He had (a) overbalanced when the power left the cable. He had (b) been stoned as the chair stopped. He had (c) been shot with a silencer.

> *God took our Johnson for a star*
> *To love and guide us from afar.*

I had lost him.

Then I saw the tree beside which Johnson's vacant chair had halted. And Johnson climbing down it, with his tennis pullover glinting like eglantine among the graceful green branches. He got to the ground and waved, just as remote cries began to issue from the rest of our immobilized party.

I was waving back when a skylight in the roof just below me creaked and groaningly opened. A ladder rose into the sky with the spectral lassitude of Jacob's dream, projected in slow motion and backward. The hens fluttered. Johnson appeared, the dog snapping about him, and called, but not too loudly. "Do you think you can climb it?"

I could climb his ladder. I wasn't sure if I wanted to. I looked ahead, to where Jacko was carrying on an acrimonious conversation with Innes, and behind, where the only view seemed to consist of two vanishing cables holding a lot of dangling seats, emphatically immobile. I lifted the bar over my waist, hitched my bottom over the seat and lowered myself till my feet found the ladder.

Johnson helped me into the house, and then downstairs and out of it, accompanied by the beatific sound of the passing of many great lire. Just as we got to the ground, Jacko turned around in his high seat and bellowed.

I was rather touched to observe that he'd missed me. Johnson cupped his hands and yelled something at him. He promised, I think, to send a mechanic. At any rate, he then took me by the hand and began running with no style but a great deal of speed down the path and back to the platform where we had started. I said, "What about freeing the others?"

"They're too high to get down," said Johnson with absolute accuracy.

We continued to belt down the pathway. "What," I said, "if they can't get the machinery started?"

"They won't get to the villa on time," Johnson said. "What a pity."

What a pity. I stopped dead in my tracks, and the jerk as he skidded me forward nearly shattered my wishbone. I started running again, but methodically. I said, "You fixed it."

"I fixed it," Johnson agreed. He didn't sound

penitent. "Who would suspect two taxiloads of bent tourists?" he'd said, or something like it. "Who," Professor Hathaway had said, "would attempt to dispose of seven people?"

"Listen," I said. I tried to speak reasonably. "What if someone is waiting to go to the villa at fifteen hundred? What if they were about to call off the meeting, and then discover the opposition has reduced itself to you and me? What if they try to knock us off? Hell," I said, hauling viciously on his pulling arm so that he was forced at least to turn around and look at me, "at least Innes Wye had his Dardick."

"Ruth," Johnson said very gently. He took me by the arm and walked me past the Hotel Europe with its voyeurs and into a dark and flowery lane all shaded with trees. "I haven't a Dardick," Johnson said, "but I have a little thought I'd like you to receive and mull over. Whoever will be in the Villa Michele at three P.M., it won't by any conceivable chance be Charles Digham."

He was an intellectual snob, a pouff and a traitor. He was also a man of great cunning. I went to heel and walked on with my trap shut.

The Villa San Michele lay on the right past the souvenir stalls. At 1430 hours, we entered it.

Tickets were sold in the vestibule. It was a quiet day, the attendant said, glad to find someone to talk to. One or two gentlemen in the morning. This afternoon, a pair of ladies with cameras and Mr. Frazer. Mr. Frazer, did we know him, the playwright?

Indeed, said Johnson. He showed no surprise and quelled with a douche of his glasses the open-

286

eyed stare I was trying to throw him. We turned right into the small white-walled rooms and enclosed patios of the villa itself and he hissed each time I spoke until I lost patience and confronted him. We were in the monumental bedroom, as I remember, beside the monolithic uncanopied four-poster and the statues and the heavy carved seat-pieces. "All right," I said. "All right. I'm here and you're here and Maurice is here and everyone else is dangling in the air above Monte Solaro. To protect Charles, maybe, but that isn't everything. Can I induce you to tell me what's happening?"

"I have an idea," Johnson said. "Perhaps Maurice has the same one." He touched the chairs, walked around the bed and went and stood under the arch by the window, peering about him.

He made me nervous. Ever since we had entered the villa he had explored it as if he were going to buy it, prodding the statues, passing his hands over the carved fragments plastered into the walls, lifting the cushions. The guide hadn't come with us, and it was just as well. I've seen a few bus parties in my time, but none as ferrety as Johnson Johnson.

"I have an idea," he continued now, peering out of the window, "that there is to be no nasty encounter in the Villa San Michele at the hour of fifteen hundred today. I think something else entirely is going to happen. I think a message is about to be picked up."

The occasion seemed to warrant a little grammar. "From whom to whom?" I asked, whispering flutily. "And what?" I added, as an afterthought.

"From whom, I can't prove," Johnson said. "But it can't have been left before latish this morning, which makes the attendant's news all the more interesting. And to whom we may never know, because whoever is going to lift it will make quite sure he is not observed doing it. But what, is a different matter. That is what I hope we are going to discover."

"A message," I said, helplessly mourning. The rooms connected like a jigsaw puzzle; up and down steps, through little piazzas and terraces. And outside, acre on glamorous acre, stretched the gardens, with the white gleams of statues and fountains.

"A written message, tucked somewhere known to the searcher. Come on," said Johnson. "We haven't all day. Let's do over the chapel."

We did over the chapel, which was full of holy paintings and open-pored wooden statues and atmosphere. We walked over mosaic and peered between barley sugar columns of marble and, emerging, climbed the flowery paths to the summerhouse. We nosed our way through the loggia, its white pillars twisted with greenery.

Axel Munthe had built his crash pad on what remained of a big Roman villa, and into it he had squirreled all of ancient Rome that could be found on the island. Leaning over the wall between the Korda pillars you saw the sea lying burnished beneath you, with the yellow-gray of the cliffs rising from it, and the pale broken arms of the harbor. A white tourist liner moved in, as big as my finger, and the Sorrentino ferry, and the white wakes behind them. The other islands floated sugar-pale on the water and the Italian coast showed, blue and low far behind them. A woman's voice said, "Oh,

Mr. Frazer. Oh, Mr. Frazer, how can we thank you?"

Johnson started to laugh. It was so irritating I could have cuffed him.

I straightened and so, more smoothly, did Johnson. From the distant curve of the loggia stepped the noble figure of the owner of the Frazer Observatory, blandly smiling. Two ladies in tweed suits and felt hats and cameras were backing before him, genteelly driveling. Maurice stopped, cigar in hand, by a statue. The soft white hair, freshly cut by the artist, strayed across the magnificent forehead. "In this haunted bower, what impulses cannot flower; what encounter does not have its meaning, deeper than any we poor mortals may reach for. You have a right profile, dear lady. You may, if you wish, take my left. Various, I fear, as a chameleon. The curse of the mummer."

He posed, pouting smoke, for a further exposure, and as they bagged their photometers, shook their hands warmly. They walked slowly past us, flushed and moonily smiling and I wondered, as Johnson glanced at them, if either man envied the other.

Maurice had style, panache, courtship, indeed adulation. Johnson had more woolly jerseys, and the recognition due to his profession. If you discerned in him anything remarkable, he forced you to recognize it with the eye of the intellect.

The snobbery which once I had accused him of. Or perhaps merely the requirements of his other, confidential profession. Perhaps he yearned for tight pants and chain belts and contact lenses. Perhaps he indulged in them secretly, with a round bed and a blond fashion editress in Hampstead. "Johnson! And Ruth darling," said Maurice, allowing us to approach him. "I worry too much, and so does poor, motherly Lilian. There you are, hand in hand and perfectly happy." Only Maurice at his most elvish would think of calling Lilian Hathaway motherly. He added, "I thought you were all coming at three. Where are the others?"

"Held up," said Johnson vaguely.

"I know. I saw the chair lift stop. My dear boy," said Maurice, "haven't you done anything yet to release them? One would think you were here with an ulterior motive."

His pink, preserved face with the bright eyes and the actor's vivid lines surveyed us maliciously. Maurice was making the running. Maurice, who had nearly ruined the assignation outside the Castel Sant' Angelo. Maurice, who was supposed to be reposing on *Sappho,* and who was here instead, prudently in advance of the multitude and no doubt caught only because two ladies with cameras had happened to be in the Villa San Michele's interesting gardens.

Johnson was not put out in the least. "I am," he said. "I wanted to see who would be here at three o'clock."

"Exactly my intention," said Maurice. "I thought of squatting behind the splendid statue of . . . is it Hymenaeus? Timothy would know exactly. But this is one of those days when my cigar will only draw in the open." He surveyed Johnson. "If you wish to squat, dear boy, please do not hesitate."

"Thank you, but I'm not allowed. It bags my trousers," said Johnson. His trousers were ruched like Harris Tweed window drapes and so, I make no doubt, was his underwear.

"I told your man Lenny," said Maurice. "I said, don't lurk about bagging your trousers. Come in the taxi with me. He did. I just dropped him off in the doorway. I take it we are *all* being followed?"

"I'm not," said Johnson peacefully. He stood, hands in pockets, looking through his glasses at Maurice.

"Yes, you are. I'm following you, dear boy," said Maurice. "My intuition told me you were in this, on one side or the other. I trust for Ruth's sake, it is on the side favored by Lloyd's, Baring's, Interpol and the American Constitution. It also seemed to me, while the Submerged Tenth were prattling, that you were looking for something. Or is it a small Sponsored Litter-walk?"

Johnson began to laugh. He took his hand out of his pocket with a pipe in it. "You've found it?" he said.

"On the contrary," said Maurice fruitily. "I came to tell you there was no need to investigate further. The meeting has taken place. The communication has passed. The evidence, to be sure, lay about for the taking."

He placed his cigar in his mouth and, holding open his jacket, removed from an inside pocket an envelope which he handed with simplicity to Johnson. He lifted the cigar from his lips and watched, smiling, while Johnson tapped the envelope open. Into his palm, glittering, tumbled four minute pieces of film, densely figured. Johnson tipped them, without touching them further, back into the envelope.

"If I asked you where, when and who," Johnson said, "you would doubtless refuse, for the sake of your health, to tell anyone?"

"That is right," Maurice said. He looked twenty years younger. I hated them both, because they were speaking in riddles.

I said, "What, then. What is it? What was on the film, Maurice?"

"Do you know," said Maurice, "I was going to ask the same dynamic question. What *is* on this film, Johnson?"

"The traffic regulations for the city of Turin for the year nineteen fifty-four. At a guess," said Johnson Johnson. "If you are still following us, Maurice, we're going to have a beer in the Europe."

"Are we?" I said. "Aren't we waiting until three o'clock?"

"It was three o'clock, dear child, half an hour ago. And no one came, except Johnson and you. Look," said Maurice with gentle pleasure. "There is Lilian."

The chair lift, it was clear, was now functioning. I wondered what delay Johnson had stipulated, and how much in hard cash it had cost him. I worry about these things for more reasons than one, I can tell you. Then Charles came striding along, and Innes, cagily, and Timothy, with a late geranium held to his cheek. "So here you are! You both climbed down, how agile. And tell us, who came at three? I forbid you to say," said Timothy petulantly, "that nobody came, after everything."

"Maurice came," Johnson said. "But he didn't meet anyone but two camera maniacs, and he had a lot of good excuses."

Innes scowled at Maurice, who, supported by the agile buttocks of Hymenaeus, was conversing airily with the Professor. Charles also, I observed, regarded him with the deepest suspicion.

Timothy sighed. *"No one* in sneakers with spike mikes and tapes and transmitters?"

"We blew it. Where's Jacko?" said Johnson.

"In the Hotel Europe," said Innes Wyes curtly. "Close to the bar, I rather imagine."

"What a good idea," Johnson said. "Let's all join him."

The sunset from the boat was stupendous: a sort of pink and amethyst light with the sun an orange ball on the sea behind the headland we had all climbed that afternoon. Before an hour had gone by the most beautiful island in the world was only an outline in black, with a necklace of lights strung across it, ending in the golden arcades of the Villa San Michele. I said, "What now?" to Johnson.

Since our return from Anacapri he had been at his most aggravating. To all my whispered questions about the incident in the Villa Michele he had merely responded with pipe smoke and platitudes. Maurice, appealed to on the subject of the torn film, had been equally bland and equally unforthcoming.

Neither of them referred to the passage in public. It seemed to me that Maurice, having meddled in something which didn't concern him, had backed discreetly into a Jiffy bag of deliberate ignorance, and Johnson was letting him do it.

Or maybe, of course, Johnson knew where the torn film had come from. But if he did, he wasn't prepared to tell me or anyone else. I assured Charles, Innes, Professor Hathaway and Diana, each of whom took me aside, agog, that there was no reason to suspect Maurice of being a front man for the Mafia, and that truly Johnson and I had seen nothing suspicious. Jacko didn't ask because now he had Di he was specializing.

I kept the bit about the envelope of film to myself. My instinct, as I remember, was to let the whole thing die a natural death. Charles was free. Our guess about the appointment in the Villa Michele had proved to be groundless. Tonight *Sappho* would sail for Naples, taking Professor Hathaway to her morning encounter with Bob and Eddie. Tomorrow *Dolly* would follow and, united, we should all pile into Johnson's and Maurice's cars and drive back to Rome and the observatory. Whatever Johnson was up to, the rest of us would be home for Christmas. I said, "What now?" to Johnson with the dim idea of inviting a summing-up.

"You mean there ought to be something else?" inquired Johnson. Di, with her hair spectacularly done, was lying full length by his knees on the cockpit cushions dressed from head to foot in burgundy velvet with pierrot ruffles in white organdy around her neck and both her wrists. Charles said she looked like a hambone but I could see he was itching to photograph her.

I said, "I mean, shall we ever find out what really happened?

"It's hard to say," said Johnson, considering. "It seems unlikely. Two days after you get back, you're due to leave Italy anyway, aren't you? If I hear anything, I'll send you a postcard."

"You mean," I said suavely, "that you're painting the Pope all through Christmas?"

"No. You're right," Johnson said. "I shall be busy. I'll send you a card *after* Christmas."

Then Di proposed bridge and I went below to start packing. I could hear them revoking all the time I was cleaning my teeth.

To hell with Johnson. And Capri. And the Finnish Observatory. I fell asleep, thinking forgivingly of poor Charles's watch.

It was the last time I remember feeling forgiving. I was a nice, simple girl up to that evening, refreshingly clear of the current mainstream of received opinion. The twentieth-century equivalent, emotionally, of the horse. It is a handicap I no longer suffer from.

We got halfway to Naples, as I remember, when we saw the red flags on the horizon. They were lying out of our way, but it was early morning and we had time to be Good Samaritans and investigate. *Sappho* was already in Naples and Professor Hathaway at this moment would be in the hill post studying Eddie's log-book.

The rougher ethnic element on *Dolly* were in rather less of a hurry, and in any case Charles, asleep in the saloon, was a formidable obstacle to anyone attempting to prepare breakfast. In the end, I imagine Lenny simply laid the table around him. I know he was still in his pajama bottoms when Di and I eventually stumbled out of our stateroom. I was glad to know he had pajama bottoms. I had never seen them before.

We had had breakfast when Lenny whistled up Johnson. All you could see at that time was a stretch of empty blue sea with a streak of black and white in the distance. "I can't quite make it out," Johnson said. "It may be some wreckage."

"Or a net?" Innes suggested. Fishing nets sometimes broke adrift from their offshore weights and anchors, and the ferry traffic would be at its height very shortly.

"Or a wreck *and* a net?" Charles suggested. He gave me the binoculars. Johnson moved to the cockpit and, turning the wheel, pointed *Dolly* straight for the flag sticks. I could see them now very clearly, and a lot of black and white balls knocking about at their feet. They took a long time to become any plainer.

Johnson cut out the engine. He said, "It's farther away than it seems. I rather think this is a job for the speedboat."

We had been trailing her, the narrow *V* of her wake inside ours. Lenny moved aft to pull her alongside and before he had her tied up, Charles and Jacko and Innes were in her beside him.

Johnson stood and looked down at them all. "Christ," he said. "The last treat of the hols. You'll capsize her."

But he let them stay and waved Lenny back to the cockpit. "You take her. Keep her screw out of the nets, that's all I ask you." A moment later, in a shower of spray the speedboat had abandoned the three of us.

> *You have crossed the flowing river*
> *To the land of evergreen*
> *Each day I long to see you*
> *But the river runs between.*

"Spoilsports," said Diana vaguely. She was painting her feet in the cockpit. They looked rather nice; like paper doilies as supplied to the International Society for Krishna Consciousness. Johnson went below, having put the wheel on automatic. The speedboat, diminishing, was hitting the wave-tops like a jumping bean and I could hear snatches of sea chantey—Charles, at his most exuberant. Innes and Jacko weren't singing and I felt sorry for them, but it was their own fault for being so far forward. I said, "If there's fish in those nets, it'll stink to high heaven."

Di looked up with her brush full of henna. "I know what you think," she said. "You think they're going to find that net wrapped around a body."

"Never crossed my mind for a moment," I answered. I drew a trembling line down to my shin with her dipstick.

"A body," said Di with satisfaction, "with a scrap of cardboard still in its dead fist. A scrap of cardboard saying *S.M. Capri* twenty/fifteen hundred. Go and watch them through the bincoulars and tell me the moment when Jacko sicks up his corn flakes and uova." She had got The Marmalade on the radio and I couldn't hear Charles singing anymore.

I took the binoculars and walked around the side deck to the long polished stretch in front of the coach house. Below the hatch I saw Johnson moving about in his cabin. I got the speedboat into focus just as she slowed down to circle the flag sticks.

There was a fingerprint on one of my lenses. I had lowered the glasses to wipe it when I noticed an empty boat in the sea under *Dolly's* port beam.

There had been no sound of engines. I was trying, I believe, to work out its possible link with the wreck when I saw it was the launch from *Sappho*. I was still looking at her when a man's arm snapped around my waist hard and held me, and a man's hand struck down my arms and dug itself sweatily over my mouth.

I kicked the hatch, as I remember. I bit the dirty hand holding my face together and I got my nails in and I dredged up my three bits of mail-order jiujitsu, but Johnson didn't sprint up with the anchor chain and it didn't alter the outcome by a whisker. Someone raised a club and someone brought it down on my cranium, sharply.

I fell face downward on the deck of the *Dolly*, and left the roll call of active participants.

CHAPTER 17

I WAS KNOCKED OUT once before, playing hockey, and the first time I woke, I rather expected to see the games mistress looming above me. Instead, I was in a kind of fuzzy darkness which made my nose tickle. I let out a volley of head-splitting sneezes and light entered as the fuzz lifted suddenly. Someone spoke in Italian, there was a prick in my arm, and I went to sleep again. Looking back on it later, I thought of four other things I might have thought of doing which would have altered the course of events quite considerably, but I really wasn't up to it.

The next time I woke wasn't very much better, but I did have the sense to keep my eyes shut and listen. I was indoors, on a bed with a coverlet under me, and I could sense electric light on my eyelids. I was still, I was glad to find, fully dressed. I could hear someone breathing, and a chair creaked in front of me. I turned, sighing reposefully, waited, and opened my eyes.

I was facing a wall. It was bare, whitewashed and heavily finger-marked, and on it, in green felt pen someone had written EXP 62, QSS C9D B ABnv C Bnv I'VE GOT TO MEET DI WILL YOU PUT IT IN THE LOGBOOK.

I was in my own bed in the rest room of the Frazer Observatory, just as I had been when Jacko walked in on me the day it all started. The door opened behind me and I turned, still half awake and thinking, I believe, that it was Jacko all over again and this time when I met Charles and he suggested the zoo I was going to say No and change the whole course of history. A man in a black sweater and trousers came in, glanced at me and said to another man, sitting in the rest-room straw chair, "That one is awake. What about the other?"

They spoke in Italian but they were not, I thought, the two men who had attacked me in Ischia. They didn't look as if they would trouble to call anyone "little darling" before they socked it to her. I said, "What other?" and the man in the chair got up and they both walked, shoulder to shoulder, toward me. I wished I hadn't spoken. Then I saw they were both gazing at the other bunk which lay up above me.

"He's awake, too," said one of the men, and lifting his arm, brought it down suddenly on the bedding above me. The mattress bounced and Johnson's voice, rather breathless, said, "I want a pot of

Indian tea and some toast, lightly done. My friend, I believe, would prefer coffee and cookies."

I was starving, too, but I shouldn't have had the nerve. I could feel my nose beginning to swell, I was so glad I wasn't alone. I said, "Hullo," huskily to the bed up above me.

"Hullo," said Johnson. "What exciting lives astronomers lead. Does your head hurt very much?"

I was about to answer him when one of the Italians said something and the other, bending, took me by the arm and pulled me over the edge of the bed. I said, "Johnson!" and Johnson's voice, perfectly calm, said, "They're taking us into the kitchen. Do what they say, and leave all the rest to me. They understand English."

One of them kicked him when he said that; he was just sliding down and I saw it. I didn't see why either of us had to put up with that. We were two against two and I can kick people too, if I have to. Then Johnson arrived on the floor and I saw his hands were tied together. His jersey was torn and he had bruises all over his face and his glasses were cracked. He looked a mess. He looked at me over his splintered bifocals and said, "I'm afraid there are at least three more unsporting gentlemen outside. Whatever do you think they can want?"

There was, then, no point in resistance. Particularly as I knew as well as Johnson just what they wanted. I walked erratically out of the rest room, propelled by one of our captors, and found myself pushed into the kitchen where Jacko and I had had so many companionable breakfasts, eating Innes's goodies. There were two other rough types in the room lounging about, and a man, sitting in the chair where I had sat, poring over the film advertisements in the *Messaggero*.

He looked the sort of man who had his own manicure arrangements and others would appear out of the ground if he snapped his fingers. There is nothing quite so chic in the world as a handsome, gray-haired Italian in impeccable Savile Row suiting with a fluent command of endearingly accented English. I had been trying to collect one for years before I met Charles and I know people who cultivated Di in the sole hopes of being able to prise one out of her collection, but she hung on to them all like grim death, and I don't blame her.

This one was like all the others, smooth and hard-eyed and smiling, and he had my bullwhip in his fingers and was idly snapping it at the feet of one of his minions, who stood there, grinning stiffly. It was the sort of thing that keeps people interested in the wide-screen cinema and I should have adored every minute if I hadn't been in the same room, instead of watching it. He turned his head when he came in and said, "Ah. Miss Russell and Mr. Johnson. Please come in and sit down. I hope we shall not need to keep you for more than a moment."

"I hope not. We are rather hungry," said Johnson severely. They had put him in one of the observatory chairs and were tying his arms to the back of it. In a moment they did the same to me, and we sat pointing our chests at the doorway. The two men who had brought us in stood in front of it, smirking, and the two others had stationed themselves behind our chairs, exuding garlic.

The room seemed full of men, and judging from the cigarette stubs lying everywhere, they hadn't just come there. On the table at the gray-haired man's elbow stood one of our precious bottles of vino and a chipped glass, half empty. All our glasses were chipped, and I was glad of it.

He picked up the tumbler while I was watching him and said, "I am sure you are both hungry and thirsty and that you would both prefer to make yourselves tidy before we hold this conversation. I cannot, however, afford to allow either of you out of sight just for the moment. Mr. Johnson, I rather think you have something of mine which I am going to ask you for in a moment. But first, Miss Russell, I want the photographs from Lord Digham's Zeiss Icarex camera."

> *We talk the old times over*
> *We laugh and joke the same*
> *But still it hurts a lot inside*
> *When someone speaks your name.*

"She burned them," Johnson said.

The bullwhip, moving idly, circled around and then snapped in his direction. I could feel the draft of it, and it was less than an inch from Joynson's face. "When I speak to Miss Russell," said the gray-haired man agreeably, "it is Miss Russell I wish to answer. The photographs, please."

"I burned them," I said.

"So you have been saying. Lord Digham is your cher ami and you were anxious not to embroil him in anything troublesome. But I believe, Miss Russell," said the gray-haired man, "that you did not destroy that roll of negatives."

"Don't be silly, of course she destroyed them," said Johnson irritably. "She thought at first Charles

303

himself was involved in it. Naturally, she would destroy all the evidence. And so if you don't believe me, count the number of times the Dome has been searched, and her possessions. You got in today. Don't tell me you haven't gone through the entire building to find it."

The gray-haired man listened quite patiently, I thought, and then, lifting the whip, looked along the handle in Johnson's direction, one eye narrowed. I said sharply, "Stop it!" The gray-haired man smiled, and then with a savage flick of his wrist, sent the hide flying toward Johnson again. The tip coiled like a spring around his spectacles and, snatching them off, flung them clattering to the far side of the kitchen. "I said," continued the gray-haired man, smiling, "it is for Miss Russell to answer. Miss Russell, where are the photographs?" The handle of the whip came up again, and this time it was pointing to me.

I was wondering, if I got marked like a mixed grill, whether Charles would still love me. I wondered why Johnson was sticking to my story, and whether the police would get on our tracks and if there was a chance that Jacko and Innes and Professor Hathaway would decide to come on to Rome and do a good evening's work in the observatory.

Thinking it over, it came to me that there wasn't a hope. Wherever Johnson and I had been landed, it wouldn't have been in Naples harbor, but some nice secluded beach with a fast car near it, waiting. And no police force in its senses would hear a story like that and wave goodbye to the yachtload of foreigners who reported it. They would be setting up roadblocks and searching through Naples. The one place no one would ever think of looking for us was inside the Frazer Observatory. "Miss Russell?" the gray-haired man repeated more softly.

I decided Johnson was playing for time, and I had better help him. "You see," I said, "there were pictures of girls. I was angry with Charles. I didn't care about his couture photographs. I burned the whole thing to teach him a lesson."

"When?" said the gray-haired man.

"Monday," I said. "Monday the sixth, after Charles and I had had our row and he went off to Naples." I didn't look at Johnson.

"And where," said the gray-haired man, "did you burn them?"

On Monday, November 6, I had been all day in the Dome. "In the Dome," I said quickly.

"Indeed?" said the gray-haired man, smiling again, and this time I did look at Johnson.

It didn't do me any good because he wasn't looking at me. He was studying the other man, watchfully. "But," said the gray-haired man gently, "you could not have burned it in the Dome that Monday, Miss Russell. That Monday the stove was out of action and you did not have any matches." And the whip, snaking out, curled itself hard around the leg of Johnson's chair and flung it sideways. It fell toward the sink with a crash of splintering wood and a grunt from Johnson, as he struck the floor with his shoulder and head. He was still tied firmly to it.

They left him there. "And so," pursued the gray-haired man, his voice hardening, "where are the photographs, Miss Ruth Russell?"

I stared at him. I had forgotten it, but it was true. I had worked all day at the Dome, and Jacko had gone off with the only box of matches. I hadn't even a light, I remembered, for Maurice's cigar.

Maurice. And the launch . . . the launch, of course, had been *Sappho*'s launch. And who else, of course, had the key to the Frazer Observatory but Maurice Frazer? Who else could have nets left by bribery—who else returned early to Naples especially to do so? Who else at 1500 hours had been in the Villa San Michele but Maurice? And who but Maurice could have removed Johnson's dummy film from the vase in his own bedroom and, having developed it, initiated the search for the real film which was ending here, back in the observatory . . . ?

And it was ending, for Johnson's voice, rather muffled from the floor was saying, "Tell him, Ruth. It isn't burned. You know and I know it isn't."

And it wasn't, of course. I said, "Pick him up, and I'll tell you."

The gray-haired man laughed. "You will tell us or your friend will be made still more uncomfortable. Are the photographs here in the Dome?"

I looked down. I wanted time to think, and I also wanted time to slide my eyes around to Johnson who proved, with the slightest possible movement, to be shaking his head. I said, "No. I posted them to England."

"Miss Russell," said the gray-haired man sadly, and at his tone, the two men by the door moved across and stood one on each side of me, looking inquiringly at their master. "Miss Russell, we know what letters you have posted. There have been none to England."

"Tell them," said Johnson from the floor. It came

306

to me that he had always known I hadn't burned them. I remembered that exhaustive search of the Dome he had launched with Jacko and me after the dud film was stolen. I realized it was my film he'd been looking for. I wondered if he'd spotted it.

The men on either side of me moved restively. On the other side of the room, the door handle moved slowly.

"I need a drink of water," I said.

"Afterward," the man in the chair said sharply. He had stopped being suave.

"I feel dizzy," I said, allowing my eyeballs to slip upward slightly, a thing Charles and I frequently practiced, to the distress of soft-hearted onlookers. The door handle paused and then continued to turn. The door eased forward slightly. The gray-haired man turned and looked at it.

It was a bad moment. On the floor, Johnson wriggled abruptly, his chair creaking, and one of the men aimed an absent-minded kick at his body. The man at my side, in response to a nod from the mastermind, walked softly forward and stood, silently waiting, one hand on the doorknob. The door, pushed slowly from outside, moved another fraction toward us.

I yelled. I didn't know who it was, but if it was one of ours, I couldn't let him walk in unsuspecting and cop it. I yelled, I think, "They're waiting for you," but it didn't do a bit of good, for at the sound of my voice the person outside flung open the door and charged inward, to receive a full karate chop on the back of her plaited leather choker. A tiny gun went flying and took a chip out of the breadboard.

It *was* one of ours. It was, for heaven's sakes, Di Minicucci, who was on board *Dolly* when we were kidnaped and whom we had all forgotten. She somersaulted like a hedgehog and ended up full length on her back by the stove with her eyes shut. She had on a midi coat in blended fitch slung over her playsuit and a handbag that didn't match, but still a handbag. I take off my hat to Di Minicucci. For sheer presence of mind and tenacity she made the whole of "Star Trek" look like pikers.

Then the gray-haired man in the chair snapped his fingers and was given a heavy revolver. He fondled it once or twice, checked his aim, and settled down with one elbow negligently on the table and the other held in his palm. The muzzle of the gun, thus handsomely supported, pointed straight at poor Di's European hairpiece, just back from the cleaners, and poor Di, reposing gently where she had fallen, was in no situation to dodge it.

"Now," said Gray-Hair calmly to me, as if nothing had happened. "Perhaps we may finish our business. The photographs, or your pretty young friend will receive some unwelcome attention." And stretching down he unzipped, smiling, the top half of Di's Pucci playsuit. The men standing around her grinned and fidgeted.

Half Italy at one time or another has seen Di either half clothed or starkers, but by Di's choice and in front of Di's friends, not thugs of this variety. It might not seem like it but Di had something to lose, and that was dignity.

So I was going to tell them, but Johnson got in before me. "They're in the grounds," he said. "She buried the negatives out in the flower beds. Show them, Ruth."

The man in the chair turned and looked at me. "Is that true?" he said sharply.

Without any volition of mine, my eyeballs began to behave in a very queer manner. "Yes," I said rather thickly.

"Where? Can you describe it exactly?"

I shook my head. I wasn't feeling very well. "Give her some water," said the gray-haired man harshly. He waited while I drank it and said, "Then you will show us. Dimitri will untie you. He and Pietro will then take you out into the grounds, and I shall follow you with this revolver. The slightest attempt to mislead us and I will signal Giorgio here to commence broadening your charming young friend's education."

I looked at Johnson and Johnson winked and suddenly, for the first time, I saw a gleam of hope in the operation. For the photographs were not in the flower beds and Johnson clearly knew that they weren't. He wanted us out of the way. And with us out of the way, that left only two men in the kitchen, to guard himself and Diana.

Except that Johnson was tied to a chair, and Di was knocked out.

If indeed Johnson was still tied to the chair. And if indeed I had not imagined, just then, that Di's false eyelashes flickered . . .

I made a long, long job of getting to my feet. I crawled to the door and staggered out into the hall and leaned against the front door while they unlocked it and dragged it open. I wondered how Di had managed to follow us. I wondered if she had brought the rest with her and then realized that she must be on her own. Lilian Hathaway might be an eccentric, but she knew when to call in authority. If the others knew where we were, the grounds would already be ringing with police whistles.

Unless, for example, Di had rushed to Naples and asked someone there to send the police up to the observatory. Unless she had asked Maurice to do it.

It was dark outside, and very clear. The lights of Velterra were cozily visible, and at the foot of the hill a window glowed in Maurice's villa. The garden itself was perfectly silent, save for the trickling of a small fountain by the swimming pool. A light breeze, swaying the poplar trees, hid and disclosed the white flanks of some of Maurice's statues and, further off, the ghostly pillars of Innes's Folly, rising like a Necropolis above the hanging gardens ripened on grave-mold. Maurice's gardeners, unalarmed, would have buried a corpse there. Next year, who knows what bumper crop would dazzle the neighbors.

I put off time as best I could. I wandered up and down marble staircases, pausing here and exclaiming doubtfully there until the gray-haired man, losing patience, pulled my arm tight and high at my back and said, "Enough. You show us now, or your friend suffers. What is that?"

It might have been a compatriot loosing off at the sparrows but it wasn't. It was the sound of gunfire back at the observatory. I found myself flung back into the arms of Dimitri and his colleague while, gun in hand, the gray-haired man began to run in the darkness to the squat black shape of the Dome.

My arm aching, I ran dragging after, in the grasp of the other two men. Then the grip on one of my arms disappeared and I turned, in time to see Dimitri stagger off and sink in a flower bed.

> *May the winds blow gently.*
> *On that quiet and peaceful spot*
> *Where the one we love lies resting*
> *And will never be forgot.*

The man holding my other arm whirled around and released me, his hands reaching out to someone I could not quite see, dodging and ducking around us in the darkness. Then Johnson's voice said, "Ruth! Run like hell, sweetie . . ." And I did.

Feet trampled the ground all about me. Near the door of the Dome there was a burst of shouting and another shot. A little flame bloomed in the darkness to one side of me and I swerved away as the sound of the shot exploded in my ear. Johnson's voice said breathlessly, "It's all right. It was my gun. Make for the villa."

"No," I said, and stopped. "We've got to get Di. And listen . . ."

Johnson said, "I'll look after Di. Run for the villa. I'll draw them off."

The firing was nearer now, and the shouting. Someone came racing up beside us and I saw Johnson's arm rise in the gloom and descend with the revolver in it, butt downward. There was the sound of a thud and a fall, and Johnson grabbed my arm again and began ushering me at a brisk downward canter in the direction of Maurice's villa. I said, "Maurice is on the wrong side, you bloody idiot."

I should have known better. I should have kept

my mouth shut and trusted him. The gray-haired man was out there somewhere in the darkness, and the man Johnson had just felled, and probably three others beating about, but all I could think of was Di lying helpless there in the Dome, and Maurice waiting behind the lit window for us all to walk into the limelight.

So I bleated out, and a figure rose from the bushes in front of us which had nothing to do with the shouting men from the Dome just behind. A neat figure which blocked out the stars and waved its revolver so that it flashed just once in the dimness.

"It isn't Maurice you have to worry about," said Innes Wye. "Drop your gun, Johnson. I'm taking you both where no one can get at you until Ruth has told me just where those photographs are."

Johnson dropped his gun. He could hardly argue with the barrel of Innes's Dardick pointing straight at him and a recollection of the fate of the fish tank. Then we were making a stumbling run through the garden. I had forgotten we were near the door of Mouse Hall until I was thrust through it, with Johnson blundering after me.

I thought it was plain myopia, and then I realized what he had tripped over. The body of Di, groggily shaking its head, lay across the threshhold in the winking light of Innes's banks of electronic instruments.

Innes bent and, pulling her inside, closed and locked the door, his revolver trained on us without ceasing. He switched on the light. "Yes. I thought she might be better here than lying in the Dome," said Innes Wye. "How lucky we all met. You see,

Johnson, I needed you. I needed you for a hostage."

I should have known. Anyone who killed locusts and lobsters the way Innes did was bound to be kinky. The fact that he kept white mice as well just went to prove it. I wondered why he needed hostages and then I didn't wonder anymore because far in the distance through the locked door and shuttered windows came the sound of more firing and the shouting of many more voices. The police had arrived at the hill. And Innes was here by arrangement, waiting for his friends so that they could all beat it together. With us as his insurance against accidents.

The lights popped in and out and the thin green lines wiggled and Di sat up and said, "How the hell did I get here . . . Oh!" as she saw Innes.

Johnson stayed where he was, under Innes's gun with his back to the white foam plastic blocks of the Incubator, but I knelt down beside her and Innes let me. I said, "Di. You did tell the police, didn't you? Somewhere?"

She pulled her wig off with one hand and fanned herself with it. Even dumped on the floor in a mess of torn fitch, she looked like the front cover of *Harper's Bazaar*. "No," she said blankly, looking around her. "I didn't wait for the others. When they hauled you two away I upped anchor and sailed *Dolly* after you." She looked at Johnson. "I picked the lock on your car and followed in it. What is he pointing a gun at you for?"

"I think he's going to shoot Johnson if I don't give him Charles's photographs," I said wildly.

Di got to her feet and held her neck, swearing.

"Then for Christ's sake, give them to him, darling," she said testily.

I knew she had a crush on Johnson. I had a slight one myself, except that he didn't seem to be handling this situation with any particular aplomb. I mean, for God's sake, to be held up at pistol point by Innes. I said, "The negatives are on the shelf, in the fourth bag of Poppy's Cuddle."

"They aren't," said Johnson, suddenly stung into speech. "I searched every inch—"

"I know you did," cried Innes, equally outraged. "That bastard Timothy laid me out and you pinched my key. Where did you put the photographs?"

"I didn't get them," said Johnson viciously.

"They're in the fourth bag of Cuddle," I repeated with patience. "I cut them all into strips."

There was a silence. The sound of shouting and firing, which had receded into the distance, became suddenly noticeably louder. "Get them," said Innes.

To cover us all, he made Di and Johnson back beside me until we reached Poppy's cage. Behind the bars, the tin container full of shredded white bedding was bulging and still. Poppy was having a nap. On the shelf up above, labeled in Innes's methodical way, were her pails of sawdust and her packs of rolled oats, her bag of sunflower seeds and her hamster dinners. Beside them, in an orderly row, were the bags of Cuddle, shipped out from England.

I reached behind me for the fourth, and handed it over to Innes. Then we stood all three in a row while he tried to open it.

Someone banged on the door.

Innes swore. You can't open a bag of Cuddle one-handed. I know, because I have tried it.

Someone banged on the door again. Someone pumped a shot into the door and a voice said, "Open up. Open up or I'll shoot the lock off."

It wasn't the police. It was the voice of the gray-haired man who had threatened to have Di assaulted. Di said, jeeringly, "You'd better open up, hadn't you?"

Maybe she thought it was the police. Maybe Innes himself wasn't sure if it might be a trick. In any case, he didn't at once let his friends in. He backed, bag and gun in his hands, to the window, edged a shutter open with a jerk of his elbow and peered outside.

A shot smashed the glass and sang into the room, ending its life in the base of the Incubator. Innes inserted his gun in the hole and fired back instantly.

"Innes," said Johnson gently.

The Dardick, smoking, swung around and trained on Johnson before he had stopped speaking. "Your friends won't get in," said Innes firmly. "You may as well get used to the idea. You're beaten, Johnson." Another burst of fire came from outside the building and he swung around to the window, pressing the trigger. A figure in a dark jersey and trousers appeared for a moment, illuminated by the light from the window, and dived into the bushes, firing. Innes fired back three more shots. I said, rather slowly, "That was Dimitri."

"The bastard," said Innes feelingly. He looked back at Johnson. "How many more of your chums are waiting outside there, eh? Six? Twelve? By God, I'll give them a run for their money." Giorgio, looming into his sights, took a quick potshot and raced out of them, followed by a hail of Dardick bullets from Innes.

I said, "Innes. They're on your side."

"*My* side?" said Innes, laughing gratingly. "They're on the side of your friend Johnson. D'you know how I got here tonight? I followed Lenny. He knew where to come."

"You should have asked him whom he was following," said Johnson mildly. "Innes, whom do you work for?"

"Who?" said Innes. He fired off three more shots. I reckoned it made twelve altogether.

"Whom," said Diana. The gray-haired man appeared, calling something, and Innes fired another shot, followed by a second. Someone battered at the door and he looosed off two more. The second time the gun only clicked.

"He works for the American security service. Don't you, Innes?" Diana said. "Open the door, darling. We don't want anyone hurt."

Innes turned, bag in one hand and Dardick uselessly in the other, and Diana looked at him smiling, a little gun perched in her fingers. The one we had seen her lose in the Dome when they pounced on her. "I'll take the bag," she said, and held her hand out to Innes.

Innes produced a number of very pale think-bubbles and looked at her. I looked at her too, but I was mainly concerned with watching Johnson. He was standing where he had first taken his stance with his back to the Incubator, and the way he was looking at Di was neither staggered nor baleful, but just mildly satisfied. The banging on the door increased and Di, letting drop a swearword which made even Johnson blink, backed and opened the door, keeping the gun trained with profound expertise straight upon us.

The gray-haired man walked quickly in, followed by three of his henchmen, the last of whom barred the door quickly. Spreading out, guns in hands, Giorgio, Dimitri and Pietro manned the windows. The gray-haired man, also gun in hand, turned to Di and said in Italian, "What the hell took you so long? Have you got it?"

"In the bag," said Di calmly. Still keeping us covered, she gave him the packet of Cuddle. He kneaded it.

"The girl cut it to shreds. You will have to piece it together," said Di prosaically. Other than making sure she could kill us if necessary, she gave us no more of her valuable attention.

She was always a clever bitch, with the brightest attributes of both her nations. Only Innes, staring at Johnson, seemed still to be totally at a loss. Johnson smiled at him. "Let me introduce you," he said to Innes mildly. "Miss Diana Minicucci and her father, His Highness the Prince. Are you really one of Joe Grady's roving scientists?"

"Yes," said Innes. He looked very shocked. I wondered if he really was an American agent, and decided that if Johnson said so, he probably was. Johnson said, "Congratulations. Was it your two thugs then who gave Ruth the going-over in Ischia?"

"Yes," said Innes defensively. He turned to me. "I have to explain that."

"Not now," said Johnson. "After they examine

the contents of that bag, you realize, they are going to shoot us."

"Ruth and me," said Innes gravely. "I expect that."

"And Mr. Johnson," said Prince Minicucci, lifting his handsome gray head from the Cuddle bag. "Since introductions are in order, perhaps I should make you known to one another? Dr. Wye, Mr. Johnson is a member of British Intelligence. If you hadn't stopped him just now, he would have been safely in the Villa Sansavino with Miss Russell. A basin, Diana."

Which was a pity. Because when she brought it and he up-ended the Cuddle, there were no strips of negatives in it. They left Dimitri at the window and they all came and stood looking at me—all except Diana, who kept her lashes and her revolver unwaveringly on my friend Johnson. Johnson said, "Ruth, you deserve the British Empire Medal and I shall worship you forever, but don't confuse anybody any longer. Tell them where the photographs are."

"And then they shoot us," I said.

A voice in the distance, speaking first in Italian and then in English said, "We know you are inside. If you open the door and come out, unarmed, with your hands resting on your heads, we will spare your lives. Otherwise we shall blow the door down."

"And then," said Johnson, "they can use us as hostages. Go on."

The voice outside began painstakingly all over again. "We know you are inside . . ."

Prince Minicucci walked to the window. Through the crack in the shutters we could all see the floodlights: lights surrounding Mouse Hall in its entirety, and shining on uniformed heads and the long barrels of rifles. It reminded me of the day the Chief of Police discovered he had been riding for half an hour in the same limousine as a gas balloon. Diana's father cupped his hands and called in Italian, "We have here Mr. Johnson, Dr. Wye and Miss Russell. We demand to leave this building and quit the country without molestation. Otherwise they shall all die."

"I am afraid Miss Russell," said Di, "is going to perish before anyone if she doesn't hand over that film roll. Don't be mad, darling. It is here, isn't it?"

She looked at me as she had always done, cool, superior, vaguely friendly, with no evil intentions toward anyone so long as they didn't interfere with her creature comforts. I said, "Yes, it's here. Behind the power cables. I put it there that day Johnson and Jacko and I unmanned the Incubator."

It was true, this time. If they shone a light where I pointed they would find it: the original film from the Zeiss Icarex, tucked in behind the hank of 2000-volt cable that festooned the three walls of Mouse Hall. I had put it there when Johnson had switched the power off on that one day we all came to search here. Unless someone switched the power off again, it could not be removed.

Johnson had searched for it, and perhaps seen it, but if he had removed it, every one of Innes's instruments would have recorded it. And Innes himself, of course, was the last person to switch off the power, even if he had dreamed of anyone choosing his private locked Hall as a hiding place. Outside, someone with a loudspeaker said, "You are invited to come out unarmed, with your hands resting on top of your heads. Provided the three people you mention are quite unharmed, I promise a cease-fire immediately."

The Prince said, "They will use tear gas. Close the shutters. Dr. Wye, I desire a battery spotlight . . . Dear sir, why should I hesitate to shoot one of you now? Ah, that is wise."

He switched on the light Innes had given him. "Now, Diana." And Di, bending, turned off the power.

All the machines, as once before, fell totally silent. Outside, the voices of the polizia could be heard very clearly; inside you were aware of heavy breathing, and the half-lit circle of faces, intent and sweating like a Rembrandt etching at Sotheby's. Minicucci walked out of the circle.

He was a short man, and the bank of instruments made it awkward to reach to the cable. He looked around for a stool and, finding one, pulled it over and climbed upon it.

Even Di watched him. That was how she failed to see Johnson lash out and kick over the battery lamp. One moment we were there, isolated in our pool of light and our silence. The next, darkness fell, and bloody chaos.

Someone fired a shot and someone shouted. Someone started a scuffle and someone, raising his voice, ordered Giorgio and Pietro to stand guard at the door. A voice outside, self-consciously sonorous, said, "Unless by the count of twenty you emerge unarmed from your doorway, we shall with regret have to make use of both gas and explosives."

Prince Minicucci's voice, clear and final, said, "Diana. Put on the power."

The arc lamps of Mouse Hall, blinding, dazzled us. They shone on Innes, astride Dimitri and thumping him, and Pietro, ceasing abashed to attack Giorgio, who continued punching. They shone on Diana standing still by the switch and wringing her hand, from which I had just twisted her revolver. They shone on Prince Minicucci, still and straight-backed and triumphant on his flat stool-top, bearing in his right hand the roll of film which would make him welcome, I supposed, in whatever country he intended to end up in. And they showed Johnson, standing in the spot from which he had only once moved, by the Incubator. Only the white blocks of the Incubator were all tumbled askew and in Johnson's hands, and pointed at Minicucci's breast was the red laser. "Thank you, Diana." he said. "Perhaps you will join your father and Pietro and Giorgio. Innes, you might release Dimitri and relieve Ruth of the gun. Minicucci, I'll have that film, please."

"Will you?" said Prince Minicucci. He looked with distaste at Johnson and at his laser. Then, with a flick of his thumb, he sent the film flying, to flash and sizzle to nothing in the mesh of cables over his head. "So," he said. "Some of the evidence has disappeared."

I didn't know what I felt. I dared not look at Innes who, with Diana and the three men to cover, had no time for Johnson's affairs. Minicucci, still under the threat of the laser, was descending with care from his stool. It was only then that I remembered Professor Hathaway saying something about Minicucci's laboratories.

If he had laboratories he would know, as Innes did and I did, that the red laser used in our astronomy is utterly and totally harmless.

He did know. He reached the ground, paused, and without warning dived for Johnson.

And Johnson, miraculously, was expecting him. Instead of becoming a shield for Minicucci he sidestepped and, swinging the gun like a club, cracked it across the Prince's fine, tailored shoulders and then caught him under the chin. Innes fired. The Prince staggered, grunted, dropped and rolled over.

Diana didn't run to him. Maybe she saw he was dead. Maybe she didn't care anyway. Maybe her wits were sharper, on the whole, than her father's. She didn't utter a sound. Instead, she hurled herself on the floor and flung the power off again.

We were girl against girl and three men against two. I couldn't fight Diana, although you could tell where she was by her Le Galion. I couldn't even help Innes and Johnson: among the fighting, buffeting bodies it was impossible to make out anything but, occasionally, Innes's aftershave. Soon, the police were going to shoot the locks off and burst in on us, firing. Soon, someone else was going to be killed, and I didn't want it to be me or Innes or Johnson.

I knew what I had to do, and it seemed a pity I couldn't warn anyone, but it took all my energy to reach the side of the room where the crank was. Then I fitted it into its socket and, toiling, rolled back the roof of the workshop.

A yellow glare from the sky split the darkness.

For a moment, the struggle slackened, and then with fresh vigor renewed itself. Even if Diana and her friends realized what was happening, they were far too busy to track down the mechanism. The ratchets ground and rumbled like a trailer going over a cattle grid. I hoped the police outside would notice it.

They did. I had cranked the roof a yard back when the first gas bomb arched through the opening, and I went on cranking until three more came and burst on the Incubator. Then I did my best to crank it shut again, to keep in the full body and flavor. I got within a foot or two as well before I had to give up, coughing and retching, by which time the police had the door broken.

Inside they found no opposition. Only seven very sorry people, and a mouse that had died in the course of its duty.

CHAPTER 18

"I PROPOSE," Johnson said after the police had gone, "an Anglo-American funeral with full military honors, and crossed Cuddle bags on the gun carriage. Hard cheese, Innes.

> *A little flower, lent not given,*
> *To bud on earth and bloom in heaven."*

"I only kept her for amusement," said Innes stiffly. "I am a scientist, you know. I assist my country on occasion, but I am expected to place my own work first."

He had been apologizing ever since we arrived at Maurice's, which we did about midnight, leaving Di and our complete personal histories in the hands of the police. The first thing they had done was advise Naples and the Villa Sansavino that we were alive, which pleased Maurice and Timothy and Professor

Hathaway and Jacko, who had just arrived there, having been told quite simply by Diana that I had fallen overboard and Johnson had drowned trying to save me.

They had remained in Naples all afternoon while the police and harbor people were looking for us. Charles and Innes and Lenny had reacted differently. Lenny, following a hunch, he said, of Maurice's, had followed Di when she left the others in Naples, saying she wished to avoid the photographers. And Innes, convinced that Johnson and his friends were the villains, had followed Lenny, to whom, in fact, we owed the arrival of the police at the observatory.

Charles hadn't followed anybody. Charles, knowing who Johnson was, had discerned a dark plot to kidnap me and wrest from me the supposed hiding place of the film and had lit out wildly for Rome, driving up one-way streets and plunging through yellow-taxi lines until finally he ended up in the British Embassy, begging them to put the Prime Minister on to finding me.

By that time we were at the Questura, making our statements. The moment when Charles burst in and collected me in a grip like a waffle iron was not one I am likely to forget. After years of cackling at moonlight on water he went completely to pieces and cried into my Capri cruising wear while I patted his shoulder. Innes went bright pink and went away for the fourth time to phone the American Embassy while Johnson stayed right there, enjoying it. Even now, sitting in Maurice's study with one of Professor Hathaway's Tricosa cardigans over my shoulders, I was wearing more of Charles than another single garment. I didn't expect to be kidnaped again, but it was reassuring all the same.

Everything was reassuring: the meal we had had at the Trattoria Sinigaglia in Parassio, where Charles announced he would discard me if I did not at once renounce my diet, and where we had pork stuffed with rosemary and garlic and liters and liters and liters of Castelli wine in tall waisted jugs with glass seal and no handles. I discarded my diet. Worry can do more for you any day, dimagrante-wise.

It was reassuring to be welcomed into the villa by Timothy, even if he did pour coffee for Charles and Johnson, bending over the silver, lightly sunkissed by Sicilian skies, before bringing me mine.

It was nice to be squashed by Jacko and receive a hirsute kiss fragrant with seafaring aromas. It was unexpectedly disconcerting to receive a dry embrace and a touch on the hair from Professor Hathaway who saw, withdrawing, the drip on my chin and dispersed it. "Early to bed," said my Director with some briskness. "You've done very well. Early to bed, don't you think, Johnson?"

The time being midnight, the suggestion was more well-intentioned than practical, particularly as Johnson seemed to be for some reason included in the program. Johnson himself paid no attention, being occupied in filling his unpleasant pipe and lighting it. He had found another pair of bifocal glasses and had changed his seagoing gear for a Clydella shirt and cable-stitch pullover. Seated on the base of his spine he was thus immune to the frequent glances of Innes, who had not changed at all and whose kipper tie was blotched with blood and tears and spit from the polizia's gas bombs. At length Innes said, "Must you?"

Johnson, Professor Hathaway and Maurice himself all paused in the act of striking fresh matches and gazed at him. I was reminded of something. "Maurice," I said. "I owe you an apology. At one point this evening I had nasty thoughts about you."

"How delightful," Maurice said, puffing out Avana smoke forgetfully in the direction of Innes and smiling with that particular silvery sweetness which has endeared him to generations of nubile young visitors. "How delightful to be sixty and still have nasty thoughts entertained about one. Unquestioning adoration is only for the angels, and so are all the boring sorts of devotion. I know you thought me guilty, and I am pleased by it. Innes, on the other hand, is offering you sugar and will shortly give you a brandy because he is overcompensating. He thought you were guilty, and is now ashamed of it."

"Innes! Did you?" I said, fascinated. A shower of demerara sugar slid down the Tricosa cardigan as Innes knocked the spoon sideways. He put the bowl down crossly and took his seat between Johnson's pipe and Professor Hathaway's Manikin. He said, "When the cameras became so suspiciously mixed, yes. And your presence at the Fall Fair was unexpected."

"I don't see why," I said, mildly astonished. "It was in my balloon after all. We wondered, come to that, what you were doing at it. How, by the way are your calluses?"

Innes looked bemused.

"She means, How are your Trappists?" said

327

Johnson kindly. "Don't listen to her, she will only confuse you. Innes was at the Fall Fair, Ruth, because he had offered to help track down some rather worrying leaks from our brave nuclear physicist boys in the Palassio Institute. Everyone felt he had spotted the gentleman responsible, but no one knew how he was getting the dope passed on to his opposite number. Then it turned out he had this nineteen-three Baedeker . . ."

There was an awed silence. *"Intercourse with Italians?"* said Timothy.

"Which Di bought at the Fall Fair from Mr. Paladrini," I said. "Di. Of course. But Innes, you left."

"I left," said Innes with dignity, "in order to follow Diana in due course unobserved and witness what happened to the Baedeker."

"Which you might have done," said Johnson understandingly, "if . . ."

"If Diana hadn't given him the Organizer's crocodile handbag," I said. I looked at Charles and then remembered he hadn't been at the Fall Fair and collected instead Johnson's modified approbation. "So he was pushed down the steps and . . ."

"And drugged," said Innes coldly, "by Mr. Harrogate."

Timothy looked contrite. Maurice said, "By Timothy? What with? Timothy, I will not have you white-slaving in Italy."

I said, "With Jungle After-Shave, the Essence for Men Born to Conquer. Timothy didn't mean any harm. Truly. But, of course, it allowed Di to get the message out of the Baedeker." Light broke upon me. "Innes! You dragged that Baedeker all through

328

Ischia and Taormina. It doesn't go any farther south than Central Italy."

"I had a theory," said Innes coldly. "It proved wrong. I've already told you. I deeply regret what occurred in Ischia."

Professor Hathaway sat up abruptly. "You are not referring to the fish tank?"

"He is referring," I said, "to the two thugs he set on me at the Aragonese Castle. You thought I had the film from Maurice's vase, didn't you, Innes? Or was it even the contents of the Baedeker? At any rate, you paid these two characters to search me and they did rather more than you bargained for." I had been nursing, since I realized that, a rather endearing vision of Innes getting drunk on the strength of it.

Charles said, "Wait a minute. Innes, was it you who searched all our belongings? By God . . ."

His face, during the account of the attack in the Aragonese Castle, had been growing blacker and blacker, but at least he wasn't smoking. Innes said, through a mild fog of tobacco ash, "Naturally, I was interested to see who had stolen the film. I searched the vase for the film as soon as I woke up and heard what had happened—"

"I remember," said Maurice blandly. "You called to ask me to explain a line in Act Two of *The Willowhunters*."

"—And it had gone," said Innes stiffly.

"Di," I said. "I suppose. Did she come and visit you, Maurice?" I had a vision of Di next morning at Renati's, drifting over and embracing Johnson. And another, too late, of something Johnson had told me already, in the Hotel Quirinale one evening.

"She always comes to see me in the morning," said Maurice. "Came," he corrected himself. For a moment, as he studied the end of his cigar, his expression was less than regal. Then he looked up and drawled, his voice bright with malice, "So they tricked you, dear boy, into going to the balloon seller's flat? How you must have surprised Di with your Dardick."

"I suppose I did," Innes said. He sounded undeniably sulky. "It was, of course, merely a device to throw suspicion on someone else. They did not know who I was at that time."

"More fool they," Johnson said. Under the glasses, his bruises were turning crimson and purple, but his pipe continued to burn with even placidity, and you would almost have said he was enjoying it. "Of course, after all the fun in the Corso and the photographing of Mr. Paladrini they couldn't afford to let him live. They killed him and faked the suicide note, and cleared the flat in a hell of a hurry. In so much hurry that they missed the fish with the Capri date on it. Then Di or a friend switched the gas cylinders. It was easy. Ruth was off duty after midnight on the Wednesday."

I thought of Di switching the gas cylinders and then tried not to think of it. I said, "They forgot something else. They forgot the list you found, with the dates in Ischia and Lipari and Taormina."

"Ah," said Professor Hathaway. "Now I find this of extreme interest. You have just mentioned the route followed by *Dolly?*"

Johnson didn't say anything nor did he look at

me. I looked at Charles. "Yes," I said. "Well. We didn't tell you. But there was a timetable in Mr. Paladrini's flat which implied that the Capri date was the last of a whole series of meetings. Johnson thought we ought to pursue it. But nothing happened."

Professor Hathaway said, "I wonder why nothing happened?"

"Because I faked the list," replied Johnson mildly. He cleared a space in the smoke with his hand and looked with some concern at Innes, who had doubled up, sneezing and coughing. I said, "I think after the gas . . ."

"Dear me. Of course, how thoughtless," Maurice said smoothly. "Johnson, put out your furnace. Do I understand the whole cruise on *Dolly* was a whimsy? Not that I am complaining. Your company and that of your friends was delightful. But the Tyrrhenian Sea in November . . . You have not been kind to Jacko."

Nobody had been kind to Jacko. I think it was the first time it struck me, so self-centered had I become, that the person who must be suffering most from all this was Jacko. Retired in his chair, silent against the twitching wall panel, he had spoken to no one since he kissed me. It didn't need much effort of the imagination to know what he must be feeling. He had loved Diana. Really loved her. And she had merely employed him.

"I apologize," Johnson said, "to Jacko and to anyone else who may have regretted the voyage. But I did have a purpose, and that was to transport anyone who showed signs of wishing to attend the

331

only assignation on that cruise which was genuine. The meeting in the San Michele Villa on Capri."

"Which I attended?" said Maurice richly. "Timothy, you are being parsimonious with the brandy. I wish to mark the occasion when I outguessed a member—you are a member, I understand?—of Her Majesty's Secret Service." He drew on his cigar and then, resting his smoking hand on the chair arm, smiled at us all with that fine actor's smile, unchanging, timeless and triumphant.

"You argued," he said, "rightly—let us give you all credit, with perspicacity—that no one in our presence would attend such a meeting. You argued that all the persons you suspected had, however, an excuse to pay one visit at least to the villa. So, you argued, the person with information to sell might quite possibly leave a message for the person intending to buy it. Hence your appearance with dear Ruth in advance of your party. Only it happened . . . It happened to those of us with experience of life, that another possibility presented itself."

"What?" said Jacko badly. Maurice cast him a look of melancholy dislike.

"Human nature," he said, "is the dramatist's business. One rounds one's characters. One studies how they should behave. I felt Sophia Lindrop was behaving . . ." He hesitated. ". . . *theatrically.*"

"So?" said Charles. I remembered he had been engaged to Sophia, and the things she had said to him on the quay, leaving *Sappho*.

"So I followed her," said Maurice mildly, "to the barber's. She was having her hair done in the feminine quarters. She didn't see me, but it was quite possible to watch what she was doing. And that, of course, was talking to Diana Minicucci."

"They were friends," Professor Hathaway said. "At least—"

"At least," I said, "Di appeared to put up with her, but most certainly gave her a ducking in Taormina. It put me off the scent, I can tell you. Maurice, what were they talking about?"

"Now that," said Maurice regretfully, "I couldn't tell you. But I can say the subject was distasteful. Sophia was plainly angry and Diana, after listening, became angry as well. In addition, something was passed to Diana. She studied it for a moment, and then tore it up. I was interested," said Maurice calmly, "and my barber was kind enough to save me the fragments. You saw them. A small piece of film of no significance."

The pebble glasses of Professor Hathaway were trained on the pink face of Maurice. "Hence the anger," said Lilian Hathaway slowly. "Both Sophia and Diana expected something different. What? There can be only one answer. The material which was concealed in the Baedeker."

Charles said, "Or Ruth's roll of film. It had disappeared, remember. Innes was looking for it. And Ruth, sweetie, you're a hell of a liar. Even Johnson knew bloody well you hadn't burned it."

"No," said Professor Hathaway. "That was a roll of film. This was a single negative. Large enough, when shot on an eight-millimeter camera, to encompass several pages of manuscript. And small enough to slip within the binding of a Baedeker." She turned her lean, adenoidal face upon Johnson, and Johnson, lying back, met her regard without flinching. "What Sophia had obtained was not what she had expected. Who, then, had substituted one film for the other?"

The electric fibers on the wall panel shivered. The used coffee cups littered the tables, between the skyphoi and the kylikes and the psykters. The tobacco smoke, lightly veiling the ridgepole, dropped again like Jupiter's shower in search of a virgin. Johnson, rolling slowly to starboard, produced from one hip a small square of dark gelatin. "I did," he said. "This was what they all wanted."

Even Maurice, I recall, straightened like an elderly spring and sat bolt upright, his cigar charring the bedcover. The rest of us stood up, jumped, or, like Charles and me, merely craned forward. "What?" Innes said. Below the pale hair and the bruises his eyes were shining like dome screw covers. "What is it? Have you seen an enlargement?"

"Yes," said Johnson. He sat back as he had done all along, his pipe in one hand, and held the film like a fag in the other. "You have to see it through an enlarger. That's why Sophia didn't know she had the wrong thing until she got it into the Capri Observatory. This is the stuff Innes was after. The leaked data from the Palassio Institute."

"That?" said Charles disbelievingly through my hair. In the heat from the tall marble fireplace his arm around me had sealed itself to my cardigan. Where we had been two, we were one. Where we had been at odds, we were at peace.

"Yes, that," said Johnson lightly. "You're a photographer. You know how much they can cram onto one frame of movie film. Look." He held it up to the light. "You can see the pages on it. Like miniature postage stamps."

"May I see?" said Charles, and, loosing me, crossed stiffly to Johnson. Bending, he took the film and held it, in his turn, against the light.

"You can't distinguish it," Johnson explained patiently. "To do that, you need an enlarger."

"I know," said Charles, and taking his hand from the lamplight he walked across to the fire and dropped the film, steadily and defiantly, into the flames.

Innes gripped his wrist as it fell. A second later Jacko, crying aloud, was on his knees beside him. I heard Maurice grunt and Timothy gasp and saw Professor Hathaway, the pouches deepening under her eyes, clasp her hands on the arms of the chair till the knuckles stood out like plaster beading.

As the film frizzled into gas, I sat and watched it and, unlike the others, had no impulse to move. Nor did Johnson.

Charles said, "I couldn't let you. It's the only evidence that Sophia was mixed up in it. I was engaged to her once." He looked as if he hadn't had any stuffed pork in Parassio, or any food at all for a very long time.

"It doesn't matter," Johnson said. Unlike the others he hadn't even flushed with excitement: on his dark skin his bruises stood out like shadow cretonne on a chesterfield. Charles looked at him, and then at me, his mouth wry, his eyes appealing. He said, "She was a silly little cow. Always listened to the wrong people. I take it you will want to arrest both of us now."

"Should we?" said Johnson.

Charles straightened and Innes released him. Jacko got up. Timothy, his kind face puzzled, was looking from Charles to Johnson and then, appealingly, back to Johnson again. Charles said, his voice tired and level and very final, "I had nothing to do with it. I suppose Sophia had. But what it was, she never told me."

"Then you have nothing to fear, have you?" said Johnson with equal gentleness. Charles looked at me and dropped suddenly on the arm of my chair.

"Poor dear," said Timothy, who had begun pouring out brandies. I saw Innes looking at the time. Maurice followed his glance and said, rather accusingly, to Johnson, "Aren't you arresting anybody?"

"Who would you suggest?" said Johnson. His pipe, between his teeth, was giving him trouble. I recalled that, until pushed, Maurice had kept his counsel about the complicity of Di and Sophia with all the chivalry due to his station. But Lenny had gone after Di with his blessing, and I felt sure the wires from Naples to the British Embassy, one way or another, had been humming.

"Well, there are a few little questions," said Maurice. Professor Hathaway glanced at the circling eyes of the blackamoor clock and took a brandy; Charles and Jacko were already sipping theirs. "Such as, where did Sophia find the negative she showed with such disgust to Diana on Capri?"

"Surely you guessed that," said Johnson. He finished drawing his bonfire with a matchbox, laid the box down, took the pipe out of his mouth and said, staring into the bowl, "Of course, it was in Ruth's borrowed wristwatch."

I could feel, around my shoulders, Charles's arm slacken with astonishment. The veil of smoke lifted as a number of people breathed heavily into it and then dropped again. Innes said, "Of course. Ruth's wristwatch, which you made her give Sophia. Presumably," he added crossly, "you had already substituted a worthless film for the Palassio one?"

"On the journey to Lipari. Professor Hathaway kindly gave Ruth phenobarbitone in the course of the evening. You tried to take her watch yourself just before breakfast, you may remember. Not to mention . . . Innes," said Johnson severely, "I did take exception to your making the poor girl swim about in her evening dress."

"It was Di who shouldered me in," I said rather colorlessly. They had all wanted the watch. I hadn't quite realized it at the time. I hadn't realized it until Sophia snatched at my wrist by the swimming pool.

Maurice said, "How fascinating it all is. Have I grasped it? At the Fall Fair, Diana receives the nuclear film in the Baedeker. It is then placed in Ruth's wristwatch from which Innes, Di and Sophia successively attempt to remove it, not knowing that Johnson has already done so. The intention, one might suppose, was that Ruth should deliver the film to some other party, presumably in the Villa San Michele at three P.M. yesterday. But Ruth, poor dear, does not appear to know she is to deliver the watch to anybody, or that the contents of the watch have been tampered with. On the contrary, she goes so far as to allow Sophia to sink her teeth into her ear, an episode of unforgettable pageantry, in order to protect it. Therefore Ruth is an unwitting courier. Who, I wonder, was the Institute's nuclear film intended for?"

"Sophia, of course. Don't be so script-minded, Maurice," said Professor Hathaway. "She ought to have had it, no doubt, the weekend Ruth and Jacko were to have spent down in Naples; I expect the San Michele rendezvous on the twentieth was a holding date, in case anything went wrong. In fact Sophia went into action, as we know, long before the twentieth."

"Premise accepted," said Maurice blandly. "Then, second question. Who placed the nuclear film in Ruth's borrowed wristwatch?"

Charles took his arm from behind me and put his brandy glass down. His hand, I noticed, was perfectly steady. "The film wasn't put into Ruth's watch," he said. "It was put into the watch while I still had it." He turned to me. "I told you I saw Sophia in Naples? And that she wanted her presents returned?"

I nodded.

Charles said, "I made up my mind to take them. She knew I was coming with you and Jacko to visit the hill post that Saturday. I knew I should be able to find her, either in Naples or in Capri. Ruth, I'm sorry I didn't tell you, but there was no point in dragging it all up. I was on my way to finish with her, and I'd never have seen her again. So on Friday I put on the watch, to take it to Naples."

"The Friday you were arrested," said Johnson.

"Yes. Then Ruth discovered hers was cracked and, God help me, I gave her Sophia's to put on. I remember getting a kick out of it. Through no fault of mine, I wasn't going to have to see Sophia again.

338

And instead of going back to Sophia, my girl was wearing her bloody timepiece."

His voice split and he drank some brandy quickly. Innes said, lucidly, "Then when and by whom do you consider the nuclear negative was inserted?"

"By Di," said Charles. "I've worked it out. While we were with the police after the balloon cart business on the Thursday, Di left Rome and went back to Jacko. The watch was in my digs. There was nothing to stop her from opening it."

Everyone except Maurice and Professor Hathaway looked at Jacko, who blushed and went a shadowy white behind his mustaches. He said, "That could be right. I don't know when she actually got back from Rome. I was out having a bite to eat when she said she rang me. She came around to the Dome a bit later."

"For a photographic session?" asked Professor Hathaway.

There was a lurid silence during which the disinterment of criminal nastinesses was replaced by the auguries of professional disaster. Jacko thought deeply, rapidly and wistfully and answered, "Yes."

"Ah. Of Diana, in various traditional attitudes," said Professor Hathaway, gazing at him through the pebble spectacles with the mesmeric firmness of one about to pin back the ears of a multitude. "Of course," said the Director of the Trust, glancing to the wan form slumped in thought on her left, "Doctor Wye had torn up all your pictures."

I wondered through what grapevine she had learned that, and decided it was probably Johnson. Recollections of Poppy, smothered in Johnson's three-ply Geelong underwear made me reach, in a sophisticated way, for Charles's nearest hand. He let me take it and then squeezed mine, at intervals, in between allowing Timothy to give him more brandy. Professor Hathaway said, "You have no idea, James, what a wide audience your studies of Diana have been reaching. Chile. Germany. Pretoria. Egypt. Okayama. Argentina. Zelenchukskaya even; or so I am told. Does it embarrass you?"

It embarrassed me, I can tell you. I looked from Professor Hathaway to Jacko with my brain wheezing. I said, "They went to other observatories?"

"From the Zodiac Trust," said Professor Hathaway mildly. "In exchange for other material *from* them. You wouldn't expect astronomers to have such a lively interest, would you, in earthly bodies? But they apparently did. Every now and then, from among a pile of plates arriving or departing for comparison or specialist reduction, there would slip out a disconcerting picture which would find rapid cover without, of course, being reported to the head of the observatory. And that, as it happens, was only one method of exchange employed by these extraordinary persons.

"You must be aware, James," said Professor Hathaway, tipping the ash from her Manikin, "that in the worldwide network of observatories, there exists a ready-made system of communication which lends itself to a number of telling abuses. Who would put a flawed photographic plate through an enlarger? Yet they are sent to the center for reduction with the good plates, and who knows what microprints they may not incorporate in some hazy corner? Astronomers are excellent photographers.

And if they cannot doctor the plates, there is always the parcel of undeveloped plates which passes periodically from one place to another without fear of broaching by customs. And if that fails, there are Jacko's pictures and their like: good harmless fun which causes no more than a giggle if they fall into the wrong hands and would never, in a sporting profession, be reported to the authorities. Maurice?"

"I am listening," said Maurice. "Agog."

Narrowing her eyes above the belching tip of her half-consumed Manikin, Professor Hathaway groped with both hands through her large tapestry handbag and handed something to Maurice. "Perhaps," she said, "you haven't yet seen one of James's productions."

It was a picture of Di: an old one, in which she was wearing a fringed outfit someone had brought her from Cairo. I recognized it upside down as Maurice studied it at arm's length on the four-poster. I said, without thinking, "He's altered her necklace."

I saw Jacko go slowly scarlet at the same moment as I felt the tide of red rising over my own neck and face. Charles, rigid beside me, was staring at Jacko.

"The necklace—Ruth is right—is certainly the most interesting part of the photograph," said Lilian Hathaway calmly. "In fact, I found it so interesting that I decided to share my interest with Johnson. He is here because I asked him to come here. Pass around the photograph."

No one spoke as it went around. Everyone looked at the necklace, and avoided looking at anyone else. Very few of them looked at her face; the smart, beautiful, likable face we had been friends with.

"You said," said Professor Hathaway, "that the necklace had been changed. It had, in a very alarming way. Each of these circles, which once contained round clear stones of a pale character, is now filled with approximately four manuscript pages of classified material. The photograph arrived at the Trust from this station a month ago. The person who received it has been under observation. More pictures were to go, I am sure, with the packet due to go off ten days ago. Unfortunately, Jacko's pictures were destroyed and I appeared, to supervise the rest of the packing. That was why it was decided to entrust the rest of the information to Sophia."

"To send from Capri?" said Innes. "Through her network of communications?"

"Of course. She was already suborned when she worked at the Trust. She only left when her place was taken by another."

Johnson had lied to me. Jacko stood up. He said, "Wait a minute."

"We're not going anywhere," said Johnson coolly. "Are you going to try and convince us you knew nothing about this?"

The fire roared up the chimney, dark red behind the gauzy curtains of tobacco. A trickle of sweat, hovering over my neck, suddenly made a cold dash down my back. I shivered and sought in vain around my hip for a handkerchief. A clean one appeared before me, which I recognized as Timothy's. Timothy said, "Maurice. I think it is bedtime."

Maurice smiled. "What? Before the last murder? Timothy," he said, "you have no soul in the matter of exits."

"You said," said Johnson to Jacko, "that you could defend yourself."

"Dear boy," said Maurice regretfully. "I always said your hobbies would lead you into nothing but trouble. Much better stick to stump work, like Timothy."

"I also prefer stump work," said Professor Hathaway, surveying him, "but I doubt if any court would accept it as a character reference. You understand, James, that it is the connection between the Minicucci family and the Zodiac Trust which is exercising us. Prince Minicucci, we are led to understand, was the head of a select organization which dealt in the exchange of illegally acquired information, whether military or industrial. In this he made use of his daughter and of people like Sophia, I make no doubt, and Mr. Paladrini. But information has been coming from this observatory and elsewhere into the Zodiac Trust since Sophia left us. We are left to wonder therefore who is responsible."

Charles said, "Isn't it a matter for the police? It seems hard luck on Jacko to have to pull himself together in the middle of the night and start defending himself. We're not a court."

"It is a matter for the British police," said Professor Hathaway. "The police in Rome are at present mainly occupied with tracing and arresting all of Prince Minicucci's associates. I prefer to clear my own doorstep. James, have you been sending doctored photographs in the parcels to England?"

"No," said Jacko. His flowered shirt had come untucked from his trousers and his mustache had flecks of Maurice's cigar ash in it. He said, "This is a hell of a—"

"You have only to answer me truthfully," said Professor Hathaway. "Did you, or Diana with your knowledge, transfer the lethal gas cylinder from Mr. Paladrini's flat to the Dome?"

"No, I didn't," said Jacko. "Listen, was it likely? Ruth uses that mixer gas. I was as likely to get blown up in the Dome with her as anybody."

"Unless you disconnected it when she was about. Did you give or lend Diana the key to the Dome, so that her friends were able to break in or search it as they pleased?"

There was a slight pause, during which Jacko breathed heavily through his nostrils. I stared at the ground. I knew he was thinking of his Orals. The strict voice, the impersonal questions were so reminiscent I could feel the same low, queasy feeling in the pit of my stomach.

Jacko said, "I did lend her a key. Once or twice. But that's got nothing to do with it. Look, if I wanted to search the Dome or bust Charles's camera or anything, I didn't have to hire someone to do it. I could do it myself and fake some sort of tale of a break-in. In any case, the man who pinched the film and broke up the camera busted the door to get into the observatory. My God, he tied me up and got away while I was still on the floor of the developing room. You were there, Innes. And Ruth, and Charles and Johnson. There you are. The bloody film was stolen and that proves I had nothing to do with it."

"Of course it does," said Johnson cheerfully. It was a tone that I distrusted and I saw by Jacko's wary scrutiny that he wasn't buying it either.

Johnson said, "The man who smashed Charles's camera and took the film was a security agent, the partner of the man who was killed in the toletta at the zoo. He had nothing to do with Minicucci and the fact that he broke in and attacked you does nothing whatever to prove you weren't in with the Minicuccis up to the hairline. The only thing it does prove is that you didn't shoot him. In fact, the puzzle is, who *did* shoot him? Di and her friends weren't around, and there wasn't time to summon them. I suppose you didn't put the body into the meat safe?"

"I didn't know it was there," said Jacko indignantly. "My God, ask Ruth what we both felt when we saw it. Look, what about that break-in? If I hadn't been there, I suppose Ruth would have joined the other bloke in the meat safe. If I hadn't found the key to the meat safe, they might be there yet. Try and get out of that!"

"My dear boy," said Maurice gently, "you are the one whose extraction is in question. Am I not right in thinking that on that occasion entrance was effected by a key to the Dome? And that the intruder was aware of the presence of a trapdoor, and therefore was either a member of the observatory staff, or on intimate terms with one? What about that, my poor children?"

"All right," said Jacko hotly, glaring around at his tormentors. "Tell me one thing. What do you think he had come for?"

Again, it was Innes, no friend of his, who supported him. "The body," he said. "The fact that he had the meat safe key on him proves it. Also, he did not know, Jacko, of your presence. You had expected to go home after your duty. Ruth had just come on duty and was safely locked in the Dome making exposures. It was pure coincidence that on this one night she left the door open, and that the subsequent events forced the criminal into the open. I do not believe," said Innes, "that there was any prior intention of harming Ruth. Up to that moment, Minicucci's party had shown themselves most anxious to avoid police interference. The trapdoor was merely a desperate device to insure his own escape through the Dome roof. If you had both fallen through it, there would be no absolute proof that it wasn't an accident."

"All right," said Jacko. "Then if all he wanted was to remove the body, you can count me out of that one as well. I spent half my nights in that Dome. I could have carted out and buried the entire Inter football team and no one need have been any the wiser."

"I remember suggesting it," said Maurice mildly. "In fact, truth to tell, I began to worry a little about the possible contents of my refrigerator. Johnson, I think the boy has made a case for himself."

Professor Hathaway leaned forward and stubbed out her cigar with a movement of sudden decision. "Yes," she said. "I do believe he has. Now, where does that leave us? Johnson, Innes and myself are not under suspicion. On circumstantial evidence, Jacko may be largely absolved. Who, then, doctored the pictures and slipped them into the packages intended for the Trust? Timothy and Maurice?

346

They didn't need to leave bodies in the Dome: they had their own ample resources."

"Of course," said Johnson mildly. "Also, neither of them made the slightest attempt to ensure that Ruth's valuable wristwatch was safely transferred to Sophia. Indeed, it was through Maurice's amateur sleuthing that we got the shredded film back from the barber's—thereby, I will say," added Johnson reprovingly, "much upsetting Lenny, who was already having a steam treatment—you may not have noticed—in another part of the salon."

"How did . . . ?" began Maurice.

"Added to which," said Johnson, paying no attention, "neither Maurice nor Timothy was sufficiently intimate with the posting details of the Dome, nor did either know anything whatsoever about photography. Indeed, once you rule out Innes and Jacko and Charles, who was in Naples or in prison half the time all the crimes were being committed, there is really only one person left who possesses every qualification. Ruth, come over here."

Charles's hands dropped from my shoulders. My heart, which had been beating in a succession of quick, heavy thumps, had a logjam and began to shake me like an uneven trip-hammer. I looked up at Charles and he was staring at me with a face I had never seen before.

Everyone was staring at me. I got up very slowly and walked to where Johnson had risen. "I'm sorry, Ruth," he said. "But it had to be done." And taking me by the arm he drew me beside him, so that I could see the loving regularity of the cable stitching and the bristle where he needed shaving and the bulge in his trouser pocket which was either his pipe, or his matches, or something which was bigger and neither.

His hand on my arm was very tight. "I couldn't have him using you as a hostage," said Johnson. "Charles. It is, I'm afraid, the end of the joyride."

CHAPTER 19

"AND THAT," said Charles with a breathless kind of angry amusement, "is what is wrong with the British Intelligence Service today. I beg to inform you, Johnson. You've made a ripe, newspaper-worthy, libel-incurring cock-up of this one."

"Charles?" said Jacko. He came over and stood beside me and glared at Johnson. "You said yourself, he was in prison half the time."

"I know. I put him there," said Johnson. "To keep him out of Ruth's way. To isolate him from his associates. And to see what he would do with the nuclear film from the Baedeker which Di had received at the Fall Fair and given him. What he did, of course, was put it in his watch and make Ruth unwittingly carry it to Sophia."

"So you say," said Charles. "Who can prove it?"

"I can," said Johnson. "What you burned just

now was the second part of the Turin Traffic Regulations for nineteen fifty-four. The nuclear film is safely in England, with your fingerprints on it."

"Bluff," said Charles.

"You think so?" said Johnson. "You have an eight-millimeter-film camera. You not only take fashion shots. You have industrial contracts for photographs. The two security agents in the zoo were from such a firm. They wanted to see what was in your camera because they had suffered a leak and were suspicious of you. And what was in your camera, as Ruth well knows, were retakes of Jacko's pictures of Diana, with certain microfilm additions."

"Prove it," said Charles. "If you can, from the ashes."

"Or Ruth's testimony," Johnson said. "She can testify against you, you know. Despite your persuasiveness, she wouldn't marry you. You had hoped to make Ruth into another Sophia. Instead, she realized you had lied about the ownership of her camera, and, finding yours in the Dome, developed what was in it. What she found must have reeked of industrial espionage, but she was more than fair to you. She hid them, and even when at one point she thought I might help you out of your trouble, she didn't give you away."

"Because there was nothing to give away," Charles said. "I was a cretin, no doubt. I didn't know I had muddled the cameras. But when I realized I had, I thought I ought to pretend that mine was the one which was pinched at the zoo. After all, my own was lying about loose for anyone to take. I wanted to make that secure first."

"Then why not tell Ruth at least?" Johnson said. "Or were you afraid of something happening which would cause the police to investigate and develop the contents of both cameras? I can see that it would be better to get hold of Ruth's camera and destroy the film somehow, so that the question of developing it could never arise. And mixed up with it all was Mr. Paladrini, who had appointed to meet you with the balloon cart outside the zoo on that day, and who duly handed over to you the balloon bearing the rendezvous advice for the Fall Fair.

"Only, Ruth got the balloon and managed to interpret what it meant. And Mr. Paladrini, knowing you were being followed, took the law into his own hands and gave your pursuer the lethal balloon. Whose fragments you removed, of course, when you went into the zoo toletta. What a shock it must have been to see that someone had got away with the contents of Ruth's camera already. That meant that when he developed it, he would realize he had the wrong film. And he would then look for the right one, which was still lying in the Dome.

"You did your best to get it that night," said Johnson. "The night of Maurice's party, do you remember? But Jacko had exposures going on in the Dome, and it was blacked out. And none of us, as it happens, left you for a moment. And then, when you got away from Maurice's party, it was to find that the other security agent was already in the Dome and had found your camera with the film in it. You even caught him, and had him locked in the bathroom, when he unfortunately escaped.

"Or did he escape?" said Johnson reflectively. "Who knows? He might even have remained in the bathroom, a bullet hole in his head, until it was safe to remove him to the meat safe. But the film had gone, and that frightened you. You appointed Di to go to the Fall Fair in your place and you forced a quarrel with Ruth to account for your departing to Naples, to meet Sophia and arrange for the nuclear film, when it came, to be passed to Sophia when you and Jacko and Ruth came to Naples at the weekend.

"You came back to Rome on Tuesday evening, hoping to find things had cooled off, and that it would be possible to remove the shot man at last from the Dome. The locks had been changed, but Di always had access to Jacko's key and of course by now had copies. Unfortunately, in your absence Mr. Paladrini had been spotted at the Fall Fair and since positively identified. Prince Minicucci decreed that he now represented an unnecessary risk to the organization, and on Tuesday night or early on Wednesday morning he was taken away and killed and equipped with a suicide note. A little later, for reasons which had become rather compelling, you made the exchange of gas cylinders from Mr. Paladrini's flat to the Dome, but left the Dome cylinder insufficiently connected, so that until you chose, nothing fatal could happen."

I said, "You're wrong there." It didn't come out very well and Jacko, on my other side, shot a glance of hatred at Johnson and put his arm around my waist. Johnson, without looking, opened his fingers and freed my near arm. I wanted to sit down but I didn't. I stayed exactly as I was.

Johnson said, "No. If even I knew you were worried, do you think Charles wouldn't observe it? And something appalling had happened. He had entered the Dome after you left him at midnight, and had been discovered even before reaching the meat safe. Instead of covering his tracks, he suddenly had both you and Jacko in full cry after him. He left that trapdoor open praying you would both fall into it, for he thought you would certainly have recognized him. In fact you didn't recognize him, and didn't fall into the trap. Then, of course, when he retrieved the film from Maurice's vase the next morning, he saw that it was a dud and guessed you had found and developed the right one. From then onward, it was too dangerous to leave you with him. I told the Rome police my suspicions and had him arrested until further notice, quite incommunicado but for the one meeting with you when he gave you his wristwatch. He received no letters and received and made no telephone calls until the moment of the Capri appointment, when I released him so that he could incriminate himself and, if possible, all his associates.

"By that time Sophia compromised herself by attempting to seize the watch, which she recognized as Charles's and which they had already used for exactly this purpose. She lost her head over that rather, because I think she was truly jealous of you anyway. She left the Trust, as you know, when Charles became interested in you, and he must have had a hard time persuading her to continue helping him. He succeeded. It seemed to me that having lost the watch, as she thought, and also her chance of helping Charles, Sophia would quite cheerfully have allowed herself to fall over that wall at Taormina."

"Excuse me," said Maurice politely. Because they had all stopped smoking, the air had cleared oddly. Maurice, reclining on the Rape of Persephone was able to invoke, with every line of his handsome face, the spirits of justice and moderation, tempered on this occasion with the least drop of actor-manager's acid.

"Charles, I do think you should sit down. Fascinating though it all is, I hardly think there is a shred of real evidence against you. And I do want to make two little points. Johnson, Charles couldn't have removed the signed film from the vase in this room. You know he couldn't. The Mouse Alarm was on. It had been repaired the very instant you shorted it. And if the film was so important, why did you allow Sophia to take the watch in the end, even with the substitute film in it?"

I knew what the answers were going to be. I didn't even look at Johnson as he said gently, "Ah yes. The Mouse Alarm. Charles called to see if Ruth was with you, Maurice, after she had gone with me to Mr. Paladrini's without telling him—yet another indication, to Charles, that Ruth didn't fully trust him. You didn't even mention his visit, though you knew that Innes had called at the house, and that Di had also been, but after the film had been stolen. You thought, as everyone did, that the Alarm was on, and therefore he couldn't go near your suite. But don't you remember? Even Ruth and Diana and I in Rome were inconvenienced by it. There was a power cut that morning."

I had remembered. I had remembered Di's bland voice at Renati's. I remembered, inconsequently, the way Johnson had fascinated her. It was the last high-stake rubber she would play with him.

"And you needed to hand over the watch?" said Innes thoughtfully. "To insure that Sophia rushed out and told somebody, so soon as she identified the fake on her enlarger?"

"Of course," said Johnson. "We observed everyone going ashore at Capri that day, and we placed Charles most carefully out of reach in the chair lift. So Sophia darted out of the observatory and poured out her troubles to Diana. It was easy to guess then what was going to happen. Ruth had to disappear: she knew too much for her own good, and besides, once in Minicucci's power, she could be persuaded to tell the whereabouts of that compromising film she had hidden. Charles didn't believe it was burned any more than I did.

"He also knew for the first time who I was. He was the only one among our group of suspects who did know, which made his authorship of the great abduction plot fairly plain. I hadn't expected to be kidnaped on the high seas, but as soon as I saw that wreckage, and Charles leaped so briskly into *Dolly*'s speedboat, I smelled a rat. *Sappho,* of course, belonged to Minicucci: it was only a matter of Di giving instructions to the little man who liked to sing to the engines, and the necessary R/T conversations would take place. I heard *Sappho*'s launch coming under cover of Diana's radio, and I even stayed below so that they could play it any way they wanted. But Charles wanted me out of the way. If I was an agent and had taken the nuclear film from the wristwatch, then I must be pretty sure what his share in the plot was.

"There was an awkward moment," Johnson said.

355

Sappho's launch didn't take us to the harbor, where my people were waiting, and they landed us and got us into Minicucci's car without our being followed. But luckily, Charles knew exactly where we were all going. He made some excuse to leave for Rome after Diana and led Lenny—and, as it turned out, Innes—straight to the observatory. Then having checked with Diana that all was going well, he rushed about filling in his alibi until he discovered, to his horror, that we were alive and well and baring our bosoms at the police station. I'm glad you sat down," said Johnson to Charles quite calmly. "But although Maurice means to be kind, I shouldn't like you to rely on his verdict. The case against you, to my mind, is overwhelming."

The telephone rang.

"I doubt it," said Charles. He was sitting on the arm of one of Maurice's Sicilian sofas, his blazer immaculate, his scarf neatly tied, his deep-collared shirt slightly crumpled. Because of the heat, the long hair which lay on his brow was stuck thickly together and curling a little bit at the ends. In bath steam, Charles's hair curled up all over. He didn't look at me or Jacko. He gave the impression, as it were, of speaking around us, so that there seemed no one in the room except himself and Johnson. He said, "You haven't met my mother, Johnson, have you?"

"I have," said Professor Hathaway. She got up and stretched. "I made a point of it, at a dinner at Number Ten, as I remember. I asked her where the instability was in the family."

The telephone rang again.

"Instability?" I said.

"The grandfather made a fortune and shot himself. There was a cousin who was pretty notorious as well. I wanted to know who you were tying yourself to," said my sponsor. She picked up Maurice's phone and answered it. "Pronto?"

"I take it," said Charles to Johnson, with the same casual hauteur as before, "that you have no objection if I telephone the British Embassy for my protection?" He stood up.

"I've done that," said Johnson. "There are two cars downstairs now. One from the Embassy and one from the police, to take you back to the station. It is, as I said, the end of the joyride."

"Is it?" said Charles. His eyes were full of fun. He looked as if, I thought, he was going to rip out an obituary notice and stride along, declaiming it to all who would listen. "Why, Lilian. Who was telephoning you? Lloyd George?"

Professor Hathaway put down the telephone. "The police," she said. "I thought you wouldn't object, Johnson, if I accepted the message. Diana has made a full confession."

"Bloody cow," said Charles.

"A little tribute, true and tender:
Just to show we still remember."

He stood up and hunted in his pocket and took out a revolver. I looked at Johnson but he didn't move. Innes sat up.

"Wait," said Johnson.

We waited. By the coffee cups, I could hear Timothy breathing. Professor Hathaway, moving with dignity, perched herself on the bed beside Maurice. Jacko remained where he was, beside me, with his

357

arm held tight around me. I didn't mind. He was a nice boy, and I suppose I filled a sort of Diana-shaped space at the moment. Charles said, without pointing the gun at anybody in particular, "We can't all be perfect. You made one hell of a mistake yourself." He pointed the gun at Johnson. "The red balloon. There was gas in it."

For a moment everyone was lost, and then I remembered. The car chase from the Castel Sant' Angelo, among those balloons which Charles had assured us were gas-filled. And which had proved entirely harmless, but for the last one. "Ah, yes," said Johnson. "That was the place where I over-reached myself. Ruth should know—we had found the Paladrini address long before I took you there next morning. We found the explosive gas and we noticed the switch in the cylinders. So I set a trap.

"There was never an appointment in Paladrini's papers for the Castel Sant' Angelo. The whole thing was a fabrication of mine to induce Charles to get into that balloon cart. To save his own life, as he thought, he had suddenly to produce a new theory about the toletta death being due to a gas balloon. More than that, he had to give away the switch of gas cylinders. In fact, I had filled the balloons from the harmless cylinder, and we had already made the lethal one harmless. The only thing I didn't know was that Paladrini already had one or two explosive red balloons fastened to the pole of the toy cart. They weren't loose, so it didn't appear to matter, until the Chief of Police chanced to shoot one."

"You mean . . ." I said. I shook Jacko's hand off my arm and stared at Johnson.

"The whole ride from the castle was my doing.

I'm sorry," said Johnson. "At least . . . I'm not entirely sorry."

No. Charles hadn't enjoyed that journey. Charles had been more scared than any of us. But Charles, of course, had been convinced that each blue balloon was a killer.

Whereas the killer, I suppose, was Johnson. For prison would be the death of Charles. Not a few days in clink for an escapade. But the life of Dartmoor or Peterhead, year after year after year. No matter who his parents were.

"Goodbye," said Charles; and lifting his gun pulled the trigger, twice, in Johnson's face.

Nothing happened.

"Did you think," said Johnson, "we should let you keep it with the bullets still inside? Be a good chap and come downstairs quietly. There are police outside. You really can't get away."

Charles turned the gun toward himself and looked a long time in the muzzle. Then he shook it, and threw it down on the floor, dusting his hands afterward. *"Memories,"* he said, *"don't fade, they just grow deep. Of one we loved but could not keep."* He grinned, and putting his hands in his pockets, began to walk backward toward Maurice's study.

Through that was a door to the public rooms, and a staircase which led to the loggia. Johnson said, "Charles. You've no transport, no money, no possible hope of escape. Don't cause trouble. Come with me." And he walked quietly forward.

Two things happened very suddenly. Charles turned and ran. And Maurice, stretching out a finger, pressed on a button.

The scream came to us from the study. It went on and on, and even Johnson, caught striding over the threshold, stopped, too taken aback to move for a moment. Then he looked at Maurice and Maurice said, "He deserves it."

I wondered afterward if he did deserve that. If you have ever seen a drugged fly hurling itself buzzing from wall to wall, blind and deaf and insensible to all but its agony, you will know what it was like to look at Charles in that room, howling, twisting and staggering, with all thought of escape stricken from him.

Beside me was the coffeepot. Not far away was the wall panel: the famous wall panel of history, slowly twitching. I looked at the doorway and saw Johnson was looking at me in turn. Then he shook his head and walked forward to his prisoner.

I don't think Charles even heard him, or saw the hand stretching out for his sleeve. He gave a long hoot, like a Sicilian diesel, and plunging from Johnson's reach, ran the length of the room to the windows.

We heard the crash of the glass, but didn't see him jump, in the darkness. It was a second floor, and there was no balcony.

I wondered if, in some rodent paradise full of sunflower seeds, Poppy knew how tidy had been her requital.

I have never been back to Italy. Maurice is dying, they say, now, and the pretty girls have all gathered around someone else, but Timothy still makes his coffee for him, and they have a new chauffeur who likes them.

Jacko left the observatory for the Surface Weapons Establishment and when last heard of, he had a Zufenhausen Flyer and a nice flat with twin baths in Croyden.

Innes finished his Incubator. It proved to be an instrument for the detection of neutrinos, and was every bit of the success that he expected. He was able to put it into production himself with the help of the United States Government and the £20,000 he won on "Rischia Tutto" just before he left Rome for Christmas.

I am working at the Zodiac Trust with Professor Hathaway, handing out and digesting projects with the help of a new computer and the extra physics man we got sanction to appoint on the strength of Johnson's check for the Mouse Hall power cut.

Johnson finished his portrait of the Pope. It was crated by the Vatican carpenters and left the Vatican station with an escort of cardinals for its sacerdotal quarters in London. They say His Holiness was so pleased with it that Johnson is to return to paint another for the Pontiff's own study. Johnson says the Chief of Police has some reservations.

Johnson comes to see Professor Hathaway on occasion, and I have had him in the computer room, watching us working. He and Conrad hit it off, which is a relief. Conrad is the new physics appointment. You never can tell, but it seems that he might be an asset.

Johnson doesn't appear to consider remarrying. Of course, he has his boat, and his painting. I'm glad to have known him. I feel quite differently, I find, about bifocal glasses. It is only obituary notices that I never read.

> *What you suffered, you told but few*
> *You didn't deserve what you went through.*
> *Tired and weary, you made no fuss*
> *But tried so hard to stay with us.*

About the Author

Dorothy Dunnett is author of seven
highly praised historical novels and five
suspense novels. She lives in Scotland.